PRAISE
SHADOW AMO

vill hold you captive until the last

iuthor of the Ladies of the Manor
ind Shadows Over England series

"When all the exoticness of the Far East arrives in the quiet country-side of Victorian England, rumors abound—and so does love. *Shadow among Sheaves* is a fresh retelling of the story of Ruth that adds a whole new way to look at the Biblical account. Poetic prose. Strong characters. And a drama that gets under your skin."
> —Michelle Griep, Christy Award-winning author of
> the *Once Upon a Dickens Christmas* series

"Set in 19th century England, *Shadow among Sheaves* is the tale of an Indian widow and her beloved mother-in-law. Amidst fear, self-sacrifice, and starvation, the young widow finds desperately needed assistance in the form of Lord Barric—an earl who soon finds himself torn between his reputation and his heart. Lovers of historical fiction will enjoy this elaborate retelling of Ruth and Boaz."
> —Denise Hunter, bestselling author of *On Magnolia Lane*

SHADOW
AMONG
SHEAVES

Naomi Stephens

SHILOH RUN PRESS
An Imprint of Barbour Publishing, Inc.

Published by Shiloh Run Press, an imprint of Barbour Publishing, Inc., 1810 Barbour Drive, Uhrichsville, Ohio 44683, www.shilohrunpress.com

Our mission is to inspire the world with the life-changing message of the Bible.

Member of the
Evangelical Christian
Publishers Association

Printed in the United States of America.

"Where you go I will go, and where you stay I will stay.
Your people will be my people and your God my God.
Where you die I will die, and there I will be buried."
RUTH 1:16–17 NIV

For Curtis—the first person to call me an author.

For Ena—who met (and loved)
Rena and Barric before anyone else did.

PROLOGUE

England, July 1861

The sun was the same, but that was all.

Blindingly hot, it hung low on the horizon as if dangled there by an invisible string. Rena studied the sun's path as it settled at the base of the sky, her fingers fiddling with a tiny glass vial which hung from her neck by a cord. As she tipped the glass, the sand scrambled within, racing from one end to the other.

Sighing, Rena settled back into her seat. She wished she could have brought buckets of sand from India. She had lived in the northwest, in Jaipur, which was a considerable distance from the sprawling Thar Desert, but she and Edric had gone there on one of his leaves. She still remembered the way the sand had felt beneath her bare feet, sharp against the balls of her heels like tiny knives; she remembered the way the sand had smelled on her skin in the morning, as if she were knit together by heat and sunlight; she remembered the way her husband's hands had felt on her neck in the evenings when they had lain down in the sand together to forget themselves and the cutting remarks of their countrymen. If she clamped her eyes shut, she could nearly taste the dry summer air of home, could feel the tiny grains of sand pressing against her shoulder blades as Edric's fingers carded her hair. . . .

But coming to England was far better, she reminded herself, reopening her eyes to glance at the seat across the compartment, where her mother-in-law still slept deeply. Nothing could grow from sand, Rena reasoned with herself. Nothing could grow from nothing.

As the train groaned tiredly along its track, she could already make out the shapes of fields and orchards, their foreign perimeters drawn jaggedly like the edges of an unfinished puzzle. Tree trunks the size of castle turrets lined the fields with a thick border of summer leaves. Beyond the trees, small buildings dotted the landscape, spread out in dark squares like a chessboard.

She looked from the fields to the unfamiliar buildings and back again. She pressed her vial of sand between two shaking fingers. *Yes*, she thought, redirecting her gaze to the sky. *The sun is the same. But will that be enough?*

"Abbotsville!" called an attendant, stepping sideways through the cramped compartment. He jostled Rena's mother-in-law, Lady Hawley, as he passed her, nudging her out of sleep.

Nell looked worn from their journey. Rena was certain she looked little better herself. The passage by sea had been brutal for both women. Half of the three-month journey was spent huddled below deck as the walls of the steamer were blasted by turbulent squalls, which had made the entire structure feel as if it were made of matchsticks. Rena had lost control of her stomach enough times that she could no longer taste her own humiliation. Somehow she had endured jarring wagon rides across sweltering Egyptian deserts, followed by cramped barges and rickety paddle steamers. If she closed her eyes, she still felt unbalanced on dry land, and she suspected she might always feel the ocean's silent sway beneath her.

The whistle blew shrill as the train slid into the station, its wheels slowing beneath them. As the train halted, Rena could hardly believe her grueling journey was finally at an end.

England awaited beyond those doors.

Edric's England.

As the other passengers began to bustle, she once again checked the contents of her bag. She had not kept much in her haste. Two plain dresses in addition to the one on her back, a slab of hard bread, and a few stacks of henna leaves pressed between the pages of a book which had once belonged to her father. She shouldered her bag and then tucked the thin cord back beneath the neckline of her black widow's dress. The vial of sand now rested against her chest beside Edric's gold signet ring, as if she had buried him there.

"I will take care of you," whispered Nell, stepping closer. The older woman settled her hand on Rena's cheek and smiled. "I promise we will pick up these scattered pieces."

It seemed an impossible task. There were as many scattered pieces within Rena's heart as there were leaves on England's countless trees. Her husband was dead. Her family lived oceans away. Now she entered the land of those who sought to rule her people, where she was as strange to them as they would always seem to her. She glanced again at Nell and forced herself to banish these regrets. Nell had lost twice as much, Rena reminded herself. Nell had lost her husband as well as her only son, and yet she smiled at Rena with eyes as bright as Edric's had once been—those lovely, almond-shaped eyes which ran in the Hawley family.

Together the two women had hardly enough money worth counting. Edric's father, Sir Alistair, had set aside a fairly comfortable allowance for his wife and daughter-in-law. With the death of his son, however, he had weakened considerably in both spirit and frame until, worried for his wife, he had scrambled to secure further savings by making risky investments in his final year. Though Sir Alistair had never known so during his lifetime, he had been ruthlessly swindled. The collectors arrived the day after the funeral, forcing Nell to hand over nearly everything she had left to cover his debt.

"Alistair was rather good at chess," Nell had remarked to Rena that afternoon, shaking her head in equal parts grief and frustration. "But he sometimes trusted his own judgment too well to foresee a checkmate. But, of course, there was always time to reset the pieces for another game."

Until now.

The rest of the Hawley fortune, including the estate and the baronetcy, was entailed upon Edric's death to an older cousin, Felix, who lived in Australia. Nell had written to him immediately for help but had received no reply. Now Nell was at last returning home, to Abbotsville, to stay with a cousin whom she hadn't seen since childhood. But Rena knew how Abbotsville must really feel—a tomb-like world, where Nell had once been young, where she had been a wife and a mother, but she could never be those things again because the ones she loved the most had already been snatched away.

Rena had felt something similar when she had knocked on her father's door to tell him she was leaving with Nell for England, when she had wrapped her arms around her mother's neck and wept that she must go. She had lived with her parents for nearly two years after Edric's death. During that time, she had been confined mostly to her own quarters, where at her parents' bidding she had fasted to the point of faintness and prayed to the Hindu gods that she might someday be forgiven for marrying him.

With time her father had hoped they might find a man to overlook her union with Edric and perhaps marry her despite of it. She *was* still rather beautiful, as was observed in town, and the laws had been recently altered under British influence to allow remarriage for widows. In many parts of India, however, widows were still beaten and shunned, cursed and spat upon, their clothes stripped away and ornaments ripped from their piercings so even their skin and flesh were broken. Though Rena's parents had been devastated by her secret marriage, they had also been merciful to bring her back into their home and harbor actual hopes for her future.

But Rena had married an Englishman, an *officer*, and even if an

Indian man was willing to look beyond her marriage, Rena could never be the same person. Never again a daughter. Never a wife. And so, nearly two years into her prayers and fasting, when Rena had learned that Sir Alistair had died and left his wife with nothing, she had rushed to the dear woman's side and pledged herself, with many tears, to easing Nell's pain. Now the rest of Rena's life stretched before her like one of her father's books, like a foreign language written in ciphers too jagged for her to comprehend.

She had married Edric impulsively. She had followed Nell to England impulsively. But her father had always said her heart was a steady strum, always guiding her forward, forward, forward.

As the train door jerked open, Rena jumped to clasp the older woman's fingers. "Don't be afraid," she said, pressing this promise deep into Nell's wrinkled palm. "*I* will take care of *you*."

CHAPTER 1

Both women were starving.

After nearly three weeks in Abbotsville, Rena's shoulder blades now cut against her skin like she was made of paper. Head pounding, she lay beside Nell in a stable which smelled of manure, desperate for any way to escape the unbreakable claws of poverty.

The sun was beginning to show through the dawn-filled haze, but Rena was too angry to look at the sky. In India she had loved watching the sun and stars unfold at the start and end of each day. She often pressed against the rail of her father's balcony, lifted up, captured by the endlessness of it all. Now everything was different. She, a Brahmin, was forced to sleep in the hay like an animal. The humiliation was nearly unbearable. Her father's home was filled with sacred, ancient texts and priceless artifacts. He was a valuable asset to the British troops stationed there. Even Rena herself had once been described as a prize.

And who was she now?

She yanked a few strands of straw from her hair—a trespasser, lying amid filthy cattle while Nell slept soundly beside her. To such concerns as starvation and poverty, Nell merely replied that all problems had their solutions. She was a sturdy woman with no intention of moping. But Rena was not convinced, even by such practiced bravado.

Many years ago, Nell had lived nearby, in a suburb of Liverpool, well before she met and married Sir Alistair. A few of her cousins were still scattered in various estates throughout the area, and Nell had written to them several months ago, shortly after Alistair had died, to announce that she was returning to England and would be much indebted if she could stay with one of their families until things were sorted.

"*Of course,*" they had all responded. "*With pleasure. You are always most welcome.*"

They'd made arrangements to stay with a Lady Harriet, who lived the closest to Abbotsville. All was quite settled ahead of time. But then Nell had arrived in England with an unexpected surprise—Rena.

"There must be some mistake," Lady Harriet had stammered, stunned to find an Indian girl waiting beside Nell at her gate. "We did not expect you so soon. We haven't enough room for two houseguests. . . ."

Rena had counted at least two dozen windows from her place beneath the gate. Two dozen windows in Lady Harriet's home, and yet not a bed for two widows to share. Nell had made her way down her list of cousins and second cousins, but all had given the same answer with varying degrees of shock and disgust as they stared at Rena in her plain widow's dress.

Rena rolled onto her side and studied the careful way Nell now slept in the hay, with not a single hair out of place. Nell had come from one of the most estimable families in northern England. She didn't belong here, sleeping like a vagrant with a foreign castaway. But even those sorrows paled in the face of another—before Nell had fallen asleep that night, she'd mentioned the workhouse.

"It is always best to consider all options," Nell had said bracingly, but Rena also read the terror thinly masked in the woman's eyes.

Restless, Rena pushed herself up from the ground, burying her face between her hands. Several times she had passed the Liverpool workhouse during her daily search for work. Cramped and full of sickness, it was a glorified prison for the hapless, desperate souls who needed it. If Rena and Nell were even admitted, they would be forced to turn over their own clothes, to bathe supervised, to work their way through a system dead set on breaking them.

No. Rena climbed to her feet. She could not let that happen. She *would* not.

With one last anxious look at Nell, Rena left the stable and marched straight into town. People were already beginning to gather on their way to the fields, and they watched her steady approach with alarm. Rena wanted to spit on them. When she and Nell had knocked on every door in town, no one had looked either of them in the eyes. When they had slept in doorways, alleys, and barns, the people of Abbotsville had pretended not to see them, not to notice. But now they watched Rena, their gazes pinned and direct.

As she turned the corner at the edge of town, three field hands jumped quickly to the side to avoid running into her. Rena fisted her hands. She was so hungry. So tired. She wanted to tell those men her family belonged to the highest caste in India, that her father was far more eloquent and learned than any of them would ever be. But Rena knew, even if they believed her, they would not care. They would still leave her and Nell to starve in gutters. All the money in the world would not make them look at her with any less disgust.

And why should they? The Indian Mutiny was painfully fresh in everyone's mind, only a few years past. When Edric left England in pursuit of colonization, no one could have expected him to marry an Indian woman. That she had returned in the wake of his death was an unspeakable scandal.

When the English looked at Rena, they saw a tapestry of evil: Indian soldiers rising up and shooting their British officers, British women and children hacked to pieces in defiance of westernization, Christian converts hunted down and murdered at Delhi for forsaking the Hindu faith.

It did not matter that Sawai Ram Singh, the Maharaja of Jaipur, had sent nearly all of his troops to aid the British. Or that he had housed the wife and children of Major Eden in the Badal Mahal, refusing to hand them over to the demanding rebels who had then marched onto Delhi. The people in Abbotsville only knew that Rena was Indian. She had lived in the north where the mutinies had raged the hardest. She could never be trusted.

In times of weakness, Rena still considered sneaking off in the night so Nell might live with her own family in comfort. But Rena loved Nell too much to abandon her in such a way, and she knew Nell would never allow them to separate. An even weaker part of Rena was too afraid to starve to death alone.

She came at last to the door she was searching for and froze on the threshold, feeling herself approaching a precipice from which she could never draw back. At Nell's warning, this was the only door she had not visited in her relentless search for lodging. *"Edric."* She whispered her husband's name, just to hear it spoken. Then she shoved through the weathered door and stepped inside.

She had heard many rumors of the Gilded Crown, an establishment well known for thievery and prostitution, though it masqueraded as a common roadside inn. Splintered tables and benches were scattered about the dining hall, half the tables still not cleared from the previous night's revelries. A dingy portrait of a rather severe-looking Victoria loomed above the sooty stone fireplace—as if the queen herself actually cared to know what went on in such a place.

The dining hall was mostly vacant, save for a few passing travelers who ate breakfast in the corner and a scattering of women who lounged on benches along the farthest wall with bored, waiting expressions. Rena tried not to look at the women, but she could not help noticing as one of them stood abruptly and stepped across the room to lean against the bar. The woman wore a gaudy dress, wrinkled and slightly too big for her slender frame. The heavy smear of bright rouge on her cheeks made her appear perpetually tired but no less pretty. To Rena she looked like a butterfly wing someone had accidentally stepped on.

Rena froze as the woman met her eyes. She was the first person to have really looked at Rena since she'd arrived in Abbotsville, and an unspoken understanding hummed between them. Rena wondered if this woman had been homeless too. Cast off by relatives, or perhaps born illegitimate.

"Who is loitering there?"

Rena stepped back at the nasty voice but turned her eyes toward the staircase, where a woman with a stack of faded blankets was descending the stairs. This woman was much older than any of the other women there. Her graying hair was tied tightly at the back of her head, and she had the beady eyes of a badger, dark and unusually close together.

Rena's voice came out in a painfully fragile thread. "I came to see if you have a room." The words flooded her with shame. She wondered what Edric would have said if he had seen her in such a place, practically begging for crumbs.

The older woman shook her head. "No," she answered in a clipped voice, then stabbed a thumb at the door. "Leave."

Half-relieved to be cast out from such a dismal place, Rena turned toward the door but stopped as she remembered the stable where Nell was still sleeping like those in India who were born too unclean to merit a caste at all. From the highest to the lowest was a dizzying fall, and Rena still couldn't feel the ground beneath her own feet. Could they plummet lower still? She thought of how it might be if she and Nell faced winter without a home. What might happen if the chill in the air journeyed to their bones and then to their lungs?

"My mother-in-law is starving," Rena managed, half turning back to the woman. "We both are. We have nothing. We are desperate."

The woman looked at Rena the way Nell's family had looked at her, as if the whole of the Indian mutinies were carried out at her behest. "*Put the Indian chit back on a boat,*" one cousin had whispered to Nell when he thought Rena was out of earshot. "*Send her home at once.*"

"Even we have standards," the woman said scornfully. "You must find lodging elsewhere."

But Rena had already been everywhere. Nearly delirious from sparse food and even sparser sleep, she felt unbearably thin beneath the woman's gaze. "*Wife!*" growled a voice, and the woman winced. Rena turned and watched as a thin man with a dirtied apron crossed through the kitchen door. "See to the storage room," he ordered, jerking his head toward the back. "Make it ready."

The woman hissed then spun around and disappeared through the back hall. As soon as she was gone, the man folded his arms in front of his chest and gave Rena a dubious look. Hard work had given his skin a blotchy appearance, but his eyes were clear. Scraggly white whiskers hung in a long, wiry tangle along his jaw. Rena had once heard them called *Piccadilly weepers* by British soldiers who had worn the style with a bit more class.

"Have you not heard of what happens in our upstairs rooms?" the man challenged. "Or is that why you're here?"

Rena's humiliation climbed, undercut by a stab of raw fear. "I have no interest in what goes on in any of your rooms," she responded. "I left my mother-in-law, Lady Hawley, sleeping in a stable. All I am looking for is a roof to put over her head."

At her stiff reply, his face softened, as if discomfort was something he didn't often see in his line of work. He measured her anew, the corners of his mouth pinching as he glimpsed her black mourning gown and trembling hands. With a slight wince, he asked her, "This mother-in-law of yours. Can she wash dishes?"

Half-breathless with hope, Rena jumped to answer, "We both can."

"My wife will never let you in her kitchen." He shook his head with an embittered frown. "But if your mother-in-law can wash dishes and floors, if she can sweep and clean tables, then you can stay in our storeroom."

Rena was too stunned to answer immediately. With the looming threat of the workhouse, she was certain Nell would accept the arrangement, though it still smarted to imagine her mother-in-law scrubbing floors in such a place. "I am. . .indebted to you, sir."

"It's not exactly posh lodging—a drafty produce closet with a narrow bench."

"We've slept in gutters," she answered, steadily meeting his eyes.

He quirked a bushy eyebrow then nodded. "And the men? The ones hereabouts who drink too much, they might take an interest in you."

She hesitated, glancing back at the pretty, albeit rumpled, woman who still watched her with unease. Was this their silent understanding, then? Was Rena looking at her future, or was this poor woman remembering her own naive past?

"I am not to be touched," Rena insisted, mortified to have to set such a stipulation, regardless of whether it would be followed. She turned back to the innkeeper and lifted her chin. "If you can promise me that, then we will gladly accept your offer."

"Ah, so here you are setting our terms now." He nodded his approval then extended a veiny hand. "I am Mr. Bagley, and I accept your terms. It's only fair warning to you, though, that my wife does not and likely will never like you."

If such was the least of Rena's worries, she might actually sleep through the night for the first time in nearly two years. "I am growing rather used to being unliked," she confessed. "And I would rather sleep among humans who despise me than horses who don't."

Oats, barley, wheat.

Rena ran her fingers with wonder along the sheaves as she followed the main road out of town, passing foreign fields and grand estates as she journeyed. So much food, she thought bleakly, and yet she and Nell were both starving.

It certainly wasn't for lack of trying. For four weeks, Nell had scrubbed dishes and floors to pay for their place in the shabby storeroom at the Gilded Crown. But money was scarce, barely enough for a loaf of bread and some watered-down milk every few days. And while the Bagleys had allowed them to stay in their produce closet for practically nothing, they were not about to feed them as well. To Rena generosity was becoming a land with uncomfortably tight borders.

Hunting for work of her own, she had knocked on enough doors to scab her knuckles a hundred times over. No work was beneath her, she vowed, no prospect too small. But all doors closed as if on phantom hinges, blotting out her desperate pleas.

Since Edric had died, Rena wondered if she was being punished for something she had done. For marrying a foreigner, perhaps. For leaving her family behind so she could look after Nell. For watching Nell starve and finding herself too weak to find an answer. *Karma.* The word unfolded like a flower in her mind, whispered in her mother's careful, instructive voice. As a child, Rena had learned that her actions had the power to haunt or reward her, to shape who she would become, possibly even in future lives. And Rena felt haunted in many, many ways.

She pressed deeper inland, hoping to come upon a farm willing to pay half price for a milkmaid. With fewer buildings and trees left to block the wind, she pulled her gray shawl tighter around her shoulders and tried to brace herself against a shiver. It was only August, and Nell often said the country air would become crisper after the harvest was gleaned, then turn bitter. Though Jaipur certainly had its colder evenings in the winter months, Rena had spent much of them indoors. She was still too used to the heavy air, the kind of heat she felt deep in her throat every time she swallowed. Abbotsville's leaves were dazzling in their own way, the fields a lovely shade of burnt sunlight, but the shivers still jumped along her skin and made her wish for a warmer, more inviting place.

"You think your desert sands are everything, Rena, but there is a whole world beyond this heat. Someday I will take you to England. We'll pluck apples from the trees and lie in the grass all evening while we eat them. And then I'll whisper in your ear all the ways I love you."

Rena gripped the front of her threadbare dress, feeling the press of Edric's ring from beneath the fabric. He had spoken those words to her three days after their wedding, and it sickened her to hear his voice now, in a strange, foreign place where stalks of wheat stood sentinel over her aching heart. She shut her eyes, no longer wanting to see the lush leaves and yellow harvest. "Oh Edric," she sighed to the empty road. "This place is yours. I wish you could share it with me."

As if hearing her somber plea, distant voices began singing deep in the field beside her, the echoes lifting up a sorrowful dirge which matched the caws of crows as they soared overhead.

As if their voices could sense her hunger.

As if they were giving it a voice all its own.

Rena turned toward the field, closing her eyes once more as she listened. From a distance, she couldn't make out any of the words, but the vague sound gave the song a certain beauty. She took several steps toward the field, then parted the stalks, her feet crunching the ground as she pressed forward. The fields were empty.

She walked for what felt like hours, pulled toward the voices as if hypnotized. She followed the music through several plots of land until she began to see men with swooping scythes in hand and the hunched-over backs of women as they gathered. Stubs of grain fell to the earth beneath each worker, but they did not stop to collect the smallest of these fallen pieces. They worked in a rhythm that made Rena nearly dizzy as she watched. Some of the workers still sang as they gathered; some of them chattered and gossiped among themselves, wrapping twine around thick sheaves; some of them scowled as they worked in the distance, hauling dried sheaves to a massive machine that guzzled, shook, and churned.

Glancing away from the workers, Rena studied the sprawling manor on the hill above—an ancient building with a buttressed roof sloping out like the spine of an overturned book. She dipped to a knee, scooping up a few pieces of scattered grain, and cradled the buds in her hand. So much food, she thought again, and yet her stomach could not recall its last meal.

Desperation whispered in her ear that she had to do *something*, and fear guided her hand as she slipped the grain quickly into the bag at her side, which Nell had insisted she bring in case she happened upon any vegetables growing wild.

She was about to gather another handful when a hard fist clamped tight around her wrist, jerking her so hard to the side that she nearly lost her footing. Startled from her crime, she looked up into a pair of flinty eyes.

"So this is what they teach in your part of the world?" the burly laborer snarled. "To steal from those who work their own way?"

"Please!" she cried, but his grip tightened around her wrist until she gasped and her fingers spread out in terror, dropping the few snatches of grain she still held. "Please, they were just left on the ground!"

She hardly realized she was struggling against him until he tossed her to the ground. Her arms thrummed with pain as her hands shot out to break her fall. For a moment, she could barely move. No man within her father's house had even seen her face, not until Edric had at last pulled aside her veil, and no other man had ever touched her either. Now she was thrown aside as if she had never been cherished, never been set apart in her father's world of books and satin, but was made only to be beaten.

"You think you're worthy of our leavings?" The laborer laughed at her startled expression. "I'll throw you to the magistrate before I let you touch even the scraps from Lord Barric's table."

"That's enough."

The burly worker looked to the side, scowling as another man strode forward. The newcomer was thin but muscular, a young man with corn-colored hair parted to the side and prominent sideburns cut in the style of Prince Albert. He wore a respectable-looking suit, pressed and trim.

"She was stealing," said the larger man to the other, defensively, running a hand along his sweat-stained collar. "I know Lord Barric wouldn't like that. Not a bit."

"I can certainly deal with the situation without you putting words into Lord Barric's mouth." The blond man jerked his chin toward the other workers. "Back to work. Now."

As the worker retreated, the new man looked down at her with eyes that were all English, bright blue and glinting. "And were you stealing, as he says?" He regarded her down the length of his slender nose with a cautious expression, arms folded in front of him.

Rena crept back up onto her knees, hardly knowing if she dared stand for fear of being arrested. "He speaks the truth," she finally admitted. "I stole grain. Two handfuls."

"I see." He tipped an eyebrow. "And how did you happen to be here, stealing two handfuls of grain?"

"I heard the singing from the road, and I followed it." She realized her answer was peculiar, nearly riddlish. She met his eyes more fully and quietly confided, "And I was hungry."

He unfolded his arms from his chest, so she thought he intended to help her up, but he crouched down in front of her instead, lowering his eyes to her level. "How long since you've eaten a meal?" The pity in his voice speared right through her, made her cringe. She wondered what her father would say if he ever found her kneeling at a man's feet.

"It wasn't just my hunger," she amended, mortified by the sound of her own excuses. She stood abruptly and straightened, trying to feel less small. "I wouldn't have done it for myself alone. But my mother-in-law—I promised I'd take care of her, but we have no money."

Standing, the man pondered the grain still scattered about their feet, then glanced at the manor in the distance. "Lord Barric owns this property," he said after the thread of silence had tightened between them. "He is the master of Misthold, up at the top of the hill. But he is abroad. Gather what scraps you can while the sun is still high in the sky. Keep your head down while you work. And then go with my blessing. If anyone gives you trouble, you tell them William said it was permitted."

She stared at this man called William, not fully understanding his words. "You are giving me permission to steal from your own master?"

He measured the placement of the sun with a speculative eye. "You won't have long," he observed. "Be quick." And then he walked away.

Rena watched his retreat with a sense of wonderment. She'd been certain she was about to be arrested. Instead, a blessing of grain, offered at no cost.

She was not the only one shocked by William's offer. Work had ground to a halt around her, men and women staring at her with looks of unguarded curiosity and distrust. Tipping her eyes up at the sun, she ignored their heated stares, even as William barked one final order at his underlings to "*keep working!*"

As the workers dropped their eyes to their work, Rena dropped to her knees and hastily began to gather grain.

Jack Fairfax, the Earl of Barric, parted easily through the line of workers, his coat crisp and black against a sea of faded tan work smocks. As soon as the laborers saw him coming, they ducked their heads down, working faster. He heard his name carried through the rows on whispers: *"Lord Barric. . .Lord Barric. . .Lord Barric. . ."*

He only sporadically left Misthold to come into the fields below. His tenant farmers saw to the crop's annual yield, and his steward oversaw the farmers. Most of his peers were content to manage their land affairs from London or Bath, where they could continue with their other interests, but Barric preferred to keep a hand in his investments, to be known among those who worked beneath his title.

His friends teased him to no end on this score. *"Still working the fields, eh, Barric?"* one would ask over a game of whist. *"Don't you know that's what the bumpkins are bred for?"* To the sound of chortles, another would interject, *"I've heard milkmaids make excellent lovers, but how ever do you get the dirt out of your shirtsleeves?"*

He kept a hawkish gaze as he walked the fields, straight on course, penetrating. The workers were making good time with the harvest, he noted, their hands tired but strong as they reaped and bound the sheaves in toiling waves. Still, the end of autumn was racing toward them, and he wanted no surprises come winter.

At the end of the row, a girl with black hair and dark skin collected grain, her hair knotted tightly against the back of her neck. She wore a simple black dress which fit her loosely. Barric stopped midstep when he saw her. While he didn't know every hired hand working his field—for his steward managed such affairs—this girl was undoubtedly foreign, and after the mutinies in India, he was certain he'd have been aware of the risk involved in hiring her. He watched her tuck several handfuls of grain into a bag at her side. Not once did she look up at the workers milling about her.

She was trespassing, he realized darkly. Stealing from him. With skin and hair as dark as hers, did she really think she could go unnoticed?

He cut forward a few steps but stopped when he heard the girl was singing under her breath as she gathered. Music, he thought. From a throat so thin he could wrap his fingers twice around it, from lips so parched they were nearly bleeding.

He considered the girl's face. Her expression was intent and focused, her gaze bright despite its weariness. Dirt lined the edges of her jaw, where she had often stopped to rub her hands. As she stooped to gather a few fingers full of grain, her slender back curled into the shape of a question mark.

His eyebrows rose.

"Lord Barric."

He redirected his gaze as William stalked toward him.

"I didn't know to expect a visit so soon after your travels."

Barric returned his steward's greeting with a smile that rested subtly on his thin lips. He had no wish to talk about his lengthy trip to France, even with William. The whole sordid business had already left him in an especially dark mood. Barric replied, instead, with sarcasm, "You know how I like to be surprising. But so, it seems, do you. That girl—" He inclined his head toward the end of the field. "Who is she?"

William's eyes followed the path of Lord Barric's gaze for barely a second. "A foreigner," he supplied without embellishment.

Barric looked back to the girl who knelt on the ground like a shadow spread low beneath the grain. Her hair was the blackest he had ever seen, nearly the same color as her deep-set eyes. "Yes," he replied flatly, studying her hands as they swept through the fallen stalks. "I can see as much for myself. But who is she?"

"She's a beggar."

No sooner were these words spoken than the girl straightened her back to lift her eyes toward the sky, seeming to measure the sun by its warmth on her face. Beggarly though she was, her movements were slow and thoughtful, as if her skin was but a somber veil draped across her back. His voice sounded suspicious when he finally asked,

"Where did she come from?"

"One of our workers caught her stealing grain. I told her she could take what scraps she wanted—just for the day."

Barric's gaze swung back to William. "And you thought it right to give to her out of my pocket?"

William stood his ground, unflinching despite the edge in Barric's voice. "It didn't feel right," he insisted. "Sending her away. And I've heard talk of her in town these past few weeks. Let's just say folks haven't taken too. . .kindly to her arrival."

Barric made a sound behind his closed lips. "I see. And have any of my workers given her trouble?"

"For stealing out of your pocket, you mean?" William smiled faintly. "I'd have thought you'd be the first one in line to give her trouble. My lord."

Most days Barric couldn't stand the blunt way his steward spoke to him, as if he matched Barric rank for rank. It had been that way ever since they'd been boys, when William's father was brought to Misthold to serve as steward to Barric's. For years Barric and William were surly playfellows, until William was sent to a middling class boarding school and Barric to study at Eton.

When Barric's parents had died in a boating incident, he had risen from a boy of fifteen years to a landed earl in a single, wretched morning. From the young Jack Fairfax, as he'd been named by his parents, to the imposing and powerful Lord Barric. He had left off with school and returned at once to oversee Misthold. His father's title had fit him rather poorly, then, like adult clothes too large for a child, but he had still managed to accomplish far more as *Barric* than he ever might have as *Jack*.

Then William's father had died, a year after Barric's, of consumption. Almost as soon as William had returned to Abbotsville, Barric found himself at his door, all but demanding that William step into the position of steward. It had seemed a logical choice at the time. Surely William knew his father's work as well as Barric knew his own, and he was familiar. But perhaps there had been more to it than that. Though Barric usually glowered in its presence, he had always admired pluck.

"If I'm going to give anyone trouble," Barric said at last, "it would surely be you."

Again, the steward glanced at the beggar. "True enough, but I'm not the one your men are making eyes at."

"Your point is noted. So, tell me—what is our little thief's name?"

"I didn't ask her," William admitted. "Of course, if you are curious, you can go ahead and ask her yourself."

William tipped his head toward the girl, daring Barric to ask her, but Barric scanned the other workers in a show of feigned disinterest. As if an earl would deign to speak to a foreign, thieving beggar, he reminded himself somewhat reluctantly. As if he owed the girl anything when she was already walking away with pockets full of his grain.

CHAPTER 2

Rena walked quickly, eagerness spread across her face like a banner. She cut through the patchwork clustering of fields, trying to reach home faster than the winding roads usually allowed. Though her bag was now weighted with grain, she felt far lighter than she had in many months, with the threat of starvation held at bay momentarily. She now carried enough food to feed both herself and Nell for a week.

The fieldworkers were beginning to turn in for the day, the sun barely lighting them from an inch above the horizon. She pulled the bag's strap tighter across her chest, breathing in through her nose. Most days she closed her eyes and imagined the smell of India still lingered on her hands and neck like a perfume. She missed the scent of India's impressive heat. She missed the Eastern color palette which swirled in serpentine ribbons across her memory, smelling of citrus rinds and black spice.

She studied the English horizon as she pushed her way through a prickly hedgerow separating one master's field from another's. Jogging roads connected coastal cliffs to sprawling fields. The line of earth teemed with a patchwork of various crops, many of them tall enough to brush her belly, some towering even higher. Hills plunged downward toward the fields, the highest slopes topped by the occasional grand estate with high-arched entries and sculpted casements—each structure stood watch over its valley like a great imperial eye.

She pondered all of this vastness, willing herself not to be impressed. She could not attach herself too much to Abbotsville's lovely trees, though they blushed with golden leaves, rich with color.

Nor could she find comfort in the rows of sun-kissed crops or the hills shrouded in greenery. For what would be left for her in this foreign place when all of that grandeur was dead and barren, buried in snow? The trees flashed the brightest right before they died. Much like Edric, she thought with a shudder, England was a young world forever dying, its bursting colors draining slowly away into a muted shade of drab, English gray.

Parting through one final stretch of wheat, she stepped back onto the main road, leaving the labyrinthine fields behind her as she turned at last toward town.

"Well, now, who do we have here?"

Two men stood in the road. Rena nearly plowed into the one who had spoken, startled from her private thoughts, but then her hands came up at the last moment, pushing her back from his wide chest. Two gray hunting dogs lurched forward and began barking up at her. The bouncing sound rubbed at her nerves and made them feel raw.

As she stepped back from the dogs, the man's companion smiled his smooth agreement. His face was half-hidden in shadow, slanted with the faltering light. "It must be that little Indian chit we've heard so much about," he observed, tapping her in the ribs with his walking cane.

Even more than she despised the man's amused grin, Rena hated that he had called her an *it*. The men were both handsome, young, and well dressed, their features angled in twisted amusement. Edric too had inherited power and youthful charm. But these men were nothing like Edric, and it grieved Rena to remember her husband while pinned in place by their sly, hunting smiles. She glanced down the lane, toward the bridge, trying to think up an excuse for leaving quickly. How many steps would it take for her to reach the bridge? Ten? Twenty?

The second man's eyes flickered toward the field and back to Rena. He was tall and lanky, as ramrod straight as the walking stick still dangling from his hand. "She's been strolling through your fields, Thomas."

The accusatory note in his voice wedged between Rena's ribs like a spike. "*You're* Lord Barric?"

The man smiled his slow answer, but she still doubted him. "I didn't realize the field was yours," she explained, trying to sound polished and poised. The dogs meandered curiously, moving in tighter and tighter circles around her. She eyed their slavering snouts, but even with the snorting growls, the beasts did not seem nearly as dangerous as their masters. She redirected her gaze to the men, watching their teeth flash white in the dusky air.

Sensing her scrutiny, Thomas shifted his eyes to hers. His thick black hair was elegantly tousled, with trim sideburns angling low around a sharp, pointed chin. "I think you ought to pay me for tramping your Indian feet across our land." He smiled dangerously. A subtle mustache cut a thin line above his slender lips.

The sound of horse hooves clattered somewhere in the distance, but neither of the men marked the sound. Rena clutched the bag of grain closer to her chest, still reeling from the man's fiendish insult. "I haven't any money," she said stiffly, trying to sound like her father. Influential. A woman of words, commanding respect. "Let me pass."

Stepping into a spot of dwindling sunlight, Thomas scanned her speculatively. She flinched when she noticed his eyes were blue like Edric's and yet held not a scrap of his kindness. He smelled sharper too, as if he dabbled on too much cologne, the *eau de toilette* Englishmen so often used as aftershave. "Friend of ours had a *bibi* back in India. A little thing like you. Perhaps you could take off those shoes and dance for us. Dance like her."

Rena's blood heated as he all but called her a concubine. The horse hooves, which had begun as a muted thud moments before, began to sound crisper, nearer. The taller man looked curiously in the distance, but Thomas did not pull his eyes from Rena's. She wondered if whoever was coming would even bother to deliver her, or if it might be another man like them, cruel and entitled. "Leave me alone," she said at last. "Bibi or not, I'd never let you touch me."

"Look at that chin," Thomas scoffed and touched her anyway, flicking his fingers beneath her jaw. "How high she keeps it lifted—as if she isn't as sullied as the dirt soiling her dress."

Rena ignored the itching urge to wipe her face with her grimy hands. She didn't need a mirror to know she looked wretched. For the first time since marrying Edric, she missed the veil she had worn in her father's house, which had shielded her from hungry eyes like theirs, commanding respect and honor. Though many of the English had denounced the Hindu practice of *purdah* as cruel and slavish, wearing her veil had also made Rena feel like she had held some unspoken worth, a secret.

But there was no veil when Thomas's friend swooped forward, seizing the bag from her grasping hands. "And what are we guarding so carefully, eh?" He threw open the flap. His fingers were thin and long as he reached inside. Skeleton fingers, Rena thought dizzily. He lifted his brows as he tipped the bag upside down, littering the ground with her grain.

"Stop it!" Rena choked, and for the first time she heard her own desperation, a shrill sound which was unfamiliar to her tongue. "That was given to me! As a gift!"

But the man simply smiled, malevolence gleaming beneath his shadowed eyes. The dogs were circling closer to her ankles, throats burbling low with growls. Unwilling to beg any longer, Rena turned on her ankle to run.

"Hold on to her!" ordered Thomas, stepping over Rena's fallen bag. The other man's walking stick fell to the ground as his hands locked around her forearms from behind, pulling back on her limbs like levers until she struggled to remain on her toes. She shrieked, desperation climbing up her throat as Thomas stalked toward her.

She bit his hand when she found it too close to her cheek—and Thomas swore explosively, striking her hard across the face. Rena swallowed another scream. Her blood boiled and churned as it rushed to the skin. In India, she was her father's daughter, beloved and shrouded; here she was bruised, a worthless girl with foreign eyes whose only wealth was in the abundance of her own grief.

The horse and rider were now nearly upon them, kicking up a deafening clatter in Rena's ears. From behind, she felt the man who held her draw a nervous breath, his hands slackening slightly as he hissed Thomas's name in subtle warning.

But Thomas ignored his friend, fingers pressing like spikes into Rena's cheeks even as the soft whinny of a horse could be heard from a few feet behind. "We ought to tie you down in that field," he spat in her ear. "Let the crows play with you. How long do you think it would take people to notice you were missing? You think anyone would even care to do anything about it?"

"I would."

As Thomas spun around to face the intruder, Rena's eyes darted right, where a suited man sat upon a black stallion, watching them with a stony expression. In the emerging moonlight, his hair gleamed copper red, stylishly short but still messy along the arch of his brow.

Ignoring Rena's slight cry of protest, Thomas jostled her behind him and lifted his chin to the horseman. "Cousin," he greeted at last, a cordial smile on his lips that didn't reach his eyes. "Didn't expect to see you back for several weeks yet. Tell me, how is Charlie these days?"

Rena closed her eyes, feeling the cold fingers of defeat brush across her skin. *Cousin.* As if she could place her hope in a man who shared blood with either of these monsters. The newcomer's expression cooled even more, until, surprisingly, Thomas released her.

She didn't want to hear what Thomas and his friend might say to the red-haired newcomer. Perhaps they would call her a harlot for the lodging she'd taken at the Gilded Crown. Yes, she'd heard that title whispered on more than one occasion as she hunted for work through town. Or perhaps Thomas would say she had stolen the spilled grain from his field. Without an ally, she could be hurled in prison or worse for such an offense.

"We were just having a bit of fun," the friend explained feebly when he realized the rider would not answer Thomas's question. He inched back a few steps from Rena, putting distance between them, and snatched up his walking stick from the ground. "Perhaps things got out of hand."

The rider angled his head as he slowly replied, "Perhaps."

"Oh, don't be such a bore," Thomas chided. "You remember Sir Ellis Andrews, yes? From Oxford."

The rider did not mark this reintroduction. Sir Ellis Andrews fiddled his walking stick from one hand to the other.

"And what are you about this evening?" Thomas challenged in a far less obliging tone. "Aren't you usually rolling up your shirtsleeves to muck around with the field hands?"

"As chance would have it, I was on my way to call on your father." The rider spoke in a voice so bored it sounded half-dead. He raised a brow. "Give him my regrets, won't you? It seems you will be arriving without me."

Sir Ellis nodded his anxious agreement to the veiled dismissal, but Thomas would not be cowed. "I haven't yet concluded my business here." He inclined his eyes at Rena. As his gaze touched her skin, fear muddled her mind, until she could hardly sort out his words against the pounding in her own ears.

At that, the red-haired man swung down from his stallion, his booted feet connecting sharply with the ground beneath him. He and Thomas matched stares. Thomas was shorter than his cousin, scrappier of build and perhaps a few years younger. For a moment, Rena wondered if they would come to blows, but Thomas must have sensed in the other man's gaze that he lacked some upper hand, for he nodded his head in slight acknowledgment and signaled for Sir Ellis to follow him up the road. Rena drew a steadier breath as she at last saw Thomas's back turned in retreat.

"Fair bit of warning," Thomas added, angling a look over his shoulder. He nodded his head at Rena and sneered at his cousin. "The girl bites."

"Fair bit of warning," the red-haired man replied, his steely gaze boring into Thomas's back. "So do I."

Even after Thomas and Sir Ellis had skulked away, mortification and fear lingered heavily in Rena's chest. The red-haired stranger watched his cousin's retreat with a tight frown. When he raked a hand distractedly through his hair, Rena followed the gesture, staring slightly. She had never seen red hair before. Edric's was a dusty brown color, the same shade as the earth when faded by the sun. But this man's hair was red. Different. Foreign. The color of copper.

As Rena waited for him to speak, she pressed both hands to her face. There she felt the sting of Thomas's blow on one cheek, the flush from raw panic on the other, which was all she needed to remind herself she was still quite alone with a man. "I must go," she announced stiffly. "I'll be missed."

The man stirred as if he had entirely forgotten she was there and turned to face her. He scanned her in quick appraisal, his gaze darkening as it came to rest on her face. "He struck you," he said as if he had only just remembered, and stepped closer to her.

Rena jerked backward, not wanting to show him the spot between her shoulder blades for fear of exposing herself for another assault. "I need to go," she repeated, completely ignoring his remark. "I'll be missed. My mother-in-law will be waiting. She'll have noticed I'm late, and—"

"Look at me," the stranger ordered, cutting her off. After what had happened with the other men, it took Rena a moment before she felt daring enough to meet his gaze dead on. When she did, the corners of his eyes creased slightly. "Do you think I am like them?"

She studied him for a slow moment, watching his eyes shift and narrow as they awaited her answer. He did seem different from the others. Not just in his appearance but in bearing. His eyes were hard, but they did not seem cruel. Though he stood proud and tall, he did not feel dangerous. She released her pent-up breath and slowly shook her head.

He broke his eyes from hers. "You were in my fields today."

Lord Barric. Though this man matched far more closely whom she'd pictured than the cruel and entitled Thomas, Rena was nonetheless back on her guard. The steward had said Lord Barric was the master of Misthold and all the fields surrounding it. Such a man would have considerable power. He would have both money and influence, would brush shoulders with the local magistrate. And she *had* stolen from him.

"I was given permission," she explained hastily.

"Yes, so I was told." He paused, his eyes missing nothing. "I was also told my steward caught you stealing first."

Ashamed, Rena's eyes fell to her feet and stayed there. "I did not mean to steal from you."

"Explain yourself, then." This time she didn't mistake the edge in his voice. He was not interested in hearing vague excuses. Only the truth.

"My mother-in-law hasn't had a full meal in days." She broke off, still feeling the weight of his stare even though her face was tipped down toward her feet.

"Your mother-in-law is hungry," he repeated slowly. Then, in a harder voice, he demanded, "And what of your hunger? You're practically a skeleton."

Now she felt ashamed in quite another way. "Yes," she admitted tightly, her throat clenching as though he held a fist around her windpipe. She stopped to banish images of the full woman she had once been, so safe and well cared for. She had been beautiful too, shapely and pretty enough to have caught Edric's eye even while hidden beneath her veil. Now she was a skeleton, as this man had so bluntly noted, covered in dirt. *Vanity*, she warned herself. All that was vanity.

"Yes, I am hungry," she went on, "but I am not responsible only for myself."

"What are you doing here?"

Weary of defending herself, Rena spoke more frankly. "Surely you've already heard more than enough stories of the Indian *trollop* who has come to invade your precious England." She heard the burst of bitterness in her words and winced. Most days hunger frayed her nerves and made her speak and act in hasty ways. She was so tired of being stared at and whispered about, of being treated like some beastly thing which made families unwilling to open their doors. But she didn't want to be bitter or inwardly frayed or even hurt. She wanted to be stalwart like Nell, immovable like Edric.

"I have no taste, nor time, for gossip," the man volleyed, sounding irritated by her answer. She was ready, then, to leave and return home, but his expression relented, his tone nearly gentle as he asked her, "What is your name?"

"Rena." As soon as she said it, she winced, realizing her gaffe. To have introduced herself to a lord by first name on first acquaintance—why, it was unheard of.

Lord Barric's eyes widened slightly as if he too was taken aback by the introduction. But then his expression smoothed, and he bowed, graciously overlooking her misstep.

"Rena." He tested her name, a slow pronunciation, then met her eyes as if measuring its sound against her wraith-like appearance. Edric's voice had always held a laughing quality, her name soaring whenever he spoke it, but this man gave her name a strange cadence, soft and rolling in a way she'd never heard.

"Yes, Lord Barric." She tried to sound formal, dipping into a slight curtsy so they might both forget her threadbare dress and dirt-marred cheeks.

Her halting accent probably mangled the sound of his name. He was as foreign to her as she was to him, and yet he flashed a faint smile at her words. "Ah, so you've heard of me."

In truth, she knew very little of the man standing before her. Only that his steward had said she could pick the grain *because* the master was not at home. Would she have been allowed even to set foot on the land had Lord Barric been there? Or would she have been cast out before he'd see her?

"I can repay you for what I took," she promised suddenly. "If you only give me time, my lord."

He stooped to pick up her bag and held it out to her. When she did not move to take it, he pressed it into her hands, and she noted how horribly light the satchel felt now that the grain was littered in the road.

"You may pick from my fields," Lord Barric finally said, a low-spoken offering, "however often as you and your mother-in-law have need. You needn't think of paying me back."

Rena's eyes startled wide. She wanted to ask why a lord would make such an offer, especially to someone as strange and out of place as she was, but it seemed unwise to do so, in case it prompted him to change his mind. "I am grateful for your kindness," she whispered instead.

Lord Barric threw a glance over his shoulder, in the direction of town, and stared distantly at the path the other men had taken, presumably toward home. "And I wouldn't go asking for help in any of the other fields." His voice was much grittier now, as it had sounded before. "Do you understand?"

She followed Lord Barric's gaze down the road, where the wind howled as if echoing his cousin's snide laughter. She understood all too well. When she bunked down for sleep that night, she was sure she would once again feel the press of Thomas's icy fingers digging deep into her skin—would feel the startling crack of pain as his hand had connected with her face. "Yes," she whispered, tucking the folds of her shawl even tighter around her elbows. "I understand."

Lord Barric glanced back down and studied her. He was much taller than she, but she kept her chin held high to meet his eyes. Thomas had jeered at her lifted chin, had mocked her for her grubby hands and defiant expression. Barric's eyes trailed from her eyes to her jaw, as if measuring her pride by the lift and angle of her face. "Good," he remarked, then looked away once more as he said to himself, "Yes, good."

Thinking this was as kindly a farewell as she'd been offered yet in Abbotsville, Rena shouldered her bag and moved to leave, but Lord Barric kept in step with her as she headed back toward town. "Shall I escort you home?"

Rena struggled with his question. *Home* didn't seem like a befitting term for a storage closet which often smelled of moldy produce. With a sidelong glance, she measured Lord Barric one last time. He wore a long black frock coat with glinting buttons and a fashionable set of high riding boots, barely worn. He walked beside her with the casual gait of a man who in his life had inhabited many great halls. She grimaced, imagining the moment he would duck beneath their splintered door-frame to inspect their dusty hovel. Perhaps he would even wonder *how* she survived at the Gilded Crown, when so many other women led men upstairs just to pay their way.

"I'd much rather go on alone," she decided, dipping her head as she tried to pass him.

He followed still. "Where is it that you live?"

She shook her head, trying to sound dismissive as she said, "It's not far."

"And you are alone?" Barric pressed, matching her quickening pace with ease. "You and your mother-in-law?"

"We live with. . .with kindly people." She faltered on the outright lie. Though Mr. Bagley had shown her mercy, he also made his living in the most unscrupulous of terms. And his wife, true to his promise, hated Rena and seemed to awaken each morning with the sole aim of tormenting her.

"Are they relatives?" he demanded. "These *kindly* people who apparently let you starve?"

She eyed him sharply for pressing the issue, thinking a gentleman ought to allow her *some* bit of privacy.

"They are relatives to someone, I'd imagine."

Lord Barric inclined an eyebrow.

"Are you playing a game with me, or do you really refuse to answer my questions?"

Once upon a time, Rena had played games with Edric, had teased and smiled because he was kind, and she wanted to seem spirited and interesting. Feeling Lord Barric's shadowy presence beside her, she sighed and shook her head, feeling the grit between her fingers as she rubbed her hands together.

"I *live*, Lord Barric," she replied bleakly, "not particularly well, I'll admit. But I do live, and that is more than answer enough."

CHAPTER 3

Bag still in hand, Rena shoved against the front door of the Gilded Crown. The door's red paint splintered and stuck beneath her clammy palms, its wood peeling from years spent standing against rough wind. Rena faltered in the open doorway, cringing as the room reeled in its familiar chaos.

The usual men were drinking that night. Side by side, their elbows on the bar formed a thick, impenetrable chain as they murmured together. Beyond them, a cluster of painted women circled the tables, their eyes searching, lingering, promising. Rena knew that several of them, the particularly pretty ones, lived in the rooms upstairs. The rest lived in various other holes throughout town, drifting from bed to bed to stave off starvation.

Rena's fingers were stiff as she slipped her shawl from her shoulders and shut the door behind her. As she entered, the women avoided her eyes more than the men, drifting away and scattering as soon as she neared. Rena studied their tangled hair, which was pinned against the backs of their heads in elaborately wild designs, as if it had only just now been tousled. Self-conscious, Rena smoothed her fingers over her own hair, which was parted smoothly down the center of her head. Her simple plait was tucked up in a tight bun at the back of her neck, as would have been in style several years before. As she moved, the line of women continued to fold away from her. Did they know how deeply it hurt for her, a Brahmin woman, to live in a shelter of prostitutes? She didn't belong in Nell's world, but she certainly didn't belong to theirs either. Even here she was somehow beneath.

A man knocked against her as she approached the bar, and she stiffened out of instinct. By now every eye in the place viewed her as a possibility. *How long?* the men seemed to wonder. How long could she starve before considering it? Work was work, as the women often said. Rena's eyes panned warily to the shadowy staircase, her stomach clenching in fear of her own desperation.

"And what wickedness have you been up to?" Rena glanced toward the bar, where Mrs. Bagley was drying water glasses with a grubby towel. Rena often imagined the woman's stubby fingers could turn to claws when provoked. "Surely you haven't been up to anything useful."

Though weary from her encounter on the road, Rena would not allow Mrs. Bagley to tempt her into a foul mood. Instead, she swept forward, splaying both hands on the bar in front of her, and managed a weak smile. "I have two pence." She dug the pennies from a scrap of fabric in the back of her shoe. As she slid the battered copper coins against the bar, two men on either side of her shifted in their seats. Could they tell it was all she had left in the world? "Won't you fix us a plate?" Rena pleaded. "Just for tonight?"

"For two pence?" Mrs. Bagley humphed, her eyes fixed on an invisible spot on the glass she was holding. Not once did her gaze flick to the worthless coins in front of her, which scraped together were hardly enough worth a boot cleaning. "You'd think we weren't already giving you lodging out of our own generous pockets."

Rena bit back her irritation. Nell had worked slavishly hard those last few weeks to pay their way, and Mrs. Bagley could hardly rent the produce closet to regular customers regardless.

"Please," Rena said, softer, carefully tempering her words so the other guests would not overhear her begging, "let me do this for my mother-in-law."

There was nothing Rena would not give for Nell, nothing she wouldn't do. True, she was now to be a beggar at Lord Barric's feet, but his offer was also a salvation of sorts. Tonight was the beginning of something new. She could feel it. Rena wanted to feast as she had in her father's house, as Nell had done on holidays, as they had both done when she married Edric.

"If you wanted to do your mother-in-law favors, you'd have stayed in India where you belong."

Rena winced as Mrs. Bagley's voice rose, knowing the other customers would be sure to overhear every insulting syllable. "What could you do for her, anyway, a little waste such as yourself? Another mouth for her to feed, that's what you are. Why, I ought to take those two pence as payment for the room I'm renting to you at practically nothing. As if two pennies scraped together are enough for a plate from my kitchen."

"Perhaps two shillings would be enough to make up any remaining cost." Rena startled when a hand placed two silver coins on the bar beside her own. Glancing up, she joined gazes with an older man, nearly her father's age, who wore a thick white neckcloth.

"Parson?" Mrs. Bagley nearly stammered in disbelief as she shook her head and sweepingly said, "That is hardly necessary. I did not mean for you to be in any way disturbed by my tenant."

Everyone was staring now, and Rena suspected for once the attention had little to do with her. Men and women alike cast uncertain glances at the parson, evidently shocked to find him standing beneath the inn's scanty light.

"I am just fine." Rena whispered the words tightly, mortified to be caught, again, with nothing. "I will not take your money."

Her words moved nothing in his expression. He had intelligent eyes, cast in a subdued shade of misty gray. As he glanced over his shoulder, the patrons went about their usual business, pretending not to notice his presence.

"It is not a question of what *you* can afford," the parson assured

Rena, speaking loudly enough for his voice to be heard all the way down the length of the bar. "But if the innkeeper's wife cannot manage to feed you for two pence, then it is certainly a question of what *she* can afford."

Heads turned again. Mrs. Bagley's hand shot out at once and claimed Rena's two pence, leaving the parson's two shillings behind. "I assure you we can certainly afford to feed anyone who comes in our doors."

The parson nodded slowly before plucking up his two shillings and slipping them back into his pocket. "I am quite relieved to hear you say so," he said, then glanced distractedly over Rena's shoulder, once again scanning the crowd.

"Is there. . .anything you need?" Mrs. Bagley hedged hesitantly.

The parson settled his attention back on her. "In fact, there is," he admitted. "I'm looking for Miss Janet Dawson."

"She frequents this place well enough," Mrs. Bagley agreed with some surprise, eyes shifting toward the corner stairs. She grimaced. "Though she is currently. . .*working*."

"I see." The parson stepped back, frowning as he dropped his hand from the bar. He was quiet for a moment, then tipped his head meaningfully in Rena's direction. "I will kindly wait if your customer is hungry."

The dismissal was clear but kind. Mrs. Bagley clanked the glass she was holding down on the bar, scowling slightly at Rena as she disappeared into the kitchen and began barking orders at her poor, unsuspecting kitchen girl. As soon as Mrs. Bagley was gone, Rena sought the proper words to thank the parson for what he'd done. Not merely for stepping in, for offering money, but for the way he had spoken to her, calmly, as if there was nothing at all peculiar about her. Nothing different. It was certainly a change to be regarded with more respect than pity.

But the words did not form in time, nor did the parson seem to expect them. In a moment, his attention was drawn across the room, where a thin young woman with plain brown hair and tired eyes was descending the stairs. As soon as she spotted the parson, a spark of unsettled recognition flashed across her features. The fear in her eyes made her seem somewhat younger.

"Must be about the child," someone whispered from just behind Rena's shoulder.

To which another grimly answered, "They summoned the doctor this morning."

The parson stepped through the chaos of the pub to meet the woman—Janet—at the bottom of the stairs. He tipped his head in greeting, and her hand found the banister, clutching tightly. Even over the din, Rena heard her sharp words. "What is it?" Janet demanded. "What's happened? Why have they sent you?"

The parson stood very still. He did not reach out to touch her, though she looked at him, wide-eyed and fearful, as though he'd grabbed her by the arms. The parson motioned gently toward the front door, but the woman shook her head and asked him something else, words which were lost to the murmur of the crowd. The parson's eyes were soft and dreary as he whispered something back to her. Immediately she half sunk against him, her hands clawing against the front of his coat as she shrieked out an unintelligible name. The parson grasped her shoulders, continuing to whisper in her ear.

The voice over Rena's shoulder spoke again. "What would the poor lad have thought, to know he had a mother such as her?"

"Probably better off that he didn't."

Janet swayed, then fell, her hands pressed tightly against the floorboards as she heaved. Rena knew enough of death to know that this was what it looked like. This was how it felt. Rena had hit the floor too when the doctor had emerged from Edric's room to tell her it was all over. Even after two years, she still felt as though she hadn't managed to stand fully ever since.

From all corners of the room, women left their men on various benches as they rushed to grab ahold of Janet. They ran their hands over her hair as they whispered quiet words to her. Senselessly, she shook her head, over and over and over, as if to clear it. But when all else cleared, Rena knew this one truth would never change: the woman's child was dead.

Familiar with the press of grief, Rena moved toward Janet, wishing to soothe her, but Mrs. Bagley grabbed her hand in a vise grip and stopped her from taking another step. "Get back to your room," she snapped, shaking her head in rebuke as she hurled a tray of food into Rena's arms. "What makes you think she wants comforting from you? Indian witch."

Rena fiddled with the storeroom's doorknob, first wiggling it to the right and then pressing the tip of her foot firmly against the bottom left corner of the door—a frustratingly familiar ritual. At last the door swung free on its rusty hinge, admitting Rena into the narrow space.

She paused in the entryway. Nell had not heard her come in. The woman sat alone at the table, both of her eyes clamped closed, her hands pressed tightly against the marred wood of the tabletop.

Even beneath the vulturous talons of starvation, Nell's strength and vibrancy filled the room. Though more than twice Rena's age, Nell was remarkably beautiful, her blond hair woven with wisps of elegant silver which would not dull into gray. Her back and shoulders had turned bony in past weeks, but even hunched over the table in her strange vigil, the woman seemed sturdy and unbending. Hunger had not stolen the light from her eyes or the strength from her brow. Colored only by candlelight, Nell wore a determined expression that swept away the dusty gloom of the room and made her mistress of even the cobwebs.

Clenching her fingers together, Rena studied the crisscrossed veins on the backs of Nell's bony hands, then considered the woman's palms as they pressed prostrate against the table. On Nell's third finger rested a thin, gold wedding band set with amethyst, which had begun to fit loosely in her hunger. A talisman, Rena thought, against the pangs of widowhood.

Rena had not known Sir Alistair well. He was a stern-looking man who wore a suit like a badge of honor. He was quiet and forceful, and *bloody good at chess*, as he liked to boast. He smoked cigars only on the back terrace where his wife couldn't complain about the smoke.

When Edric had brought Rena home that first morning, and introduced her as his wife, Sir Alistair had not thundered as he seemed likely to do, or demanded if Edric was joking. Instead, he had risen from his chair, smelling strongly of tobacco, taken Rena's hand, and asked her if she played chess. To her startled reply that, no, she had never played, he had told her she must learn. And that was that. As a baronet, Sir Alistair had seemed too rigid to be Nell's husband, and yet he had watched his wife often with a faint smile on his lips, and when she beat him at chess, he had howled with delight and called her a cheat.

Rena focused again on Nell's empty hands. The poor woman had lost her husband and son barely two years apart, but she hadn't spoken of either of them since she and Rena had left India. Edric and his father seemed to live and linger in these moments, filling up the quiet and pressing outward, as if both men were pushing at them from behind a glass wall. Was Nell aware of this? Perhaps this was why she closed her eyes and sat in such silence. Did she feel closer to them?

Rena balanced the tray of food on her hip as she slid into the room and shut the door quietly behind her. "Are you speaking to your husband?" Rena asked the question before she could consider the strangeness of it. Rena had watched her own family meditate each morning for lost family members—her mother prayed for their peace and her father strove to do good deeds in their names so they might each find their way in the next life. But, of course, Edric's family followed other paths with their prayers.

As if awakened from a much deeper world, Nell's head jerked toward the door, and her eyes widened as they flashed from Rena to the overflowing tray and back again. "Speaking to. . .my husband?" She let out an amused, breathy laugh. "Goodness, child. I was praying for our stomachs!" Her eyes dropped once more to the tray, and she quirked a suspicious eyebrow. "Although it would seem my prayers have been answered. Unless I am hallucinating those pork pies—"

Rena grinned down at the feast, the smell of meat and warm bread filling her belly with foreign longing. Wanting to quash any suspicion she was stingy, Mrs. Bagley had loaded the tray with a sampling of nearly everything the kitchen had on hand—meat pies, cheese, and pickled eggs; shreds of roast with slabs of bread; two short glasses of dark ale, rimmed with foam.

But Rena had never touched meat before, nor eggs, nor even tasted alcohol. She had always been a meticulous follower of the Hindu diet, even after she had married Edric. Cows were sacred to her people, and eggs forbidden, and so much of the tray's contents were off-limits to her.

Did she really dare?

Rena caught the desperate hunger in Nell's eyes, knew it mirrored her own, and felt her stomach tighten. Realizing she was far too hungry to starve on her own uncertainty, she slid the tray to the middle of the table and dropped into the seat across from Nell.

"I assure you the food is quite real," she said, stretching her aching muscles. "Well, either that, or I suppose we both could be hallucinating."

Nell ignored Rena's tired attempt at humor. "Yes, but how on earth did you afford this?" Eyebrows lifted, she gestured to the closet they had come to call home, which would forever smell of rotting turnips. "Last time I checked, we were scandalously destitute."

Rena smiled sheepishly, pressing her fingers against the deep scratches in the table's surface.

"Please, don't be cross with me, Nell. I had two pence I've been holding back, just in case." Her smile grew as she plucked up a steaming pie and held it temptingly out to Nell.

Nell did not take the pie but glanced at it as if it could not be trusted or might vanish if she tried to eat it.

"Two pence would never have purchased all of this," she disagreed, shaking her head in disbelief.

"Perhaps Mrs. Bagley was of a generous bent this evening," Rena offered, trying to sound hopeful as she placed the pie back on the tray.

Nell pointed at Rena, her tone suddenly crisp. "That is as brash a lie as ever I've heard. Now you tell me the truth. Where did this come from?"

This conversation was not going at all as Rena had hoped. She knew Nell would be mortified if she learned the parson had stepped in publicly and forced charity on their behalf, and Rena had no wish to prod the woman's already wounded pride. Besides, they should be celebrating. Laughing. Feasting. Their bellies should be full of warm bread and cool ale.

"It really doesn't matter where it came from," Rena said, waving a dismissive hand. "What matters is why I purchased it in the first place."

The suspicion did not fade from Nell's eyes, but she sat silently, patiently awaiting Rena's explanation. Leaning across the table, Rena grabbed her mother-in-law's hand and squeezed her withering fingers.

Nell's hand tensed. "Have you found work, then?" She sounded skeptical. Rena had been trying for weeks to no avail. Of course, it seemed too perfect to be even remotely possible.

"Not exactly. But someone has discovered our situation, and he has welcomed me to pick from his field however often as we are in need."

Nell broke her hand from Rena's and stood abruptly. "You are to be a beggar. That is how we are to survive?"

"How could I refuse such an offer? Nell, this man has saved us."

"Who?" Nell demanded. "Who is this man?"

"He's called Lord Barric."

Nell's eyes widened. "Lord Barric," she repeated incredulously. "Why, you cannot possibly mean Jack Fairfax?"

Rena began to feel uneasy again. "You know him?"

"The Earl of Barric? He is a relative of ours, though I myself have not met him. Sir Alistair's mother was a Fairfax before she married into the Hawley line, but our two families have not mingled on familiar terms in many years."

"Did something. . .happen?"

The older woman waved a hand. "It is an old fight," she said, as if it signified nothing. "Sir Alistair was always grieved not to have seen the families reconcile in his lifetime."

Nell glanced at the wall beside the bench, where a small portrait hung from a rusty nail. Rena followed her gaze. The picture—which captured the Hawley family before disease had struck, snatching away two of their strongest—was one of Nell's few remaining possessions, apart from a crucifix she had hung over the doorframe and an intricately woven shawl she had once made under the tutelage of her mother. Nell's jewelry had already been sold, all but her wedding ring, to pay for their passage to England. Everything that could fetch a price was gone, leaving the room as barren as the women living within.

Nell crossed to the portrait and stared for an unnervingly long moment at the painted figure of Edric, who stood tall beside his father, right hand resting firm on an imperial sword. The colors in the picture were clear and vibrant, as Edric's smile had been before death had dulled it. Despite Edric's regal pose and solemn expression, the artist had somehow captured his laughing eyes, the secret look of a man who was never entirely serious. Rena clenched her teeth, trying to blot out the sound of her husband's murmuring laugh. "*I don't mind a little scandal,*" he had whispered in that coy way of his, "*if it means I can call you wife and find you in my bed every morning.*"

"I cannot allow this." Nell spoke quietly, as if she'd said the words directly to her son. She placed two fingers on the gilded frame and shook her head one last time before softly deciding, "Rena, you must go home."

Rena nearly knocked her chair over as she rose.

"*Go home?*" she repeated, stunned.

She knew Nell had been anxious those past few weeks, often sitting by herself in marked silence. Rena had thought the woman was grieving. Was this what Nell had really been thinking in those moments? Of shipping Rena off and away? Of being rid of her? Rena's heart began beating harder from the inside of her breast, as if tearing through her chest would give it more room to feel.

"Yes." Nell turned and met Rena's eyes directly. "You must return to your parents. To your family."

Rena's mind journeyed back to everything she loved and missed most about her childhood home: an earthen city sprawling beneath the sunbaked horizon, bookshelves lined with ancient volumes written in every language imaginable, luxurious tapestries slung from the walls in shades of apricot and pomegranate, her father's mustache tickling slightly as he kissed her cheek and called her *my child.*

Her father was raised in an aristocratic family before the British takeover. Since he was well read and had studied hard in his youth, he was singled out to assist in translations for the British officers. For a

Brahmin to carry out any act that smacked of servitude was degrading. Though Rena's father often suffered guilt for siding so strongly with the British after the mutiny, like many others he also saw crown rule as an opportunity to strengthen India, and—far more importantly—his family's place within it.

But Edric had changed all of that.

Her father had cursed the British crown in every language he knew when he realized one of its officers had stolen away with his only daughter. He had been hard as stone and withdrawn when Rena had returned to them in the wake of Edric's death. But then Rena had packed her bag and told him she was leaving with Nell.

"*Rena,*" her father had rasped, a broken man, grief left in the place of his rage. It was the first time he had spoken her name in over two years, since before she was married. His fingers had clutched at her shoulders, then her fingers, then her hair, reaching and grasping as if his flesh-and-blood daughter had turned to sand beneath his pleas. *"My child, you must not go. You must not go to England. . . ."*

"There is no future for you in England," Nell went on, an unpleasant echo of Rena's father. "I have no connections. No money. An earl may allow you to pick in his fields, but that does not mean he may not trample you in the process. I'll not have you so degraded."

Rena opened her eyes, staring bleakly across the room at Nell. Once again she traced the woman's features, finding poignant similarities around the eyes and brow to the man Rena had once called her husband. Rena had given up everything to follow Nell to England. Her family and her home. Yes, even her future. And when her parents had demanded a reason for this strange departure, she could name no other reason than love. For as long as Rena cleaved to Nell—for as long as she loved her and looked after her—she clung, in a way, to Edric.

"I cannot go back," Rena insisted, tears rising up despite the firmness of her voice. When a few tears escaped, trickling down her face, she ground out the next words: "India is not my home anymore."

Glancing at the cross above the door, Nell continued on. "And after I am gone?" Rena knew the woman was trying to sound practical, but her voice betrayed her with a quaver. "You will never marry so long as you stay here, never have a family of your own. If you return to India, there are still men who may offer you a life worth living."

Rena still felt this was unlikely, though her parents had entertained similar foolish hopes. Her eyes panned once more to the portrait at Nell's side, glimpsing Edric's painted half smile.

In their wedding vows, she and Edric had promised each other all they had or would ever have. In the moment of his death, all Edric had left behind was his mother, a woman who had clutched his right hand as Rena had held so desperately to his left. She remembered watching Nell's grief from the other side of his fresh corpse. She shivered violently and leaned her weight against the table, feeling as if Edric's clammy skin was still coupled with hers.

"I *have* a family."

An aching belly, an empty room, skin pulled tight over hungry bones—all of these sacrifices were worth it, she knew, if it meant staying with Nell, if it meant her family would be her family forever.

Nell crossed the room and placed a steadying hand on Rena's damp cheek. "Edric begged me to look after you," she whispered, as if she could read and anticipate the direction of Rena's thoughts. "It would kill him all over again to see you as a beggar, for his proud bride to be brought so low."

Rena's hands found Nell's, and she gripped the woman's fingers achingly tight. "You must not send me away," she pleaded, beginning to weep when she saw the determination in Nell's expression. The woman was as stubborn as Edric had been and would certainly send her away if she thought it was for the best. "I would rather beg in the field of every lord, to be trampled over and mocked, to be hated by every person who sees me on my knees, if it only means I may remain at your side."

Nell opened her mouth, eyes stern as if to chide her daughter-in-law for her passionate words, but Rena fell to her knees, clamping her hands to the woman's shabby skirt. "You must not send me away," she cried again, pressing a tearstained cheek to Nell's feet. "Your home is my home. And everything you are and everything you love—that is all I ever wish to be."

Nell placed her hand gently on top of Rena's head as if to offer a silent blessing. "Then God help us both," Nell breathed unevenly, her fingers trembling slightly as she combed them through Rena's hair. "For I am no match for these tears."

Barric had not been looking for the girl as he strode through his fields, but his eyes found her anyway. Wearing the same dull black dress, she stooped beneath thick stalks of grain, gathering a few fallen buds into her bag. She moved steadily, her eyes carefully neutral, shoulders guarded as she bent low over her task. Though she kept mostly to herself, two male workers on either side of the row stole surreptitious glances at her as they made their way down the line. A few other workers whispered to each other, their voices low over their working hands. Barric tore his eyes away from the girl before any of them could notice where his gaze had strayed.

He still wasn't entirely sure what had made him offer his fields to her in the first place. He was certain his peers would find rich amusement in the unusual arrangement. Why had he allowed a beggar to glean from his crops, especially one who had previously been caught stealing from him? He could already hear their mocking speculations. She was a pretty little thing, they would say. Surely that had something to do with it.

Barric's eyes drifted back to her. He wasn't sure what, exactly, Thomas's intentions were, or what he and Sir Ellis might have done if he hadn't happened upon them on his ride. Sometimes Barric almost wished he might forget that he and his cousin shared blood. They had been educated together as children and played together. As they grew older, they had shared in games of whist and bottles of brandy. Thomas had never been a monster, exactly, though he had always been monstrously arrogant, the product of a negligent mother who had taken too much laudanum and a father who had never quite settled into his own place as a second son.

Thomas's mother had died when he was very young, well before the boating accident which had claimed Barric's own parents. Though Barric's uncle had made too many allowances for Thomas, university had unleashed him entirely, giving him an even more heightened sense of entitlement. Too often for Barric's liking, Thomas flaunted his education and extensive travels, insinuating in subtle ways they made him a better man than Barric. Of course, there was far more standing between the cousins than education. Barric had inherited everything from the Fairfax line; Thomas only had what was left to him from his father's marriage to a moderately wealthy heiress with extravagant tastes.

If he were honest with himself, Barric pitied the man Thomas had become. Feeling the empty hands of one who did not stand to inherit title or fortune, Thomas had developed a deep-rooted anger which often acted without reason. His schoolfellows had not helped matters. Most of them were knaves like the cowardly Sir Ellis Andrews, who was, lamentably, not the worst of Thomas's associates.

Still, Barric could not believe his cousin had gone so far as to hit the girl. As soon as he'd seen it happen, something dark and unpleasant had burst within him.

Crossing his arms, Barric once again considered the girl's progress. Her skirt was rimmed with dirt and her face was layered with sweat. Even her movements seemed stiff and achy, as if her small frame was unused to manual labor. If he gazed upon her back, Barric suspected he would be able to see every notch of her spine.

Rena, she had called herself, with eyes strangely stripped. The name fit her well, an uncommon but lovely slip of sound. He knew she had been afraid of him, and for good reason. She had stolen from him. His peers would have thought it only right if he had acted toward her in anger or had her tossed into prison—or at the very least, looked the other way while his cousin had his sport with her.

He watched her move to the other side of the row, where one of the men had let a few extra kernels fall from his bundle. Barric frowned. The hollowness from the night before seemed gone from her eyes. Gone, he wondered, or just artfully covered? It would serve her well, he supposed, to seem strong in the presence of those who might hate her.

"Looks like our little thief has returned," William observed out of nowhere, clapping Barric on the shoulder. "An interesting development."

"I fail to see what's so interesting about it." Barric broke his gaze from the girl to consult some notes he held in his hand. "I told her she could return."

William's eyebrows shot up, and he took a small step back. "Indeed?" He stole a secret glance at Rena, his expression ponderous. "I wonder what's in your mind, Barric, to allow such a thing."

"Aren't you the one who let her help herself to my grain in the first place?"

"Yes," William answered slowly. "I told her she could take enough food for the day. But I am a steward and you are an earl, and you must consider. . .appearances."

Barric frowned. As if he hadn't thought the same thing the previous night, that he was opening himself up to a world of gossip and impossible scandal. After years of managing his affairs with an iron fist, he might as well paint a target on his back to anyone of rank and title. And all for what? For a foreign girl who sang to herself as she picked from his fields.

Barric did not lower his own voice as he firmly replied, "As long as she is hungry, she is welcome."

Let his workers do with that as they will.

"You could have offered her work," William suggested, eyes darting around to gauge the reactions of those working closest to them. "Such an arrangement would certainly be a little more. . . orthodox."

Barric snorted. Of course he had thought of that.

"Ah." William nodded as if reading Barric's thoughts. "Except that I fired several workers just last week."

Barric frowned his frustrated agreement. His brother had racked up a nasty line of debt in France, and Barric had asked William to let go of a number of field hands to compensate for the sizable loans. They had been turning away interested workers for months. To hire an Indian woman in their place would cause a nastier scandal, perhaps even put her in direct danger, especially after the mutinies in India. Too much British blood was spilled to make Barric risk seeming at all unpatriotic.

"She is welcome to return for as many days as she needs," Barric repeated, intending to put an end to their conversation.

"You surprise me, Barric. Of course, I know she's very pretty, but—"

Had anyone else made such an insinuation, Barric might have taken a swing. "Your toes are approaching an invisible line in this conversation," he said instead, voice darkening. "You should restrain yourself before I have to do something about it."

William dropped his eyes. "Of course. Still, I can't help but wonder what the other peers might say of such an arrangement. Or your uncle, for that matter."

Barric bristled unpleasantly. Yes, Uncle George would certainly have a lot to say.

"They are as free to speak as I am to conduct my affairs as I see fit. I would assume this arrangement won't be a problem for you?"

"Oh, I always welcome a good challenge," the steward said, his lip curling slightly. "I quite like it, actually. Since Charlie's left, it's been years since Misthold has had a good scandal of its own."

Scandal. It was the last thing any lord worth the title welcomed willingly, though many might risk it for a pretty set of eyes and a shapely frame. It had been years since Barric had taken such a risk.

"You haven't done anything unholy, have you?"

Taken aback by the question, Barric glanced sharply at William, who had folded his arms in front of his chest and was peering over Barric's shoulder with a strange expression. "Not recently. Why?" Barric turned to find Parson Richardson strolling toward him with a weary smile.

"Good morning to you both," the parson greeted, removing his wide-brimmed hat as he bowed his head in humble greeting.

Barric squinted at the older man in some confusion. "And to you as well, Parson. Though I must wonder what brings you here this morning."

If the question sounded forward, so too was Parson Richardson's sudden presence there. True, the parson had once been a particular friend to Barric's father, which granted him an invitation to the occasional party at Misthold. But aside from that, the parson almost never visited Misthold—certainly never on social calls. Though the parson was always friendly toward him after services, Barric sometimes wondered if the parson thought he was as good a man as his father or if he found the younger lord somewhat lacking in the graces of the older.

"I was told I could find you here by a rather surly footman." The parson halted in front of him and edged a look around them. "Might I have a private word with you, my lord?"

Barric scanned the overly tight shoulders of those working directly around him. Most made a task of not glancing at him as they pretended not to overhear.

Nodding a quick farewell to William, Barric stepped back to gesture the parson toward the road. "Walk with me," he said, and the parson followed half a step behind.

The two walked in companionable, though confused, silence until they'd crossed the road, well out of earshot of Barric's other workers.

"No doubt you're perplexed to see me," the parson remarked at last.

"No doubt," Barric replied.

"It's a matter of some. . .delicacy." The parson paused, his forefinger tapping thoughtfully against his mouth before he glanced at Barric again and asked, "I wonder if you have any tenant homes currently vacant."

Barric stopped midstep. The question was unusual. And though he had always liked the parson well enough, he felt strangely defensive. "I'm afraid to say I do not."

It was only half true. Though the tenant houses were indeed filled, William had a small cottage behind his house, which had been vacant for some time after the death of William's mother. Still, Barric wasn't going to mention *that* until he understood exactly what they were discussing.

The parson frowned, his eyes falling to his feet as he clutched the brim of his hat. "Yes, I was afraid that would be the case. I have someone in need of housing. A very desperate situation I'm afraid."

"Who is the person?" Barric asked, with a touch more interest.

"New to Abbotsville," the parson answered, slowly, as if drawing him in. "Two widows have recently come to the area. One is rather young."

Barric's defenses flew up. "You are speaking, of course, of the Indian woman." He had not realized her mourning dress was worn in honor of a dead husband, though perhaps he had seen as much sorrow in the darkness of her gaze.

The parson met Barric's eyes and spoke with equal frankness. "The one picking in your fields right now. Yes."

Barric found himself uneasy again. He had offered to escort Rena home the previous night, in case Thomas and Ellis still loitered, but she had adamantly refused him. He could tell she was embarrassed about her home, and the parson's inquiry only solidified his suspicions that she lived in conditions which were likely hellish.

Despite himself, he asked, "Where are they staying now?"

"The Gilded Crown."

Barric made a sound of disgust. "You must be misinformed," he disagreed tightly. "The Gilded Crown is. . . Well, it's a—"

"We both know very well what it is." The parson shook his head. "And I am not misinformed."

Barric battled a burst of indignant anger. The Gilded Crown was a filthy place, though not unpopular among those who lived for distraction. The girl had not told Barric where she lived because she clearly had no wish for him to know or to intervene. She could have begged him for deliverance from such a place but instead kept herself shrouded in secrecy.

Another thought crossed his mind. With more urgency, he demanded, "She doesn't. . .*work* there?"

He realized how little he knew about her.

Again, the parson shook his head. "That was not the impression I was given. Regardless, we both know she doesn't belong there."

Barric was beginning to believe the girl did not belong *anywhere*.

She certainly did not belong in his fields, covered in dirt and surrounded by staring eyes. Yet, if he were honest, he could not imagine her in India either.

"This news is troubling," he agreed. "But I'm afraid I cannot help you."

He struggled only briefly with the lie. Of course, William's cottage would suit the two women rather well, but he also knew housing her in such a way would open them both to another wave of speculation. How would it look, if he swept a woman out of a brothel and housed her on his land for free? Wouldn't it be a logical assumption that she might be a live-in mistress? As William had said, he was a lord who had to consider appearances. Especially with a brother like Charlie who welcomed all manner of scandal.

"I am very sorry to hear you say so." The parson's tone betrayed a bit more than disappointment—did he suspect Barric was holding something back?

"Have you made inquiries elsewhere?"

"I have spoken with some of the other gentry," the parson answered vaguely.

"And? What were their replies?"

The parson offered him a dry look. "Suffice it to say your refusal is the kindest I've heard."

Barric could only imagine what his peers might have said or suggested, even in the presence of a parson. Still, he reminded himself, the woman's home wasn't any of *his* concern. He had done more than enough on her behalf already, and he still wasn't entirely sure why. Of course he felt sorry for her. She seemed too young to suffer the way she did.

Noting Barric's silence, the parson nodded his knowing farewell. "If you hear of anything, Lord Barric, you will come to me, yes?"

Barric grunted his farewell, frowning as Parson Richardson took his leave. A passing whim of pity for the girl almost made him offer up the cottage, but he could not bring himself to speak the words. The Barric title had come to him at a high price, and he would not let any woman, however pitiful, muddy his dead father's good name.

CHAPTER 4

Barric was getting trounced. Never had he been dealt quite so many miserable hands in one night, and present company was not helping matters. Even after what had happened on the road the previous week, he had, quite begrudgingly, welcomed Thomas back into Misthold. For Barric, playing nice with family was too often a necessary evil, especially if it meant avoiding a scolding from Uncle George.

They sat around the table with two of their mutual friends—Sir Anthony, a portly gentleman who shared Barric's property line, and Roger Fiddlestone, the local magistrate, who was uncommonly good at cards. Barric had also invited William, simply because he liked his resolute steward far more than any of the other men who could have been getting drunk on his brandy that night.

"Ah," Fiddlestone murmured, mouth curving with raw delight as he studied his own hand against Barric's face. "Judging by Barric's stormy expression, we've stayed long enough to steal away his last pound."

Barric lifted a brow at the pathetic cards in his hand before making a small sound of agreement. "Perhaps I ought to turn in while I have some dignity," he mused, setting all three cards down in a formal pass. "Return to my room to lick my wounds."

Ignoring the hint, Thomas helped himself to another dram of Barric's brandy. "Word has it you have someone *else* to lick your wounds for you these days," he remarked, balancing the glass elegantly in his hand. "That is why the girl is in your fields, isn't it?"

Sir Anthony smothered a burst of uncomfortable laughter, eyeing

Barric nervously when he realized his blunder. "Well, I'll say—" the squat man began but chose not to elaborate further.

Barric's hand stiffened around his glass. Of course he knew this conversation would come up eventually. Rena was the one subject none of the men had brought up since sitting down. He was impressed Thomas hadn't spoken of her sooner but not altogether surprised. Though his cousin might best Barric at the occasional hand of cards, he had never once bested him in a fight, not since they'd been children. Thomas must have been further in the bottle than Barric had noticed to finally mention her.

William studied his own cards coolly, his expression uncharacteristically dark. "Your cousin," he said to Barric, "is especially vile this evening."

"Really, Barric," observed Thomas, gesturing widely at William as if the steward wasn't even in the room. "I'm not sure why you feel the need to invite the hired help to a *gentlemen's* game."

"Well, I'll say!" Sir Anthony exclaimed again, and cleared his throat in agitation at the snub.

Fiddlestone shifted his cards, eyeing Barric carefully as if he thought he might knock the table out from between them. "Perhaps we ought to focus on the game," he suggested. He looked very like a magistrate with his hard-edged smile. "I think we all have rotten hands this round. Shall we start over with another trick?"

Barric ignored the magistrate's attempt at burying the conversation.

"William is here at my personal request and invitation," Barric said, flitting his eyes briefly toward the steward before smiling faintly. "And, gentleman or not, he is walking away with a good deal of your money tonight, Thomas."

"And a good deal of mine too," Sir Anthony agreed with a lumbering nod.

"You're changing the subject, of course." Thomas shook his head as if sensing a trick. "You don't need to be bashful with us, though, Barric. It isn't as though the girl would be overly delicate after having been married. I certainly don't begrudge you your little arrangement, though I am surprised it was you who made it."

Barric briefly imagined punching Thomas straight through his even teeth; his cousin spoke far too audaciously not to be sauced.

"She works in my fields," Barric explained tightly. "And then she leaves, and that is all."

It was true. Rena had returned to Barric's field three times since he had told her she could. That was a week ago. Each day, she came into his field, chin tucked low against her chest. She worked quickly and left well before the sun set. Not once had she spoken to Barric or even glanced his way. He suspected her encounter with his cousin was the reason for her haste, the reason her proud eyes rarely ever lifted from the ceaseless work of her hands. Though no one would have guessed it from the steady look in her eyes, she was afraid.

Fiddlestone shook his head in genuine sympathy. "Poor lass seems a bit too young for a widow's dress, if you ask me."

"Not *so* young," Sir Anthony disagreed, rubbing a handkerchief over his ruddy face. "I heard from my wife she's nearly twenty. Don't they have child brides over there? Married at eight or ten?"

Thomas was enjoying this conversation immensely. "Yes," he interjected, smacking his hand emphatically on the table. "And you'll never guess the witless sod she gulled while she was over there."

Ignoring Thomas, Barric poured himself another glass of brandy, trying to busy his hands and appear uninterested. Thomas showed all of his teeth as he smiled. "*Edric Hawley.*" Thomas raised both brows and sank back in his chair, delighted by the sound of scandal on his lips. "Can you believe that? *Hawley.* Married him for his money, she did, and then he up and died, he and his father both."

Barric felt his eyebrows shoot upward in surprise. Edric was their second cousin. It had been many years since they'd all been boys, and nearly ten since the Hawleys had left for India, during which time he'd heard very little of their family. Edric's grandmother had been Clarissa Fairfax, sister to Barric's own grandfather before she had mortified the family by marrying a near-nobody lawyer named Maxwell Hawley.

Some speculated that her husband, who later went on to become Sir Maxwell, had blackmailed his way into the baronetcy, his title and property allegedly granted for some delicate legal matter he'd handled for a relation of the prime minister. It would have been a very delicate matter, indeed, to be rewarded with Hawthorn Glen, a comfortable estate situated on some three thousand acres of land. During his time, Sir Maxwell had acquired an unflattering reputation as a hard-edged miser, and Barric's grandfather had cursed the fool daily for carrying off with his only sister and buying his way into the gentry.

By all accounts, Sir Alistair, Edric's father, had been a far better brand of Hawley, who bore the baronetcy much more graciously than his father before him. Many said Alistair was much more like his mother, his wily nature and shrewd discernment allegedly inherited through the Fairfax line.

"Poor Edric," Thomas went on with an exaggerated sigh. "Died before he could ever hear himself called *Sir* Edric." He tipped his now-empty glass meaningfully at Barric. "Seems the girl doesn't mind, though. Seems she's more interested in trading up—from *baronet* to *earl*, eh, Barric? I suppose one must admire her resourcefulness."

Barric glanced down at the glass in his own hand, his fingers tightening again. Unlike his dissolute cousin, Edric had been the kind of man worthy of Barric's brandy, a bit flashy and careless, but a man strong of principle. Last Barric had heard, the Glen was vacant, and Sir Alistair and Edric still alive. And he had heard absolutely nothing of an Indian wife. News ought to have reached them by now, but the rift between the Hawleys and the Fairfaxes, which had never quite healed after Clarissa Fairfax's defection, probably had much to do with the family's general silence.

Realizing the men at his table were awaiting his reply, he took a brief sip from his glass. "You say all of this as if I'm interested."

"You sure seemed interested when you played the chivalrous knight to her damsel in distress." Thomas drove those words at Barric like the sharp tip of a sword. Barric ignored the way William looked between the cousins in obvious confusion.

"Shall I pay you in kind for what you did?" Barric's eyes glinted as they rose to Thomas. When Thomas did not answer, Barric said, his voice low but controlled, "Stay away from her."

Angling his head toward the other guests, Thomas practically slurred, "As if I'd dirty my boots in *that* disgusting hovel—"

"*Thomas.*" Fiddlestone caught the man's eyes and shook his head in warning.

Barric's frown deepened. So his cousin had discovered Rena lived at the Gilded Crown. He wondered, with a stab of unease, what Thomas might do with that information. What *other* men might do if they saw her on the road and realized where she lodged.

Thomas leaned over the table toward Barric and spoke in a low voice. "If you want my advice, I'd make a convenient transaction out of her. Make her *pay* for that grain. It's not really fair, after all, to be giving her for free what so many others must work for. I promise you'll sleep far better for it. Might even take that temper of yours down a notch."

Barric stared blankly at the cards in front of him. Such arrangements between lords and workers were quite common, but that didn't make the idea sound any less monstrous.

"And if you want *my* advice," he cautioned, "I'd stop guzzling my brandy before you say something that might truly provoke me."

There was a sharp pause. A muttered oath of offense. Pocketing the money in front of him, Thomas pushed back from the table, his chair legs screeching against the wooden floor. As he gained his feet, he stumbled, upsetting a few of the cards and knocking over his empty glass as he caught himself against the table's edge.

Fiddlestone jumped up to assist, grabbing ahold of Thomas's elbow. "Easy there!" he said as he steadied Thomas.

Enraged by his own fumbling, Thomas shoved off the magistrate's touch. "Get your hands off of me, man!"

At that, Barric shot up out of his seat, grabbing Thomas by the collar. "Perhaps I ought to sober you up myself," he suggested, dragging his cousin closer. He'd sooner force his cousin's head into a bucket of cold water to sober him up than allow him to insult the guests at his own table.

From over his shoulder, Barric heard poor Sir Anthony observe the squabble with some distress. *"Well, I'll be. . ."*

Thomas did not drop his eyes from Barric's, his insolent gaze all but begging Barric to take a swing, until at last Fiddlestone placed a steadying hand on Barric's shoulder. "It's all right," he said, his tone deliberately flat, obviously affronted but not wishing to make a scene of it. "I think it's time we all turned in."

Thinking this was a fine suggestion, Barric relaxed his fingers, allowing Thomas to jerk back and straighten his jacket.

Naturally, Thomas was the first to leave. Without making his excuses, he slammed out of the room, followed closely by the nervous Sir Anthony. Only Fiddlestone lingered at the door, turning back briefly to meet Barric's tired eyes.

"I'll see to it he gets home," he promised, then pulled the door shut behind him.

Barric let go of a heavy breath. The whole point of this miserable card game had been to put well enough behind them; instead, matters had been made much, much worse.

He started when he heard the sound of someone's throat being cleared on purpose and whirled around, surprised to find that William still remained. Standing by the window, the steward crossed his arms and narrowed his expression pointedly, eyes shifting to the door. "They won't keep this to themselves."

"No, they won't, but I know you to be a discreet man."

There was a question there, unspoken, and William eyed him with a measure of surprise. "You know I am."

Barric tipped his glass, swallowing the rest of his brandy in a swift punch. "Good," he said, setting the glass back on the table. "Because I need your advice."

"Absolutely not." William shook his head, pacing back and forth across the carpet as he grappled with what Barric had just said. "You cannot lodge her. Not on your own property. Not after she's lived in that brothel."

"Is this a general rule of yours, then? Not helping people who have lived in brothels?"

William flattened Barric's wry humor with a rebuking glance. "Come, now, Barric, you know exactly how it would look."

Barric sighed and shifted back to lean against the windowsill, feeling the cool gusts of wind as they battered against the casement. Of course he knew. Well before he'd even set the matter to William, Barric had already known exactly what the steward would say. Wasn't that why he'd asked him in the first place?

But why, then, did the parson's request keep niggling at him?

When Barric didn't speak, William met his eyes. "It would look like you are setting up your mistress," he clarified with an accusatory frown. "You'd appear to be worse than Charlie. At least he has the decency to carry on abroad."

Barric scowled at the mention of his younger brother and glanced distractedly out the window. Usually, he couldn't stand when people dragged his brother's name into casual conversation. Yet again, this conversation was far from casual, and the fact they'd known each other since boyhood had always granted William certain leniency.

"The parson is worried about her," Barric explained. He watched as a particularly rough gust of September wind blew against the stalks of waiting grain. "Perhaps he is right to be worried. The girl has no one here to turn to."

"Why should that matter to either of us?" William challenged, half wincing at his own reply. He tried again. "Surely you've done your Christian duty by her. We both have." When Barric didn't answer, he drew closer, placing a hand on Barric's shoulder. "The cottage is at the center of your property, Barric. Everyone will think you are bedding her. What was the phrase Thomas used? A transaction?"

Barric certainly didn't like hearing this word in his steward's mouth. Irritated, mostly because he knew William was right, he lifted his chin and pinned his steward's gaze with his own.

"So, you're saying you refuse?"

There was a brief pause, the crackling fire the only sound for several moments.

"We both know I would do anything you asked of me." William dropped his hand from Barric's shoulder. "So I'm asking you, as a friend, not to ask me. Your peers will rip you apart if you step any closer to the girl than you already have. And I've no interest in getting my daylights darkened just because I have to roll up my cuffs and defend your blasted honor."

Barric snorted. "I don't need anyone fighting for me. Least of all my steward."

"Just. . .give this some time," William pleaded with a sigh. "Let things be as they are for a spell. The girl will survive."

When Barric made no reply, William lowered his eyes, murmuring something under his breath, which sounded an awful lot like "stubborn blighter."

When William turned toward the door, Barric's gaze flicked down to the ledger now tucked tightly beneath his steward's arm. He felt his lip cut up into a tight, familiar smirk. "Retreating, are you?"

William's hand was already on the doorknob. "Has it not occurred to you that *your* good name is *my* good name? Think about it, Barric. Part of my job is making sure you don't make yourself out to be an utter fool."

Barric smiled ruefully, even as he waved a careless dismissal at his mouthy steward. "I'll not say you've done a tremendous job of that thus far."

The line of laborers moved at a grueling pace. Scythes in hand, a group of seven men tore through the wheat. Behind them, men and women raked up the fallen crops, then bound them into thick sheaves with scraps of straw. An unbreakable rhythm was set by the steady swoosh of blades leveling one row of crop and the next and the next. The workers left behind them barren, stubbly ground, with bound sheaves propped up in strange, tented structures—called *stooks*—to be dried by the sun and later hauled for threshing.

Behind the fieldworkers, Rena stooped to gather any scattered kernels of wheat, then slipped them into her bag. She gathered quickly. Stooping, then rising, careful to keep her face angled down toward her hands. The workers pretended not to watch her progress, but Rena felt their gazes, could hear the whispers which followed her movement.

With a sigh of embarrassment, she sidestepped briefly into a patch of shade, closing her eyes against the bright afternoon sky as she swiped a few beads of sweat from the side of her face. Though she was no stranger to warmer climates, she was unused to toiling in open fields or feeling the relentless press of sunlight against her neck and shoulders.

Several workers made throated sounds of relief as two women appeared at the end of the next row and hastened toward them with large buckets of water balanced at the hip. One by one, the men halted their reaping, thrusting aside their tools into the fallen stalks as they waited for the women to reach them. Those who bound also set aside their sickles, watching the sloshing buckets with hopeful eyes as everyone stepped away from their work.

Flitting from worker to worker, the women ladled out water in tin cups. The workers drank quickly, water trailing down their throats.

At last one of the women neared Rena. She held out the cup to a thin worker beside her, who drank deeply, chugging off its contents. Swiping a sleeve against his mouth, the man nodded his gratitude and handed the cup back to the woman as he bent again to his task.

The back of Rena's dress stuck to her shoulder blades, and her throat was scratchy, but she ignored the women and doubled back toward the nearest stooks, crouching low to gather some kernels of wheat which had been dropped there. She refused to think of the women with their buckets of water, or any of the field hands who had already quenched their sandpaper throats.

Rena turned in surprise as one of the women approached her, ladling a cupful of water and holding it out to her. Rena stared at the cup thirstily, but she did not move at once to take it. The woman would not meet her eyes but stared somewhere over Rena's shoulder.

Rena's fingers lifted toward the cup, but another worker shoved through those gathering up their tools. "What do you think you're doing?" he demanded of the water woman.

The woman blinked, lowering the cup slightly. "We are all thirsty."

"Sure, sure," he agreed. "But the water is for the *workers*. Those who *contribute*." He turned his eyes on Rena. "And how do you contribute?"

Rena stared at the man's grubby smock and scrawny frame and could not help thinking such a man would *never* have been admitted into her father's house. He was too dirty, too coarse. . .and yet there she was, fated to stand beneath such a man when it counted most.

"It's only a drink," she said stiffly, and at last took the cup from the woman's hand.

Before she could lift the tin to her lips, the man knocked it from her hands. Rena watched, crestfallen, as the water splashed against the brittle stubs of ground where wheat had grown just that morning.

"I think we all agree you've taken plenty enough of what isn't yours," the man replied coolly. The other workers watched the humiliating exchange, though no one came to her aid. One of the men had the decency to yell something out to the man—about "letting the poor lass alone"—but the rest were empty whispers. Nothing of substance. Nothing that helped.

Rena felt her fingers curl into tight fists. She wanted to lash out at the man, to strike him as hard as he had struck this rising chord of shame within herself. When had she become dirt beneath a field hand's shoe?

With a satisfied smile, the man shrugged at her empty expression and stalked away. Rena swore under her breath, a feverish release of pressure, and bent back to her task. Her fingers were caked with dirt, each nail coated in filth. She thought, again, of her father. Would she have been admitted into his house if she had looked this way? Certainly not. She would have been shut out by a servant before she could ever have announced who she was.

Out of the corner of her eye, Rena saw another cup of water extended toward her. Unsure if she should expect another round of mockery, she settled on her knees and glanced up, but it was not the same woman who had filled her last cup. The other girl had been simply dressed, hem lined in dirt the same as Rena's; this one wore a clean, high-necked cotton gown, fashionable in its tight bodice and wide crinoline. The dreamy blue fabric stood stark against the brown and gold colors of encroaching autumn.

The young woman did not attempt a smile, but neither did she glare like so many others. "So," she said, not quite able to hide her curiosity, "you are the one they've been talking about."

Rena didn't quite like this introduction. "I suppose I would be, yes."

The girl nodded, then gestured for Rena to rise. Rena did as she was instructed and stood, then took the offered cup. "Thank you," she said, and took a deep drink.

Shifting back on her feet, the girl cleared her throat. "My brother could have gotten into a nasty bit of trouble for helping you," she said, half-accusatory. "Letting you steal from Lord Barric's field like he did."

Lowering the now-emptied cup, Rena studied the girl, recalling the young man who had first let her pick from the field. Of course they were siblings. Brother and sister shared the same eye color, a royal English blue, which seemed to outrank them slightly. And though this girl's hair was much curlier than her brother's, an unruly tumble pulled into a loose bun, it was the same shade of dusty blond. She was a pretty girl, perhaps only a year or two older than Rena.

"It was not my intention to get him into trouble. But I thank you for the water—" Rena hesitated, realizing she didn't know how to address the girl. She was well above Rena in station, squarely middle class if her spotless dress indicated anything.

"Miss Wilmot," the girl finished for her, her eyes creasing at the corners as if strained by the introduction.

"Miss Wilmot," Rena repeated, and handed the cup over. "I thank you."

Rena turned away with every intention of returning to her work.

"There is a lot of talk," Miss Wilmot put in quickly, "about *why* Lord Barric lets you pick from his fields. The talk will only get worse if you stay here. There isn't an eligible woman from here to Liverpool who hasn't set her cap at Lord Barric."

Rena had never heard this phrase, "set her cap," but she gleaned the meaning of it from Miss Wilmot's suspicious eyes—the women of Abbotsville were jealous of Rena. She turned to face Miss Wilmot, her voice hardening. "Then I wonder that he hasn't married one of them."

Miss Wilmot went on as if she hadn't heard her, "He is an earl, a gentleman of fortune and property."

Rena sighed and shook her head. "You may rest assured I have no design upon Lord Barric. I have a husband. He may be dead, but he is still mine. As such, any man in Abbotsville would find me a fairly sad conquest."

Miss Wilmot's mouth clenched into a tight frown. "Yes," she conceded, "but even a sad conquest can be beautiful."

CHAPTER 5

Barric rode Samson idly through town, removing his hat for the chirping ladies who stepped out of storefronts to greet him.

"Good morning, Lord Barric," said one lady.

"How long it has been?" lamented another, who was usually as chatty as a church bell in town but deliberately shy in his presence.

Her mother hovering close at her hip, Lady Angelina was made bolder than the rest. Wearing an impossibly purple gown, belled wide around her legs, she drew close and placed a gloved hand on Samson's black snout before tipping her head up to meet Barric's gaze. "I hope you have had a successful morning shooting," she said, discreetly eyeing the gun which now rested flush across his legs. He had been out partridge shooting with Roger Fiddlestone since dawn, a successful outing, and now had three brace of the unfortunate birds bound to the side of Samson's saddle.

"And won't you join us for our dinner party next week, Lord Barric?" Lady Angelina sought to sway him with a cloying smile. "We have not yet received your reply."

In general, Barric had no wish to attend dinner parties. The ladies who arranged them were easily as skilled at hunting men as he and Fiddlestone were at hunting partridges. Still, he often attended for the sake of connections, or even hosted his own at Misthold to placate Uncle George, who often criticized him for being too withdrawn with his father's title.

He made some noncommittal reply to Lady Angelina's invitation, smiling drolly as he signaled Samson to ride on. Eventually, of course, he would have to marry one of them. He was nearly thirty, already older than his father had been when he had asked for his mother's hand. It seemed impossible to imagine another mistress of Misthold—even more impossible to imagine himself focusing his attentions anywhere but on his land.

Still, he had no interest in marriage, at least not pressingly. Charlie had once joked that Misthold was always to be Jack's mistress, and he was probably right. Barric worked the land, or at least saw to its workings, more often than he entertained society or women. And after years of watching Charlie fumble, Barric had seen exactly the kind of trouble a woman might bring.

"Curious, are you?"

Barric pulled back on the reins as he heard his cousin's voice behind him. The two had not spoken since the disastrous card game, and Barric had hoped to keep it that way. Sighing deeply as he braced himself for another confrontation, he angled in the saddle, reluctantly allowing Thomas to catch up.

"And what is it I am supposed to be curious about?" Barric asked blandly.

Thomas extended a dramatic arm to the red door directly to Barric's left. With wary eyes, Barric read the weathered sign hanging over the entry: THE GILDED CROWN.

His hands tightened. He had not intended to ride so close to the edge of town, nor had he realized he was so near to the inn.

Thomas didn't even have the dignity to lower his voice as he crowed, "Couldn't stay away, could you?"

In truth, Barric had not allowed himself to think about that door or the girl who lived on the other side of it. Instead, he had taken William's advice and agreed to remove himself from the situation. He didn't even frown when he found her gleaning in his field but made himself tend to his ledgers or the other workers instead.

But now she was not so easy to think away. The door shot open with a clatter, and a man stumbled down the two front steps, openly drunk, his smug eyes squinting against the morning light. Barric's insides twisted. Rena walked through that same door every day. She called it home. She lived in the smoky noise, where men like this drunkard either wanted her favors or scorned her presence. He realized he had been staring too long at the door when he heard Thomas snort with amusement.

"I hear from a few of my gaming mates she's found work outside of your fields." Thomas nodded to the man who had just left. "Of course, you aren't the only man with deep pockets, and the Gilded Crown is ripe with opportunity. It makes sense that she would follow the money."

Barric wanted to believe his cousin was lying, wanted to spit the lie right back in his face, but he also realized he had no way of knowing for certain that Thomas wasn't right. Barric still kept an eye out for Rena in the fields, but he never spoke to her. Never approached. Never asked how she fared or tested her desperation to see how deep it ran.

Just then, Sir Ellis came sauntering down the road, a self-satisfied smile plastered on his lips. He wore a ridiculously dandyish suit, with a gaudy orange waistcoat and narrow trousers cut of checkered tweed. Sir Ellis tipped his head as Lady Angelina paused with her mother to greet him. Lady Angelina proffered a white-gloved hand, all but preening as Sir Ellis bent over her fingers. No doubt she was extending the same dinner party invitation Barric had brushed off, and judging by her answering smile, Sir Ellis had accepted.

Barric stiffened as Sir Ellis made his farewells and headed in their direction. As soon as Sir Ellis eyed Barric down the road, his swagger stiffened, and he seemed at once to be a smaller man, less studied. He was exactly the kind of schoolfellow who might have weaseled up to Barric too had he made it to Oxford. Barric recalled the evening Sir

Ellis had held Rena still for Thomas to strike and cursed the man for a coward.

"Good morning, Fairfax." Sir Ellis forced a chipper grin as he came to stand beside Thomas, touching his hat in greeting. "And good morning to you as well, Lord Barric."

Barric did not bother dismounting from Samson. "I've forgotten your name," he lied with a downward glance.

The man colored at Barric's greeting. "Sir Ellis Andrews, my lord."

Before Barric could say anything in reply, Thomas turned Sir Ellis at the shoulder to steer him away, perhaps fearing what Barric might actually say to his friend in public if provoked.

"I think we should leave my stodgy cousin to his *pleasure*," Thomas suggested as they stepped away, eyeing the red door with a knavish grin. Before they had walked out of earshot, he added, with a bit more relish, "Perhaps you and I might take dinner together at the Gilded Crown this evening, Sir Ellis."

As soon as they were gone, Barric dismounted so hard the balls of his feet stung. He hated that Thomas's practiced taunts still successfully peeved him, even after so many years. Barric imagined Thomas and Sir Ellis sitting at the Gilded Crown's bar with those smarmy smiles. They would watch Rena return home from Barric's own fields, her cheeks marred with dirt. They would mock her. They might even follow her to her door—

Bristling at the image, Barric led Samson to the other side of the road and tied him up outside the mercantile. He felt the Gilded Crown's door waiting behind him, but he busied himself with securing his gun to Samson's saddle and did not turn around.

He reminded himself of what William had said. The girl would survive. It needn't matter to him what she did with her own time, in her own home, if it was what she'd chosen. He had already done more for her than anyone else of his station would. What did it matter to him where she lived or how she sustained herself?

But it must have mattered.

He had already offered his fields to her, against his better judgment, in part to protect her from men of his class who might exploit her—men like his very own cousin. And while he doubted she had actually taken up work at the Gilded Crown, as Thomas had suggested, the insinuation still bothered him.

All he had to do was go into the Gilded Crown, and he could have his answers. Making up his mind to go in, Barric turned toward the inn, tugging off his riding gloves as he strode across the street.

Then he came to his senses. Three steps from the door, he halted. How would it look for a respectable man like himself to be found in such a place, inquiring after a vagrant who for all he knew worked as a prostitute at that very inn? No. He would not go in. Clenching his teeth at the indignity of it, he turned back to Samson.

After her interlude with Miss Wilmot, Rena left the fields early, well before lunch, without speaking to anyone else. She'd taken the long way home, ambling at a slogging pace, which matched the slow churn of her thoughts. Was Miss Wilmot right to be suspicious of her and her place in Lord Barric's field? Like his workers, Lord Barric often watched Rena when he thought she wasn't looking, but she suspected it was because, like everyone else, he did not fully trust her yet.

She pulled open the door to the Gilded Crown and passed through a small cluster of revelers. Though she had already steeled herself for Mrs. Bagley's newest round of insults, Mrs. Bagley had no interest in speaking with her because she was already deep in conversation—with Lord Barric.

Rena stumbled to a halt when she spied him standing at the bar, his hat resting on the chair beside him. What could he mean by coming there? Had he been looking for her? Had he come to retract his offer, perhaps, or had he come with new terms that demanded payment for access to his lands?

Ignoring the drink in front of him, Lord Barric stared at the wall with a flinty expression as Mrs. Bagley hissed to him about something or another in her waspish voice. One of the working women, her face heavily painted, leaned next to him, whispering in his ear. As the woman touched his arm, Lord Barric stiffened.

Avoiding his eyes, Rena ducked her head and walked by as quickly and as quietly as possible. She crossed close enough to the bar to overhear Mrs. Bagley complaining, "A bleedin' thorn in my side, and you'd think she'd be more grateful!"

As Rena rushed for the back hall, a man emerging from the staircase bumped against her. She stumbled back as the man grabbed her arm to steady her. Rena knew exactly why he had been upstairs, could read the truth in his muddied eyes. He smelled stale, like alcohol and sweat, and his hand lingered even after she had pulled back from him.

"Pretty thing like you," he murmured, "could do good business in a place like this."

This wasn't the first time Rena had been sought out in such a way. Her first night at the inn, she'd been mistaken by a drunkard for a "new girl" and tugged toward the staircase until she had found her voice and hissed at him to let her go. For the most part, the innkeeper stepped in whenever someone made advances on her, but there was also much he did not see. And as Miss Wilmot had astutely said, some found the prospect of conquest, no matter how sad, alluring.

"Release my arm," Rena ordered in a tight voice.

"Some business might put some meat on those bones of yours. I know a lot of men have said they might pay more money for something a little. . .*different*. Surely you aren't a stranger to such things."

In Jaipur there were similar theories among the soldiers, that the Indian women had darker appetites than their British female counterparts, that their veils and separate quarters left them repressed and full of wanton desire. These women either needed to be saved, as the missionaries believed—or else they were available to those men who could purchase them. Many in Edric's own regiment had whispered that such had been Edric's motivation for marrying Rena, and had looked at her as if she were a member of a harem rather than a loyal wife to a loving husband. This was the way the men at the Gilded Crown looked at her now, and it made her tremble with rage.

Tightening her jaw, Rena glared up at the man who held her arm until he released her and stalked the other way. Still shaking from the man's touch, Rena refused to look in Lord Barric's direction. Would he think she served as the other women there served? Though she had done nothing to feel ashamed of, she still felt disgusting.

Somehow she made it to her room without catching anyone else's eye and closed the door carefully behind her, checking the hall first to make sure she had not been followed. Setting her bag on the table, Rena searched the room for any sign of Nell but found none. Nell often walked during the afternoons while Rena was out picking, or visited with the parson, who had sent them small baskets of vegetables from his garden whenever he was able. Lowering herself onto the bench, she pressed her head lightly against the wall behind her and closed her eyes.

A firm triple knock at the door scattered her completely.

Rena stood so fast the bench banged back against the wall. Her eyes darted frantically about the room, and she fought off a moan of misery at the idea of admitting anyone into the space. The dusty shelves still held some of Mrs. Bagley's rotting produce, and a bunch of threadbare blankets were piled messily beside the bench. Her eyes traced the cracked walls and the fractured window frame, which admitted a harsh English draft on cooler nights.

Another knock. Firmer this time. Demanding. Nell would never dream of knocking, and Mrs. Bagley usually just burst in whenever she was looking to pick a fight.

Resetting her gaze, Rena stared down the door in a silent challenge. She was *not* opening the door.

The last two knocks were short, as if the person on the other side had finally given up. Thinking they had gone, she crossed on silent feet to lock the door. As her fingers brushed the latch, however, the door swooshed open, and Lord Barric ducked through the low casement, hat in hand and eyes immediately trained on her.

Rena reeled back several steps, far too stunned to speak straightaway. When he closed the door behind him, her mind splintered into a million different pieces. Shock wore off, and anger rose up in its place.

"You cannot barge into rooms when you have not been welcomed, *sahib.*" The Indian word flew out before she could stop it, the deferential title for a white man, one with wealth and influence.

Lord Barric shuffled back a step, eyes creasing slightly. "Mrs. Hawley." He bowed stiffly. "Forgive my intrusion."

Rena did not return his greeting with a curtsy. "You should not have entered. Open the door at once, sir."

His mouth tipped into a frown at her forceful tone, but he had to know exactly how it would look to anyone who had seen him shut himself in there. Rena's reputation was already ruined, and now he had compromised his own, tangled it up with hers. But to what purpose?

Barric's hand closed on the handle as if to obey her command, but then he seemed to remember where he was, and his eyes raked briefly over the room. From the bench to the table to the window with the cracked frame—his expression was unreadable as he took a quick but thorough assessment of her lodgings.

His hand dropped from the handle. "You live here?"

She couldn't quite place his tone. She heard no pity, not even disgust, but what other response could there be to such a dismal dwelling?

Her toes curled as she studied Lord Barric's meticulous fashion: high boots, black morning coat, and a slate-gray cravat. He moved his riding gloves from one hand to the other as he eyed the stack of threadbare blankets by the wall, which Rena used to build her nightly nest on the floor while Nell slept on the bench. Lord Barric was much too tall for the space, she decided, his clothes far too fine for a world of dust and cobwebs.

Rena searched his features for any hint of his intentions. She hadn't observed him this closely since the night he had saved her from his cousin, but he was as tall as she remembered, his red hair an unpleasant shock of color against the closet's drab walls. Rena folded her arms in front of her chest.

"This is a house of prostitution," she said, her uneasiness making her bold. "I trust that is not why you are here."

He sighed at her challenge, pulling his eyes from the room to rest on her. They were green, she realized, brighter than jade and striking. "No, Mrs. Hawley. That is not why I am here."

She waited for him to go on, but he didn't. Noticing something on the far wall, Lord Barric crossed the tiny space, stepping up to the family portrait still hanging from the rusty nail. His eyes panned the picture, eventually coming to rest on Edric.

Wanting to end the taut silence, Rena kept her voice flippant. "So. What did Mrs. Bagley have to say to you?"

"Nothing which does her any credit."

Rena could easily fill in the rest. "Wicked," the innkeeper's wife called her. "Useless." Back in India, Rena had often passed the untouchables in the street—the poor wretches who worked in filth, who were beneath the caste system and therefore trampled underfoot. As a Brahmin, she had not given them much thought.

But then she had become a widow.

In the Indian state of Punjab, the term for widow—*randi*—was synonymous with the word for prostitute. Rena had faced similar scorn in Jaipur, where it was widely considered a curse to be touched by a widow's shadow. Rena looked at her hands, still dusty from the day, and imagined she could see the touch of this shadow curse on herself, with wrists and fingers crawling with unseen filth.

Yes, she thought with a sigh. Now she knew exactly how it felt to be untouchable.

When she glanced up, Lord Barric was watching her. She dropped her hands to her sides as he stepped back from the portrait.

"I should not have come." His mouth tightened as he seemed to consider saying something else. But then, to Rena's bewilderment, he tipped his head in a thoughtless bow and moved to leave without another word. The door opened before he even touched the handle, and he and Nell nearly collided in the entrance.

Quick and cool, Nell's gaze swept from Rena to Barric, who straightened and met the older woman's eyes straight on.

"Lord Barric," Nell greeted, dropping a quick curtsy. A basket was hooked beneath her arm, their evening loaf of bread nestled inside with a small cluster of flowers. "I did not realize Rena was to be called upon today. Had I known, I would have ensured I would be home to help her greet you."

There was a stabbing silence.

"I beg your pardon." Lord Barric tipped his head again in formal greeting. "I merely came to call on you, Lady Hawley. Our families have not been close for some time, but I wanted to extend a formal hand of friendship to you both."

Nell's eyes maintained their shrewdness as she stared him down. Though the older woman was in more than reduced circumstances, she still managed to angle her chin indolently and smile at the lord, as if she was privy to some unspoken joke. Or else was wise to his falsehood.

"How kind you are," she said. "It has been many years since our families have spoken on such friendly terms."

Barric's eyes swept over to Rena one last time, his voice lowering slightly. "Pardon me. I do not wish to take up any more of your time." Then he calmly strode out of the room, pulling the door shut behind him.

Nell followed his retreat with an unsettled expression, her lips pulling a thin line. She plopped their usual order of bread on the table, then at last rounded on Rena. "What on earth was he doing in here? Why was the door not left open?"

Rena stood stiffly and crossed to the table, leaning her weight on her elbows.

"It was as he said," she said, following his story. "He was merely making a social call."

"And this is the man who has supposedly *saved* us," Nell grumbled. "To use you so carelessly in this place."

"Lord Barric is not a careless man," Rena disagreed. Though Lord Barric had surprised her twice now, he did not seem the type of man who did anything by accident or carried on thoughtlessly. He had come there with a reason, but she still wasn't sure what his reason was.

"You must be careful," Nell cautioned, arranging the flowers she'd picked in a chipped glass between them. The colorful petals seemed amiss in the drab space, which was cold and unreasonably drafty, even for September. Rena knew they would take only hours to wilt, as if choked at the throat. "Not all men are as kind as Edric."

Nell handed Rena a bread knife and a plate, a clear order in her eyes. Obeying, Rena began slicing into the loaf, dividing it into equal slabs. "You think Lord Barric is unkind?"

"I know very little of Lord Barric." Nell eased into her usual chair. "But I overheard in town that his brother has taken three mistresses in France and has ruined as many here in England. You must guard yourself well against a man with such relations."

Rena blinked, her knife hand hovering over the bread as she sorted through this new information. If Nell was right, then Lord Barric's family was indeed of a dangerous stock, especially with a cousin like Thomas keeping him company.

Realizing that Nell was still watching her, Rena set down the knife and tried to sound offhand. "Surely, you don't think I'm in any danger—"

Nell took up a piece of bread. "I think you ought to be careful. Allowing you to pick from his fields could be kindness—and you should never turn your back from true kindness—but keep both eyes open with him. Guard yourself."

Though Rena felt uneasy, Nell's warning still felt out of place. Lord Barric had been nothing but kind to Rena, offering her food and protection. And though the man's gaze was direct and often severe, though many of his words were stern, his workers still respected him, listened to him, and they always obeyed his orders. Such was the man who had told his workers Rena was to be left alone.

Taking her first bite of bread, Rena finally relaxed her anxious shoulders. She would trust Lord Barric, she decided. For now.

His cousin called her Edric's Indian whore. His workers whispered that she had married her husband entirely for his money, perhaps even killed him herself before she realized nothing from his will could pass to her. Mrs. Bagley called the girl an ungrateful, useless beggar. A leech.

Barric had thought of Rena as a shadow the first time he'd seen her crouched beneath the grain. Now it was as if her shadow had brushed shoulders with him in the field and followed him home, and it had a peculiar habit of gathering around his shoulders when he ought to be thinking of other things.

Sitting at the desk in his bedroom, Barric ran a hand through his hair, the horrible names and rumors banging around inside of him as he pretended to review the month's expenditures. He kept thinking of William's spare cottage, turning it over and over in his mind like a coin he couldn't bring himself to spend.

As she'd entered the inn that day, she had lowered her eyes from him and hurried past, obviously trying to avoid him. As if she could go unseen with her black hair and copper skin. And then that man, who had clearly come from upstairs from the arms of another woman. The drunken fool had grabbed her arm and looked at her in a way that made Barric unaccountably nervous—looked at her as if she belonged there the same as any of the other women did. As if he wanted her. Did it bother Rena to be regarded in such a way?

Or did she encourage it for the sake of survival?

Barric had followed her to her room because he wanted an answer to that particular question. He had tested her against the gossips, to see what she would do if she found herself alone with a wealthy man. But as soon as he'd caught her open expression, so startled and angry, he'd known everyone else was wrong about her. There was no deceit in her expression, no drop of cunning in her eyes, and not once had she smiled or begged him for anything.

The numbers on the paper he held blurred together in one long, senseless line. Frustrated, he dropped the paper, stood from his desk, and crossed to the window. From the casement, he could see all of his flourishing fields covering the ground below him like a thick blanket. He balanced his hands on either side of the sill and leaned toward the cool glass.

He had spent weeks in France trying to encourage his brother to return to England, where he could finally keep a closer eye on him. But Barric's younger brother had been obstinate since birth, and with the death of their parents, Charlie had severed the leash and rushed off in search of pleasure at the first opportunity. Barric was tired of paying off Charlie's mistresses, of sweeping away his rakish indiscretions. He had just set things back to rights in France, for the time being, when he'd returned home to find Rena beneath the stalks of grain.

Stepping back from the window, Barric reminded himself, again, she was none of his business. As William had already said, he had done his duty, and surely that was enough. Yet no one speculated about Charlie's income. No one batted an eye when Barric paid all of Charlie's debts or made his mistresses disappear with a few well-placed pounds. And yet Rena's name was smeared at every opportunity. *Harlot*, they called her. *Leech*.

And then there was her room, if it could even be called a room. Where the poor girl slept on the floor amid moldy blankets, her skin kissed by brittle air rather than her late husband's lips. And somehow she'd still had enough pride to challenge him as he tested her, though he was a lord and she was nobody. Enough pride to scold him, to make him hesitate and feel actual shame for suspecting the worst about her as everyone else had done.

Such pride would draw attention in a place like that, would stand out. The men at the Gilded Crown might let her alone for now, but they still watched her. They still smiled at her and talked to her. Anything might happen with time.

Barric wasn't sure where he was going when he pulled into his boots and grabbed for his jacket. He still hadn't made up his mind when he saddled Samson and darted out of the stables at a reckless pace. But the beast seemed to know its master's course without being prodded in any certain direction. Perhaps because they had made the journey so many times when Barric was in a thunderous mood.

The ride lasted but a few minutes, leading Barric to a modest stone house at the center of his property. Vines scaled the home's rustic walls, creeping up toward the high roof. The yard was well manicured, though most of the foliage had already crisped beneath autumn's warning frost.

Dismounting, Barric tied up his stallion and crossed through the wooden gate, his hands easily unjamming the stubborn latch. He was just about to knock when William opened the front door, already awaiting his lord with a tired, albeit mocking, smile.

CHAPTER 6

India, August 1858

Rena watched the soldiers from her usual place of concealment in the upper hall, the lantern light tangling strands of gold against her veil. She wore a traditional Indian gown, the *sari* hung loose around her chest and shoulder, with tight flowers woven in deep indigo.

As the soldiers made their greetings, her father's handsome features became lined with the strain of subservience. It had been more than a year since the start of the Indian uprising, when a dangerous rumor spread that the new Enfield cartridges, to be used by Indian foot soldiers, were oiled with pig and cow grease—a taboo for Muslims and Hindus alike. In answer, *sepoys* from the Bengal army had risen up against their commanding British officers and launched a battle for independence which had already left thousands dead.

"We need these translated," ordered one tall soldier, thrusting a parcel at her father. "Urgently."

As her father nodded, glancing through the documents, another mentioned a series of nearby riots, which, as always, required a local's particular insight.

The soldiers' accents were strange, and they spoke quickly, but the language itself was not altogether unfamiliar to Rena, whose father had spurned tradition by teaching her much of the language in her youth.

Then English women had begun entering the *zenanas* to minister to upper-caste women who lived in far stricter purdah than Rena. *Zenana schools*, they called them. These British women, missionaries in their own right, taught the English language to their cloistered charges, as well as the basic tenets of Christianity, even seeing to medical needs which required a woman's touch.

While Rena's father had never demanded she and her mother be confined to the zenana, as many households did, he had secured a matronly British woman—Mrs. Price—to come into their home and sharpen Rena's English. To her father's delight, Rena learned quickly, her English far more advanced at age seventeen than any of the other women in Jaipur. Granted, Rena's father could not have suspected she would use her knowledge to eavesdrop from upper corridors while he spoke business with British soldiers, but she did.

"We want to end the rest of this with as little bloodshed as possible," one of the soldiers remarked.

"Of course," her father agreed in a bland voice. "Come with me. Let us talk."

Watching the soldiers move in a powerful line across the tiled floor, Rena pulled her purple veil closer around her face so that only her eyes gleamed through the gauzy layer. She was generally unimpressed with the soldiers who frequented their front hall. Many spoke to her father as if he was an incompetent fool who could barely understand them, though he understood very well. Others wore their suspicion of him openly, as if he was reporting back to the rebel rousers, though he certainly wasn't.

She lingered in the upper hall long after the uniforms had disappeared into her father's study, where the voices were reduced to murmurs, then returned to the sanctuary of her mother's garden. There she paced the halls of the vaulted terrace, allowing the desert heat to sink through her veil and caress her skin as she thought of her father, so proud, now forced to serve the Crown.

Very few were actually surprised by the hard nature of Britain's unyielding fist. Westernization had been seeping into India for years—altering the country's practices, amending its laws, even usurping the princely states of their rights to self-rule. India had found itself in a battle for its own traditions, and many feared the battle was already lost.

From the end of the terrace, Rena spied two soldiers moving slowly in her direction from the inner hall and pulled back into the shadow of the stairs. "He says there's a back entrance to the stables up ahead," explained the one on the left. "You're to go at once to the commander and give him this translation."

"Of course, of course," said the other, slipping the proffered parcel into his coat pocket.

The first man nodded his farewell and returned inside, presumably to join the others in her father's study. The other scuffed his toe against the tile before continuing his course for the stable.

Rena could easily have slipped away, up the stairs to her chamber, and she and the man would never have met. But there was something uncommonly bright about his eyes, clear as the sky, even from a distance. And so, instead of disappearing to her room, she slipped behind a pillar for a foolish, closer look.

The man was apparently well trained at feeling the weight of an unseen enemy's gaze.

"Who is there?" he demanded, coming to a stop.

Rena froze, her breath held deep in her chest. As soon as he sensed her on the other side of the terrace, he approached. She knew at once he could follow her, catch her if she tried to flee. It felt more foolish to run than to face him.

The soldier's eyes widened as she stepped out of her hiding place and lifted her chin to see him better. He seemed even brighter in the open sunlight, with freckles around his nose and a thin, white scar above his right eyebrow. She considered the sword at his side, which was sharpened to a gleam, and wondered how many of her countrymen had been gutted on that very blade for their insurrection. Eyes narrowing reluctantly, he darted a quick glance to the other end of the hall, presumably to make sure they would not be seen. Assured they were quite alone, he settled his eyes on her more deliberately.

"Good afternoon," he said by way of greeting.

To which she tipped her head and solemnly responded, "Good afternoon, sahib."

His eyes glinted. He seemed bemused by the title, as if he already knew formality would not become either of them. When he stepped closer, she felt stuck between two heartbeats and reached reflexively to fix her veil, to make sure her face was still covered. But the man halted her, curving his hand carefully around her wrist.

"Your eyes," he said. "They're lovely."

She jerked her hand away from him, flustered by how softly he had spoken, as if a lowered voice could mask such brazenness. "Your boldness does you no credit, sahib," she replied, this time striking him with his title to make him go away.

"I have plenty else to do me credit," he answered vaguely. "And my name is Edric."

She glanced around the terrace, pulse spiking. She wondered if her father might confine her in the zenana forever if he overheard such words.

She ducked beneath an archway, into the nearest inner hall, heading quickly in the direction of her own chamber. The man called Edric followed, his soldier shoes tapping a steady rhythm as he pursued her. "I'm surprised they don't keep you locked up, away from me and my kind." His words were now sharpened like the weapon at his side, but Rena ignored the jab and kept on walking. "Your father is either much more negligent than his countrymen," he went on. "Or he loves you a great deal."

"You know nothing of his countrymen," she said over her shoulder, and instantly regretted her words. Clearly, this soldier knew what everyone knew—her countrymen had risen up against the Crown, had slaughtered women and children because they were British. And they had lost. Her people would always live in fear of British revenge.

"I know you will marry one of them," he said, waving a dismissive hand. "And he'll lock you in a room and take a mistress, maybe two. Does that not frighten you more than I do?"

His words were unsettlingly accurate. Though Rena's father was kind, he also brushed shoulders with many powerful men and warriors, *rajputs*, some of whom had supported the rebellion and saw her father as a useful political alliance. Rena had often thought about how it would be for her if she was married to a cruel man who supported such bloodshed. She made it to the steps, her hand curving around the banister as she willed herself to leave the soldier and his cutting words behind her.

"I'm curious," the man said in parting, "if it's the color of my uniform that makes you so afraid of me? Or perhaps it's my accent that has your armor up?"

Rena halted with her foot on the lowest step. "I am *not* afraid of your uniform," she lied, rounding on him. "I have no armor, sahib, nor would I need any. I'm not afraid of you at all."

"What about my lips?" He drew near enough to grab her arm and command her attention entirely. "Surely they frighten you, at least a little."

Rena did not answer that particular question.

But she did meet him in her mother's garden later that night.

For nearly three weeks, she met the mysterious soldier at the fountain to talk, to listen to his laugh, and sometimes just to sit in companionable silence. Once he asked if he might be permitted to see her face, but she would not move aside her veil, would not allow him to glimpse anything more than her eyes.

"No matter," he said. "Your eyes are enough."

And so she began to love him.

The other soldiers knew. When Edric disappeared from the barracks each night, most presumed he'd taken Rena on as his mistress, though this was not the truth. When Edric confided his true intentions to a few of his fellow officers, they tried to talk him out of it—and very nearly succeeded. There were two especially difficult nights when Rena received notes from him and waited in the garden as he'd asked, but he didn't come to see her. She thought he had finally listened to reason, and perhaps this was for the best. But then he appeared on the third night at her bedroom window, smiling tiredly as he asked one final question of her.

Their midnight ceremony was officiated by a tall missionary who had been sent over with Edric's battalion and eschewed his church's rules by allowing the elopement. Dazzled and slightly afraid, Rena stared at the missionary's cross as he read to them from the Bible about loving one another always. His cross was a shiny talisman which seemed made of starlight. Its foreign shape made her shiver, and her mind couldn't help drifting to her poor parents, who would find her bed empty in the morning, and a cryptic note that sought to explain what she had not yet understood herself. She still did not know if Edric's parents would welcome her or if they would sooner spit on her for bewitching their son.

When Edric's hands circled hers, her eyes left the missionary's cross to stare into her husband's open, promising expression. "I will love you always," he whispered into the silence.

And at that moment, Rena finally lowered her veil. . . .

England, September 1861

"Excuse me? Are you ready?" Rena's eyes flew open to find the present facing her like an endless stone wall. A young man with sandy hair waited behind a counter, studying her with a confused, awkward grimace.

She unclenched her hands, let out a breath, and nodded abruptly. "Yes, yes, of course. I'm sorry, I was just. . .thinking about something else."

Thinking of *someone* else, she amended in her mind, of another time, another person, another life that might have been if youth had not withered far too early.

The young apprentice offered her a half smile, then turned to the older baker, who worked in the back by the ovens. The baker was a pudgy man with gray hair, whose hands and apron were coated with a layer of sweat and flour. He wiped his forehead with the back of his arm, leaving another white streak as he offered her a tentative smile.

Following their usual transaction, she handed over her bag of grain, which had been gleaned from Barric's field and ground by the miller that morning. The baker nodded to his apprentice, who stepped forward and placed the bag on a small table scale, squinting his eyes as he read whatever number was indicated. Then he reached into a box beneath the bar and handed her a few coins in trade. With this money, Rena purchased two thin loaves of bread and, as it was market day, made her way to the stalls to buy a small chunk of cheese and some watered-down milk.

She returned to the Gilded Crown with her bundle of food beneath her arm. She strode across the front room, completely ignoring Mrs. Bagley's newest quips about "learning the art of pride and self-reliance." The old woman's voice still jangled in the background as Rena fought with the door and pushed her way into her room.

Her hand tightened on the knob as she stared at the large crate resting on the table—inside she saw their blankets, Nell's shawl, the family portrait. Even the cross above their door was placed reverently on top of the pile. Dropping the two loaves to the floor, Rena crouched to check for her dresses beneath the bench, and her father's book, but even these were gone, packed away in the crate.

She was leaving, she realized, her stomach clenching.

When someone placed a hand on Rena's shoulder from behind, her emotions were knit together so tightly she nearly cried out in alarm. But when she pivoted, it was Nell who slid into the room beside her with a strangely serene expression.

"You said you wouldn't send me away," Rena reminded her quickly, swinging her body like a door between Nell and the crate. "You promised I could stay with you." Her voice pitched higher with desperation as she finally begged, "Please, Nell, I don't want to go back to India."

Nell placed two fingers to Rena's lips and fondly whispered, "Hush, child."

Then a third person joined them in the room, stepping over the loaves of bread she'd let drop in her startled confusion.

William's shoulders were stiffer than normal when he nodded his silent greeting to Rena. She stared back, mouth slightly agape. Over the past three weeks, she had seen very little of Lord Barric's steward, neither had he spoken with her since the first day he'd let her pick from the field. He seemed a sharp man with a catlike smile, and many in the fields said he was the only one who ever challenged Lord Barric and got away with it.

"Mr. Wilmot!" Though she was mostly shocked by his presence in her room, her voice came out harsh and demanding. "What are you doing here?"

Ignoring her question, he glanced at Nell and spoke pointedly. "Are you packed, Lady Hawley?"

Rena frowned, her gaze darting from William to Nell. "What does he mean? Where are we going?"

Nell placed a hand on Rena's shoulder. "We have been offered lodging on Lord Barric's estate." Her voice unwound slowly, the words incredibly soft, no hint of the shock which ought to accompany such an outrageous offer.

Rena's eyebrows slanted together. Just last night Nell had told her to be on her guard when it came to Lord Barric; now she was encouraging her to move onto the man's property?

"But you told me Lord Barric couldn't be trusted."

Nell looked sidelong at William and laughed awkwardly, as if she'd been caught saying something she shouldn't.

"I said no such thing!" she exclaimed, trying to sound surprised, though her cheeks flushed slightly. "Now, I've just been speaking with Mr. Wilmot here, and I think we ought to accept his very generous offer."

But was this an offer made of honor or of pity? Rena remembered too well the way Lord Barric had studied her home with that unreadable sharpness.

Barely even noting Rena's unease, Nell rummaged through the crate, pulling out her shawl and slipping it over her bony shoulders. Following Nell's cue, William grabbed the crate off the table.

"If you will follow me," he mumbled over his shoulder, "my cottage is not far."

"What?" Rena scoffed. "We are to live with you?"

"I live with my sister," William explained. "I have a small cottage out back. My parents lived there before the larger steward's home was completed, and my mother preferred to stay there after I became steward. She died earlier this year, and so the building is now vacant."

"You see?" Nell's eyes seemed rather peaceful. "It's all quite settled."

Rena still faltered. "But—"

William set the crate back down with a thump and turned to Nell. "May I have a word with your daughter-in-law?" He flashed a tight smile. "It'll take but a moment, and I'll bring your things out when it's time to go."

Rena didn't really expect Nell to leave her alone with William, not after how upset the woman was when she'd found Rena alone with Lord Barric. But then, surprisingly, Nell crossed the room, placed a hand on Rena's cheek, and softly murmured, "An answer to prayer."

Then she calmly strode out of the room, leaving the door wide open as she exited.

Rena's eyes shot back over to William, who crossed his arms.

"Don't be a ridiculous fool," he warned. "You ought to accept my offer."

It couldn't be that simple. Rena had been in England long enough to know it couldn't be that simple. "And what do you want. . .as payment?"

Eyes narrowing, William put a mocking hand to his chest as if she'd struck at a chink of invisible armor.

"Perhaps I merely like to help my fellow man," he challenged. "Or women, as the case may be."

But William's eyes did not seem as generous or pitying as they were the first day she had met him, when he told her to keep her head down and gather whatever fallen grain she could. That had felt genuine. Kind. But now his eyes felt distant. His voice was harsher, more in line with how he addressed the field hands when they were giving him grief. Honor clearly had nothing to do with it.

Rena stared him down, waiting for the truth, until at last William sighed, his voice grudging as he reluctantly admitted, "Lord Barric did not exactly give me a choice."

Which meant William was offering his cottage to her out of obligation. Not kindness. Not even pity. Shaking her head, Rena mused bitterly, "You advised your master otherwise, I take it?"

Sighing, William spoke more candidly.

"Come, now, Mrs. Hawley. My motivation for coming to you is of no bearing on what's to be done. You'll want a warm cabin when winter arrives, might even find your death in this hovel if that window isn't fixed up proper. Offended or not, I think you're far too sensible to turn down a rope when you're clearly drowning."

Rena frowned. "I'm not *drowning*."

"No," he volleyed. "You're living in a whorehouse."

Wincing at the bluntness of that particular remark, Rena pivoted and imagined seeing her room through Lord Barric's eyes. The man lived in a sprawling manor, perched high above his toilsome fields. He probably had more rooms than he had workers, and marble halls decked with paintings, and shelves lined deep with books, their spines as colorful and varied as her father's own robust collection. Now that she lived in poverty, her previous life in India clung to her like a tattered robe.

She should be grateful for William's offer. Nell could keep warm in the evenings, in a room with a stove and a comfortable bed. To turn down William's offer because her pride had been wounded would be incredibly selfish. Rena had once stood in a crowded train and vowed to take care of Nell—here was the perfect opportunity to fulfill her promise, offered at no cost.

William was right. She had swallowed her pride once already, to beg for Lord Barric's grain. Just one more gulp, and Nell could have a home.

Reading Rena's defeat well before she spoke it, William hoisted the crate up into his arms and nodded.

"Wise choice, little thief."

Rena awakened from a slumber so deep and secure she barely remembered her own name when she finally opened her eyes. The sun was low in the sky, thick shafts of dwindling daylight pouring through the casement. It must have been nearly five.

Realizing she had fallen asleep, Rena sat up abruptly, nearly spilling out of her rocking chair. Miss Wilmot had extended an invitation to her and Nell, welcoming them for tea between the hours of four and five. Nell had pleaded a headache after lunch and lain down for a nap while Rena settled in the rocking chair to tend to some necessary sewing. She glanced down at the quilt she'd pulled up to warm herself. All she'd wanted was to be comfortable, and instead had fallen asleep. Groaning at the idea of arriving late to her first social call, Rena clambered to her feet, nearly yelping as she moved against a sudden crick in her neck.

She crossed the room in two quick strides, about to jostle Nell's arm to wake her, but could not bring herself to do so. Nell slept soundly on the bed, the heavy quilts pulled all the way over her shoulders so only a few wisps of silver hair poked through. After all the evenings they'd spent sleeping in barns, and then that drafty closet, Rena could not bear to wake her mother-in-law. She wanted the lady to sleep, snug and safe, until the exhaustion of destitution seemed nothing more than another passing dream.

Leaving Nell beneath the blankets, Rena padded soundlessly across the room. Compared to the closet at the Gilded Crown, the cottage was a palace, twice as nice as William had described. The plaster walls were freshly painted, and the dark wooden floors were smooth and spotless, even in the corners. Nell and Rena now had a cozy kitchen table, surrounded by four sturdy, high-backed chairs. They'd traded their drafty window for a charming little casement, uncracked, with flouncy needlepoint curtains draped on either side. In the corner, two mismatched rocking chairs were angled toward the coal range. The room was well stocked too, with thick blankets piled inside a traveler's trunk at the foot of the bed, and a wooden hutch beside the oven, which was full of various kitchen essentials.

Rena washed her face and hands with brisk water from a basin, then changed into the stiff dress Nell had washed in the creek the evening before. She kissed Nell on the shoulder through the quilt before leaving, hoping she would not be too cross with her for calling on Alice alone.

As Rena opened the front door she swallowed a dagger-sharp thrust of air. The afternoons had been unusually brisk for mid-September, and the workers tore faster through the fields as the diminishing harvest growled at them to finish. Everything would be done by week's end, William had announced the night before. And then the harvest celebration, in which all the farms would join together for a night of reveling to usher in the winter and shutter closed the barn doors.

Rena made her way across the yard to the steward's private house. William and his sister lived in a sturdy stone structure, which was connected by a wooden fence to a small outbuilding. A cluster of chickens loitered in the yard, watched by a prowling rooster. At the far corner of the property was a sty cluttered with fat, fly-pestered pigs, who watched Rena's approach with expressions of dumb boredom.

Holding her breath, Rena knocked on the front door. She did not have to wait long. A young girl with honey-red curls pulled the door wide, bobbing a quick curtsy as she said, "Oh, you have come to see Miss Alice."

"Yes." Rena slipped her shawl from her shoulders and smiled. "Hello."

Without another word, the maid ushered Rena through a narrow hallway, leading her into a snug but cheerful parlor. Several chairs flanked a lovely fireplace, which was already lit and crackling. "I'll tell her you've come," the maid said with a curious glance, and vanished back into the hall.

Rena paced the room as she waited for Miss Wilmot. All was orderly and well detailed, manicured to perfection. The tabletops gleamed, scattered with brimming vases and various knickknacks. She touched her fingertips to the mantel, where not a speck of dust was to be found, then made her way to a bookshelf in the corner, where a menagerie of volumes was tucked together in no obvious order. There were several novels with cracked spines, a newer volume of Dickens, and one three-volume set titled *The Book of the Farm*, which she presumed belonged to William.

Rena dropped her fingers from the shelf as the parlor door opened and her hostess swept into the room wearing a high-necked dress with lace cuffs. As Miss Wilmot moved, her magenta skirts billowed and shifted over the bell-shaped crinoline, and Rena became even more aware of her own simple dress—utterly black—which was shaped only by a layering of petticoats beneath.

"Mrs. Hawley, forgive me for keeping you waiting. I was seeing to something in the kitchen."

"I was not kept long," Rena replied with a gracious nod. "My mother-in-law begs your pardon for declining your kind invitation."

Miss Wilmot closed the door behind her, then gestured Rena toward the fireplace.

"I hope she is not unwell?" she asked, genuine worry crinkling her brow.

As Miss Wilmot drew closer, Rena caught a scent which had clung to many of the officers' wives in India—bergamot and lemon oil—a sharp, clean scent. Not unpleasant, but distinct.

"She is quite well," Rena assured her. "Merely tired."

Miss Wilmot nodded, but she still seemed stiff, her smile forced as her eyes briefly trailed the ground between them. Rena almost regretted not waking Nell. Perhaps the older woman's company would have made this meeting a touch more comfortable, if only for Miss Wilmot's English sensibilities.

"I've already asked Betsy to bring us our tea." Miss Wilmot nodded to the two chairs with emphasis. "Please, do be seated."

Rena obeyed, lowering herself into the one nearest the fire. "You have a charming home," she remarked. "Have you lived here very long?"

"Nearly all my life," Miss Wilmot admitted, perching on the edge of the plush blue chair that was angled toward Rena's. "For several years, we actually lived in your cottage, while this one was being built. Our father was steward to Lord Barric's father when we were children."

"Really?" Rena was surprised. "But that means you've known Lord Barric—"

Miss Wilmot smirked and straightened her skirts. "Since he was a child. Yes."

Rena had a hard time imagining Lord Barric as a boy of seven or eight—racing through his father's fields with a tumble of red hair or sitting down begrudgingly to learn his letters with a stiff governess. At first she thought he might have been an ornery child, as serious in his younger years as he was now as an adult, but perhaps this was not the case. Perhaps he had followed closely at his father's heels, or was mischievous, or rather loved to play with wooden swords with the brother she had heard so much about.

Miss Wilmot smiled, angling back slightly in her chair. "You are wondering what Lord Barric was like as a boy."

Glad to see her hostess suddenly more at ease, Rena cracked a sheepish smile of agreement. "It *is* rather difficult to imagine, isn't it?"

Miss Wilmot nodded, her eyes drifting to the corner as if imaging the younger Lord Barric playing there, just on the other side of her sitting room. "In truth, he was much the same as he is now, though he smiled more freely."

Yes, Rena thought, the past certainly did that to people. Most days she found her own past too painful in its vastness. Too often she felt as though her smile had been left in her father's study, misplaced, or perhaps stolen away entirely by Edric's smile and carried with him into his grave.

As if sensing Rena's thoughts, Miss Wilmot leaned forward and lowered her voice. "His hair was redder too," she confided. "If you can imagine that."

Miss Wilmot's smile coaxed one out of Rena, until both women laughed a bit shyly.

With a faint clatter of dishes, Betsy pushed through the door, balancing a silver tray with kettle, pot, and various floral cups. The maid crossed the room, set the tray on the table between the two women, and tipped another quick, though awkward, curtsy. Did it strike the maid as strange, Rena mused, to be bowing to a beggar?

"She seems a good sort of girl," Rena commented after Betsy had left.

"Yes, Betsy does enough work to shame any of Lord Barric's field hands." These words were barely finished when a second tray was carried into the room, laden with warm scones, clotted cream, and a selection of paper-thin sandwiches.

As Betsy bowed and took her final leave, slipping the door soundlessly closed behind her, Rena watched Miss Wilmot's methodic hands work an intricate process which had likely been known to her since girlhood. She poured scalding water from the kettle into the finer, earthenware teapot to properly warm the vessel, then discarded this water and replaced it with a fresh batch. She measured out the tea leaves—three teaspoons—and added these to the teapot to brew. When all was at last quite ready, Miss Wilmot asked how Rena took hers, but Rena hesitated. It had been so long since she had taken her tea in *any* way, let alone with cream or sugar.

Miss Wilmot touched her fingertips lightly to the sugar bowl and raised a questioning eyebrow.

"Please." Rena nodded, trying not to sound too eager.

As Miss Wilmot at last handed Rena her cup, she said, rather quickly, "I'm sorry if I was suspicious of you when we first met. I do hope I did not hurt you."

Rena might have wondered how a woman like Miss Wilmot, so pretty and kind, had not yet been married. The answer, Rena knew, was not so far below the surface of this very conversation. Miss Wilmot had known Lord Barric since he'd been a boy with redder hair and a more eager smile. Had she been hoping on him all this time?

"It is all right," Rena murmured. "It is in the past."

"It cannot be easy for you here."

"I survive," Rena answered, but Miss Wilmot's look of curious concern was not altogether unfounded. Every time Rena braved a glance in the mirror, her own bleak eyes stared back at her, rimmed with exhaustion.

"I saw you eyeing the books when I came in," Miss Wilmot said. "You enjoy reading?"

"My father was an academic," Rena replied. "It was my joy to sit and read with him in the afternoons." She smiled, remembering. "At one of our first meetings, Edric told me my skin smelled of ink and paper. . ."

She broke off, realizing she had spoken far too openly, and dropped regretful eyes to her cup. She hated herself for speaking of Edric so candidly to a woman she barely knew. As the clock on the mantel counted the seconds, Rena become increasingly frightened to look at Miss Wilmot or to say anything else. Miss Wilmot was a kind woman, if a bit forceful at times, and had extended a hand of courtesy by welcoming Rena into her parlor. But that did not mean Miss Wilmot wished for friendship. It did not mean the woman even *liked* her.

"You are welcome to our shelves," Miss Wilmot offered at last, setting down her teacup. "They are sparse, I'm sure, compared to your father's, but they have often helped me pass the tedium of winter."

Rena's eyes lifted. She was grateful for the change in conversation and, when she met Miss Wilmot's gaze, grateful also for the quiet sympathy in the woman's eyes. Rena glanced at the bookshelf in the corner.

"You are sure you and your brother will not miss them?"

Miss Wilmot's mouth curved. "My brother has not held a book in years," she said. "He is kept very busy with his work. He often leaves early or returns rather late, either seeing to the fields or meeting with Lord Barric."

"They must have a good deal to talk about."

Miss Wilmot's smile tightened at the corners. "Yes, Mrs. Hawley. I would imagine they do."

After everything that had happened, Rena still couldn't bear to be called *Mrs. Hawley*. That life, Edric's life, was never again to be hers. The name now felt like a mockery of her heart, though she was certain Miss Wilmot had not intended it to sound that way. Rena sighed, knowing she was about to cross yet another line of propriety.

"Please," she said. "My husband's name feels heavy at times. Won't you call me Rena?"

Miss Wilmot fiddled with their teacups, setting them straighter on the table between them. Of course, Rena and Miss Wilmot were hardly close enough for a first-name friendship. Miss Wilmot glanced from the teacups to Rena's work-worn hands, and perhaps she was imagining a time when Rena had smelled of paper and ink, when she'd had a husband who said such things, but now he was dead.

"I will," Miss Wilmot promised, then met her eyes. "And you may call me Alice."

Barric's coat had been discarded hours ago, strewn in a heap beneath a row of trees. His back was now drenched in sweat, shoulders blasted by late September wind. He was used to the unpleasant contradiction of sweat and ice on his skin. Scythe in hand and sleeves bunched to the elbows, he swooped through the rows in perfect rhythm with his workers, their comrade in arms as much as their lord, and for once a man with similar interests. He always worked his own fields the last week of the harvest, despite the derision of his peers.

In truth, he welcomed the labor. He enjoyed the aching in his muscles, the smell of the earth on his hands, the crisp taste of the air as he breathed sharply through his work. The fields of Misthold had once been a sprawling maze to him as a child, a place to run and explore, until his father had commanded him to learn its workings. Now he *owned* that land, pushed himself in the interest of its upkeep, usually in the form of figures and ledgers. But for now he enjoyed the way his heart beat faster as he worked those fields, the way he felt his whole body focus toward the single task of persisting.

Rena moved somewhere down the lane, into Barric's line of vision, circled by some of the other women. Barric trained his eyes to avoid her. According to William, she had moved into the new house two nights ago, though she seemed no different that morning for having slept in an actual bed. Her eyes were still tired, rarely ever lifting from her work, and she avoided Barric as if nothing at all had changed between them.

He thought of the innkeeper's wife and the drunken man who had grabbed Rena's arm by the stairs. He thought of all the foul rumors he'd heard about her, of the filthy closet and the pile of thin blankets he'd seen scattered on the floor—a bed more suited for a dog than a person. And had she once complained about her situation?

The girl ought to have been cursing her situation, fighting back, showing some teeth as she had when he'd come to her room and startled her out of her reverie. But her expression remained strangely subdued, so much so that Barric still wasn't sure if she'd been broken or was just incredibly resilient.

Barric tipped his head back to catch his breath and watched Rena move, again, out of the corner of his eye. That particular morning, she had bound stacks of wheat with the other workers rather than filling her own bag, which surprised him. He had never demanded, or even suggested, she work for him, yet she'd hunched and hauled all morning, binding sheaves with the rest of them. Now that the day was nearly over, she worked on the other side of a narrow road, helping the field hands hoist dried sheaves into the wagons to be hauled to the threshing machine. Her back seemed brittle from the labor, ready to split.

"Make her pay for that grain," his cousin had said. Was she trying to pay him back for the cottage? Barric had never requested payment, but the idea of her being indebted to him sat heavy within.

Tossing aside his scythe, he left the small patch of field he'd been working and crossed the road to the closest wagon. He helped one of the younger men jostle several stacks of dried wheat deep into the back, thwacking the worker appreciatively on the shoulder after they were in place. As he jumped back down from the wagon's edge, he intended to reach for bundles of his own but found himself approaching Rena instead.

She worked quickly, scraping together some scattered wheat which had come unbound from a stook. Though she didn't look at him, her shoulders stiffened as he approached, and her fingers faltered briefly with the scrap of straw she used to secure the sheaves. So, she *did* notice him. He leaned in as if to help her secure the knot, then murmured, barely loud enough for her to hear, "You do not have to work like this."

Her chin jerked up at a sharp angle as if surprised to find his was the hand assisting hers. He waited for a response, testing her again, but she dangled for only a second under the challenge. "You would have me only beg from your hand?" She tied off the knot quickly, without his assistance, then raised both eyebrows.

"I am not your employer," he went on, straightening out of his crouch. He kept his voice stiff and businesslike, watching as the other workers began relocating to the other side of the field. "The cottage is already yours. You do not need to pay me for it."

She shook her head. "I cannot take anything more from you than what you have already given."

He leaned closer, grabbing a few of the bound sheaves, his voice dropping again. "Is it your pride that makes you so stubborn?"

Finally, her eyes rose to him. They were a deep blackish shade, the pupils a thick veil barring him from her thoughts.

"I do not have the luxury of pride, Lord Barric. Nor do I wish to." Her words were not sad or harsh but spoken as naturally as if she had commented on the state of the weather or the color of her dress. She scooped up several bundles in her arms and inclined an eyebrow at him. Reading her request, he grabbed the last few bundles and carried them toward the wagon.

Rena climbed up into the empty wagon first, stacking her haul into the farthest corner. From the ground, Barric tossed his own in beside her, nearly knocking her over in the process. When Barric held out his hand to help her, she braced her fingers in his and clambered back to the ground. Immediately Barric's fingers felt the raised scars and calluses on Rena's hand. He glanced down, expression tightening as he tilted her fingers to observe the fresh white cuts and blisters lining her reddened palm.

Rena fisted both hands and drew them out of his hold, clasping them behind her back, her expression shuttering closed as Barric slowly studied her again. Her hands were those of a new laborer, the skin rubbed raw from the sharp bite of the sheaves.

"You are not used to working," he observed.

"I am not used to many things," she countered, turning her back to him as she moved to join the other workers. Her words were clipped and final, severing their conversation.

But Barric was not accustomed to being dismissed, nor was he finished.

He intercepted her before she could reach them. "That's not entirely true," he disagreed. "You seem especially used to running."

Rena spun around to face him. Gone was the subdued, tired look from her eyes. She wore a flashing, searching expression that indeed wanted to run but seemed instead made to fight.

"Isn't that why you came here?" he pressed, first peering down the row to make sure none of the other workers could overhear them. "Isn't that why you ran from India? Did your parents cast you off for marrying Edric?"

She winced and stepped back as he spoke Edric's name, and he immediately regretted how casually he had spoken it, as if her husband's name was nothing more than lifeless gossip on his tongue. Rena's gaze clouded, and she lifted her face toward him. "They did not cast me off. They loved me. They begged me to stay with them in India."

"Then why come to England?" He shook his head, uncomprehending. He had no idea where these questions were coming from, or why he cared, but he barreled on anyway. "Why come to a place where you would be hated? You must have known how it would be for you here."

She sighed heavily. Either she was not sure of the answer herself or she was not sure he would understand, for she struggled to formulate a response.

"My parents have each other," she explained slowly. "My father has his work and his books, and my mother has her garden. They are rich in many ways, Lord Barric, as I might have been had I stayed with them."

Rena's eyes drifted to her feet as if her gaze had been weighed down with an anchor. Barric was surprised to learn she had come from such a wealthy family, though perhaps he had always seen as much in her keen eyes. And, of course, she'd had enough resources in India to be taught English. But to marry Edric Hawley—she had cast aside a life of ease and affluence for one of mockery and disdain. He thought again of her hands, rubbed raw from labor. Did it mortify her to be seen covered in dirt, to be counted lower than everyone else around her? Did she regret her choices?

"But Nell. . ." Rena whispered after a moment, as if hearing his questions. "I could not watch her board that ship alone, with nothing. She begged me at the docks to stay behind in India. But Nell is my family too, as much as my parents, and I must take care of her."

"But who takes care of you?" Rena's eyes flew to Barric's, her expression startling wide, and he clenched his teeth, already wishing he hadn't asked such a deeply personal question.

He opened his mouth to amend what he had said, to twist his words into something less intrusive, but she cut him off, shaking her head.

"I don't need to be taken care of."

"Ah." He smirked ruefully as he foresaw the second half of her predictable answer. "Because you can take care of yourself, I suppose?"

This time her eyes did not budge from his.

"No. I have spent more than enough time being taken care of. We all must suffer now and then, Lord Barric, and I am strong enough to bear it. There is no other option than to endure."

We all must suffer. The words sunk beneath Barric's skin, unsettling him more than he would have liked. He glanced toward the other workers, who kept up momentum on the far end of the field. Though they pretended to ignore him, he knew he'd drawn unnecessary attention to himself and to Rena.

He swept back a step, placing more distance between them.

"The sun will set within the hour," he remarked dismissively, nearly flinching at how cutting his words sounded. "If you really wish to help, you must do better to keep up with the others."

Rena stood when she was supposed to stand.

She sat when she was supposed to sit.

She pretended to listen attentively, back rigid, never once braving a glance over her shoulder. But she still felt eyes boring into the back of her neck, still heard the occasional murmurs which were out of place from the rest of the prayers and petitions. She squinted her eyes against a shaft of light streaming through the stained glass. Alice shifted beside her, hand close enough for Rena to touch. On Rena's other side, Nell knotted a worn handkerchief between her knobby fingers. Her eyes seemed mistier than normal.

For William and Alice to share their pew that morning was an act of extreme kindness, when so many others had passed them by with looks of obvious avoidance. Though Nell said many churches still rented their pews, reserving them for families of class, Parson Richardson had adopted a newer, more controversial first-come, first-seated rule which allowed even the penniless—even Rena—a place with all the rest.

From her spot in the southernmost wing, she could see much of the congregation. Many of the parishioners seated near them frequented Barric's land or other farms nearby, and she passed them often on the road to town. In one of the front pews, Thomas sat beside an older gentleman with slightly graying hair and a lavish gray waistcoat beneath his suit of black. Like others had done, Thomas used an opportune moment to ease a surreptitious glance back at her. His eyes were narrowed, perhaps surprised she'd had the nerve to come.

Rena sat up straighter, trying to pay attention to the service but struggling beneath its weight. So many words she'd never heard, so many songs.

Standing then sitting. Chanting then reading.

There were watchful eyes and dubious murmurs, and the organ's melancholy groan as it conjured up a somber dirge to clench at her heart.

Lord Barric sat on the other side of the aisle, his gaze sharp but thoughtful as he listened to the parson read. He seemed the only one not trying to figure out her presence in the sanctuary. After the way he had dismissed her in the field, so cuttingly in front of everyone, she wanted to be angry with him. But did she have the right to question his words when he had given her everything she needed?

He could destroy her world, she realized, and Nell's, in a moment if he wished.

Pride would get her nowhere.

Nell looked down at her then and offered a kindly, reassuring smile. Rena struggled to return it, feeling as though she'd been dug up by the roots and planted in the wrong kind of soil. For weeks Nell had pleaded with her to come to church.

"I do not wish to be stared at," Rena protested nearly every week, though they both knew it was a weak excuse. She suffered the stares of strangers every day in Barric's field and yet returned to work each morning. "The parson may not even want me there," she'd also tried. "He knows who I am. What I am. He knows where my prayers have been spent."

But even that lie was no good. More than once, he had paid them a visit, urging her attendance with unreserved kindness, and when he went fishing, he sometimes brought them a portion from his daily catch, if not more.

The truth was Rena had been afraid of following Nell through the church doors. Not because she was foreign to them, exactly. What really gnawed at her were all those years spent prostrate in prayer to other gods. She was a pagan to every set of English eyes watching her from the pew. She had made the pilgrimage to the holy river Ganges with her parents; she had listened to her father as he read to them from the *Vedas*; she had watched her father leave for temple, had knelt before their household shrines and joined her parents' prayers to Shiva. Rena had never been as devout as her parents, but she had also never doubted what they had taught her.

She averted her eyes from the altar, the familiar barrage of guilt assailing her mind. What would her father say, she wondered, if he could see his only daughter standing beneath the church's buttressed ceiling, kneeling now before Edric's god? Or if her mother knew she had left off praying to the gods and goddesses enshrined in the corners of her home? Rena still wasn't sure how she felt about any of it or where she fit in. She'd been thrust into a maze of foreign prayers and incense, wall after wall of guilt staring her down, and she could not see her way out.

In the end, Rena's own words had persuaded her to follow Nell to church that morning. "*Your home is my home,*" she'd said all those weeks ago, when Rena had begged to remain at the woman's side. "*And everything you are and everything you love—that is all I ever wish to be.*"

She'd meant those words, and her vow had made her somewhat stronger, bound to Nell by something other than grief. But there was still an invisible line stretched between the two widows, which formed a wall of sorts whenever Nell said her prayers and Rena tried not to listen, whenever Nell went to church and Rena stayed behind. And so Rena had come. For Nell, she told herself.

Shifting in the pew, she gazed once more at Nell's Bible and thought of Edric's missionary friend, the one who had married them in the garden all those months ago. Rena had stared at him so openly, not merely as a young, nervous bride but as a strange native who had been thrust into an entirely new world. Did the missionary have reservations, she wondered, about allowing his friend to marry a pagan girl who worshipped strange blue gods and goddesses? Had Edric forced him to marry them against his better judgment?

"Blessed are the poor in spirit." Rena's eyes snapped forward, where the parson was reading from a thick black book on the pulpit. "For theirs is the kingdom of heaven."

She sat up a little straighter, the words snagging somewhere in the back of her mind like a frayed thread caught on an unseen nail. *Blessed?*

"Blessed are they that mourn"—he went on in his straight, even voice, his black robes gathered around him like shadows—"for they shall be comforted. Blessed are they which do hunger and thirst—"

"Rena." Alice touched her hand, jostling Rena's attention away from the parson. "Are you ill?"

Rena realized she'd stopped breathing. *Blessed.* The word clanged around inside of her. Blessed to mourn? To feel empty? Blessed to be poor and starving, she added bitterly, to have nowhere else to turn?

The parson was still reading, but Rena had stopped listening. She didn't wish to believe such things. After Edric had died, she had fasted and prayed until her head swam and her knees ached, as her parents had instructed, but it had only made her feel emptier. Instead of poor and small, she wanted to be strong and full, to grow beyond the grasp of her own grief. Blessing was invisible, something she could never snatch up in her blistered, beggarly hands. But strength? Strength was seen. Noticed. Respected far more than suffering or hunger ever was.

With an unsteady breath, she met Alice's concerned frown. "It's just warm in here," she whispered.

CHAPTER 7

At last the harvest was at its end, the final sheaves gathered, hauled, and stored. Barric made rather a show of carrying off the last of the sheaves, a small parade following him with banners and music, and then all the workers were offered fresh cider pressed from an orchard on Barric's property. Even Rena was offered a cup, her first taste of crisp, English cider. Embarrassed to have been included, she quaffed off the pewter tankard in nearly one chug, wincing slightly at the unfamiliar tartness. She lingered but a short while before making her way home. All the workers were extra noisy on the road, made jovial by the satisfaction of a job well done and the contents of several shared flasks. One of the older men even smiled at her in kindly greeting.

The biting air which sometimes warned of winter had relented that day, and so Rena walked without a shawl, appreciating the trees which were at last crowned in full autumnal colors. She crossed by the stables as she often did when she took the back way home, away from searching eyes, and was surprised to come upon Lord Barric as he led his tall black stallion toward the stall. She wondered that she had not seen him slip away from the other workers.

"Good evening, Lord Barric," she greeted in a low voice. Though she often avoided him, she did not wish for him to catch her avoiding him now, especially after he had been so stern with her the last time they'd spoken, insisting she learn to keep up with the others. She was still learning to keep up.

He turned, his eyes flashing with surprise. His auburn hair and jacket were both rumpled from the day's work, and there was a faint scrape of dirt along the side of his jaw, as if he had raked his work-worn fingers there. His eyes seemed especially tired, rimmed slightly from lack of sleep. It'd been a long week for everyone. "Ah, Mrs. Hawley."

Strangely, she was reminded of the evening they had met, when he had first inquired after her name. She remembered the deep sound of *Rena* on his lips. Now she had slipped from "Rena" into "Mrs. Hawley," as was only proper, but it was still strange, in a way, that the name her husband had given her had outlived him.

She stiffened when she realized Lord Barric was watching her. "I ought to congratulate you on a successful harvest."

His lips quirked slightly at her formal tone. "It has been an interesting season, to be sure."

She considered moving along, leaving him to celebrate his harvest with a pipe or a bottle of port or some such thing, but then she paused, watching the way Barric's gloved hand smoothed along his horse's mane. "Your horse is rather beautiful," she noted.

"Do you ride?" Barric asked, leaning down to check the beast's hooves. "Or did you, in India?"

"Only once," she admitted, recalling the time Edric insisted she learn, several weeks before he'd taken ill. "And was unsaddled very shortly."

A passing smile crossed his face as he straightened. "Now *that* I cannot picture."

"It was rather mortifying," she agreed, shaking her head as she remembered the burst of chortles from Edric's soldier friends. "Knocked flat and covered in mud. Your horse, however, does not seem the type to unsaddle a lady."

"He'd surprise you," Barric warned, then gestured Rena closer. "Come. He would be glad of some attention. Samson is rather a vain brute."

She smiled, stepping closer and placing her hand on the horse's wet snout. Samson was a pretty beast with wide, ponderous eyes and a few splotches of gray around his nose. The soft puff of air Samson snorted into her palm brought a delighted smile to her lips, and she gasped as he bowed his neck to nuzzle his nose against her stomach. She felt her smile leap into a grin. It was a delightful change, to feel joy so deep it finally showed.

Barric circled around Samson to stand beside her, his hands never leaving the reins. "He's fond of you," he remarked as Samson dropped his snout against her hip.

"Unsurprising, I suppose. Though he could also be searching you for a carrot."

Surprised to hear Lord Barric speak so teasingly, and pleased by the gentle light she found in his otherwise tired eyes, Rena laughed her faint agreement. "That will teach me to come empty-handed, won't it?"

Their smiles both dropped as a young, lanky stable hand came rushing out to take Samson, and Barric relinquished his hold on the reins, nodding his silent thanks.

As soon as the stable boy had disappeared with Samson, Barric glanced back at Rena. "Are you going home?" he asked, nodding toward the dusty road looping down the hill to William's house.

She stepped back, realizing she had dawdled longer than she'd first intended. "Yes," she answered. "I often come this way to avoid the other workers."

"Might I walk with you?" He turned to hang his whip on a peg. "Just a short stretch of the road?"

Stunned by his request, and a bit suspicious of his motive, she nonetheless nodded. "Yes, of course."

Barric drew up beside her, his even strides betraying no unease, though he was silent for some time as they made their way down the golden-colored hill.

"You have seemed tired these past few days," he observed. Rena did not bother to deny it. She'd been working hard to keep up with the others, as Barric had told her she must, and felt wearier for it. She had tried to split her days in half, the mornings spent binding sheaves with the women and the afternoons spent picking for her own stores, but the work was backbreaking, and, as he had already pointed out once before, she was not used to hard labor. "I realize I haven't really asked you how you are settling in," he went on.

"Perhaps you've been too busy provoking me," she answered before she could stop herself.

Barric's eyebrow inched up as he slanted an approving smirk down at her. "Perhaps."

Rena cursed her honest tongue. She must have been more tired than she thought, to speak so freely to a man of title. "I have been well," she tried again, a bit more diplomatically. "The house suits us, if that is what you are asking."

"The people here do not speak to you unkindly?"

"The people do not speak to me at all." She had meant to sound casual, unaffected, but heard the hurt in her own voice she hadn't been able to weed out. As Barric's expression tightened, she hastened to amend, "Except for you, my lord. Of course. And the Wilmots."

"They are good people," he agreed quietly. "And will you be coming with them to the festival this evening?"

She hesitated. According to Alice, harvest home was a yearly tradition, a night of raucous drinking and dancing to celebrate the close of the harvest. All of Abbotsville would be there—landowners, stewards, even tenant farmers and common laborers. But Rena was none of those things, and she and Barric both knew it.

"Come," Barric teased, "do not tell me you are afraid to go. I would never have thought it of you."

"I am not afraid," she insisted. "I just had not thought about it."

At her defensive tone, he smiled—a true smile—one that

pinched the corners of his eyes and pressed grooves along the outer edges of his mouth. "You ought to come," he decided. "Everyone in Abbotsville is welcome, and many are the men who would feel lucky to dance with you."

But, of course, Lord Barric knew this was not true. The men in his fields regarded her mostly with contempt and made no secret of it— they would not count themselves at all lucky to dance with her. Was Lord Barric trying to offer her words of comfort? Or was he trying to convey a message?

Did *he* want to dance with her?

This was hardly a safe question, and so she asked another. "Do you dance, Lord Barric?"

When he met her gaze, so direct, she was all the more glad she had not stammered in her reply. The man walked a dangerous line whenever he deigned to speak to her. Far too close, she'd think, and then stern enough to cool her blood with a word.

He surprised her with another smile, this one a faint twist at the corner of his lips. "Perhaps you would have to come to find out."

The evening air was unusually mild for October. From the cottage window, Rena caught the heavy smell of towering bonfires smoldering in the distance. All of Abbotsville had gathered for the festival, but Rena had ignored Lord Barric's invitation and dressed instead for bed. She was now curled into the caress of her favorite rocking chair, both feet tucked beneath the fabric of her nightgown as she read one of the books Alice had lent her. Music began tumbling across the now barren fields. The notes were thick and plucky, sticking to the window like hands pressed up against the glass.

"You ought to go to the festival," Nell prodded, looking up from her knitting and glancing to the window. "You are young and made for dancing."

Rena cradled her cup of tea, feeling the steamy rim press warm against her chest. "I have no interest in dancing," she disagreed, turning a page to show she was otherwise employed. "Besides, the festival is for the masters and those under their employ. I am neither."

But that was only half of the matter. The other half involved Edric and how she had not considered him once when she had spoken to Lord Barric of the festival. She was not ready to forget him. No, she was not yet ready to dance.

Nell's fingers were steady on her needles, but her eyes twinkled in the dim light as if she was privy to some secret joke. "Lord Barric invited you, did he not?"

Rena sunk deeper into the chair. "But I am not his employee. I am his beggar."

Nell opened her mouth to disagree, but three light knocks sounded at the door, cutting her off midword. Startled by the intrusion, Rena grabbed the blanket from her chair back and pulled it quickly over her nightdress as Nell bustled to the door and flipped the latch. Alice entered, wearing a wide-skirted satin dress made in the most fashionable shade of emerald.

"I've come to collect Rena," she announced.

Setting her book and tea on the table beside her, Rena pulled her braid nervously over one shoulder and sat up in her chair. "What are you talking about?"

"The festival," Alice explained with a confused frown. "Lord Barric told William you'd be coming."

Rena was surprised Lord Barric had said any such thing to William and wondered how much of their conversation he had shared. Letting the blanket fall down a fraction, Rena gestured to her nightdress. "As you can see, Lord Barric was mistaken. I am not coming."

Alice matched the gesture by holding up a lovely dress. The satin was rusty red, like autumn—like the blood moon. "I have no intention of letting you carry out the rest of your days like a hermit." She crossed the room and dropped the fabric into Rena's lap. "You *are* coming."

"You've shown more than enough kindness," Rena disagreed. "There's no need to—"

Alice's eyes narrowed. "If you stay locked up in here, everyone will know you were too afraid to come."

Barric had suspected the same when he'd asked her about coming to the festival. And the truth was that Rena was afraid. Afraid of betraying Edric by living her life too soon after his death. Afraid of the whispers that still followed her wherever she went. Yes, even afraid of Thomas and Sir Ellis, that they might be there too.

But she had sworn to be stronger, and maybe this was the moment to prove it.

She pulled herself up out of her chair, raising her eyebrows as if to say, *Satisfied?*

When Alice nodded her approval, motioning for Rena to strip out of her nightdress, Rena's eyes fell back to the dress in her hands. "Oh, but it's far too fine," she protested, and reached for her usual black gown.

Nell stopped her, a gentle hand pressed against her shoulder. "It's been well past two years," she said softly. Rena's eyes dropped. It was the first time Nell had called attention to Rena's black garb, which she had already worn several months beyond the customary mourning period. Some days she wore it for penance, feeling like she had more to atone for than could possibly be done by earthly means, but she had to try *something*. Other days she wore it because she was not yet ready to release Edric, in much the same way Nell had wept over the graves in India, knowing once she left she would likely never visit them again.

"Edric would not want for you to wear it forever," Nell whispered. Before Rena could disagree, Nell turned from her. "I'll draw up a fresh basin of water," she said, and then disappeared out the back door.

In Nell's absence, Alice turned, giving Rena a modest moment to undress. Surrendering, Rena pulled out of her nightdress and climbed into her cotton chemise, followed by her drawers and stockings. Clearing her throat to signal she was through, Rena shuffled, cold on her feet, as Alice stepped up to fasten the corset.

"Not too tight," Rena instructed as the boning cinched against her rib cage, pressing up and inward. Though she had begun wearing the British fashion when she'd married Edric, it still felt like a cage to her small frame, full of layers that clung in unnatural ways.

"Where are your petticoats?" Alice asked, a diplomatic question. She must have already known Rena did not own a wire crinoline, as was the current style, which made Alice's own frame appear so impossibly bell-shaped. Alice shimmied the red dress over Rena's shoulders, pulling the hemline down to brush the hardwood floor. Rena's petticoats added some lift and width to her skirt, but not enough to make her look like any less of a skeleton, as Lord Barric had already once named her.

"I knew this color would look lovely with your complexion." Alice smoothed out a few creases as she straightened out of her crouch. "Here, let's undo your braid."

Alice grabbed a few pins from the nightstand, then brandished a small jeweled net before signaling Rena to sit. As Alice fussed with her hair, Rena observed her friend's bountiful curls, which were tied into a loose chignon at the back of her neck, with several careful spirals covering both ears. Rena winced against the scrape of hairpins, pulling her eyes away from her friend. Polished and poised and smelling faintly of lemon, Alice shimmered even in the dim candlelight. No matter how they dressed Rena or primped her, she would always stand out against Alice's elegant, English beauty.

Alice briefly smoothed the top of Rena's hair and stepped away to signal she was finished. Standing, Rena straightened the long sleeves and stole a surreptitious glance in the mirror across the room. She was surprised to find she looked like an entirely different person, her complexion much brighter now set against color. The sleeves hit low on her shoulders, but the dress was modest enough. Her hair was pulled into a gentle coil at the nape of her neck, secured loosely in the net so several waves escaped along the side of her face.

Nell slid back into the cabin, her smile curling as she shut the door quietly behind her. "You look incredibly beautiful, my child." With gentle hands, she washed Rena's hands, neck, and face with a wet cloth. Rena avoided Nell's gaze, embarrassed to be trapped in such a dress while her shrouded heart was still very much that of a widow.

Rena pursed her lips as she slid into her shoes, the worn leather far too battered when set against the rest of her elegant ensemble. Then she pressed a kiss to Nell's cheek and stepped outside. After weeks of enduring the chill of impending autumn, she was grateful for the evening's warm wind, surprised when the thick air stuck to her skin and reminded her, strangely, of early mornings back home.

Like pursuing thunder, Rena's feet followed the drumbeats rolling in the distance, a half step behind Alice as they made their way to the festival. They did not have to journey far. From the top of the hill, Lord Barric's manor was brightly lit, its gray walls standing guard over the valley of rolling fields below. At the bottom of the hill, brushing the far edge of the tree line, six large bonfires roared, rimmed with people.

As they neared the first fire, Rena's nose crinkled, unprepared for the heady mix of cinnamon and smoke that stung each nostril. Tables lined the festival's perimeter, piled with enough food and drink to make Rena sick for a week. Since arriving in England, her stomach had become a stranger to nearly anything but bread and water. She remembered the feast she'd shared with Nell after Lord Barric had offered his fields to her. It had been the first time she had ever broken her family's dietary laws and eaten meat—a decision she had made out of loyalty to Nell—but Rena had been so nauseated she had hardly slept that night and could barely drag herself out of bed to glean in the morning.

Frowning at the sickly memory, her gaze drifted over thick baskets weighted with apples to the hulking pork roasts skewered on spits. Every platter seemed slathered in sweet sauces and rich gravies, so different from the diet of spices and vegetables she had eaten at home. Everywhere Rena looked, she saw indulgence masked as celebration. Casks of deep autumn wine flowed freely into glasses, and those not drinking danced in lines near a low dais which was wreathed in orange and yellow flowers.

A fiddler ripped his bow against the strings, his eyes slicing sharply as the drummers carried the music into a crashing fever pitch. Nearly tripping over a stack of bulbous pumpkins, Rena watched the musicians, feeling their wild music as if their fingers and bows stirred her blood rather than strings.

It was a miracle the girls were not plowed over by the crowd altogether. People gathered in every open space of grass, their glasses full and eyes deliriously merry. Most of the masters gathered together, murmuring and laughing in expensive black suits, their waistcoats cut of every fine color imaginable. Alice smiled and nodded to William, who stood where a few of the tenant farmers had flocked to their own corner of the celebration.

As they circled the second fire, Rena spotted Lord Barric standing on the other side of the pit. Glass in hand, he stood close to the fire, his eyes trained on the flames as if he could see the wall of heat rolling toward him. A band of young women, several ranks above Rena, tangled like flames nearer to him, with teeth and ribbons flashing. Finally turning from the fire, Lord Barric offered a rare smile to one woman who was wearing a rich, jewel-colored dress. Immediately the woman broke into a feline grin.

Rena dropped her gaze to her hands, allowing the image of spitting flames to overlay Lord Barric's casual expression as he spoke in the woman's ear. Alice had said there wasn't a girl from there to Liverpool who hadn't set her cap at him, and here was the proof.

As if sensing the direction of her thoughts, Alice slipped her hand around Rena's arm and tugged her along. Before they reached the other side of the fire, however, a young man with playful eyes pressed briefly to Alice's side, leaning at the waist to drop a few words into her ear. A slow, pleased smile drew across her face, and she squeezed Rena's hand with a silent message.

"Forgive me," Alice whispered. "I'll be but a moment. Eat something in the meantime."

Rena did not wish to eat. She wished to go home. She felt like an insufferable traitor to Edric for wearing Alice's red dress, unsettled by the way it hit low on her shoulders and made her copper skin glow.

She trailed Alice and her partner to the end of the makeshift dance floor, watching the young couples stomp out the steps to a raucous, fast-paced dance. Alice's young man seemed harmless enough, albeit a flirt. He wore homespun clothes, clean and pressed, and his dusty hair shadowed his eyes as he led Alice to the lines of dancers. He made Alice laugh, his hands eagerly searching out her waist each time they were rematched at the end of the row, and he had a habit of whispering when they were very close.

Rena wondered again that Alice had not yet married. Several men openly watched her friend, as though pleased by her laughing eyes, and Rena hoped with a pang that Alice was not saving her heart for Lord Barric, a man far too high in rank to consider marrying his steward's sister.

Rena was about to turn away from the dancers when she sensed a presence beside her. She didn't have to lift her eyes to know the voice when it spoke. William. "I see you've come out of hiding."

"I wasn't given much of a choice," Rena replied, following William's eyes to his sister, who stared at her partner with a bold, immovable smile.

The steward looped his arms loosely in front of his chest, his eyes not once leaving Alice and her companion. "Ah. So, taken hostage, then?"

"Your sister is very. . .persuasive."

William barked a laugh and shook his head.

"She is kind," Rena observed. "I like her."

Arms folded against his chest, William continued watching Alice and the other dancers with a look of bored detachment. "You should know that people talk," he said. "About you. And him. About your. . .arrangement."

Though surprised by the boldness of the remark, Rena still managed to answer his suspicion in a steady voice. "Do you think I did not know that?"

The angular lines of William's face sharpened into an expression that seemed oddly foreign to his usually reserved features.

"You may be prepared to martyr yourself to gossip," he said tightly. "But I'm not ready or willing to see Barric make a fool of himself without good cause."

Rena heard a burst of smothered laughter nearby and glanced to the side, where a group of men watched her with open, curious eyes, clearly amused by her conversation with William. Drink in hand, one of the men leaned closer as if hoping to catch their words.

Darting a glance at the men, William sighed, took up Rena's hand, and led her with startling abruptness to the dance floor. "And what do you think they are saying about *us* now?" he challenged, pulling her toward him as he inclined his head to the murmuring men.

William did not let her answer. In perfect time with the other dancers, he spun her around. Rena stiffened, feeling oddly brittle, as if the sun had dried up her bones.

"*Dance with me,*" Edric had said to her once. He had spent two weeks teaching her the steps to his favorite dances, insisting she accompany him to one of the military balls. Oh, how people had stared at them. His comrades had called him a brazen fool for bringing his Indian wife to such a place. The English women who had come to India seeking British husbands of their own—*memsahibs* as her people called them—had watched her with clear disdain, spitting epithets to one another as she and Edric had passed them. Did those women think she had stolen a prospect from them? Did they think he was under her spell? But Edric had pressed Rena's hand, silencing her thoughts as he murmured, "*They're just jealous of your beauty. Dance with me.*"

She shook away the whisper of Edric's ghost when she realized William was watching her.

"If you don't think I'm worth the trouble," she said, circling around him and taking his outstretched hand. "Why have you given us your cottage?"

"I just want to make sure you don't do anything stupid." William leaned closer so she could still hear him over the raucous music. "Barric's a good man, the kind who can take care of himself, but as with any man he's also the kind who could get a young woman into trouble."

"For a steward, you sure have a lot to say about your master." She heard in her defensive tone the words of a spoiled aristo, latching onto rank and twisting it to her advantage.

William did not seem angered by her reply. His hand parted from hers just long enough for her to catch hands with the man adjacent to them. The other man spun her quickly, his fingers barely touching hers, as if afraid her skin might burn him. As she and William met in the middle, William replied, "Our fathers died within a few years of each other. You might say Barric and I both returned to finish what they started, and I do not wish for anything to impede that end."

Rena nodded, her throat constricting. "It is difficult," she agreed, "to pick up after the dead."

Sometimes, when Rena teetered on the verge of sleep, she still felt like she was spinning, faster and faster in Edric's hold as he led her through the next unfamiliar dance. Sometimes she awakened dizzy and needed a moment to settle her eyes on something steadfast. Now Rena wore a strange red dress and danced with a young man she barely knew, her steps heavy and awkward.

"This husband of yours," William began, then frowned as if already regretting his prodding question. "Would he have wanted you to come to England?"

Edric had always talked about England and how desperately he wanted to bring her there, though neither of them could have guessed she would return without him. Sorrow rose up, the familiar beast, and choked her. Rena dropped her gaze. She did not wish to speak about Edric. She wanted to feel weightless again, to spin herself dizzy as she had two years ago in her husband's arms.

"Never mind," William whispered, his hand tightening around hers. "Don't answer. Just dance."

William led her through one more reel. They didn't speak again, and Rena almost enjoyed herself. William was a confident dancer with a reserved smile that slipped its guard now and then and ended in genuine laughter. Rena followed his lead, though the steps of the second dance were mostly unfamiliar to her. Still, it was relieving, in a small way, to race against her own heartbeat, to feel noise and chatter and lose herself within it. At one point, she forgot which way was right and which way was left and tripped against him, laughing for the first time in many, many months.

At last the music beat like rapid wings to a steady close. With a reluctant smile of approval, William stepped back to bow. Rena curtsied, then moved to take up her previous post at the floor's perimeter and wait for Alice's return. Before she'd made it three paces, however, cool fingers locked around her forearm and pulled her half a step off balance. "I believe I have the next dance."

Rena turned at the waist and found Thomas waiting behind her. Each lock of his black hair was swept carefully over his brow and his mustache impeccably trimmed. He might have been handsome, in an angular way, if only his eyes weren't so uncomfortably cold. He dashed her a swooping bow and tipped his head in obvious question. William's lips tightened as he glanced sharply at Rena. "You don't have to dance with him," he said with a baleful glance at Thomas.

Thomas sighed dramatically. He still hadn't released Rena's arm. "You don't have to play watchdog for Barric," he rebuked. "I promise he is not watching."

"It's fine," Rena said, refusing to be shaken by someone who obviously wanted to watch her cringe. She smiled faintly at William, though her throat felt unbearably tight. "It's just one dance."

Without another glance at William, Thomas led Rena to her place in line with the other ladies. With unnerving focus, he stared at her across the aisle, waiting for the music to begin. The fiddle pitched to life, and as the other couples moved across the floor, Rena was obliged to cross to Thomas, to hold her hand out toward him. At the first chance he had, Thomas pulled her tightly against him and lowered his eyes to her saffron-colored dress. "It would seem you have come out of mourning," he observed, and smiled again.

Rena made no answer but followed the motions as he danced her down the line, past other men and women who watched their progress with uncertain expressions. His heavy cologne stung her nostrils as it had that first night on the road, and she ticked down the seconds until the dance would end and she could at last escape him.

"I almost envy Barric," he continued as she returned to her place beside him. His arm locked around her waist as he dropped the words in her ear, "He must enjoy the pretty vision of you slaving in his fields—how especially if you were to wear that dress as you begged."

She clenched her teeth, relieved when he released her. She switched places with the lady beside her and was allowed three seconds respite before her hands were again joined with Thomas's.

"We don't have to talk," she commented frostily, snatching her hand back as soon as she was able.

"Prefer a man of few words, do you?" He smirked, his eyes markedly pointed in Lord Barric's direction.

She tried not to react to his needling, but her fingers clenched briefly against his coat sleeve, betraying her frustration. She already knew what people thought of her. *Trollop*, they called her, and her short stay at the Gilded Crown had certainly not helped matters. Would people think, because of this dance, she was somehow involved with Thomas? She frowned at his glinting eyes.

"You needn't play so coy with me," Thomas goaded. "You'd think Barric would show more discretion. Oh, his brother has kept many mistresses too. I wouldn't be surprised if some of them were from your neck of the woods. Barric and Charlie have always had a liking for dark-haired beauties. . . ."

She kept her expression loose and unaffected, refusing to rise to his taunts. Clearly, Thomas wanted to anger her, but she would not willingly hand him words he could twist against her later. When it was clear she wouldn't answer, Thomas's fingers tightened.

"Perhaps he is not the only one who could loosen your tongue," he whispered in her ear, pulling her to an abrupt halt. "I might not be an earl, but I'd still be better business than what you had at the Gilded Crown."

Rena lost her footing. Lurching back from Thomas, she brought up her arm to strike him as hard across the face as she could, but her hand was caught at once from behind.

Thomas saw him before she did.

"Ah, Barric!" he greeted with a sly expression which was razored at the edges. "We were just speaking of you."

Rena's hand was shaking in Lord Barric's. He released her at once and stepped back. She couldn't bring herself to look at him. Had he heard? Had he heard the vile words his cousin had said to her?

"She dances rather well for a heathen," Thomas purred. "Don't you think so, Barric?"

Rena did not wait for Lord Barric's reply. Without another word, she turned and fled the dance floor.

Rena heard Barric calling out her name, a brash sound against the hollow drum of her ears. She moved faster, ignoring him. She made it several yards past the festival's edge, passing into a small thicket, where the music's beat was reduced to dead thuds beneath her tired feet. After spending time in noisy chaos, every other sound pealed louder as she hurried home. The wind felt like deafening shrieks. The pitch of crickets was as shrill as fingernails on tin.

When twigs snapped several steps behind her, she whirled around to find Lord Barric standing before her. His skin matched the moonlight gleam for gleam, and his red hair was that mysterious shade of firelight which felt familiar and foreign to her all at once.

"What did he say to you?" He was slightly out of breath from running after her, but his words were iron tight in his throat.

"Nothing I care to repeat," she replied, trembling slightly from anger and her own useless sprint.

He nodded grimly, perhaps guessing easily enough what his cousin might have said. Of course he could guess. They were family, after all. Might not Barric have been raised to entertain the same thoughts as Thomas, the same arrogance, even if he treated her with more kindness? Even William had warned her, hadn't he? Barric was the kind of man who could get a young woman like her into trouble. And now here he was, standing right in front of her.

She loosed a humorless laugh, a tired breath that rattled—a rusty sound. Barric's expression creased slightly. He stepped closer, still a few paces away, and paused. His eyes felt too hard against hers, so she shifted to the side and looked back at the glinting fires still blazing like watchful eyes in the distance. Covering the last few steps separating them, Barric's eyes drifted across her face as he clasped a tendril of her black hair between two of his fingers.

"Barric and Charlie have always had a liking for dark-haired beauties. . . ."

She shoved back against the intrusion of Thomas's voice in her mind, not wanting to believe his words but also not sure she had a reason to doubt them. She snapped her mouth tightly closed and pictured Lord Barric standing on the other side of the fire, surrounded by girls as bright as midnight tapers. And he had smiled at those girls, his face a fiery mask of shadow and reflected flame.

She opened her mouth but couldn't force a word up her faltering throat. He smelled like campfire, the smoke still thick on his coat, seeming so casual and ordinary in the thicket as if torn from his powerful world like a page from a book.

A few tendrils of hair had escaped the net at the back of her neck, and Barric swept them away from her shoulders. Nell had told her to keep both eyes open around him, to tread carefully because they weren't entirely sure what kind of man he was. Rena thought she knew, but then Lord Barric tipped her chin, searching her face.

"I should go." The words barely registered in her own ears; she half wondered if she had spoken them at all. His head dipped down, closer, and his touch was soft, like the grain that brushed her skin when she worked in his fields. As he shifted his hand to cup the side of her neck, his fingers accidentally brushed the thin cord still hanging there.

Edric.

Barric's touch to the necklace hit her like a physical blow, curdling her blood in an instant. With a sharp gasp, her hand flew to her chest, where the vial of sand still dangled beside Edric's signet ring. Barric noticed the frantic movement, his eyes creasing when he read whatever pained expression had crossed her face.

He brushed her hand aside, lifting the cord carefully to examine the two trinkets. Rena wanted to jerk back, flustered by his nearness, but she felt pinned in place by a strange mix of embarrassment and sorrow. And so she waited as he inspected the vial of sand, closely, as if peering through a magic glass into another world. His lips tightened. Then his attention shifted, his fingers taking hold of Edric's ring. There it was. Edric's initials. His crest. Another man's legacy curved into a simple circle of gleaming gold. Rena choked back a sob as every memory of Edric began splitting behind her eyes, until the man seemed to stand between her and Barric, an impenetrable wall.

Closing his eyes, Barric severed the connection by dropping the ring, letting the cord fall back heavily against her chest. Rena seized the vial and the ring in her palm, staring down at the ground with a pounding shame. He'd been about to kiss her, and she'd been about to let him.

"I shouldn't have done that." Barric's tone was overly formal, his jaw so tight the words seemed forced from him at knifepoint. "I've had too much wine, I think."

Rena was still shaking her head when he'd finished speaking. "I can't," she whispered, pleading. "I won't be your—"

She broke off, horrified by what she'd been about to let slip. But Barric caught the words before she could retract them, his eyes pausing suspiciously on her face. "Won't be my what?" He spoke slowly, drawing her out. Shaking her head, Rena garbled out an apology, but he snatched her hand. "Won't be my *what?*" he repeated.

"I won't be your mistress." She tried to sound blunt, as Thomas had been when he'd brought up the topic in the first place, but her throat closed at the last moment, clenching the sound.

For a moment, Barric's expression flashed with a stab of unmistakable shock, his mouth parted slightly, his eyes a stunned shade of shadowed green. But then, like thunder following the lightning, his expression darkened into tightly held rage, his hands fisting at his sides as his eyes narrowed on her face. "My. . .mistress?" He practically choked on the word. He scuffed his heel backward through the dirt, nearly laughing until the harsh sound betrayed his black mood. "I let you take from my fields. Offer you housing. Protection. *Eventually, he'll come to collect.* Is that what you think?" He stalked a few steps away from her.

"I only thought, because of your brother—"

Those were the wrong words to say too, and Rena knew it as soon as she'd begun. Lord Barric rounded hard, grabbing her arm to keep her from stepping back. When he spoke, the words rumbled in his throat. "What *about* my brother?"

"I've heard he has. . .many. Mistresses." Her eyes fell from his as she repeated what she'd heard. "In France. And that you—"

"You know, for someone who despises gossip so much, it certainly falls readily enough from your willing tongue." His accusation cost Rena the last few scraps of control she held. Her mouth flew open to protest, indignant, but the words caught in her chest when she realized he was right. She was holding gossip against a man who had shown her nothing but kindness—gossip she'd heard from Thomas no less. Shame kept her from replying.

"But you see, I can be just as direct as you. Yes, Mrs. Hawley, my brother has bedded *many* eager women. And when he tires of them, I pay them for their trouble, along with his debts. And there will be many more to warm his bed, I'm sure. My brother is a very charming man."

Rena stared carefully at his knotted cravat, refusing to meet his eyes. Lord Barric had been very direct, indeed, had said things which ought to have made a decent lady blush. But then she thought about those poor women, discarded one after the other, and she shook the silence away. "Do you believe these women love him?"

His sharp expression slackened, confused, perhaps even surprised by her sudden change in direction. He dropped her arm and shrugged as if he'd never considered the possibility. "Some do, I'm sure."

"Do not pay them. Let your brother see how cheaply he has used their love—he ought to see the true price of a heart."

Lord Barric's gaze dropped again to Edric's ring. Uncomfortable, Rena tucked the necklace back beneath her neckline. Barric gave her a tentative look, but he didn't speak. Feeling as though they had both mortified each other enough for one meeting, she sketched a quick curtsy—a pathetic semblance of formality—and turned to continue her path toward home.

"Where are you going?" His voice sounded uneven. Unsure.

Again, she turned and said, "I do not belong here."

As though to punctuate her statement, drunken laughter sounded through the trees, unnervingly close. Shaking her head, Rena stepped farther back from him. What would people think if they found her there in the trees, alone with Lord Barric? Just like his brother, people might say of him. Or worse, that Rena had seduced him.

"I must go," she whispered urgently. "Now, my lord. Think what people will say if they discover us here together."

He took a step closer to her. "Dance with me before you go."

Still slightly untrusting, Rena made no reply.

"What's wrong?" He tilted his head to glimpse her downcast eyes. "Afraid I might actually make you smile?"

Rena sighed, feeling the same traitorous pull she'd felt when they'd spoken outside the stable, when he had smiled so broadly as she had not seen before or since.

"Yes," she answered truthfully and turned again, away from him.

Barric returned to the festival in a stormier mood, his hands and jaw clenched tight with irritation. He had surprised himself in the thicket, embracing a woman who clearly needed time to grieve, making advances on her without a thought for her wishes or reputation. Such was not the behavior of a gentleman. Even Rena must have thought poorly of him, trusted him so little she thought his generosity was merely a guise for taking her to bed.

Now he marched back to the other revelers, his temper slipping its stronghold. He was sick of watching the way she was forced to take the town's barbed whispers, with head bent down and muted eyes, as if she were taking a beating. He could only imagine what his cousin had said to her, words awful enough that she nearly struck him, right there in front of everyone. Barric half wished he hadn't intervened, that he'd let her leave an angry mark on Thomas's deserving cheek. But he *had* stepped in, caught her strike lest Thomas return the blow, and Rena had run from them both, suspecting Barric was little better than those with whom he shared blood.

Shaking off his frustrations, knowing they were likely written too vividly on his face, he refocused his attention on the festival. From a small distance, William caught his eye, inclining his head meaningfully toward the perimeter of the dance, where several unattached young women waited with hopeful eyes for someone—anyone—to ask them to dance. Breathing out the rest of his irritation, Barric took William's cue and reminded himself that he *was* still host that evening and needed to act the part.

He approached the small cluster of women, all of whom were openly delighted by his unexpected advance. They tittered among themselves, smiling shyly, until he came to a stop directly in front of them. He narrowed in on the one with the kindest smile and extended his hand in silent question.

Of course the girl wanted to dance with him. He didn't even have to smile at her. Every woman at the festival wished he would ask her. He had a title and a fortune and was young enough to seem exciting despite his stern demeanor. Yet their eagerness wearied him, and the ones who were interested only in his money amused him even less.

With a tired smile, he took the girl's hand and led her to the row of dancers, hoping the music might help drown out his thoughts. The only light left to guide them flickered down from lanterns, the stray firelight fragmenting the girl's features as she tilted her chin up toward him.

His thoughts turned, disconcertingly, toward Rena. Though he had shared in several dances that night, none of the women had worn so elegant a frown as Rena. She had looked quite exquisite in her crimson gown, the first time he had ever seen her out of mourning. Barric told himself his interest in her didn't mean anything—he was only trying to be kind. But two seconds more in the thicket, and he'd have pulled her into his arms and kissed her. His fingers had ached to curve around her waist. Too much wine, he told himself again. Still, there had been no twinkle of flirtation in Rena's eyes when he had snared her in the thicket, no hint that her mouth was at all enthralled by his.

He focused his attention back on the girl now in his arms. With blond hair tied up in ribbons, she seemed younger than Rena, though he suspected there was very little difference between their ages. Rena's sorrow had altered her youth, though certainly not her beauty. She'd seemed small beside him in the thicket, and yet there was something formidable about her. Though her shoulder blades still pressed like rolling pins beneath her skin, pride ran a strong line from her shoulders down her spine. Would she seem younger, he wondered, if she smiled?

He led the young lady through the dance, but he felt stiff and out of sorts. Too old for her, though he knew he wasn't. As he took her hand at the end of a row, she leaned in, said something to him about the warmth of the evening, then the stars, and he smiled obligingly but didn't answer. She didn't seem to mind his silence. She seemed to wish only to smile up at him, to relish the feeling of his hand at her back, which made him feel slightly guilty for asking her to dance in the first place.

He simply couldn't hold on to his thoughts long enough to think up something to say, or to care that he couldn't. Instead, he thought about the moment Rena had matched his stare out in the thicket. From that close, he had been able to make out every golden fleck glinting from her otherwise black eyes. Yes, he thought to himself, those eyes were unreasonably inconvenient. Depthless and dark, they sorrowed. It had been her eyes that had snared him in the thicket; it was her eyes that snared him now. . . .

"Lord Barric?" His dancing partner frowned hesitantly, as if she could sense his thoughts were not with her at all.

He blinked and nearly laughed at himself. He was, as William had warned him, an utter fool. Wanting to kiss Rena meant nothing, he told himself one last time. A ridiculous fancy. Besides, if Barric were to be carried away by a woman, it certainly wasn't going to be a foreign outcast with miserable eyes.

He smiled apologetically at the heart-swept girl still watching him. He made a few light comments about the harvest and the festival, and finished the dance with far more presence of mind. When the music ended, he wished her well, made a low bow, and strode away.

He did not dance again.

CHAPTER 8

Rena had searched everywhere. She'd turned out every drawer, crawled beneath every piece of furniture, even checked the weathered cracks in the floorboards until her fingertips were splintered and her thoughts were shuffled, impossible to regather correctly.

Her necklace was gone.

The contents of their home were now a scattered menagerie, items stacked in odd corners of the room. Nell sat at the table, her face crumpled as she sought to console Rena. "It will turn up," she soothed. A heap of blankets was strewn carelessly beside the bed, and she slowly began to fold them, taking time to smooth the wrinkles with her fingers. "Things like these go missing, but they usually turn up."

Rena slammed the drawer she'd been rifling through, rattling every cup and plate within the cabinet.

"What if it *doesn't?*" Her voice sounded harsh and angry, but the catch in her voice betrayed her. She was frantic, not angry. She wanted so much to be angry.

She hadn't even realized the necklace was missing until the afternoon. As soon as she noticed its absence, she had turned into a windstorm, unsettling every item in their small home. She knew it was unfair of her to snap at Nell, but she hadn't realized how Edric's ring had kept her anchored until it had vanished, and now she was plunged deep beneath icy, punishing thoughts. She had been careless at the festival. She had been reckless. She had allowed another man to touch her. She had *wanted* him to touch her.

"Rena." Recognizing the regret in Rena's eyes, Nell rose from the bed and crossed to her, pulling her up from her knees. "You haven't lost him. It's just a ring. Just a small scattering of sand."

Just a ring. Just sand. Rena pressed both hands to her eyes, knowing, of course, the necklace was trivial—two small trinkets joined together by a cheap, fraying cord. But now the necklace was gone, the sand and the ring, and Edric's smile was in the grave, and she felt a great chasm opening within her chest, like a gaping mouth prepared to swallow.

She'd felt the chasm first beckoning the night before, when Lord Barric had discovered the necklace. She disciplined her mind, trying not to think of him or how he had come upon her from the mist, smelling of smoke and wealth, or how he had matched her gaze in the thicket, as if he hadn't matched eyes with a dozen other girls that night.

She must have dropped the necklace at the festival. This realization stiffened her spine and gave her direction. Breaking her shoulders from Nell's hold, Rena spun toward the door, catching a thick shawl up in her hands.

"Where are you going?" Nell's voice turned hard as she trailed Rena's steps, trying to catch up.

"I had it on at the festival," Rena explained, grasping the handle. "I'm going to look."

"But it's raining!" Nell looked worried now, her forehead lined with heavy wrinkles as she sunk into her familiar widow's frown. "And cold!"

"Then I will have to look quickly." She shut the door on Nell's next protest but teetered on the threshold, her skin already fitting tighter against her bones because of the icy rain. She pulled her shawl closer and barreled across the yard, forcing the gate's rickety latch to let her through.

Rena squared her shoulders as she walked, her eyes scanning the wet ground. Led by raw intuition, she checked the thicket first. She knelt down, her fingers stiff as they tore through the wet grass. Tufts of it were matted, where she and Barric had stood, but she found nothing there. She sliced her fingers on a scattering of fallen brambles which had been dislodged by rough wind. Still nothing.

"Mrs. Hawley!" When she heard her name, she rose and headed in the opposite direction, refusing to slow as she eyed the giant pits which had been alight the night before. There was the bonfire where Lord Barric had stood surrounded by all those girls, with a drink balanced casually in his hand. There was the stretch of grass where Thomas had taken her hand and pulled her against him. Her fingers curled as she fisted her trembling hands. How had the balmy festival air turned to ice so quickly?

When she didn't answer, William did away with decorum and tried her first name. *"Rena!"*

She felt him come up next to her, but she refused to look at him as she ran her fingers through her now sopping hair and methodically scanned the ground.

"I wish to be left alone."

She tried to sound pleasant, but her words cracked like a whip as she crouched to inspect the muddy grass once more. She splayed a hand against the ground and imagined she could still feel the crash of heavy drumbeats from the night before. Though the chaos had vanished, she still felt incredibly off balance.

"It's freezing out here." William sounded worried as he reached for her arm. "You're soaked. Please, come inside."

She kept her eyes trained on the ground, still searching for any glint of Edric's ring. Nell had told her she hadn't lost him, but it felt like she had. She had opened her fingers and let him slip through the spaces. "I'm. . .I'm just looking for something."

"This is madness." William hooked a hand around her arm as he tried to guide her to her feet. "Let me walk you home. I promise I'll help you look tomorrow, when it's dry. Alice will help too."

She slapped William's hand away and finally met his eyes. "I'm *not* leaving," she snapped, hating that she wasn't making any sense, hating the frightened, uncertain look now moving in William's kind eyes. "Go!"

William muttered a soft string of pleas that Rena didn't allow herself to hear. His voice was uncharacteristically worried, but she couldn't feel guilty. Not yet. Blotting him out, she crammed her hands deeper into the icy mud, not caring that her fingers felt bitten or that she could no longer feel her own skin. After a few moments, she stole a glance over her shoulder and realized William had indeed gone. He must have thought she had lost her mind. Maybe she had.

Time hovered above her, crushing in its slowness, the darkness thickening around her by slow shades. As the shadows deepened, she at last allowed herself to remember the look of the missing ring on Edric's hand. Commissioned in India, set with a prowling tiger around his initials and family crest, the gold band had glinted subtly in the low light as he made his usual cup of tea in the morning. It had cooled against her cheek whenever he cupped her face. It had hung awkwardly about his knuckle when he'd lost several stones of weight and turned gaunt with fever.

"I'm sorry, Edric," she whispered to the ground. "I'm so sorry." Would she even have lost his ring, she wondered, if she hadn't dallied with Lord Barric in the thicket? She wondered if maybe she was being punished. For wearing that dress. For dancing. For taking her eyes off Edric, if only for a moment.

She ought to go back inside. Nell would be so worried about her, and her chest was beginning to tighten.

"Have you lost your mind?"

Rena froze. She didn't have to glance upward to know Lord Barric had come—or that he was furious.

"Please, leave," she all but ordered, stiffening her shoulders as she continued to search. She knew she was behaving erratically. Madness, as William had said. But she had sunk into a dark, irrational place, where to give in was to give up on grieving. She couldn't leave Edric's ring in a field that was soon to be covered with mud and snow. It would be like burying him all over again.

Without prelude, Lord Barric stepped forward, slipping his hands beneath her elbows and hauling her to her feet. "You're finished," he commanded, tugging her in the direction of Misthold.

Rena rebounded quickly, jerking her arms from his hold and shooting backward. "I wish to be left alone!" she shouted, desperation climbing.

She finally met his eyes, flinching slightly at his tight-jawed expression. He looked as if he had left his home in a hurry, his coat unbuttoned, ginger hair a mess, drenched two shades darker with the rain.

"Mrs. Hawley," he scolded, shaking his head as he gestured to the trampled field around them. "Come to your senses! You are stronger than this."

"*Stronger?*" She bit down a wild laugh as she repeated the word back at him. It seemed her life's ambition to be stronger, stronger, always stronger. Had losing her husband not been enough to endure? Or following Nell into this strange world, away from her family, where everyone thought she was nothing? Had starving for weeks, or sleeping in gutters, or prostrating her pride at Lord Barric's feet—had none of that been enough? She remembered what she'd wished for in church, to be strong rather than blessed, and cursed her foolish heart.

She knew she was really lost, broken in nearly every way, when she brought up her arms to shove him. Barric foresaw the blow, grabbing a firm hold of her arm and using it to pull her flat against him. His skin was soaked through his shirt, frigid beneath her fingers. Startled,

Rena tore back from him, coming to a stumbling halt a few feet away as she clutched at her dress and nearly shrieked, "I am sick to death of being strong!"

Barric froze, lifting his gaze to meet her eyes. For a moment, there was nothing but ragged breathing between them, the drag of angry exhaustion, and Rena was pinned by just how much she wanted him to leave, just so he wouldn't see her like this, but also by how much she hoped he'd stay, just so she wouldn't have to be alone.

But Barric didn't leave. Though Rena was covered in mud and raving, though she'd screamed at him and nearly struck him, though he didn't even know what she was looking for, Barric dropped to both knees with a withered curse and began to search the frozen ground.

Barric found the blasted necklace. It took him nearly an hour to find where it had been stomped beneath a muddy tuft of grass. He flexed his unfeeling knuckles, the bite of icy air sharp against his skin. He had no idea how Rena had withstood the rain for so long when he himself nearly gave up at least a dozen times. Though he had tried to convince himself she wasn't worth the trouble, he'd seen the moment when she'd been about to hit him, her anger coiled tightly within her like a spring. She needed someone strong enough to withstand the grieving madness with her, if only for a moment.

And so there he was, hunched over frosted stalks of grass, and all for what?

His voice was gruff as he finally held up the cord and barked out the words, "It's here."

Fighting his temper, he watched Rena scramble to her feet. There were tears in her dark, lovely eyes, and a hunger on her face. She pressed both hands tightly to her chest, where the necklace typically hung, clearly waiting for him to hand it over. He had half a mind to hurl it at her and leave, but she seemed half-wild in the rain. Her hair was made brittle by frost, her lips a ghostly shade of white. Still, she held herself well, straight-backed and poised as she extended her thin hand. "Thank you."

He didn't care to learn what he might say to her if he opened his mouth to answer. Half a dozen curses were pressed tightly against his tongue. Swallowing them all, he spun away from her and strode toward Misthold, the necklace still dangling from his fisted hand.

"Wait!" Rena called out, hastening to his side. Her voice sounded half-dead, raspy. "Let me have it. . .please!"

He refused to answer. Instead, he barreled on, and she followed after him, silently, all the way up the steep hill to Misthold. He wasn't entirely sure where he was going when he led them both to a back entrance, jerking on the wrought-iron handle. When he finally met her eyes, she drew back from whatever she caught in his expression. Could she tell he was furious? He hoped so. If he was going to feel this angry, then she could just as well know it.

He held the door for her, and she entered, her movements slow and stiff as if it hurt to move. He took a moment to shake the rain from his hair with his other hand.

"Infernal fool," he finally muttered, slamming the door. He wasn't sure if he meant himself or Rena, who trailed him all the way to his study, her hands clasped tightly together in front of her stomach.

"Come in," he said, yanking the door open.

Hesitating only a moment, she obeyed, instantly drawn toward the fire which was still lit from when William had come to find him. She took several steps, eyes on the flames as she clutched her shawl closer about her. Water ran down the soft edges of her face, hitting the floor in an odd pattern.

"You'll be lucky if we both don't catch our deaths." He bit out the words, grabbing her arm and leading her to the couch nearest the fire. He practically flung her down onto the red, upholstered seat. "William said he'd have gone with you tomorrow. Why didn't you wait?"

Her eyes flew up to him, and her voice was still a faint scratch of sound as she explained, "I had to find it."

This time he couldn't stop himself from hurling the necklace at her. She caught it against her chest, her eyes wide and startled. "And was it worth it?" he seethed, shucking off his sopping coat and slinging it over the back of a chair. "Was it worth nearly killing yourself in the cold? People die from getting caught in weather like that."

He froze, wondering if that had been part of her plan. She wouldn't meet his eyes again, which made his heart beat uncomfortably fast. Had she subjected herself to the cold on purpose, knowing it could make her sick?

"I wasn't trying to die." She still avoided his eyes, running her fingers over his couch's rich upholstery. "I—" She broke off, the words falling dead on her tongue. Then she stood, teetering on her feet as she shook her head and said, "I wish to go home."

He sidestepped, cutting off her path to the door. "No," he said, hardly knowing what he planned on doing next. "Not just yet."

Rena clutched at her shawl, pulling the fabric tighter over her hands, and only then did he realize she was trembling all over. He wanted to be angry with her for her recklessness in the cold, but there was a terror in her eyes, which he prayed had nothing to do with him. He loosed a pent-up breath, taking her icy hand in his and tugging her toward the fireplace. He motioned for her to sit on the warm stone hearth. As she did, she angled her face toward the flames, which illuminated the gentle planes of her expression. She wouldn't look at Barric as he crouched beside her, not even as he lifted the soaked shawl from her shoulders. He noticed that the dress she wore was no longer black but a much softer gray; her eyes were still black as mourning.

"I will call for tea," he suggested, his voice more even as he set the shawl aside. "Something warm?"

She stared emptily at the necklace still resting in her palm. "You must think I'm crazy," she finally whispered.

Head bowed, hand screening her eyes, Rena's hair fell like a black curtain between them. She often seemed this way to Barric. Boarded and shuttered, stumbling around in the dark, alone.

Deciding the most he could do was make sure she was warm, he crossed to the hutch beside his desk and rummaged among the bottles.

He decided on a fat bottle of brandy, pouring two generous glasses before returning to the fire. "I don't think you're crazy." He crouched at her side, and she eyed him suspiciously. He knew, of course, how this situation would look to outside eyes—the two of them dripping on his plush carpet, half-frozen by the fire with drinks in hand. Oh, how his cousin would mock him. He held out a glass anyway. "You're frozen," he explained. "This will help."

She slipped her hand around the glass and brought it to her lips for a tentative sip. Immediately her face scrunched into a hard wince. Barric took a swig of his own, relishing the heat that pounded through him.

"I didn't mean to shout at you," she said after he had lowered his glass.

"You were upset."

She ran a finger along the rim of her glass before taking another drink. "I kept very little when I left India," she explained softly. "I had to sell my wedding ring to pay for our passage. Edric's ring—it's all I have left of him. When I thought I had lost it, I just. . .lost myself too."

Her admission shocked him. She'd never spoken to him directly of her husband, and he still wasn't sure what, exactly, he thought of their marriage. He frowned as he watched her take a deeper drink. "You must have loved him a great deal." His words were hard to get out, even harder to believe. She seemed too young to love anyone like that—to love so deeply she would crawl through icy mud just to hold on. Her loyalty unnerved him.

"Every day, I try to love him more than when he was alive, but it never feels enough. I never feel sad enough, sorry enough." Her eyes were flat and distant. "Not very long ago, where I come from, they burned widows on their husbands' funeral biers. It has been outlawed for some time, but some women still burn. . ." She drank away the end of her sentence.

In a flash, Barric pictured Rena writhing in terror within a sea of hungry flames, and his mouth filled with the imagined taste of burnt ash. Grimacing, he met her eyes.

"Why are you telling me this?"

"*Sati*," she spoke in her own language, lowering her glass. "It is believed, without her husband, a woman loses her purpose. Her very life. And so she follows him into death. It is a great honor to die in such a way. It shows a woman's boundless love."

Though Barric had heard of such pagan rituals, he often forgot they colored Rena's world. "And?" His voice hardened as he again recalled his earlier suspicion. That maybe she wished to die. "Do you espouse the same philosophy?"

"I am empty without Edric," she admitted. "That much is true. But he cherished my life as if it were his own. It would be an insult to his memory, to our marriage, to entertain such thoughts. Besides, I am not sure it counts if one's husband is British. . . ."

Barric had never heard her speak so openly. He detected self-mockery in her voice, the nearest thing to humor he'd heard from her and yet so very tragic.

"You feel guilty," he decided, taking in her downcast eyes. "What for?"

"Widows are punished in India," she replied. "Especially those who are widowed young. It is believed they have sinned in another life or misstepped gravely in this one. My family spared me great dishonor by protecting me after Edric's death, by welcoming me home and begging me to stay. They might have cast me off. I might have been beaten and shunned. They might have said his death was punishment for our union. But my father said all might be undone by endless prayer and a life of sacrifice. That I might yet live to marry again. He risked much by saying these things. I'm not sure I deserve such love."

"Do you believe what he said?"

She shook her head. "I will never marry again. I seek only to lessen Nell's grief."

And this was the woman the people called *harlot*. Barric shook his head, considering how richly she had once lived and now how barren.

"I hope he is worth every bit of your sacrifice."

"Would you believe I had only known him for three weeks?" She looked up at him, shaking her head as if still shocked by her own actions. "*Three weeks*, and I was climbing out of my bedroom window to marry a man I barely knew. My parents had no idea I even knew him until it was already done."

Stunned again, Barric paused to sort through what he knew of Rena, which he realized was still extremely little. He had seen the tireless way she had worked in his field, the raw calluses on her hands, the lifted chin which so outraged his cousin. An unbreakable thread stitched her up and made her whole.

"You don't seem the type to elope," he observed carefully. "To be swept away. Why marry anyone so quickly?"

She was about to take another sip, but her glass hovered as she eyed him sideways. "I didn't marry him for his money, if that's what you mean, nor did I need to."

"I didn't say that, and I would certainly never think it."

She took another drink, then set down her nearly empty glass.

"Edric was. . .charming. Different. When he first looked at me, it was as if he'd known me all my life. He was exciting and dependable, and I knew as soon as I saw him that nothing in my life would ever make sense again."

Barric downed the rest of his drink and set the emptied glass beside hers. When he glanced back up, it took him a moment to collect his thoughts. The rain had crinkled Rena's hair around her high cheekbones, and as the firelight now danced with her shifting expressions, he allowed himself to admit—though not for the first time—that she was remarkably beautiful. Not that it mattered, of course. It was the kind of reflection brought about by a bottle of brandy on a cold, rainy evening. The kind of reflection he ought to keep entirely to himself.

Rena didn't seem to have noticed anything remiss in his gaze.

"Have you never been in love, Lord Barric?" The question was inappropriate given their relationship—far too personal—but he found himself flashing a wry smile anyway. They had already stepped well beyond the line of what would pass for appropriate conversation.

"No," he replied. "But Charlie has been in love enough times for both of us, so I consider myself more or less covered."

"Charlie. Your brother?"

He made a distant sound of agreement.

"How did the two of you end up living so. . .differently?"

Barric wished he had a fast and easy answer for what had separated him from Charlie. His brother was not a bad man, not like their cousin, Thomas, who seemed bereft of any moral guide whatsoever.

"I wanted to be like my father," he answered truthfully. "Charlie did not. It would seem we both got our wishes."

"Did your parents disapprove of your brother's choices?"

He stiffened at her question, his eyes trailing the stonework pattern of the hearth.

"My parents are dead. Have been for a good many years."

He sounded less affected than he was. It had been many years since his uncle had slammed through the front door, face pale, to bring them news of the accident. Still, there hadn't been a day Barric hadn't stopped to remember them. His father's low rumble of a voice, his proud even strides as he sauntered through the fields. As a lad, Barric had trailed his father every day, studying the artful way he conducted his business and instructed his field hands. He had pored over his father's mysterious ledgers until the numbers would blur and his mother would gently call his attention back to his studies. She smelled of tea and book pages, and Barric missed that too.

"I'm so sorry. Have I upset you?" Rena's words emerged in a quick, embarrassed tumble. "I did not mean to upset you."

He shook his head, the memories scattering like bits of dust that had gathered too long on his weary bones. "You have not upset me," he said, attempting a rare smile. "I don't usually speak of them. My parents were good people. I feel their loss often."

Actually, he had never spoken of them. Not really. The loss of his father, especially, had sent Barric spiraling headlong into strenuous work; he had wanted the fields to be run exactly as they had been under his father's watchful eyes, for his father's money to be used in ways which would have pleased him. Sometimes he still felt lost beneath his father's shadow.

He tousled his damp hair, focusing on the heat of the fire as it rolled like a wave over his back. He did not want to think or talk about Charlie or his parents or how he had come to be the kind of man he was. He was much too cold and far too wet to deal with such things, too dizzied by the girl still crouching beside him. But Rena was staring at him as if she'd heard everything anyway.

"You should speak of them more often," she recommended quietly, after giving him a moment to collect himself.

He released a humorless laugh, sending her an arched, sideways look. "You're going to give me advice on grief? You aren't exactly an expert yourself, are you?"

His slighting words sobered her in an instant. Sitting up stiffly, Rena straightened her wrinkled skirts as if preparing to leave. Before he could reconsider, he reached down, clenching her fingers tightly, frowning when he realized how clammy and cold her skin still was.

"I'm sorry," he said. "It's a hard task, grieving, but I've found it's necessary. I suppose we could both learn from each other."

She didn't pull her hand away from his, but her eyebrows rose. "You don't think I've grieved?"

He tipped his hand toward the window, where drops of rain cut fast lines down the foggy glass.

"I think you might have started to, out there. Or maybe you were punishing yourself for not grieving enough. Either way, I think Edric would understand."

She nodded distantly as if his words had found a place somewhere within her. "May I ask you something?" she asked, her voice slow, hesitant.

"Certainly."

"My mother-in-law said your families—the Hawleys and the Fairfaxes, that is—that you don't carry on well with each other. Why is that?"

Barric challenged her query with a wistful grin. "Afraid to be found consorting with the enemy?"

She shook her head, her nose scrunching up in a near smile of her own as she dismissed his jest. "Nell told me you and Edric are second cousins. I wonder that you have not spoken to me of him before tonight. Did the two of you not get on well?"

"It's nothing like that," he assured her. "Your husband was a good man, but his grandmother was my grandfather's sister. She married. . .unwisely. I'm afraid she has never been fully forgiven for becoming a Hawley. Our families have never been close."

"Married unwisely." Rena paused as she considered this. "Some might say Edric followed in his grandmother's steps." She lifted both brows, only half-serious. "Perhaps it is the Hawley curse?"

Without meaning to, Barric felt his fingers tighten slightly around hers. "If such a curse exists," he murmured, "I'm fairly certain Edric was not at all disappointed to be plagued by it."

Her eyes dropped from his, but he was still holding her fingers when the door creaked open and a servant in crisp uniform stepped into the room. The servant's pressed appearance reminded Barric instantly of how rumpled he and Rena must have looked—her shawl was still discarded beside him, his own coat slung carelessly over the back of a chair. Releasing Rena's hand, Barric sprang up from the hearth, knocking over one of their glasses as he rounded toward the intruder.

There was a quick, embarrassed apology, half mumbled, and then the servant's head bowed slightly with an obvious question: Should he leave?

Rena grabbed her shawl and pulled herself into a standing position, her cheeks flushed from the brandy. Strands of black hair hung limp against her shoulders from the rain.

Her eyes flashed to the servant, then back to Barric, as if waiting for him to make an explanation.

"It's time for you to leave," Barric said to Rena, trying to temper his tone but sounding fiendishly curt. "We're finished here. Go."

Rena's eyes fell to her hands, and he knew he had hurt her.

"Yes, of course," she agreed, her tone stiff and flavorless, a horrible pretense in light of everything she had shared with him.

Barric had forgotten Rena still held her necklace until she slipped it back around her neck. His eyes flicked downward to the ring, and just like that, a dead man stood between them.

He grimaced, jerking his head toward the door. The servant caught the message and stepped aside, his eyes on the carpet. Rena exited soundlessly, her eyes now as vacant as those of his servant. What would his cousin say if he heard of this, Barric wondered, or if word made it into town as it doubtless would? All would say Lord Barric had a touch of Charlie in him, after all. They'd say he'd been trying to seduce her. Or worse, that she was trying to seduce him. He felt an uneasy twist within him as he wondered what Rena thought. At her weakest moment, he'd brought her in the back entrance, offered her a drink as he sat down beside the fire with her. His eyes fell to his coat still slung across the chair back, and he suddenly doubted himself.

"What do you want?" Barric asked in a curt voice, realizing the servant still awaited his attention. The servant drew forward, offering him a thin, ivory envelope. Barric snatched it out of the servant's gloved hand, tipping it up to glance at the lazy, elegant scrawl. Charlie's handwriting. He fisted the letter in his hand.

"If I hear about you running your mouth," Barric warned. "You'll be gone by morning. Understand?"

The servant bowed his anxious understanding, then left. As soon as the door had snicked closed, Barric strode toward the window, spreading his fingers like a fan against the cool glass. He studied the property beneath the window until Rena finally came into his line of vision. Her shawl was pulled twice as tight around her shoulders as she hastened across his property.

He'd been careless, he thought angrily, and had dismissed her like a dog. He watched as she crossed the clearing and made for the edge of the hill. After the intimate details she had offered him—and he knowing what it cost her to speak so openly about her husband—he had tossed her back into the freezing rain to walk home alone, as if her grief had meant nothing to him.

He turned, leaning against the cold windowpane as he sliced a finger along the letter's seal. He didn't care much for what his brother had to say these days. But in that moment, he didn't feel much better about himself.

CHAPTER 9

"So the younger Barric deigns to visit his withering uncle, even after all these months. . . ."

Barric jostled his gaze from the bookshelf to the door, unable to hide his frown as his uncle strode into the room with two gray hunting dogs prowling at his heels. Uncle George was anything but withering, and he knew it. He was a proud man, and tall, much older than his thick black hair and arresting blue eyes would lead anyone to believe.

"To what do I owe the pleasure of this little visit?"

"I've heard from Charlie," Barric announced, lowering his hand for the dogs to nuzzle. Assured he was no threat, the hounds retreated to the fireplace, lounging beneath a mahogany table with their tails curled around their bellies.

His uncle sank into a plush armchair with a slight groan of exaggerated age.

"Ah, yes, the more indiscreet of my nephews. What trouble has he gotten himself into this time?"

Charlie's letter was still crumpled in Barric's pocket. He'd glanced at it repeatedly over the past few days, though its cryptic message was seared into his memory. Only two words were written in Charlie's lazy script: *Please come.*

Usually Charlie was a bit more specific in his letters—particularly when it came to money and just how much he needed.

"He didn't mention a reason." He tried to sound more at ease than he usually felt around his uncle. It wasn't as though Uncle George was anything like his son. Thomas was an arrogant bully, a *wastrel* as his uncle usually called him, but Thomas had taken more after his mother, a spoiled woman with a papery face and a taste for laudanum. Uncle George was an elegant, cunning man, and, though he wasn't cruel like his son, he was ruthless in his own way and often got exactly what he wanted.

"I've come to ask you for a favor."

"Of course," his uncle replied with a pleasant expression that was still slightly pinched at the corners. He had every right to be suspicious. Barric could count on one hand the number of times he'd asked his uncle for anything. Barric had always been too proud to ask for help, and, though his uncle was a decent enough man, he often felt like a cheaper version of Barric's father. Except for the fact that his father's hair had been red and his uncle's black, the two men had always looked markedly similar. They had similar profiles, similar mannerisms, and a sharp crease between their eyes—a wrinkle in the shape of a musical note—which surfaced only whenever they were vexed.

"I'm cutting him off," Barric explained. "You would, logically, be the next door on which he might knock for help."

His uncle busied his hands by conjuring an ancient, twisted pipe from within his waistcoat. The tobacco carried the same wooden aroma Barric remembered from his childhood visits, a heavy scent which hazed his mind and made him feel momentarily young. "I didn't exactly hear a favor in there," his uncle said pointedly.

"I'm asking you to cut him off as well. If he asks, don't give him any money."

His uncle took a deep drag off the pipe, resting his head against his chair back as he blew the smoke out his nose. "Turning your back on your own brother?" He shook his head. "A bit boorish, don't you think?"

"I'm leaving for France in the morning," Barric said. "I'm bringing him back to England with me. That's why I'm asking you not to help him."

His uncle cracked a faint smile, as if charmed by Barric's plan. "You really think he'll come back with you?"

"Without money, he'll have little choice."

His uncle tapped his pipe on his knee, ponderous. "All men have their dalliances, Barric. There's no crime in it." His uncle's smile reached a bit higher as he lowered his pipe again. "Word has it your mind has been addled by a woman of your own."

Barric clenched his teeth, his mood blackening on the instant.

"I don't know what you're talking about."

"An Indian woman, no less. Widowed. How droll of you, Barric, to seduce a widow."

Barric's thoughts instantly turned to the previous night. Again, his cold dismissal echoed in his mind as his uncle's word *seduce* clanged somewhere in the background.

"If you'll excuse me," Barric said, nodding curtly, and moved toward the door.

His uncle held up his hands as if he hadn't been able to help himself. "All right, all right, you can sheath that invisible sword of yours." He smiled faintly. "You know, when you're good and angry, I can see your father in you, Barric. Can you blame me for riling you on occasion, if only to see him again?"

Nearly fifteen years had passed since Barric's parents died in a boating incident in France, caught in an unforeseen storm, but he still remembered the exact way his uncle had looked when he'd slammed into the room with news of their death thick on his tongue. Uncle George's handsome face had been chalky white that morning, as if somewhere inside he was already buried with his brother in an unmarked grave. As soon as the news had broken, Charlie wept into his uncle's waistcoat, but Barric merely stared in stunned silence. Then his uncle's hand curled around his shoulder, administering a ghostly touch as he'd murmured, "*All will be well again.*"

At fifteen years old, Barric had wanted to believe his uncle. He had even sought him out in his father's library later that night, pressed his chest against the doorframe, and listened long enough to hear his uncle fill the empty room with low, angry curses. Uncle George had remained drunk for two weeks straight. He had smelled of stale alcohol and pipe tobacco at the funeral; he smelled of pipe tobacco now.

Barric startled out of his memory in time to see his uncle run a contemplative hand across his mustache.

"She could be useful, Jack."

A youthful impulse made Barric respond, "Don't call me that."

Only Charlie still called him Jack. And only Charlie was allowed.

Another puff of pipe smoke. The usual plotting arch of his uncle's eyebrow.

"*Barric*," he corrected with an acquiescing nod. "Her husband's family left an enviable estate, you know. Hawthorn Glen."

"She's poorer than dirt," Barric snapped. "Living off my own charity. She has clearly not inherited it."

"Exactly." His uncle's smile glimmered behind a thin cloud of smoke. "No one has. Yet."

Ah, thought Barric. *So, there it was.* His uncle always had a motive, which usually concerned money. The typical plight of a younger son.

"What?" Barric challenged. "You want me to forge a new will for you? You would visit me in jail, wouldn't you?"

His uncle laughed. "Visit? No. Though, if you prove obliging, I might help you escape."

"What is it you're sniffing after, exactly?"

"Sir Alistair wasn't the brightest of our cousins, but he is certainly the most stubborn. Since you and the girl are so. . .close. . .perhaps you might keep an eye on the estate for me, in case there is some lucky complication with his will?"

Barric's eyes narrowed. "To what purpose, exactly?"

161

"I once made Sir Alistair a generous offer of my own, when they first relocated to India. Oh, my misguided cousin, hiding behind his silly chess set. No price I set was high enough for him. Wouldn't it be a sad bit of irony if it fell into my hands regardless? Anyway, the money is to pass to a cousin on the Hawley side, I hear, perhaps the property as well, but nothing has been made official. I would love to have the estate if things are still negotiable. Beautiful gardens. Magnificent library. Though smaller in size, it rivals even your Misthold for beauty."

Barric hesitated. His uncle had never once complained about Barric's birthright, or that Misthold Manor had passed to him. And though Barric had inherited the property at a young age, his uncle had never once tried to tell him his business in running it, but only said he was his father's son and would surely work matters out.

Once, when the upkeep of Misthold had felt especially burdensome, Barric had said he wished his uncle had inherited it instead of him, a cruel and heartless comment.

"A bit drafty for my taste," his uncle had disagreed with a knowing smile. *"And I'd be haunted by memories of my stodgy governess. You know, my knuckles never did recover from all those rappings. . . ."*

Barric knew, however, there were other memories his uncle was far keener to avoid.

Uncle George had been wolfing around vacant estates ever since his brother had died, as if searching for a birthright of his own, though none had ever suited his interests well enough. Having secured a wife with an enormous dowry, he now lived in a comfortable house with a small property and an even smaller garden, spending very little money as he plotted for an estate to someday rival his ambition. That he had made an offer on Hawthorn Glen surprised Barric; that he still wanted the property made his stubborn mind think of Rena despite itself. How would she look at Barric if his uncle moved into her dead husband's childhood home?

"We may be doing *her* the favor," his uncle went on, reading Barric's uncomfortable silence as actual consideration. "The girl may want to keep it in the family, for her dead husband's sake. Ask her about it, will you?"

Barric most certainly would not. To do so would be to press his hand against an open wound just to hear her cry.

"I should be going," he said instead, stepping toward the door.

Sensing his retreat, the dogs stirred beneath the table, stretching their languid limbs. His uncle placed his pipe gingerly on the table, then rose to see Barric out. "You won't forget about me, will you?" He pretended to sound hurt by Barric's usual absence, but his eyes glinted. "It's been months since I've seen you. I had half forgotten your hair was that unfortunate shade of red, but here you are."

"I have been busy."

"Someday I might forget your name. Barret? Bennet? Surely it starts with a *B*. . . ."

Barric allowed himself a tentative smile, the boy in him grateful that his uncle hadn't outgrown his usual teasing. "I will come back as soon as I have Charlie home."

"Ah, yes, your mission. I'll drink to your success. And when you return, I might even wish to meet this Indian girl I hear so much about."

At that startling suggestion, Barric glanced up and was pinned by his uncle's waiting eyes. They were a riptide tangle of blue and gray—the same as Barric's father's—a family attribute which had passed to Charlie rather than Barric.

"I know it hurts you to look at me," Uncle George said. "If we're both honest, it sometimes hurts me to look at you too." He placed a hand on Barric's cheek as he'd often done when Barric was a child and he'd come with gifts from his travels. "If my son wasn't a blithering idiot, I'd hope he might someday have your backbone, Jack."

Swathed in tobacco smoke, Barric stared at his uncle silently, long enough that the dogs scented the stillness and began prowling closer. "Leave the girl alone," he finally said. "Don't go digging into what might have been hers. For her, that estate is full of nothing but ghosts."

His uncle dropped his hand and smiled wistfully. "Yes," he agreed, glancing out his window as if he could see all the way to Misthold. "The lovelier ones often are."

Go. The word felt heavy in Rena's memory, but she kept rolling it over and over in her mind, allowing Barric's voice to follow her. "*Go,*" he'd said, as if she were an animal to be dismissed by his command. As if everything she shared with him that night meant nothing. She spoke to him of Edric, of her decision to marry him, of the guilt she now carried everywhere she went.

Did he think she spoke so openly with everyone? She didn't.

Did he think she was his to dismiss? She wasn't.

Did he think, because he had provided for her, he was now her master?

A small voice in the back of her head challenged her.

Isn't he, though?

Rena's pride took another blow. She owed everything to Lord Barric. Her house, her food, even her safety when she picked from his fields. She now lived the life of less than a servant. An *untouchable.* The word floated back to her again, an echo from India. She'd grown too used to her father's house to accept her new position without temper, too used to being followed by servants of her own, to living behind her veil.

"You've been scrubbing that plate for an eternity." Alice's voice was laced with a question.

Rena looked with dismay at the dish in her hands. She was elbow deep in murky water, the whole length of her apron drenched. Glancing around the kitchen, Rena tried to remember how long it'd been since she'd said anything to Alice, or if maybe Alice had said something while she was still untangling her frustrations with Lord Barric.

"Oh," she said. "Yes. I must have been daydreaming. Full stomach, you know."

Rena and Nell had been invited to dinner that night on the pretense that Betsy had accidentally made too much stew, but Rena suspected the invitation was offered because William was worried about her—after all, she *had* screamed at him the last time they spoke, as she stood in the frigid rain while he'd tried to coax her back inside.

They'd finished eating nearly an hour ago. Nell was resting in the parlor while William fed the pigs and Betsy sorted laundry. Rena had offered to help Alice with the dishes, and though Alice seemed embarrassed to douse herself in front of company, she also seemed relieved she wouldn't have to do so alone.

Alice held out her hand, demanding the plate from Rena. "William says Lord Barric went to find you on the lawn a few days ago." Giving the dish a thorough drying with her apron, she set it back in the cupboard with hardly a clank, then held her hand out for the next. "And that you followed him into Misthold."

Rena frowned down at her throbbing fingers as she remembered her frantic search for Edric's ring—and Lord Barric's cutting command that she come to her senses. "Nothing happened," she insisted, but the words sounded mortifyingly rehearsed.

Alice dried the next plate much longer than was necessary. "It doesn't really matter if it did," she said matter-of-factly. "It wouldn't mean anything."

Those words felt like a trap. Rena eyed Alice sideways, trying to read her expression, but the girl's eyes were carefully neutral. Of course, something *had* altered between Rena and Lord Barric, and it was foolish to deny it. She spoke to him of Edric. He brought her into his home. He nearly kissed her in the thicket, and they looked at each other differently now because of it.

"Why wouldn't it mean anything?"

This time, when Alice set the plate in the cupboard, it clanked. "Because," she explained, reaching for a larger platter, "he kissed me too."

Rena didn't answer, too stunned by the admission to speak, and so Alice met her eyes. "Oh, it was years ago. I was barely sixteen at the time. It was a few months after our father had died and a year after Barric had lost his own. Well, he and William got ruddy well foxed one night. It was late, so I came looking for my brother, but Lord Barric happened upon me in the hallway."

Rena's stomach clenched as she listened. "And he kissed you."

Alice nodded, swiping her hair away from her tired eyes. "Without saying so much as a word before. It was rather ungentlemanly of him to do it, I suppose, though it was quite satisfactory, as far as such things go."

Rena submerged both hands in the cooling water tub as she struggled in vain not to picture the encounter. "What happened after?" she asked very quietly.

"He said he was sorry for doing it. I knew he was only grieving over his father. Perhaps he thought he'd try things Charlie's way for once. Or perhaps he really thought I was pretty. Either way, neither of us has ever mentioned it again."

"I'm sorry," Rena said, and she meant it. She was sorry Barric had kissed Alice. Sorry he'd apparently brushed Alice aside as quickly as he had forgotten himself. But also relieved. Relieved that she herself had not let him kiss her at the festival, for surely he would have, and could it have ended any other way?

"It was a long time ago," Alice answered loftily. "Like I said, it meant nothing. Such encounters are rather common for lords in his position, and though Lord Barric is far better than all the rest, he is allowed his moments of weakness. I have certainly forgiven him."

Though Alice sounded careless enough, Rena knew the truth. That kiss meant a great deal to Alice, and had for rather a long time. Rena knew Alice worked like a dog in their little house, cooking and cleaning and mending and hauling. Even with Betsy there to assist her, Alice's toil was written quite plainly in the tired lines around her eyes, in the way she pushed her hair out of her face with sweaty hands so that the roots matted down to her forehead from the cooling dishwater. Alice had been but sixteen years old when Barric had kissed her and was now tipping toward the more dangerous side of her twenties. Had she spent all these years dreaming Lord Barric would deliver her? That she might live an easier life? And here she was, scrubbing dishes instead, with only a poor widow and a maid-of-all-work to assist her.

"Lord Barric did not kiss me," Rena confided, wanting to ease Alice's burden in whatever way she could. "If that's what you're thinking. He never has."

Alice graciously accepted the next dish when Rena handed it to her, her expression still subdued. "I wondered if you'd maybe chased him off," she admitted, flashing a timid smile. "Chased him off all the way to *France*, that is."

"France?" Rena felt herself rising to Alice's bait. "Is Lord Barric in France?" For a silly moment, Rena wondered why he hadn't mentioned such a trip to her. But, of course, his affairs had nothing to do with her. "*Go*," he'd said. Back to her place, back to her world, back to her own thoughts and troubles. And never mind about his.

"William says he left yesterday morning," Alice went on, hauling another load of dishes to the tub. "Very unexpected. Very hurried. Not that it matters two pence to you, of course."

Rena didn't have a chance to agree. William bustled back into the kitchen, his cheeks pinched pink by cold and arms weighed down with two large pails of coal.

"Bloody pigs got out again," he griped, clanking the pails down beside the range.

Both women nodded, but neither spoke right away. Noting their strange silence, William glanced over his shoulder at them, a suspicious question in his eyes before his lips curled into a tight, knowing grin. "Ah, we've been gossiping, have we?" He leaned back against the table and lifted both brows expectantly. "And? Anything interesting?"

Alice flushed to an embarrassed shade of crimson as she splashed a handful of water at her brother, and Rena was quick to assist her by talking William into another subject entirely. For, though it was many years ago, Rena still doubted Alice wanted her brother to know Lord Barric once kissed her senseless in the grim back halls of Misthold.

As Rena and Nell prepared for bed, the two said very little to each other. Rena stepped out of her dress and left it folded in its usual place over the back of a chair. Then she set to work on the laces of her stiff corset, stripping quickly down to her chemise and tugging into her nightdress. Meanwhile, Nell brewed a pot of tea, pausing only long enough to pull Rena's hair over one shoulder and weave the strands into a durable braid. Such was their evening routine: a silent conversation transpiring in the slips of time spent between each task. As Rena put out the lamp, Nell slid into her nightgown. As Nell sat at the table and said her nightly prayers, Rena pulled out Edric's ring. Fiddling with the chain, she cast curious glances at Nell, whose thin fingers were threaded together on the table, her neck bent in silent supplication.

Rena had never prayed to Edric's god. Not even at their wedding. Not even when he had taken her to church. She usually tried not to watch as Nell prayed—it always felt like stealing into someone else's home when they weren't looking. Sometimes Rena almost wished to join her, but that felt wrong as well, even though words pounded beneath her breast, lodged halfway up her throat, and she couldn't get them out. Some nights she wanted to swear, to scream as she had in the rain at Lord Barric. Other nights she crept out from under the covers to weep beside the window while Nell slumbered. In certain moments of desperation, she had considered prayer, but Edric's god was Edric's god, and Rena was no longer sure where or to whom her own silent petitions ought to fly.

"How long do you think Edric would want you to suffer?"

Startled by Nell's quiet voice, Rena looked up from Edric's ring. It had been weeks since Nell had spoken of Sir Alistair, or of Edric, and Rena had never dreamed of forcing such a subject with a grieving wife and mother. She shook her head before finding the words to answer. "I don't suffer."

Nell rose from the table, setting a cup of tea on the bedside table next to Rena. "Do you think living well or living happily undoes your grief? That it means you loved him any less?"

"I don't suffer," Rena insisted again, staring at the cup's chipped porcelain. With gentle fingers, Nell untangled the necklace from Rena's clenched fingers and set it on the bedside table.

"Your home may not be where it once was," she said. "But it can still be filled with joy. You do not need to suffer to love him; it's not what Edric would have wanted."

"I did not follow you here to suffer," Rena protested. "I followed you here because I love you."

Nell's smile warmed. "Yes," she acknowledged. "But suffering has followed you to England, and I can see as well as anyone that you are lost beneath its weight."

Rena glanced down at her now empty hands, once again studying the thin bones in her wrists, then the raised calluses on each palm and fingertip. "Would he even recognize me?" Rena finally asked. "Would

Edric even know me?"

"He would recognize your spirit." Nell smoothed her fingers over Rena's hair. "The rest will heal with time."

"I sometimes feel like I am five different people at once," Rena breathed. "Like I have to be countless versions of myself, but none of them make sense after everything else that has happened." Her words made little sense, but they were the only way she could think to make Nell understand.

Rena had to be strong but humble. Pressed by grief but driven by love. She was a foreign girl, sick for home, and yet this was her home too.

"We do not grieve as those without hope," Nell answered softly, smoothing the blankets over Rena's legs.

Hope. Rena had once placed all of her hope in Edric, in their future together, and where was he now? Six feet beneath the ground, covered in rot. Shuddering, Rena fought the urge to pull the blankets up over her head, as she had often done as a frightened child spooked by an unruly wind. She imagined Edric snatched and dragged to the underworld by Yama, the Hindu lord of death, who by some accounts judged the good and the wicked and decided how they were to be punished. As a child, Rena's mother had shown her icons of Yama's blue skin and red eyes—he was a striking figure who yielded up a mace in one hand and a noose in the other, with which to drag the unfortunate soul down to his palace of Kalichi. For a moment, Rena tried to believe Edric had been greeted by this figure, perhaps had seen Yama's four-eyed hounds, but each of these images felt empty. Untrue. Nell told Rena to hope, but her heart was adrift within her and could not find its mooring.

"Hope," she repeated brokenly, wishing she could snarl at the word and make it scatter. "In what do we hope?"

"After all these months we've spent together," Nell said, a hint of challenge touching her voice. "And still you don't know?"

Of course Rena knew. Every time the older woman stooped her shoulders to pray, she sought to answer Rena's grief. Every time she pleaded with Rena to come to church, she sought to soothe and fix her. But Nell's god was still not Rena's god, and too many pieces of Rena had already been dashed to the wind like heaping handfuls of sand. Was she to leave the gods of her childhood too?

In answer, Rena kissed Nell on the cheek, blew out her candle, and rolled onto her side. Still, it took several hours before she shuttered her mind against the icy questions that hovered close.

CHAPTER 10

Paris, France

Barric stared at the red door for several moments without knocking. Flat 324. He'd been summoned to this door more times than he could count, like a dog called back to its master. Gritting his teeth, Barric pounded his fist twice on the door, completely ignoring the bronze knocker. The goal was to bring Charlie home, he reminded himself, where he belonged. Allowing his temper to slip his hold would get him nowhere.

The door flew open with hardly a pause, as if Charlie had been waiting for him all afternoon.

"Jack," Charlie said, the name a sigh of unmistakable relief.

Barric took a stiff inventory of his brother. Charlie's coat was lined in rich plum velvet, the rest of his clothes pressed and artfully tailored as usual. Charlie had inherited their mother's blond curls, which were left unruly over well-trimmed sideburns. An expensive-looking walking stick—encased in tortoiseshell and topped with a carved ivory eagle's head—dangled absently from his right hand, as if he'd been about to go for a midday stroll.

"Still a scoundrel, I see," Barric said by way of greeting. But there was something strangely altered in Charlie's expression, which set Barric even more on his guard. Charlie's lazy care-for-nothing grin, Barric realized after a moment's consideration—it was missing.

When Charlie didn't rise to the insult, Barric entered a bit reluctantly, tossing his hat on a table by the door. Charlie's quarters were modest in size, though they were lavishly furnished, and his ceiling-high windows overlooked the Seine. Barric took notice of several new framed pieces of art, as well as a small piano which had not been there before. He plunked out a few notes on the ivory keys, waiting for his brother to speak.

"Care for some wine?" Charlie finally offered, propping his walking stick by the door. He sounded distracted, the words merely tossed out to fill the silence.

Again, Barric dragged his fingers over the piano keys, conjuring an unpleasantly jumbled noise. "I'd care to know what I'm doing back in Paris," he retorted flatly.

"I'm in a fair amount of trouble," Charlie admitted, pouring two glasses from a crystal decanter despite his brother's terse answer.

Barric was not surprised. Charlie had been in trouble since he'd been five years old, when he had accidentally caught their drawing room curtains on fire. Still, Charlie never had any scruples about trouble. On the contrary. He almost always had a plan, one which involved a sizable score of Barric's money.

Not wanting to seem uneasy, Barric settled into an armchair and took the glass when Charlie offered it. "Unable to pay your debts again?" he guessed, taking a moment to savor the tartness of Charlie's most expensive vintage.

"No, Jack." Charlie wouldn't meet his eyes. "You've settled my debts quite well enough."

"Then a woman, I suppose."

Charlie quaffed off his own wine. "It's always a woman," he muttered darkly, palming the empty glass nearly tight enough to shatter it.

Charlie's sudden passion made Barric feel uneasy. His brother had never been very serious, except for those dark, cavernous months after their parents had died. But Charlie had created his own new world in Paris, one where he never needed to be serious again, where women kept him company and his friends kept him in the usual kinds of trouble.

"What happened to Celeste?" Barric prodded. "You were quite enamored of her in your last letter."

Matching Barric's uncertain gaze, Charlie quietly answered, "She's with child."

Barric swore under his breath. If he was honest with himself, he was surprised it hadn't happened sooner, that his brother didn't have a whole host of illegitimates scampering around Europe.

"How much does she want?" he asked at length, setting his glass on the table. He should've known his brother's cryptic plea would mean something especially sordid.

Charlie shook his head defensively. "It isn't like that."

"The devil it isn't. How *much* does she *want*?"

"She doesn't want anything. She's left Paris. My letters all come back unopened."

Typically, Charlie asked him to pay away his scandals, to make his mistresses disappear when things turned ugly or tedious—but this mistress was already gone.

"I'm sorry, Charlie," Barric spoke hesitantly. "But I fail to see how I can help. To your way of thinking, isn't the problem quite settled?"

"She won't answer my letters," Charlie said again, his tone uncharacteristically bothered. "Jack, she's having my child, and she's run off and won't even speak to me."

"Come, now, don't tell me she's made an honest man out of you."

Charlie set his glass on the piano with a clatter and stood. "Don't make jokes, Jack. I need you to find her. I need you to talk to her."

Barric shook his head, exasperated and confused. "And what, exactly, am I supposed to say to the girl?"

"Tell her I meant what I said," Charlie ordered, speaking rather fast. He ran his hand through his hair in an uncharacteristic show of loss. "Tell her I'm sorry for everything, and she can depend on me, and I'll still marry her. Just tell her to come back, and I'll take care of them both."

As soon as those words were out, the room fell into silence. Charlie would marry her? Barric had never heard anything so impossible in all his life. After a moment, he rose and closed the space between them, his voice gruff. "You mean to tell me you've proposed to this woman?"

This time Charlie didn't drop his eyes. "Yes."

"But she's an actress. And there isn't a penny to either of your names."

"Yes," Charlie said again.

Barric didn't know if he should be angry with his brother for getting into this mess in the first place or impressed by his sudden attempt at making a sacrifice for the sake of someone else. In all their years together, Charlie had never once elected to do the right or honorable thing. He was too wrapped up in his own wants to realize how selfish a man he really was.

"And what did she say in response to your offer?"

"That she'd sooner marry the devil." As he repeated her words, Charlie looked ready to toss his wine glass at the wall. Barric knew the feeling all too well—the Fairfax family temper. His father had had it too, and Uncle George had been the first to suggest, many years ago, that Barric's red hair was an omen he would out-temper them all.

"Just calm down a moment." Barric held up a barring hand. "Sit down and let me think."

"What am I supposed to do?" Charlie went on. "I never meant for any of it to turn out like this. What would Father say if he could see me now? Or Mother?"

"A lesser man would have walked away," Barric reasoned quickly, disturbed that Charlie brought up their parents for the first time in so many years. "A lesser man wouldn't have cared if she left." Which meant his brother still had a conscience—and maybe there was still hope for even the blackest sheep in the Fairfax family.

"I'm tired of feeling this way," Charlie muttered, gesturing to the lavish room. "I'm sick to death of all of it."

Barric took note of the dark rims beneath his brother's eyes. Charlie's grief seemed genuine, but that didn't make Barric any less uncomfortable to witness it. Of all the outcomes Barric had anticipated from this particular visit, an outright admission of guilt had been farthest from his thoughts. When he'd received Charlie's letter, he had thought it would be an appeal for money, but it had never occurred to Barric that his brother might need *him*.

"Then it's high time you did something about it," Barric decided. "Wallowing won't help anything."

Charlie gestured lamely at his brother. "If I was anything like you, I wouldn't even be in this mess."

Barric sighed. "I've too many faults of my own to be considered by you for sainthood."

"Faults?" Charlie scoffed. "What *faults*?"

Barric didn't wish to discuss his temper with Charlie, or the fact he'd gotten into enough rows in his earlier years to dishonor the family name a hundred times over. "Leave Paris," he said instead. "Sell everything you have that will fetch a price and send Celeste all the money. You move back home with me, where I will find you work. You send her all the money you can, without expectation of anything in return. And you live a better life until, maybe, she'll listen."

Charlie paled as he listened to Barric's instructions. He set his hand on his new piano, his fingers splayed on the royal mahogany. "Sell *all* of it?"

Barric nodded his affirmation. "Anything you don't need." Which they both knew was practically everything Charlie kept in his apartment, down to the last piano key.

"And move back to Abbotsville?" Charlie shook his head and gazed out at the river, already weighing his losses. "Oh, but it's so very dull there, isn't it?"

Not so dull, Barric answered inwardly, allowing his thoughts to drift to Rena. He pondered those last few moments they'd shared together, huddled beside each other in front of the fire.

Snagged unpleasantly by the memory, Barric blinked and looked back at Charlie, who still stared drearily down at the river. How many women had his brother brought to this very room? Barric wondered. Actresses were Charlie's usual fare, musicians and travelers, anyone with an interesting story and a pretty face. Suddenly Barric felt less confident in his plan to bring Charlie back to Abbotsville. Rena was exactly Charlie's type.

Different, exotic, with just enough of a past to hold his interest.

Alarmed by his own unease, Barric spoke before he could stop himself. "If you do come, you'll keep your hands off the women who work for me."

Charlie's mouth twisted as if disgusted his brother needed to set such a stipulation. Still, he didn't refuse.

"The decision is yours, of course," Barric went on, keeping his voice neutral as he crossed to the door and picked up his hat. "I'm staying at the Grand Hotel du Louvre; I leave for England at the end of the week. Either you're with me when I leave, or you stay here. I have no scruples about leaving you here, and I promise I'll not come back again."

No one whispered about Rena that morning or slid surreptitious glances toward her when they thought she wouldn't notice. All eyes were fixed up front, where Barric sat in his usual pew with a blond-haired stranger at his side. It'd been nearly a month since Lord Barric had mysteriously disappeared to France, and according to Alice, he had returned with his brother, Charlie. The two looked remarkably like brothers—with profiles etched of hard lines, hair slightly askew, and chins lifted at a similarly haughty angle.

As if feeling Rena's gaze, Charlie reached a hand up, scratching faintly at the back of his neck. Rena dropped her eyes, trying not to watch him like the rest, knowing all too well the weight of unfamiliar stares. But that didn't stop her from hearing the women in the pew behind her.

"So, Charlie Fairfax has returned," one observed to her friend. "You think he ran himself out of trouble in France? Or is it money that's run out?"

"Probably bored," whispered the other. "Though I have a hard time believing Barric would let him carry on *here*."

"Charlie carries on *everywhere*," her friend returned, voice twisting with delight. "And I'm sure there are many young ladies in these pews who are rather thrilled to have him back."

Rena hunched forward, wishing she could block her ears. The whispers were always worse than the stares. She wanted to turn and hiss the women into silence, but she focused on the parson's voice instead, following the litany as it unwound like a colorful ribbon in her mind.

Over the past few weeks, she'd come to admit the services *were* rather lovely. Laced with music, built on a soft rise of groaning petitions, the words often pulled at the parts of her heart which had fallen silent. Even Lord Barric's sharpness seemed affected by the service that morning, his usually stern demeanor replaced with a more thoughtful expression as he spoke his responses. Once, after communion, Rena saw his head bent in prayer when the others were singing.

When the service finished and people began to gather their things, Rena followed Nell out of the pew. People on all sides of the church paused to steal one last glimpse of Charlie Fairfax, but Rena refused to look back for even a moment.

"Another lovely service," Nell observed, pausing in the aisle as she let another young family pass. Three mop-headed children stole quick, open glances at Rena before ducking their faces down and falling in line behind their mother.

Rena did not answer Nell's observation. Instead, as soon as the family had left them enough room, she took Nell's arm and steered her toward the back of the church, where the parson waited on the outer steps to greet his parishioners. Though she realized her flight was a silly impulse, she was not yet ready to face Lord Barric, even in such a harmless setting. For weeks she had tried to take Nell's advice, to live with less sorrow, but seeing him now filled her only with dread.

"I'm sorry, are we in a hurry?" Nell placed a steadying hand on Rena's shoulder. "I thought you'd want to walk home with Alice."

Uneasy, Rena glanced toward the front, where William and Alice had been seated and were now deep in conversation with one of the tenant farmers. Lord Barric was already making his way down the aisle, two pews past their friends and gaining. Rena was trying to think of an excuse to continue home alone, but Nell didn't give her the chance.

"Unless, of course, you aren't finished avoiding Lord Barric."

Rena started, staring at her mother-in-law with unreserved shock. "Avoiding him?" she repeated defensively. "I most certainly am not."

"What a relief." Nell smiled, smoothing a flyaway lock of Rena's hair. "Because here he comes now."

Rena spun just in time to face him.

When he removed his hat in a silent, pointed greeting, she stumbled over her responding curtsy, feeling oddly exposed after their last conversation, as if he could read her thoughts without her approval.

"Good morning to you both," Lord Barric finally said, his eyes traveling from Rena to Nell and back again.

"Good morning, Lord Barric." Since the man had such a marked talent for elegant boredom, Rena made sure her voice sounded twice as bland as his. "It has been many weeks since we've spoken."

Charlie grinned. "So, you must be the one everyone is talking about."

Rena blinked over at Lord Barric's brother, caught off guard by the familiar way he spoke to her, as if he had known her a great many years.

"I might say the same about you," she remarked.

Charlie's smile grew. He was much as she'd imagined: a rake who clearly knew he looked the part. His jacket was blackish blue with velvet facing—a rather ostentatious statement for church—with not a stitch out of place. Still, his eyes were kinder, less prowling than she might have expected from his reputation, and though he walked with a confident gait, there were circles sleeping beneath his eyes.

"You are Edric Hawley's widow," Charlie clarified, as if Rena had missed a hidden point.

"Yes," she parried. "And you are Lord Barric's prodigal brother."

At last Barric cut in. "This is my brother, Mr. Charles Fairfax." He nodded to Nell. "And may I introduce Lady Hawley and her daughter-in-law, Mrs. Hawley." His eyes brushed Rena's as he came at last to her introduction.

"Ah, Mrs. Hawley." Charlie's bow was a lazy afterthought, as careless as his quicksilver eyes. "I can only imagine what the gossips have told you about me."

Rena once again took in Charlie's rakish appearance. "I've heard nothing that doesn't seem entirely plausible, Mr. Fairfax."

At her forthright answer, Charlie laughed, the sound bouncing off the polished pews and high rafters. Several parishioners glanced back at them, then murmured as they bumbled toward the door. Barric pivoted to whisper something in Charlie's ear, though the words seemed to go unheeded.

"Come, now, Mrs. Hawley," Charlie said, shaking his head. "I won't begrudge you your reputation if you don't turn up your nose at mine."

"I have no reputation worth your interest," she retorted. She took two steps toward Nell, trying desperately to signal it was time to leave.

"That's not what I've heard," he disagreed. "Your reputation is all over town. Tongues are wagging, you know."

Rena could only guess the kinds of stories Charlie might have picked up about her around town—or from his own brother, for that matter. Rena's eyes passed uneasily to Barric, but he was no longer looking at her. The day she lost Edric's ring, she confided much to him in the expectation of confidentiality. She spoke of her elopement, of widows burned on their husbands' funeral biers, of her own supposed shame in fleeing India. Had he said as much to his brother?

"We are so much more than our reputation," she finally managed to reply, her face warming. "Stories cheat; truth is found only in friendship."

Charlie's answering bow was a hint more genuine. "A pity," he said. "For I myself have many stories."

Barric snorted. "Each more boring than the last," he muttered, and this time Charlie's false smile, nearly strained, softened Rena toward him. She recognized his weariness only because she felt it mirrored back from deep within herself.

Saddened by the thought, Rena made no reply, and so Nell swooped in to fill the silence. "And how have you been these past few weeks, Lord Barric?" She disarmed both men with a serene smile, neatly brushing aside the previous conversation. "We have all missed you here in Abbotsville."

"I've been very well," Barric said as Alice met them in the aisle and looped her arm through Rena's.

"Lord Barric," Alice greeted, nodding meaningfully at Charlie. "It seems your brother has followed you home."

"France did not agree with him," Barric replied with a casual, familiar smile. Rena couldn't help wondering what it had been like when he had come upon Alice in the shadowy hall and kissed her without uttering a word. Did he even remember the kiss that Alice still cherished? Or perhaps he had just been hurting. Perhaps he stumbled upon her in the darkness of his own grief and still didn't know what to make of it. Rena knew that feeling all too well.

Charlie snatched up Alice's hand and bent over her captured fingers. "Ah, Miss Wilmot," he purred with a teasing grin. "Still radiant as ever, I see. The stained-glass light paints you very prettily this morning."

Alice's smile relaxed even more, into a sisterly rebuke. As they bantered, Rena tried to picture how it might have been when their fathers still worked side by side. The spaces between them were filled with hints of how well they knew each other—there was the way William eyed Barric over Alice's shoulder, his mouth tight on just the one side, as if they were both thinking something very particular about Charlie; the way Charlie teased Alice, clenching her fingers and daring her to protest; the way she seemed immune to his charms, as if she had known him well before such charms existed, and she probably had.

"You've not changed either," Alice noted, snatching her hand from Charlie's and smoothing it over the front of her sage-green pelisse. "Though there are those who say you are now a man of reform. This cannot be true?"

Charlie's eyes twinkled, and Rena stiffened as he looked straight at her. "Only time will tell," he answered vaguely, and she did not miss the way he grinned over at Barric.

The whole way home, Barric fought the urge to glower at Charlie, walking at a pace set entirely by his own irritation. He couldn't believe his brother. *Flirting in church*, he thought, *with Rena, of all people*. They ought to drag him off for blasphemy or sacrilege or. . .*something*.

Slowing his stride, he tried to rein in his anger. Their conversation had been spirited, he reminded himself, but not suspicious, even if Charlie had drawn the usual attention. Besides, his brother had not sounded any different than he did with any of the other women in Abbotsville. He flirted with Alice too, though they all knew that was empty posturing. Would Barric have been as irritated if Charlie had approached any of the other women in attendance? Perhaps.

Except Charlie *hadn't* approached Rena—Barric had.

As if coming to the same point, Charlie interrupted his brother's thoughts in a markedly serious voice. "Careful, Jack."

Staggered by Charlie's earnest tone, Barric glanced sidelong at his brother. "What on earth are you talking about?"

Charlie kept walking. "It's not as hard as you'd think," he cautioned. "Ruining a woman."

Barric halted. Charlie didn't have to say Rena's name for him to follow his meaning, and though Barric felt a thousand denials springing to his lips, each one fell silent before he could give it breath. Rena had entertained a similar suspicion once. "*I won't be your mistress*," she told him at the festival. Her assumption had angered him. Since then he had assured himself his relationship with her was one of simple charity, one man helping his fellow, an arrangement of concern such as he might offer to anyone in need.

Smirking slightly, Charlie shook his head. "Oh, don't give me that confounded look," he said. "After all these years, it simply won't do."

"You don't know what you're talking about," Barric lied stiffly, turning from Charlie to continue their path toward home.

Charlie kept pace with him. "Tell me you haven't thought about it," he challenged. "Tell me, and I'll never mention it again."

Of course Barric had thought about it. He'd admitted to himself long ago that Rena was beautiful; to deny it now would be an obvious, foolish lie. Her beauty was dark and quiet, like sprawling fields cloaked in shadow. Her strength was even lovelier. And of course, there had been that tempting moment in the thicket. . .

When he looked back at Charlie, his brother smiled cuttingly. "Poor, miserable bastard," he murmured sympathetically.

"Need I remind you we've just come from church? In any event, you're not exactly in a position to give me advice on such matters, are you?"

"Ah, but you see, I'm *exactly* the sort of man to give you advice. The way you look at her, Jack—I've talked plenty of women into my bed with looks like that."

"Shut your mouth," Barric growled, his eyes darting to either side of the road, making sure no one would overhear such a condemning conversation. "And after your little banter in church, might I also remind you that one of your provisions for staying here is that you keep your hands off those under my employ?"

Charlie slid his hands in his pockets and smiled amusedly. "Yes," he replied. "That provision makes *perfect* sense now."

"Charlie."

Charlie scrunched his nose in distaste, letting slip his usual act of carelessness. "You really think I'd set hands on my own brother's woman?" He shook his head. "Jack. Have you forgotten I am in the process of turning a new leaf?"

"She is not *my* woman," Barric disagreed again. "She was hungry, and I fed her, and that is all. I have no thoughts for anything more."

The words sounded like a miserable lie in his own ears, as if he'd been tasked with convincing himself and was failing. Was she really nothing to him but charity? Had his interest in her really been the effects of impulse or *too much wine*, as he had once assured himself? No, no. The lie was no good. As Charlie had said, it would never do.

Charlie's tone turned serious again. "Can you be sure that such will *always* be the case?"

Barric looked grimly at Charlie, and his sudden lack of surety on the matter unsettled him. To pursue Rena would be terribly wrong. She was wounded in unseen ways, unspeakably vulnerable, and he had no wish to interfere with her grief. All she had in life depended on him, on his mercy and restraint, and though Barric knew it was rather common for masters to carry on with their servants and underlings, he had never wished to be common.

Barric needed to stay away from Rena. That much was quite settled. For as much as Barric was his father's son, he was also his own man, and he was never carried away from himself, never driven by impulse, never one to act selfishly—until he was.

"Come on," Barric said to Charlie, feeling suddenly tired. "Let's go home."

CHAPTER 11

The winter months were a trial. Rena and Nell had done their best to save some of the food Rena's harvest labor had purchased them, but their stores were running dangerously low despite their frugality, and they could nearly see the bottoms of their barrels. Alice and William still invited them over for dinner on a regular basis, strictly in the name of friendship, though Rena had a hard time not calling it charity.

"My brother and I grow weary of only each other's company," Alice would say if Rena ever tried to decline. "Honestly, you're doing me the favor."

At other times, items would mysteriously appear on their front steps. Sometimes a basket of nuts, a bushel of apples, once even a leg of mutton large enough to split over the course of several meals. Rena was grateful to be cared for in such a way, but her pride still stung. She couldn't help feeling like a hindrance to those who had so little and still tried so hard to provide for her.

At this time, Barric would go weeks without being seen. Holed up in his tower, as people said, keeping an eye on Charlie. If she did chance to meet him in town or on the road, his greetings were quick and perfunctory, sometimes even sharp. She feared she had shared too much with him during their last conversation, overstepped her bounds by mentioning Edric, and she could only determine he now regretted his decision to help her.

So, the next time Rena passed Lord Barric on the road, she lowered her eyes, said nothing, and continued on her way. At first Lord Barric seemed entirely likely to let her pass, his steps crisp and grating against the dirt road. He was several feet beyond her when she heard him pause, and then he doubled back, catching up with her.

"You have frosty eyes, Mrs. Hawley."

She kept her tone light. "I am in a terrible hurry."

"Really?" He sounded like he didn't believe her. "In a hurry for what?"

She gestured toward town. "I am posting a letter," she said. "To my parents."

His eyes flicked down to the envelope in her hand, apparently searching for proof. "I see. And what have you told them in your letter?"

Her hand tightened on the paper. "That I am well," she said, stiffly, as if dictating the letter's contents word for word. "That I am living with good people who take care of me. That I am not starving."

He walked slightly closer to her, brushing her arm with his. "And what did you write about me?"

She studied him out of the corner of her eye. She could only see his profile, but he wore a thin smile. "What makes you think I've written about you at all?"

"Tell me you haven't, then."

"Very well. If you must know, I told them there is a fearsome, old dragon who lives in a mansion on the top of the highest hill."

His smile stretched as he continued along, ambling idly at her side. "And did you tell them you refused to dance with this fearsome, old dragon?"

Her face felt rather warm as she remembered her once adamant refusal. Would she refuse him again, she wondered, if he ever pleaded with her for a dance?

"I merely told them he is a very obliging master who swoops down upon us from time to time."

Barric slowed a few paces and glanced down the road, as if realizing he had now followed her well out of his way. His eyes fell to his feet, and he was silent for a moment. Rena fully expected him to beg his excuses and leave, but he turned to face her instead. "And will you return to them?" he asked, eyeing her letter. "To your parents?"

Rena's chest tightened. She herself had returned to that same question in many moments of distress. In India, at least she would be among her own people, her family. True, she would always be scorned for having married Edric, but she would also have her parents, her home, the smell of citrus rinds and spices in the morning.

"I will remain with Nell," she decided in a thin voice.

"Here, in Abbotsville?"

Her hesitation grew. "My home is with Nell. Wherever she goes, I will go."

He nodded as if her answer made sense, but the corners of his eyes creased as if something about it had also distressed him. "We shouldn't see each other often," he said after a moment. "Ought not to, but I want you to know this place—Misthold—it is yours too."

Rena was too stunned to speak straightaway. His uncertainty gone, Barric's green eyes settled on hers. "I would like you to stay—forever, if you wish. I want you to consider your place here your home."

His words were the kindest spoken to Rena since she had alighted in Abbotsville. She had been given food, yes, and shelter, but these were but physical things, which could not quite fill the emptiness still echoing within her. She knew what it must have cost Lord Barric to speak so openly to her, neither had she overlooked his warning—they ought not to see each other. Still, after all the months she'd spent feeling useless and unwanted, Lord Barric had offered her a sense of belonging. He was not speaking to her out of pity, nor out of obligation. He had seen her otherness as all the others had, and although they could not be friends, exactly, she would always know he *wanted* her there.

Rena felt herself open, however slightly, like the blue lotus flowers which floated in her mother's garden fountain—the sacred plant bloomed each morning and closed again at dusk, a Hindu symbol for purity. Enlightenment. How long had it been since Rena had felt anything but dusk within herself?

She opened her mouth to offer her thanks, but then a few white, frosty flecks flitted in front of her eyes, and she lost focus. Tipping her head back, she stared at the gray expanse of sky as it filled with a lively swirl of white.

"Snow," she breathed, feeling the cool melt of flakes against her neck and upturned face. As soon as she spoke the word, like an answer to incantation, the snow began to fall harder, thicker, enveloping her and Barric and obscuring their view of the road. Eyelashes now coated, Rena held her hands with palms turned upward toward the sky and watched the flecks melt on the warmth of her skin. She felt herself smile in earnest. "I've never seen snow before."

Barric cleared his throat. "I should let you post your letter," he said, but did not move to leave. He reached out, instead, and touched a gloved hand to the side of her face.

It occurred to Rena, perhaps belatedly, that they still stood in the middle of the road, visible to any passing horse or carriage that might happen to take their route.

"Thank you," she said quickly, and Barric dropped his hand. "I want you to know I am thankful for your. . .offer."

He looked unsure, his eyebrows slanting low over his eyes. Taking his hand in both of hers, Rena brought it quickly to her lips and pressed a firm kiss to his fingers for emphasis. Then she waited, anxiously, for his reaction. He might be angry with her for taking such a liberty, especially there in plain sight. He might strike her away and deride her. Yet again, hadn't he been the one to bridge the gap between them?

When she dared to meet Lord Barric's eyes, they seemed a lighter shade of green in the snow-whitened daylight, and he smiled faintly down at her.

"I shall have to hope it snows much more often," he murmured in reply.

By the time Rena returned home, the bottom of her skirt was frozen stiff and her jaw throbbed from clenching, but she was still smiling. The squall of snow, Lord Barric's words, the smiling look which had stolen into his eyes—all were enough, together, to make her feel somehow younger, if only for a moment.

"It's snowing!" she announced to Nell, stomping her feet in the entryway as she pulled the door shut behind her.

Nell was busied over the stove, stirring something in a large tureen, but she threw up her hands as she caught sight of her daughter-in-law.

"Look at you, now, absolutely covered in snow!"

Pulling Rena the rest of the way into the room, Nell stripped Rena out of her shawl, brushed a few stubborn flakes from her hair, then dragged a rocking chair nearer to the stove. As Rena sunk into the chair, Nell dropped a dry blanket over her shoulders.

Heedless of Nell's fussing, Rena stared out the window, still entranced as she watched the falling snow. "I think winter might be my favorite season of all," she decided.

"Eat some soup," Nell ordered. "Before you freeze to death in that chair." She ladled out a hefty serving and handed it over. Clutching the bowl close to her chest, Rena ran her spoon thoughtfully along the rim, breathing in the savory steam. The soup was mostly broth, with a few carrots and onions and even fewer potatoes, but she still ate thankfully.

Nell crossed to the table. "Oh yes," she remembered, snatching up an envelope. "A letter arrived for you."

At first, as Rena's hand closed around the envelope, she thought it might be from her parents. She had written to them only twice since arriving in England. Once to assure them she had arrived safely, the other letter posted just that afternoon. Nell had pleaded with her for several weeks to send them word again, but writing to her parents was a task of tears and ink, and Rena knew that useless words could never explain her choice to them or come close to easing their grief. Though post took only a few months to arrive from India, she'd been able to understand their seven-month silence. Did words feel as hollow to them? Or had there been delays, perhaps, and so their letters had simply not reached her yet?

As she flipped the thin envelope over in her hands, she knew at once it was not from them. The writing was too ornate, a flourish of green ink which was sealed with an elaborate crimson crest.

She slid her fingers beneath the seal, read the contents quickly, and frowned.

"It's an invitation," she announced, her voice muddled with confusion, as if puzzling aloud through a riddle.

"An invitation?" Nell's surprise battled Rena's as she craned her neck for a sideways glimpse of the writing. "Whatever for?"

"Lord Barric's annual Christmas party." Rena let the letter drop in her lap. The invitation did not make sense. The party was to be held the next day, and he had not mentioned it on the road. "It must be a mistake," she decided, though Barric did not seem the type of man to make such a careless mistake.

Nell took up the letter in her hands and shook her head as she scanned it. "Mrs. Rena Hawley," she read. "Seems too precise for a mistake. Perhaps he wanted to surprise you?"

Rena thought back to their interchange on the road. He had told her he wished for her to consider Misthold her home, but he had also cautioned them, rather wisely, to keep their distance from each other.

"I can't go." Rena turned her attention back to her soup, but her mind was still in a tangle.

"Oh, but you must go," Nell replied, ladling out a bowl of soup for herself. "Think of all he has done for us. You cannot snub him now."

"But your name is not on the invitation," Rena pointed out, still grasping, unsuccessfully, for a reasonable excuse to decline. "Nell, I could not think of leaving you here, alone."

"I'm sure he has his reasons," Nell answered. "You must promise me you'll go and that you'll have a wonderful time, and that you'll tell me all about it. I know you will feel easier about it once you are there."

⚭

Rena stood at Lord Barric's door, wearing another of Alice's dresses, this one a yellowish gold which matched the lantern glow. She did not feel any easier, as Nell had promised she would, and had been all the more perplexed to learn William had not been invited to this particular party, nor Alice.

"I'm not really sure what Barric means by it," William had said, frowning at her invitation just that morning. "He's said nothing of it to me, but I don't handle his parties."

Though William hadn't let on, he seemed unaccountably troubled by the invitation, brushing his fingers over his jaw as he pondered its meaning.

Alice, meanwhile, had dropped her gaze from the invitation and found something to busy herself with in the other room, emerging moments later with a dress for Rena to borrow and a weary half smile that made Rena feel all the guiltier for attending.

And so Rena arrived—alone—feeling oddly stiff in a dress that fit her like a foreign skin. The door to Misthold was opened, and a stately butler bowed her through, though his eyes betrayed uneasiness, perhaps even confusion, at finding her on the steps. She considered apologizing, leaving, rushing back to Nell before Lord Barric would see her, but she was ushered into the hall before she could consider such an escape.

The last time she had been in Misthold Manor, Barric had brought her in a back door, through a shadowy hall which had felt like a catacomb. The main entryway, however, was open and lit, with luxury written in every detail. She craned her neck, tracing the chandeliers, then the royal oaken staircase which curved at an endless angle, up to thick balustrades and a carved balcony heavily bedecked in holly.

Festive music clambered through the halls, its notes carried on lively piano keys. There were at least two Christmas trees in each of the front rooms, some decorated with ruby apples, others with ornate ribbons and shiny baubles. Rena stared at the lovely trees, charmed and perplexed by the sight of them. According to Nell, the strange tradition of decorating trees had come to England through the influence of Prince Albert, the queen's husband, who was from Germany, where such things started. When pictures had first circulated of Prince Albert's Christmas tree in Windsor Castle, he enchanted the entire country, and the tradition blossomed. Nell had already enlisted William to cut down their own tree for the cottage.

At the butler's nod, Rena stepped into the sitting room. She didn't recognize most of the people gathered. Parson Richardson was there, sitting by the fire with a drink in hand as he spoke with an unfamiliar cluster of men. In the other corner, Thomas was in the process of teasing two elegant ladies who were dressed in mauve silk and pretending to be bashful.

As soon as Rena was through the door, she knew something was wrong. All eyes turned to her in unmasked astonishment, and the lady at the piano lost her place in the middle of a trill, clunking the wrong key. Charlie lazed beside the piano, dressed in a fine suit with a daring purple velvet waistcoat, his hand balanced on top of the instrument. He'd been leaning down to whisper something to the lady seated there, but like everyone else, his gaze cut to the door as soon as the piano hushed. There was an obvious question on his face, a pressing look which was trying urgently to tell Rena something—but Rena did not know Charlie well enough to read the message written in his eyes.

No one in the room approached Rena, or said a word, but only stared at her, until Lord Barric came out of nowhere, grabbing a firm hold of her arm and tugging her into the hall.

"What are you doing here?" he whispered, all but dragging her toward an alcove at the base of the staircase. When she didn't answer straightaway, he released her, searching her face with an expression that was impossibly creased around his eyes.

Rena drew back from him, his distress making her more anxious. "I. . .I was invited. . ."

His mouth formed a thin line. There was an unusual stiffness about him, confusion perhaps, followed by a glance of peculiar dismay. He opened his mouth, clearly in protest, when a smooth voice interrupted from the doorway. "Ah, so our last guest has finally arrived."

As Barric registered the voice, his eyes softened momentarily on Rena's face, a look of near apology. Turning toward the intruder, Barric said in a low voice, "You invited her, then."

The older man wore a thick, trimmed mustache and an immaculate suit of black. He leaned against the doorframe, casually, as if he had been watching them the entire time. "Now, don't be too angry with me, Barric. What's Christmas without a little mischief?" As he crossed the marble floor, his eyes flitted over to Rena. "Let's just say I couldn't help my own curiosity."

"Mrs. Hawley, this is my uncle, Mr. George Fairfax." Barric carried out the introduction tightly, lifting an arm toward the stranger. "He is Sir Alistair's cousin." He looked at Rena more directly. "And I do believe you have already met my uncle's son"—he paused, jaw clenching slightly—"on the evening we first met."

Thomas. This man was his father? Barric's uncle George tipped her a low bow, his smile warm, but Rena couldn't bring herself to trust it. She could now see the resemblance to his son too easily. Thick, dark hair hung low on the brow. Angular features came to a point at the chin. But even more than physical features, father and son shared the same look of prowling confidence, entirely undaunted. She didn't understand why Lord Barric's uncle had invited her to his party or why he had withheld his intentions from his nephew, but neither uncle nor nephew seemed at all confused by what had happened.

"I can leave," she whispered to Barric. This time he didn't meet her eyes, anger etched in his gaze as he looked instead at his uncle.

"I had no idea," she went on weakly. "I thought the invitation was from you." Still, he said nothing, only stared past her as if waiting for his uncle to say something else.

"Barric," his uncle scolded. "Escort your guest into the sitting room."

When Barric wouldn't reply, Rena decided for him. "I will leave you both to your party," she said, tipping a curtsy before heading hastily toward the door.

"Leaving?" This time it was Charlie's boisterous voice that cut the awkward silence. He strode quickly into the room, his smile tight but strangely valiant. "You are the first interesting person to arrive, I assure you." Coming to a stop between Rena and the door, he offered his arm, then another smile. "I insist you sit beside me at dinner. We are *all* delighted to have you, aren't we, Jack?"

Jack. Rena glanced back at Lord Barric, taken aback by the unfamiliar sound of his Christian name. After several seconds, Lord Barric spoke. "She sits by me." With a solemn bow to Rena, and a last rebuking glare at his uncle, he coolly strode back into the sitting room, where the merry voices had returned, rising in volume as a new swell of music echoed through the halls.

Uncle George lingered a moment longer than his nephew. "Always had a temper, that one," he confided to Rena with a look of bemusement, then followed Lord Barric out of the hall.

Charlie gave Rena a few seconds to stand and breathe before he burdened her by asking, "Are you all right?"

Her hand tightened around his proffered arm, fingers digging into the expensive fabric of his jacket. "Let's get this over with," she answered miserably, and allowed him to steer her back into the sitting room.

∽

At dinner Rena was indeed seated beside Lord Barric—the place of honor though it felt like a farce. Like the rest of the house, the table had been impeccably trimmed for Christmas, its linen cloth decked with Christmas garlands and luminous red bouquets. Barric wore a single-breasted evening coat which was stylish in its simplicity, tailored to fit him narrowly, with a cream-colored waistcoat and a crisp white cravat knotted high beneath his chin. His hair seemed two shades redder in the candlelight.

As they waited for the first course, conversation had been sparse, generally quiet. Most of the women spoke on matters of fashion, the men of hunting, but Rena was carefully silent. When she finally braved a glance at the party, Charlie caught her gaze almost immediately, as if he had been waiting for her, and offered a sympathetic grin from his place across the table.

Soup a la Reine was the first course announced, paired with an expensive smoked salmon from Scotland. Wine glasses were filled liberally by a tall butler with a hooded gaze. To Rena everything looked and smelled unreal, impossibly lavish. As soon as the soup arrived, Uncle George took a spoonful, nodded its suitability, and turned to face her. "Mrs. Hawley, won't you tell us about yourself?" He spared a subtle smile for his nephew. "Barric has told me very little about you."

"That's because he knows very little," Rena replied, taking a quick drink of her wine and smiling, faintly, over the rim. With a crooked grin, Uncle George tipped his glass toward her as if awarding a silent point.

Barric shifted in his seat. "And am I to allow such a rebuke at my own table?" he challenged, his lips touched by a slight smile of his own. "That I know very little of my own guest?" He slanted an eyebrow in mock rebuke. "Then I will say, Mrs. Hawley, in my own humble defense, that I know enough."

Rena stared, dumbfounded as he eased back into his chair and turned to Charlie with some inquiry she could not hear. Those were the first words Lord Barric had spoken to her since they'd been seated, though his fingers had lingered on the back of her chair, brushing the side of her neck as he had helped push in her seat. At the time, she'd trained herself not to think of it, but the way he looked at her just now—and then those words of challenge—made her wonder if the gesture had been altogether incidental.

As the rest of the wine glasses were filled with sparkling claret, several of the ladies made flirtatious banter with Lord Barric.

"You celebrate in style, Barric," one lady observed, her winter-white gown laced so tightly her shoulder blades nearly brushed each other. Green ostrich feathers were arranged in the lady's chestnut hair, and a heavy gold necklace was fastened around her neck, which caught the candlelight and made it dance. Her smile was a faint curve. Playful.

From previous conversation, Rena gathered that she was Lady Angelina Prim, the daughter of a marquess, and, as such, should have been seated where Rena sat, at Barric's right side. Rena had to admit that Lady Angelina, in her fine white dress—a bold choice compared to the fashionably bright colors of the other ladies' evening gowns— would have matched Lord Barric rather nicely. Instead, she'd been escorted by Charlie and was seated beside him on the other side of the table. The rest of the party was settled fastidiously according to rank, men and ladies staggered. Lady Angelina's eyes were sharp as they fell on Rena, clearly pricked by the slight, but she addressed Lord Barric instead. "You've such an eye for elegance."

"I see a good deal of elegance at this table, none of which was my own doing," Barric answered, his smile trailing briefly to Rena as he lifted his own drink.

As Lady Angelina prattled on about the impossible task of finding the right gown, Rena stared vacantly at her wine glass, fighting the hitch in her chest that had settled with Barric's gaze. To feel anything at all for Lord Barric would be absurd. Even with his handsome smiles, he was far too high above her, and she still too strangled by grief, to entertain such nonsense.

"Tell us about India," suggested the parson from his place toward the end of the table. Two ladies across from him shared a glance. Thomas coughed away a laugh. "I would very much like to go there myself one day," the parson went on, ignoring them. "As a missionary, of course."

"Oh, it is a beautiful place," Rena exclaimed, grabbing instinctively for the thin cord around her neck, as she often did when she ached for home. Barric's eyes followed the path of her hand, but she wasn't sure if she was imagining the way his eyes creased as he looked away.

Noting her sudden silence, the parson nodded encouragingly. "And?" he pressed, holding her eyes so she would not have to look at Barric's guests as they murmured among themselves. "What do you miss the most?"

She considered the question, allowing herself to drift home inwardly in a way she didn't often allow herself to do. "It is hard to narrow to just one point," she admitted slowly. "But I miss the sand that gathers between the tiles in the entryway of our home, and the hibiscus that grows outside my chamber. I miss the way my father's study smells in the early evening, of spices and ink, and the way the endless heat drags on for forever, hazing the horizon until the monsoon season comes. And if you look just right from the outer terrace, you can see men and women as they walk to the market, or the crimson coats of soldiers as they pass. . . ."

Rena trailed off at the end of her sentence, dropping her eyes to the flowered pattern of her china bowl, but it was too late. The image of a soldier's uniform had branded itself in her mind. When no one spoke right away, she allowed herself a taste of soup, but the memory of Edric was too thick for her to swallow easily.

Uncle George leaned closer to her over the table. She was afraid he might mention Edric, but he didn't. He waited for her to meet his eyes before he asked, "Tell us of your father, Mrs. Hawley. What, exactly, does he do?"

"He assists the British with translations."

"Ah," he remarked. "Well educated. He must be a Brahmin, then?"

She straightened. Nodded. Feared falling into a trap.

He laced his fingers together in a thoughtful gesture. She could tell he was still measuring her, though she doubted he was much impressed. "And so he studies languages?"

She allowed herself another spoonful of soup before answering, "Yes."

"Yes, that explains it," he said. "Your accent, my dear, is tolerably proficient." Beside her, Barric's hand tightened around his wine glass as if preparing for something unpleasant. She forced her eyes back on his uncle, who went on casually. "And how old were you when you began to study our language?"

"Ten."

"Ten!" he exclaimed, sitting back in his chair again. He glanced at Barric, obviously impressed, but Barric did not meet his eyes.

"Very impressive, I'm sure," Lady Angelina remarked in a droll tone that sounded not at all impressed.

"You were there for the mutiny, I suppose." This time it was Thomas who spoke, his tone sharp as he eyed her down the length of the table.

The servants had begun clearing the bowls from the first course, and as hers was lifted from its place, Rena realized how little she'd managed to eat.

"Of course," she answered.

"Particularly nasty bit of business," Thomas mused. "Your people killed our women, you know, our children. Locked them in a little hut and hacked them all to pieces. Then threw their bodies down a well."

A few of the ladies gasped, though none as loudly as Lady Angelina. Barric set his own spoon down with a hard clank. "Is this really an appropriate conversation for a party?" His voice was so soft that Rena had a hard time hearing him over the din of her own rising anger.

Thomas snickered. "A bit peevish tonight, aren't we, Barric?"

As Uncle George seemed rather fond of games, Rena expected him to appear pleased as his son circled the conversation like a swooping vulture, but he frowned at Thomas and merely said, "Don't be insolent."

Thomas held up his hands as if to profess his own innocence. "I was only curious to know if her father knew any of the rebels. It's a legitimate question, I would think, given her upbringing."

"My city did everything in its power to end the mutiny," Rena said defensively. "Our maharaja sent nearly all of his troops into the fray."

"We are speaking of your father," Thomas redirected, his lips pinching beneath his thin mustache. "Don't tell me your father didn't want independence like the rest of them."

Rena nearly stood from her chair. "Just because he valued independence," she snapped, "does not mean he condoned slaughter."

Thomas raised his eyebrows mockingly. "Well, then he's practically a gentleman, I suppose," he said, and downed the rest of his wine.

"My father worked with your soldiers." Rena spoke heatedly, warmth creeping to the tips of her ears as her indignation grew. "He aided them before and after the mutiny."

"Oh, of course." Thomas grinned. "That would be how you met

Edric. Apparently, he didn't mind marrying into the wrong side of the mutiny. Though I suppose we could expect no less from a Hawley."

Barric had gone very still beside Rena, his hand fisting beside his plate as he cut in icily. "There's no need to be cruel."

At the reprimand, Thomas bowed his head slightly, though his eyes appeared far less than penitent.

"This discussion," remarked Uncle George, his voice strung tight like a bow string, "is hardly appropriate for the dinner table with ladies present. We are, after all, here to celebrate Christmas."

As if he couldn't help himself, Thomas shook his head, then looked right at Rena. "Do you even celebrate Christmas?"

She knew exactly what he was asking, and she half wished she could stab him with a fork rather than answer. "The vows I spoke to Edric," she finally said, very softly, stunned by her own resolve, "I spoke to your god."

"*Your* people, *your* soldiers, *your* god." Thomas caught up his own fork between his fingers and attacked the fish offered to him from a platter by a footman. "I hear a lot of *ours* and *yours* in there, Mrs. Hawley." He dropped the skewered fish carelessly to his plate. "Perhaps you ought to go back to India after all. Besides, I'm not entirely sure it's right for a pagan to be at a Christmas celebration."

At that, the parson swept in with a commanding voice. "This conversation is over." His hard eyes panned the table, clearly outraged. No one would meet his gaze, not even Thomas. "Now, as we are all remarkably well-educated people," he continued, tempering his tone, "I suggest we find a more fitting topic to discuss."

Everyone at the table mumbled their awkward apologies to the parson, all except for Rena, who offered him a grateful, exhausted smile and turned at last to her meal.

Barric had not released his fisted hand all evening. He knew if he opened his mouth to say anything, he'd end up knocking Thomas right out of his chair, and then there'd be no end of it. Charlie knew. His eyes often found Barric's from across the table, sending a subtle warning for him to leash his temper.

But to hear them speak to Rena of her family, of *Edric*, was cruelty beyond anything Barric had ever heard, even from them.

Lamb cutlets, beef roast, venison, asparagus, beet root—on any other night, finding such a magnificent spread on his table would have pleased Barric considerably, especially for a party, but he barely tasted even one of the nearly ten courses. And so dinner passed in agonizing slowness, the conversation forced and awkward. Barric noted that Rena said very little to anyone other than Charlie, the parson, and the gentleman seated directly beside her.

He used the first open opportunity to lean closer. "I have never seen anyone look so miserable at my table," he observed. "And I am sorry for it."

Rena hardly spared him a glance. "I'm afraid your wealth has been quite wasted on me tonight," she admitted, setting down her glass. "I'm not much for forcing conversation or ignoring impudent stares. In truth, I have enjoyed very little of your feast."

He smiled wanly, touched by her candor. "I confess I'm not much for it either," he replied. "Perhaps my wealth has been wasted on us both this evening?"

At last Rena returned his smile, and Barric was struck by the unguarded kindness he found in her expression, a gentle brightness he'd spied before, but only on very rare occasions. When he angled closer to hear her reply over the other conversations, his knee brushed hers beneath the table, and they both froze, conversation forgotten. He waited for Rena to pull back, but she'd gone quite still, as if waiting for him to move away first.

When he made no immediate move to do so, her jaw tightened.

"Your uncle," she noted pointedly, "is watching us, my lord."

Barric shifted back at once and instinctively dropped his eyes, feeling like a coward. He shouldn't care if his uncle saw him speaking closely with his own guest, or if the gossips circulated his name with hers. But there was a part of him, stronger than he wished it to be, that still minded. Rena must have minded too, for the next time he turned toward her, she studiously avoided his gaze. And so he was forced into conversation with Lady Angelina instead, who demurred very prettily to his questions, all while shooting acerbic glances at Rena across the table.

Dancing was proposed by the ladies after they had consumed their cordial and finished their champagne. Traditionally the men would have excused themselves to the study to smoke while the ladies retired to the sitting room, but none present seemed to mind the slight breach of etiquette. There were several enthusiastic dancers present, of whom Lady Angelina was the most outspoken, inspired, as she claimed, by Misthold's impossible charm.

Out of the corner of his eye, Barric watched the men stand first. He didn't think he could bear to watch Thomas dance with Rena again, but he also didn't want to lose the opportunity to confront his uncle in private. As if reading his thoughts, Charlie circled the table lazily and placed a hand on the back of Rena's chair.

"If you don't dance with me," he insisted with a broad smile, "I'll leave for France at once."

Barric watched the relief register in Rena's eyes, the glimmer of gratitude as she slipped out of her seat and placed her hand in his. As Charlie led her from the room, he shot one last glance back at Barric as he went, an unnecessary warning. The room now empty, Barric at last met Uncle George's waiting stare, and felt his mood darken as every horrible insult and cutting remark from the dinner returned to him.

"Barric." His uncle spoke his name quickly, his tone urgent in a way it almost never was, as if he could sense the weak hold Barric now had on his temper. "I know you think I'm a cad, but I only—"

Pushing back from the table with a lurch, Barric stood. "Not here," he said, stalking out of the room. With a sigh, his uncle followed. As they crossed the hall, Barric caught sight of Rena and Charlie lining up on opposite sides of the room for the first dance. Beside them Thomas and Lady Angelina had been matched, but Rena kept her eyes fixed only on Charlie, her chin lifted despite the whispers from those who watched them. Charlie smiled eagerly as if the whispers were what gave the dance its charm.

The music triggered the dancers to move, and Barric watched, unamused, as Charlie took up Rena's hands in his and spun her. The piano played at a jaunty pace, but she kept up remarkably well, as if she had practiced the steps in her sleep. Barric remembered the night of the festival, when she rejected him so emphatically. Would she reject him again if he cut in now?

Dragging his eyes away from her, Barric continued down the hall. His uncle followed closely behind as he led them both to a smaller sitting room, which had once been his mother's morning domain.

"You have every right to be angry with me," his uncle said as soon as the door was closed. He held up his hands in surrender. "Things, in there, they got out of hand. That was not what I intended."

"*Angry?*" Barric repeated incredulously. He took two steps toward his uncle, then halted himself, shook his head to clear it. "What the devil *was* that?"

His uncle rifled around in his pocket for his usual pipe, then a match, then seemed to reconsider both objects, setting them down on the table. "I needed to see what, if anything, was going on between the two of you. I didn't want to believe the rumors, but I couldn't trust your own word that *nothing* was nothing."

Barric balked at his uncle's words. "You tortured that girl," he said, half question, half accusation, "just to see what I would do?"

"Tortured?" Uncle George shook his head. "You're using your words a bit liberally, don't you think? Did you see the meal we fed her? Probably the best she's eaten in a year, poor little scarecrow. The rest will fade with time."

"You let that son of yours tear her to pieces!"

"I will have words with my son," his uncle answered flatly. "But you should see yourself, Barric. Making eyes at her in the midst of high company. And don't tell me you weren't ready to take a swing at Thomas in there."

Barric didn't deny it. He turned his back on his uncle and braced his hands on the mantelpiece, studying the whites of his knuckles.

His uncle's voice gentled. "And yet you'd have me believe this is all *nothing*? I can't blame you, of course. She is an impressive little imp."

Barric still didn't turn to face him but spoke instead to the stone mantel. "You shouldn't have brought her here, like this."

"Agreed."

"I want you to leave. And take your blasted son with you."

There was a silence but no footsteps to signal his uncle's departure. "If you can't help yourself," Uncle George murmured, his words slow and paced, "I understand. But, please, carry on with her privately. Such dalliances are to be expected of a young man, especially one of your temper. But I'd be remiss if I didn't warn you. You're an honorable man, like your father. But you must remember you can't allow it to *lead* to anything. Desperate women are often in the practice of snaring honorable men into marriage."

Barric half imagined his uncle having this same conversation with Charlie. He was certain such words must have been spoken to his misguided brother at some point, something to trigger a long line of mistresses and ill judgment. Barric barely raised his voice. "I wonder," he said, "what makes you feel entitled to come into my house and give me such advice."

"Jack, I'm your *uncle*. I have responsibilities to you, and to your parents, God rest their souls. What do you think they'd have to say about you carrying on with this girl? Wouldn't they be concerned?"

"Don't use them against me!" Barric snapped, finally turning toward his uncle.

His uncle's patience slipped a rung as well. "Can't you see how ridiculous she looks at your table?"

"She will always have a place at my table," Barric growled, advancing. "The people in this hellish town can call her whatever they want— *harlot, leech, scarecrow*." His uncle winced at his own word. "But know that at the end of the day she has a place at my table."

Uncle George raised his voice at that. "You know she must be nothing to you! That she is beneath you."

"But of course she is beneath me!" Barric thundered back. "She's a wretched beggar!"

His uncle's demeanor changed on the instant, a flash of guilt as he glanced over Barric's shoulder. With a sigh, he shook his head. "Oh Barric."

Barric turned, and there she was, framed in the open doorway, her eyes luminous in the scant light of the hallway. He swore aloud as soon as he saw her. "Rena," he said, taking a step toward the door, but she turned from him and fled before he could say another word.

"Let her go." His uncle placed a hand on his elbow. "It's for the best."

Barric jerked, throwing off his touch. Barric had never disliked his uncle, never even blamed him outright for Thomas's behavior. For years Uncle George had enabled Thomas because part of him pitied his motherless son. But that was not all. Barric's uncle was slippery. Calculating. And deeply faulted. Barric knew this was why his father had always squabbled with Uncle George, why they even came to blows one night over dinner, much to his mother's dismay. Some weeks Uncle George was welcome in their home, laughing with Jack's parents over a bottle of wine until it was nearly morning; other weeks he was exiled to his own home, waiting for forgiveness while Barric's father swore never to see him again.

But Uncle George always came back. He was like Charlie in that way.

"Stay away from her," Barric snarled. "And the next time your son says anything to her, I swear I'll break his jaw."

His uncle had no response to that, so Barric left him and took off toward the sitting room in search of Rena. The music played on, pounded out on the piano, and all of the dancers still seemed in high spirits. But Rena was no longer there. Neither was Charlie.

Ignoring Lady Angelina as she called out to him from the line of dancers, he rushed for the front door, tossing it open as he tore down the steps, onto the paved terrace below. Rena was already at the edge of the lawn, moving quickly, lit only by moonlight. Her golden dress was simple but stately, giving her a look of foreign royalty.

He halted halfway down the next set of stairs, still towering over her. "Rena," he said thickly. As soon as she heard his voice, she stilled, then straightened, then turned to meet his gaze. He expected to see tears in her eyes when she looked up at him, but there were none to be seen. Instead, she stared at him bleakly.

"Forgive me." Barric spoke urgently, saying what needed to be said, and saying it quickly. "My uncle, he makes me say things I don't mean." He saw his words moved nothing in her eyes. "I swear I didn't mean it."

"You have nothing to apologize for, Lord Barric." She hit him especially hard with the title, and he took the blow as he had deserved it, without flinching. "You said nothing that wasn't entirely true."

It would have been better if she had yelled at him, if she showed even a touch of anger. But, no. Rena believed what he had said, what his uncle had said, what everyone seemed to believe. That she was nothing. "It isn't true," he said, shaking his head. "It isn't."

"Of course it is. I am a beggar, and you feed me. That's all there is."

Though he'd said similar words to Charlie, to William, he didn't like hearing them from her lips.

She turned without a goodbye, and this time he rushed the last few steps to bar her retreat. "Don't leave," he murmured, catching her shoulders with his hands. "I'm sorry. I was a coward in there, a miserable fool."

She looked like she wanted to strike him, vindictive as hellfire in her shimmering dress. She was so much stronger than anyone seemed to realize, Barric thought, and she'd already given more of herself than he'd ever seen a person give on another's behalf. He searched her eyes for that flicker of brightness she'd let show over dinner—proof that pain had not snuffed it entirely—but found only a tempest of indignation and scorn.

Barric's hands tightened on her shoulders. Suddenly he wished he had really kissed her the night of the festival, just so he could know what it would feel like now, how it would be to brush his fingers down her throat and hold her still for a second. Edric knew how it felt to hold her, how it felt to kiss her, to make her feel whole. Barric flinched as the thought passed over him. He had no right to be jealous of her husband—no right at all to be jealous of a dead man.

"I want no part of your Misthold." Rena's voice was empty as she pulled out of his hold and turned away from him. "This place will never be home to me."

Barric stiffened as she threw his own words back at him, an unpleasant echo of their last meeting on the road, from the morning before. For as long as the dinner party had been, it might have been years since Barric stood with her in that flurry of snow, his hand curving around her cheek as he watched the snowflakes gather in her hair. Banishing the image, he spoke in a low voice. "Don't talk like this. I meant what I said."

Did he, though? He tried to make peace between them, to make her feel at last like she belonged, but at the first turn he had told his own uncle she was beneath him. *A wretched beggar* he had called her. His eyes fell from her face. What kind of man was he, to have spoken with such contempt of a woman who trusted him?

"Cast us off if that's what you wish," Rena challenged, her English accent faltering more than he had ever heard. "Ban me from your fields, or call me whatever you'd like, but you will leave me alone, sir."

He dropped her shoulders, released her as Charlie came bounding down the steps.

"There you are!" Charlie called out, coming to a shuffling stop beside his brother. "Is everything. . .all right?" One look at Barric's face, and he knew everything wasn't. "What's the matter?" Charlie demanded, looking between Barric and Rena and back again. "What happened?"

Rena stared at the tree line. "I got overly warm," she lied, her voice soft and even. "But I feel much better now."

Charlie stared at her face. "You're a rotten liar," he decided.

"Even worse than you?"

Charlie gaped at her response, and Barric coughed on his own surprise.

As the shock wore off, Charlie's eyes hardened. "A liar, am I?"

"You are unhappy," she said, defending her question. "The unhappiest man I've ever met. You may have been a rake when you left Misthold, but you have not returned the same. Why do you pretend as if nothing has changed? Do you think such lies come without cost?"

Barric was not surprised Rena had so easily seen through his brother's artifice. She was quiet but sharp and had spent as much time as Charlie keeping hurtful things buried.

In answer, Charlie held out his arm to her. "If you leave now," he warned in a tight voice, "they'll call this a lover's quarrel. Which I don't think is the case. So let's all calm down, shall we, and go back in together?"

Rena straightened a few loose strands of hair as she at last looked over at Barric. He thought maybe she would leave him standing there despite Charlie's warning and rush off to her little cottage. As if four flimsy walls could keep her safe from the reach and influence of an earl if he wished to pursue.

Instead, she accepted Charlie's proffered arm with a terse nod of acceptance. "But if your brother asks me to dance," she said to Charlie, "I will refuse him."

"Ah, but you see he can't dance with you." Darting a quick, apologetic glance at Barric, Charlie tucked Rena's hand securely in the crook of his arm and ushered her back toward the manor. "Not if you are already dancing with me."

CHAPTER 12

The church bells tolled Sunday morning, but the clamor was eerily out of place, two hours too early to summon them for service. As soon as the first bell had echoed, Nell turned from the coal range so quickly she nearly dropped a kettle of boiling water to the floor. Ignoring Rena's cry of concern, the woman held up a silencing hand and waited, as if expecting the bells to stop at any moment. But the bells rolled on and on, relentless, until voices outside gathered beneath the echoing sound.

"Step outside," Nell ordered, her face suddenly as pale as her nightdress, "and see what could be the matter."

Rena set down the teacup she had just taken from the cupboard, glad she had risen early to dress for church, and snatched up her shawl from the peg. The bells were still clanging when she stepped outside. Several early risers were milling in the road, gazing in the direction of the church, though they could not see the steeple through the trees. Rena called out to the group, asking if they knew what was wrong. But they were as confused as Rena and Nell, shoulders tight against the cold air as they began to walk to town.

Gritting her teeth against the December wind, Rena followed them up the road. Each bell toll settled uneasily in her stomach. Was there a fire, perhaps, or something more sinister? Could England be at war? Had something happened to the queen?

At the first fork in the road, they met with two young boys who had also been sent to seek out the cause of the bells. Their voices tangled together with the others gathered there, a series of demands and confusion bandied back and forth among the crowd. Then, at last, it seemed they would finally have their answer when William came wandering down the road, his gaze stripped of its usual sharpness, a vague expression which was either stricken or confused.

"Wilmot," one of the men called, his voice carrying strong as the bells at last silenced. "What do you do here?"

"I was seeing to a sick sheep on the other side of town." William shook his head as if unsatisfied by his own answer. He gestured distractedly over his shoulder. "I have just passed Parson Richardson on the road."

"What happened?" one woman demanded. "Why did he ring the bells?"

William's jaw was clenched as he lifted his eyes to those who waited so anxiously for his answer. "Prince Albert," he announced in a tight voice. "He is dead."

A silence fell, so deep and dark Rena wanted to burrow within it. The queen's husband, her beloved Albert, *dead*.

Rena knew as well as everyone else the prince consort had been unwell. They had prayed for him in church the past two Sundays. But his was just a passing illness, surely. Nothing serious. After all, Prince Albert was only forty-two in age and rumored to be of excellent spirits. Not that ages mattered, Rena reminded herself with a downward glance. Edric had been but six and twenty. Death often sidled up to the strong.

One of the women on the road was weeping now. William had already produced a handkerchief, which she dabbed gratefully against her eyes as the young lads gaped vacantly. From over her shoulder, Rena heard one of the men swear under his breath as he hastened away, presumably to spread the dismal word.

She was not at all surprised by their grief. Prince Albert had been beloved by many, spoken of highly by the soldiers in Edric's own battalion as an invaluable pillar of British progress. The German prince was still famed for his work on the Great Exhibition, where products and advances had been displayed from all over the empire. Rena had once thought on this event with the utmost scorn. Empire. Imperialism. Prince Albert had been hailed a hero for raising the rallying cry of national pride and ambition; he'd made England's reach seem endless. Had Albert been able, Rena often wondered, would he have swept her very people up into his grand exhibition hall, to be stared at by curious nationals who prided themselves on their ability to take what wasn't theirs?

But the exhibition had been ten years ago, and her father had often warned her, if the world was to be British, then her family best served itself by serving Britain. And then Rena had met Edric, and her scorn had twisted within her again, like a dagger. He had been a soldier sent to colonize. To enlighten her people. To control them. And despite her indignation at his uniform, she loved him. She loved his stories of England and wished to follow him there. After a time, she'd even seen the strengths in the royal family to whom he answered.

Though Rena had often felt conflicted about the influence in India by the British monarchy, she felt no such conflict now in terms of Albert's passing. She felt a rolling grief, as resounding within her as the tolling of the church bell. England might as well have lost its king, but Victoria had lost her husband, and for once Rena felt she understood the imperial queen. She knew exactly how it felt to have her heart cleaved in two, to weep until she thought she'd choke to death on her tears. In England two years were considered an appropriate mourning period for the loss of a husband. But two years had not been enough for Rena to reconcile herself to Edric's death, and she was sure that two years would never begin to touch the grief Victoria now felt for Albert.

"Was it the fever?" one of the men demanded in a gruff voice.

"Yes," William answered. "It was the fever."

Fever.

Rena's eyes began to burn. Edric had developed a fever too. He had been delirious in his final hours, his mind snatched away before she had prepared her heart to say goodbye. Had Prince Albert's fever driven him beyond his reason as well? Had he spoken words to his wife that made little sense? Had he thrashed and raved until the doctor held him down and told Victoria to withdraw into the other room? Was Victoria still weeping over her husband's stiff body, Rena wondered, wishing more than anything that she could pour life back into his cloudy gaze?

"Mrs. Hawley. Are you ill?"

Rena had not closed her eyes, but she felt as though she had as she blinked William back into focus. The other townspeople were watching her too, and she wondered if they could see her dead husband still floating in her gaze. As she closed her eyes, one of the men had the decency to step forward as if he might need to catch her if she swooned.

"I must tell Lady Hawley," Rena said, her words mechanical. "We are still preparing for church. She will be worried."

"Shall I escort you?" William offered, his mouth tipping with concern.

Rena waved away his unease as the other people on the road ogled her.

"No," she replied, avoiding their uncertain gazes. "I must go on alone."

Alone, indeed. What right had Rena to grieve for a man like Prince Albert? they must have wondered. She was the colonized. Albert the colonizer. She was not British. She had no stake on their grief.

But Rena would weep for Prince Albert—for the family who would ache for him, for the country that would soon writhe in confusion beneath his shocking loss. Rena turned back toward the cottage.

Never could she have imagined she would share anything with the queen or even begin to understand her. Yet, in that moment, she felt wholly connected to Victoria, even though they had never met and certainly never would.

A penniless waif and an imperial queen. Widows both. It seemed impossible that death had not seen a difference.

Rena's first Christmas in England was a somber affair. Prince Albert's death, just eleven days before Christmas, still lingered at every doorstep in England. In London the social season had ground to a staggering halt, with reports of concert halls and theatres closed. Even in a small northern town like Abbotsville, his loss was made visual—shops were closed and dark; the rich were dressed in full mourning as they went about their business; the poor wore black armbands. Several high-brow dinner parties had been canceled as well, so that Lady Angelina, wearing a satin gown of ebony, had been heard remarking in town how fortunate they were that Lord Barric's party had fallen *before* Albert's death, or else they might have missed a grand affair, indeed. The lady's irreverence had struck a chord within Rena, who could not bear to hear death dismissed so callously.

Though death tapped at the shutters, Christmas Eve still unwound like a tapestry of iridescent gold within the tiny cottage. As Rena and Nell waited for Alice and William to arrive, they finished setting their table. Both women wore their widow garb as they went about preparing the feast, and it felt strange for Rena to wear her thin black gown for a man who was not Edric.

The Christmas tree, which had been resplendent, the hallmark of Albert's German heritage, was shrouded beneath a thin black veil in honor of his loss. Still, not all was mournful; Nell had said it ought not to be on Christmas. Heady scents rose from the various tureens on the range in the kitchen, half of which Rena had never smelled before. At

---

the table, the light of tall candlesticks caught slivers of window frost and painted them with a deep amber hue. The table was decorated with polished red apples and sprigs of holly. Four large plates had been shined spotless and lined upon a starched linen tablecloth.

Nell had insisted on hosting the feast, claiming it as her inviolable right as a matriarch. William had graciously delivered a few of the more expensive ingredients earlier in the week, including a cow's tongue, which had made Rena flinch as soon as Nell dropped it into the pot of boiling water. If ever they knew, her parents would surely think she'd forsaken the Hindu faith.

The Christmas pudding was the final touch. Nell had taken special care in preparing it, boiling it in a linen to protect its delicate skin. It had been hanging in the scrap of linen near the back door for nearly two weeks, tempting them all with the scent of brandy and dried fruit. As Rena bedecked the pudding with a few sprigs of greenery, there was a brisk knock at the door, as if the hand that beckoned had been chased there by cold.

"Those must be our guests," Nell said with a smile.

Rena set down her holly and stepped to open the door.

But William and Alice weren't waiting on their step. Instead, she found the parson shuffling back and forth on his feet, valiantly trying to keep warm, though his smile needed no such prompting.

"Parson Richardson!" Rena exclaimed. "This is an unexpected surprise."

"A merry Christmas to all within," he greeted, doffing his hat. He tipped his head to indicate a covered platter on the step beside him and waited patiently for Rena to move the cloth aside. Beneath was a generous leg of lamb, already roasted and piping hot.

"We are so thankful to you for thinking of us." She stepped aside so the lovely Christmas table came into view over her shoulder. "Won't you come in and join us? We have more than enough to eat, and Nell would want to thank you."

Though his shoulders were bunched beneath his ears to fend off the cold, he held up a hand and shook his head. "As it turns out, I have a dinner of my own waiting," he explained quickly. "I wished only to add to your own celebration. And, after what happened at Lord Barric's party, I'm sure you wish to share your Christmas feast. . .uninterrupted."

Rena surprised herself by not flinching on Barric's name. In the wake of Prince Albert's death, the gossips had been mercifully silent about their interactions at the party. Still, the longer Barric's name went unspoken, the more he seemed to whisper against her ear that she was nothing to him. *Beneath him.* His voice often tangled with his uncle's voice in her memory, the words breathed in a dragonish double tongue.

"You are mistaken if I think anything at all about Lord Barric." She had spoken far too quickly, then stopped short. She had just lied to a parson, she realized. On Christmas.

The parson nodded to the rhythm of her reply, like he had foreseen every word of her lie but was not angered by it. "All the same, I hope you will not be uneasy about what transpired at his party. I've known the family for years. Barric has his father's temper, I'll admit, but he has never been one to think or act cruelly."

Rena had tried not to dwell on her angry parting from Lord Barric, and the loss of Albert had offered some necessary perspective. Still, she had encouraged an earl to cast them off, to bar her from his fields, all but taunting him to let them starve just because he had hurt her with his words—such a challenge could only be ignored for so long. Frightened by the possibility that he might act on her words and turn them out at once, she had confided the whole encounter to Nell, who had merely replied that such things ought not to be worried over on Christmas.

"I am grateful for your gift," Rena replied distractedly. "You are sure you won't stay?"

In answer, the parson slipped on his hat, the wide brim obscuring his eyes. "Please, enjoy your feast," he said. "And, again, do not allow yourself to be uneasy, especially today. After all, our Savior has come."

Though calmly spoken, his words slammed against her like a gust of wind. Rena's first instinct was to bid him farewell and slip back inside the house, to ignore such things, but her feet remained frozen to the step, and she stalled. She knew very little of this "Savior," as he called Him. She had learned from her time in church that angry men had killed the man Jesus many years ago, and that He was yet as ageless to them as any of the gods she herself had worshipped since childhood. Nell's crucifix still hung on their mantel as proof of this death, but Rena usually avoided the slipped-shut eyes of this tiny savior. Though Nell often spoke of resurrection, the statue's dead eyes made her think of Edric's eyes, forever shut, forever dead, and, as Nell had already said, such things ought not to be worried over on Christmas.

But would their eyes remain forever shut?

As if in answer, the parson's words from his first sermon crossed her mind. *"Blessed are the pure in heart: for they shall see God."*

"But your list was wrong." Still battered by exhaustion, Rena spoke the ridiculous words aloud before she could stop herself.

The parson froze at her answer, crooking his head. "My. . .*list?*" He did not sound angered by her accusation, but his brow furrowed in confusion.

"You spoke once of the meek and the pure and the peacemakers," she explained. "Those who hunger and thirst for righteousness. Your list."

He nodded. "And what about it, exactly, is wrong?"

"I am not sure I fit into your list," she admitted, then sighed as she caught the concern in his eyes. "I mourn, yes, and I am poor. But I want to be proud. I want to be strong. Sometimes I even want to be angry. And it doesn't matter however much I look, but I cannot see your god."

She realized her words might very well upset the parson. He lived by his book as surely as Edric had. Edric, who had not shared nearly as much about it with her as he'd wished to. He had told her from his deathbed that he thought he'd have more time, but there never seemed time enough for the things that really mattered.

"You are entirely correct," the parson said. "You do not fit into the list."

Rena blinked up at him in some surprise.

"Do not misunderstand me," the parson said quickly, holding out an imploring hand. "We are all proud and angry people, Mrs. Hawley. The list does not describe any of us."

"I don't understand. Why preach such a list if it is fiction?"

"I did not say it was fiction." With a gentle smile, he went on, "The list truly describes only one person—the one you say you cannot see."

The Savior, as he had called Him. *Jesus.* Rena frowned. Was there really such a man, such a god, as could raise the dead, forgive sins, and wipe the tears from Rena's widow eyes? Was Edric with this god, despite his body being in its grave? Was Alistair? Was Victoria's beloved Albert?

She wanted to believe all of it, but she was still haunted by Edric's eyes—glossy, wide, and empty before the doctor had gently brushed them shut. Were Edric's eyes still closed, she wondered, or did they gaze upon this god of his? She couldn't get these questions out, but the parson did not seem to mind her momentary confusion, nor her silence.

"Merry Christmas," he said again. And with a gentle smile and a subtle bow, he swiftly vanished into the cold.

William and Alice arrived shortly after sunset, bearing a glorious turkey on a thick, porcelain platter with gold etching. Both siblings wore the requisite black, and as they all sat at the table, Rena noticed that Alice was especially quiet, her eyes trained on the table ornaments. The two women hadn't spoken since Barric's Christmas party, and the silence made Rena uneasy. Was Alice still made somber by the death of Prince Albert? Or perhaps she had heard something of the party; perhaps rumors had been passed after all.

William made quite a spectacle of pouring a thick bottle of expensive wine, gifted to him for the holiday by Lord Barric himself. "Drink slowly," he advised, handing Rena her glass with a playful wink. "Once it's gone, it's gone."

He poured generous glasses for Nell and Alice, an even more generous one for himself, then settled back in his chair. "We drink to the memory of Prince Albert," he announced with a pinched expression. "And God save the queen."

All at the table drank the toast in reverent silence. Then William leaned forward and began to carve the various beasts. Alice still hadn't spoken a word since she'd arrived but sipped at her wine and stared blankly at the shrouded tree in the corner.

"Alice," Rena whispered, leaning closer to her friend as Nell and William fussed with the turkey. "Are you well?"

Alice nodded as she tipped back a bit more wine. "Merely tired," she sighed, setting her half-empty glass down. "I will feel better once I have a full stomach."

And so they dug into the hearty meal, doling out large portions of each dish, relishing the rich flavors in silence. At one point, Rena saw Nell's eyes mist in the candlelight.

Perhaps William noticed as well. Taking a bite of warm bread, he sighed heavily at Nell. "Lady Hawley, you must have used witchcraft to conjure up such a lovely feast."

"No witchcraft needed when you're as old and crafty as I am," Nell responded between bites of chutney. This was the only dish that even remotely resembled something Rena was familiar with, as the pickled fruits were seasoned heavily with turmeric and cayenne.

"I think it is the finest feast I've ever seen," Rena decided, and took another large spoonful of the spiced fruit.

"Surely not nearly as lovely as what you had at Lord Barric's party," Alice disagreed, and gestured for William to refill her now empty wine glass.

William's jaw tightened slightly at her request, but he obeyed, forcing a smile for Rena's sake. "True," he said. "Barric's feast would likely have put our small turkey quite to shame. Still, I'd not trade tables with him if it meant losing this charming company."

Rena returned his smile, grateful to William for turning the topic away from the disastrous party.

"Betsy heard from maids at Misthold that he hardly said a word to you through the entire dinner," Alice remarked, lowering her glass again. "That he was rather cold toward you when you arrived."

This time William didn't even try to mask his disapproval. "*Alice.*"

She avoided her brother's gaze, staring instead at her empty glass. "Did he dance with you after dinner?"

"No," Rena answered honestly. "I danced twice with Mr. Fairfax. Once with Parson Richardson."

She certainly didn't mention her argument with Lord Barric on the terrace, or how she had challenged him to cast her off, or how she had refused to dance with him. She still couldn't believe she had said such things in the presence of an earl.

"What did you think he would do?" Alice scoffed, her voice tight as she at last met Rena's eyes. "What did you think would happen?"

"*Alice!*" William stood up. "Stop."

"It's fine," Rena said, shaking her head as she realized Alice was well past the point of stopping, and maybe it was for the best. Maybe they all needed to hear the truth, even if they had to forsake their lovely Christmas feast to do it.

"Did you really think he would take one look at you in my dress and forget you are a penniless beggar?" Alice fought a laugh of disbelief. "As if you aren't here, eating off our own charity. He may want you, Mrs. Hawley, but he can't have you. Not in the way you want. He'll use you, true enough, and then he'll throw you away, and what else did you expect?"

Mrs. Hawley—Rena's throat constricted at the name. It was a cutting insult, a severing of friendship. She felt her fingers tremble slightly, losing their grip on her fork.

William rounded the table and grabbed ahold of Alice's arm. "Lady Hawley. Mrs. Hawley. I beg you to please forgive my sister. She is a bit foxed tonight and is unfortunately not at all herself."

"I am not foxed," Alice said in complaint as William pulled her to her feet. But the girl's cheeks were tellingly flushed, her eyes glossed with tightly held tears.

"The way you are speaking at this table," William warned. "You had better be foxed." He bowed deeply to Nell. "We are so thankful for your hospitality, Lady Hawley, and we bid you a good night and a very merry Christmas."

Nell nodded, her hand pressed hard to her chest. "Of course," she replied vaguely. "We understand."

William steered Alice halfway to the door before his sister halted, pulling a thin package from beneath her shawl. Crossing back, she dropped it heavily on the table, right beside Rena's plate, making all the cutlery clatter. "Merry Christmas," Alice said, her voice empty. Then she turned and let William usher her the rest of the way outside.

As soon as the door had shut behind them, Rena pulled Alice's package into her lap. She already knew, from the shape and weight of the present, so familiar, that it was a book. Nell leaned forward, smoothing a motherly hand over Rena's hair. "Open it, child," she whispered.

Did Rena dare open it, after everything Alice had said? She turned the package over in her hands several times, weighing the volume before at last shredding the golden paper aside. Nestled within was a thin volume, a collection of colorful paintings of India. With reverent fingers, Rena shuffled through the pictures—some of barren deserts and tangling forests, others of the liquid horizon as it was swallowed by the setting sun. There was even a painting of the Hawa Mahal in Jaipur, its pink sandstone walls built as an elaborate screen to conceal the royal women in the zenana as they gazed upon the city. Fanning the book pages lightly, Rena stopped only once more to brush her fingertips over a depiction of an exotic garden, much like her family's, with braided vines spreading like fingers toward the page's edge.

Rena struggled for several moments to find even one word to say. Nell said nothing either, granting her daughter-in-law enough time to face her own grief. But no matter how many times Rena's grief stared at her, she could never seem to return its waiting gaze.

"Did you really think he would take one look at you in my dress and forget you are a penniless beggar?"

"She didn't mean it," Nell said softly. "You know that. You know *her*. The girl is only hurting."

Rena winced and slipped the cover shut with a small thud. Thud, like the battering of her heart beneath Edric's touch. Thud, like the pounding of feet against hard ground or the closing of a door—or the shutting of a tomb.

Rena knew Alice had spoken from a place of grief, but this knowledge did not ebb Rena's own pain. She needed someone she could depend on, someone who wouldn't call her nothing just because they feared her. She needed to feel like her feet weren't always shifting with the sand. But all of Alice's hard words, even when stacked together with Barric's, could not compare with the hole that still ached the deepest inside of her.

Edric was gone.

Setting the book carefully on the table, Rena covered her eyes with her hands, turned into Nell's waiting embrace, and wept.

The next morning, when Rena awakened, a large package sat beside her on the bed in Nell's usual spot. The box had been wrapped in bright flowered paper with a pile of crimson ribbon knotted prettily on top. Rena frowned over at the gift, shamed by the feel of her own empty hands. She had not even thought to get Nell a present.

"Well, I've never seen anyone look so miserable about a present," Nell remarked, plopping down on the bed beside the package. "Open it. It's yours."

"But I have nothing for you," Rena admitted, feeling wretched. If she'd racked her brain, surely she could have thought of something. "I'm. . .not used to Christmas."

"Oh pish," said Nell, waving a hand. "What does an old lady really need, anyway? Open it. And act excited, won't you? I've been planning this surprise for months."

Rena obeyed, sitting up and pulling the ribbon. The ornate wrapping was thick, shredding away into a heap at the foot of the bed. When all that was left was a crisp white box, Rena lifted the lid, shuffled aside a few leaves of paper, and knew at once that Nell had done something extravagant.

With an astonished sigh, Rena folded aside layers of rich indigo silk. She knew from an experienced hand, quick to measure, the bolt of fabric was seven yards long. It would wrap her waist entirely, fit over her shoulder, and drape her body in the traditional way—with one shoulder covered, the other kept free. The fabric's outer edge was woven with whorls of gold and ruby, tiny flowers so intricate that Rena wondered at the pattern's cost.

Setting the sari gently aside, she found a *ghagra* billowed beneath—a voluminous skirt, deep plum in color—then the *choli*, a tightly fitted blouse, embroidered with golden flowers, which would hug her chest and bare her midriff. A loose veil had been folded into a square at the bottom of the box. It too was lined in gold and embroidered with flecks of silver that resembled the stars.

"Do you. . .like it?" At Nell's question, Rena's fingers tightened their hold on the veil, sinking deep wrinkles into the fabric. The gift was costly beyond comprehension, more exotic than what she would have worn even in her father's household. It felt rich to the touch, and it smelled like India, like spices and fruit, as if the fabric had been patterned by hands which had just been out picking citrus blossoms that morning.

"Oh Nell. . ." Rena shook her head, swallowing away tears as her throat tightened. She already knew how the fabric would feel against her skin, a loose layer that wrapped her up and left her bare all at once, so unlike a corset. She could already imagine the silk rustling like autumn leaves as she moved from room to room. Just from weighing the fabric between her hands, her heart was charmed into thinking she was home, even though she wasn't. Even though she was.

Rena could not understand how such a gift had even been managed, not until she glanced at Nell's left hand and realized the woman's wedding ring was missing.

The veil fell from Rena's hands to the floor in a wilting coil. "No," Rena rasped, stepping up from the bed and away from the bundle of cloth as if it might burn her if she touched another stitch. "Say that you didn't," she begged, her voice breaking. "Tell me there was another way."

"I wanted you to have it. I wanted it for you."

"Where is your ring?"

Nell's eyebrow dipped stubbornly. "Sold."

Rena pressed her fingers against her mouth, remembering her own frantic search when she'd thought she'd lost Edric's ring. She had nearly struck Lord Barric that night for standing in her way. Now Nell's ring was gone, and for what? For a marvelous dress Rena could never bear to put on, because to wear it would feel like standing in two worlds at the same time; it would feel like splitting straight down the middle. "Can you get it back?"

"Alistair wouldn't have minded." Nell almost never spoke her husband's name. To hear it now felt like an omen, like he was sitting in their room hunched over a chessboard.

Rena began piling the fabric haphazardly back into the box. "You must take the dress back," she commanded, fumbling to get the top on right, but the veil had come unwound and was blocking the corner from closing.

Nell came beside her and braced a hand against the lid, barring Rena from moving it another inch. "Do you think I have not thought this through? Do you think I do not see everything you have surrendered to come to this place? Your family. Your people. Your home. You've come here, become nothing, so you could take care of me. You have allowed yourself to be hated for me, endured beggary for me." She cupped Rena's face, stilling her even more. "That is your gift to me. And I am grateful for you, Daughter."

Rena met Nell's eyes and laid her hand gently over hers. "I cannot wear it," she confessed in a whisper. "That world, it's gone to me."

"You can, and you will," Nell disagreed, dropping her hands. "Not for Sunday service, of course, but you must save it. Save it until the time is right, until you are ready."

"Ready for what?" Rena tried to sound cynical, but her throat cut the words early, and she choked on her own question.

Nell smiled faintly. "You will know the answer to that question when you see it."

CHAPTER 13

Charlie folded his cards and scattered them on the table with an aggravated sigh. "I'm starting to think the only reason you come over here is to cheat me at cards."

"Don't pretend to be moody about it," William chided, raking in his winnings. "If you're very nice to me, I might let you win the next round."

Charlie shook his head, but he was already shuffling the deck with rapid fingers. The cards brushed against each other, well paced and rhythmic, like fingertips fanning the pages of an old book.

"I'm curious," Charlie mused as he shuffled. "Does my brother also let you take him for all he's worth?"

William's voice turned smug. "Yes," he said, not untruthfully. "Often."

Barric heard their conversation in the background as he rifled through his plans for spring. William and Charlie had already invited him several times to abandon his papers long enough to join in the next hand, but drinking and gambling never distracted Barric quite so well as his work. And after what happened at his Christmas party, followed so closely by the death of the prince, he wanted to be distracted.

"We can hire more men from the village," he finally decided out loud. "We made good money off last year's crop, and finances are finally strong again."

Charlie's hands didn't falter as he shuffled the deck, but Barric glanced up in time to see his brother's mouth press into a thin line. They both knew finances were only strong because Barric was no longer making last-minute trips to Paris to funnel money into Charlie's sizable debts. To the world outside of Misthold, Charlie had returned from France generally unchanged. He still carried on the occasional flirtation, wore his usual French fashion, lolled around like an insufferable dandy. But Charlie's outward carelessness was far too conscious of itself to be real. For months Charlie had been sending sums of money to Celeste, and though they hadn't spoken of it, Barric suspected his brother had heard nothing in response.

"What about Matthew Sloan?" William suggested as Charlie finished dealing their cards. "He found work at the mill, but he might want to return. He was a hard worker."

As soon as Charlie glimpsed his own cards, he swore in dismay and threw down a crown. The silver coin spun on its thin edge for a spiraling second before clanging down onto the table. "I've had a few others asking for work," Barric said, watching the coin fall. "I'm curious to know what you both think of the names."

"What about the girl?" Charlie threw out the question lazily, as if tossing away a card he didn't particularly like. When Barric didn't answer right away, Charlie needlessly clarified. "What about Mrs. Hawley?"

Hearing her name set Barric back on his guard. He snapped his file shut. "What about her?"

Charlie lifted his eyes from his cards and spoke more pointedly. "Might you offer her one of these positions?"

"She is already provided for," Barric said, his eyes shifting to William. For weeks William and Alice had been leaving food for Rena and Nell; Barric only knew this because he had explicitly ordered them to do it. He'd made sure there was a little extra in William's pockets to help them all weather through the winter months together.

"Yes," Charlie agreed slowly. "But might she want an arrangement a bit less—"

As Charlie trailed off, William supplied the final word, "Beggarly?"

"I understand your concern," Barric replied at length. "But I fired two Englishmen last fall; I ought to hire two Englishmen back. I have no interest in sparking a mutiny of my own. In the meantime, the Hawleys will not starve."

"Christmas is barely over, and here you are, already planning for spring?" Barric straightened as Uncle George appeared in the doorway. The man hadn't dared surface since the Christmas party, and Barric felt weary as soon as he set eyes on him. One after another, all of his old frustrations sunk into his chest like arrows. He was far too easy a target.

"Stop trying to think up ways to get rid of me." His uncle brandished a squat bottle of port, angling it slightly so Barric could read its expensive label. "As you can see, I've brought a peace offering."

Barric felt Charlie's gaze and knew without looking that his brother's eyebrows had risen incredulously. "I don't know about you," Charlie snapped. "But anything less than whiskey seems a pretty pathetic apology to me."

Uncle George shot Charlie a look of mild irritation. "You want me to grovel, is that it? Say the word, Charlie, and I'll gladly take a knee. But don't act like you've never had to make reparations for poor behavior. Isn't that the whole reason you're here?"

Charlie opened his mouth to argue, but Barric took his uncle's point and cut in gloomily. "Come in. Leave the port."

Uncle George placed a hand to his chest in a show of gratefulness, then crossed the room. He thumped the bottle on the middle of the card table, pinning down a few strewn-aside cards. Glancing briefly over William's shoulder, he grimaced at the steward's cards as he advised, half apologetically, "I'd wager low, Charlie. As low as you can."

Charlie screwed up his eyes at William, who cracked an agreeing smile. "You're cheating," Charlie accused, stabbing a finger in his direction. "I'd bet my life on it."

"I wouldn't bet at all if I were you," William advised, shaking his head. "You don't seem particularly good at it."

Uncle George looked to Barric next. "Mind if I have a word?" he asked, nodding toward the door. "In the other room?"

Barric remembered how cornered Rena had looked at his dinner table, straight-backed as she had answered his guests' questions one after another. Barric crossed his arms in front of his chest and let the moment drag.

His uncle sighed. "Barric, don't look at me like that. Will you let me speak with you or not?"

"Very well," Barric agreed. "Speak."

His uncle glanced back at the table, where cards and money were once again changing hands. "I'd prefer this stay between us," he said cautiously.

"Say what you wish to say, or don't." Barric made an offhand gesture. "It makes no difference to me."

"Really? Even though it concerns Mrs. Hawley?" His uncle waited. Barric sensed no flicker of amusement in his uncle's eyes as he dangled her name in front of him.

Charlie and William were listening more attentively now. Though William was filling two glasses with the port, his smile had vanished. His gaze inched over toward Barric, who at last took his uncle's cue and strode out of the room. As he'd done the night of the party, he brought his uncle to his mother's old sitting room. He didn't turn to face his uncle until he heard the door close behind them.

"This better be good," he warned.

"I wouldn't have poked a sleeping dragon if it wasn't," his uncle responded warily. "Could you please forget I'm a scoundrel long enough for me to say this?"

Barric supposed it would be a bit churlish not to at least hear his uncle out. He leaned against the armrest of a chair, folded his arms, and nodded his acceptance. His uncle lowered himself to the settee and hesitantly began. "I've been doing some research on Mrs. Hawley's husband's estate, and I've received word from my solicitor in London that her husband's fortune was supposed to pass to a cousin in Australia, but apparently it hasn't passed to anyone."

"What are you talking about?" Barric challenged.

"There's something wrong with the will," his uncle explained. "It seems some loose ends have been left rather. . .loose these past few months."

As he listened to his uncle, Barric's temper began to work inside of him, as if it just needed more room to move, to stretch its neck, but was trapped and beginning to claw. "You've gone digging into the will?"

"Just think, all that money, that beautiful property—it's floating around unattached." Uncle George gestured toward the ceiling, as if it were all there, hidden in Barric's rafters all along.

For some moments, Barric was too stunned to speak, muted by his rising fury. There was a growing list of details and questions he knew he ought to consider, but he was still stuck on the first. "You have contacts in London. . .looking into her?"

"Not her," his uncle corrected quickly, "the estate."

"I told you to leave it alone."

His uncle's expression opened with eagerness. "Where is your sense of enterprise?" he challenged with a bit more gusto. "Aren't you the least bit interested? If the women can't inherit it, perhaps we could—"

"No."

"Barric."

"They have nothing," Barric said, his voice as sharp a grate as boots on gravel. "They are destitute, and you want me to ally with you to rip the property right out from under them."

His uncle spoke more carefully. "I understand you're protective of the girl," he said. "But whether or not I buy the property does not change their situation if the will is ironclad set against them anyway. Has she said anything about it?"

"I would never ask."

"Well, you should know other people very well might ask her. There's nothing more romantic to small-town gossip than a missing will."

"What is your sudden interest in this property anyway?"

"There's nothing sudden about it," he said dismissively. "I've always admired Hawthorn Glen. I think it would suit me rather well."

At first Barric didn't like the image of Uncle George living in Edric's old house. He knew it would destroy Nell to have her home snatched away, and he suspected it would affect Rena in subtler ways that hurt just as much. He wondered if Rena had been to Hawthorn Glen since arriving in England or if she had stayed away out of grief.

If his uncle bought the property, he would open the windows, air out the gloom. He would turn the dead man's bedroom into a guest room, a spare room. He would tear down the wallpaper for something more fashionable, raze the weed-strewn gardens, and fill the library with pipe smoke. He would erase Rena's husband, chase away his ghost.

His uncle spoke again, in a lower voice. "Your father and I used to go riding together in the evenings," he confessed. "We'd ride up past the glen, rest at the top of the hill, and look down at the Hawley manor. I always liked the sight and said that if I could have an estate of my own, it might look something like that. Your father used to tease me—if anyone could find a way to pirate a house for himself, he said, it would be me."

Barric knew his father had probably been right, but it still didn't set well with him, this image of his uncle walking through the halls of the home that might have been Rena's had death not barred her from entering it.

Rena knew she was dreaming, but there was nothing she could do about it. Legs weighted, she stood at the counter of the Gilded Crown, pleading. Nell was slumped at a table behind her, her limbs hanging limply from starvation, her eyes delirious with hunger.

"*Pay,*" Mrs. Bagley ordered, and Rena searched and searched but could not find any coins. It was only a dream, she reasoned with herself, half-frantic, and yet she could not remember how to climb out.

"*Pay,*" Mrs. Bagley insisted and shoved Rena through a door. It was not the produce closet, as she expected, but a dusty room with a disheveled bed, standard fare for a below-average inn.

Before Rena was able to turn, to tell Mrs. Bagley she could not pay for such a room, Thomas stepped through the door, his teeth impossibly white as he leered down at her.

"*Pay,*" he repeated, holding out his hand to her. His skin was smooth, his hair soft and black, but his eyes were unthinkably hard. Cruel.

Rena's mind sloshed from side to side. "*No,*" she said, but she already knew it wouldn't work. Her words were often made empty in her dreams, and this time was no different.

Thomas grabbed her by both wrists. His lips found her face. "*Something different,*" he called her, his teeth scratching against her skin.

Rena tried to fight him back. She tried to scream.

She searched frantically for his name—for *Barric*—but the only word she could clench in her panic was "*No, no, no. . .*"

The word still meant nothing. Sounded like nothing. She screamed the word, tasted the blood beneath it until at last she bolted up in bed, startled to find herself in her usual cottage, in her usual bed, with Nell slumbering at her side.

"Rena?" Nell whispered sleepily, turning over on her side. "What's the matter?"

Rena sank back against the pillows and pleaded with her heart to find a steadier rhythm. "Just a dream," she murmured, unclenching her hands, but she still needed convincing herself.

Too many days had passed since Lord Barric's party, and she still felt its strain. If Barric barred her from his fields, as she had begged him to do, or if William turned her out of his cottage, where would she and Nell go?

The next morning, she set out for Misthold after breakfast, pulling her shawl snug around her shoulders as she considered what she ought to say to Lord Barric when she finally faced him. In the aftermath of Christmas, she had been avoided by nearly everyone she had come to depend on—Barric, Alice, even William. All nodded politely to her on the road, but none of them stopped or uttered more than the standard greeting.

She had not felt so alone since she had first alighted in Abbotsville.

She couldn't very well tell Lord Barric about her dream, of course, especially the part Thomas had played in it, but she could tell him she was still afraid and needed, more than anything, to depend on him. She approached the front door of Misthold as William was leaving and nearly bumped into him.

"Mrs. Hawley," he greeted with a drawn smile. With his free arm, he reached to open the door for her but seemed to reconsider at the last moment, his fingers dropping from the handle. "What are you about this morning?"

"I am here to speak with Lord Barric."

With an uneasy look, William pulled the door closed behind him and straightened. "Give me your message," he instructed quietly, "and I will pass it on to Lord Barric."

Unsettled by William's grim expression, Rena gaped up at him. "Is Lord Barric not at home?"

Nothing in William's expression moved. "He's home."

Panic struck as she considered her last meeting with Lord Barric. Was this proof, then, he wanted nothing more to do with her? The fright of her dream nipped at her again. She could never pay her own way, not as things stood.

"Let me in," she ordered, half considering pushing past him. "I need to see him."

William looked at her sadly. "No, Mrs. Hawley. You need to stay away from him."

She reeled back a step, her gaze lifting to the windows above them, wondering if Barric was watching from one of the high casements. Was he glad to see her cast away from his door like a vagrant? Was he laughing at her in his high and lofty tower?

Yet again, William had personal reasons of his own for barring her from Misthold. Perhaps he was not speaking on Barric's behalf at all. Her thoughts turned back to the Christmas party, and her stomach clenched. "Is this about what Alice said?"

William sighed heavily, his tone tightening. "What Alice said to you was unpardonably cruel. This is not about that."

"She thinks I've tried to seduce Lord Barric."

"No. She doesn't."

"She thinks I am beneath her."

William leaned subtly closer, lowering his voice. "My sister has been in love with Lord Barric for as long as she has known him," he confided, shaking his head in brotherly frustration.

Surprised to hear William speak so plainly, Rena studied his clenched jaw and perfect suit and saw a man who worked himself tired every day, who cared a great deal about how he appeared and what he accomplished.

"She is not angry with you," William went on. "She is angry only with herself. She has wasted many years on Barric and is only now beginning to realize it."

"She has not spoken to me since Christmas." Rena's voice could not endure the pain of this admission. Her words pinched off at the end.

William reached out and touched her arm. "She also spent a smallish fortune to get you that book of Indian art, had it delivered all the way from London." He smiled faintly. "She cares for you a great deal. Give her time."

Rena couldn't keep the accusation out of her voice as she prodded. "And you, Mr. Wilmot? You have not spoken to me either."

He stiffened, but his eyes still looked weary and spent. Perhaps Rena wasn't the only one not sleeping well those days. "I do believe I have said 'good day' from time to time," he disagreed. "In truth, I thought some space was best."

"Best for whom?"

He leaned his shoulder against the doorpost as he considered how to answer. "I've known Lord Barric—truly known him—longer than anyone else in this town. I remember when he used to get in fist fights over Charlie. I remember when he used to insult me just because he thought he had to, and I remember the way he got cross-eyed drunk after our fathers had died. In many ways, I know him better than his own family."

Rena felt uncomfortable by William's open expression. His confidence in her felt heavy in her already fumbling hands. "Why are you telling me all of this?"

"If there is one thing I know best about Lord Barric, it's that he has always been an immovable man. He does what needs to be done, and he doesn't lose sleep over it, however taxing it may be. But you move him, Mrs. Hawley. You make him act out of character. You make him go against his better judgment, and that cannot end well. Not for either of you."

"You think Nell and I should leave Abbotsville," she guessed weakly, her thoughts spiraling faster than a spinning top. Perhaps

Nell's cousins would take Nell in, she thought, if she went to them without Rena. Then Rena could find another way to support herself alone. But what if the only way was to return to the Gilded Crown? She could not bear to live out her nightmare, allowing men to touch her just to stave off starvation.

William held up his hand as if he sensed her tumbling thoughts. "I didn't say that. Things will continue as they have. You'll live with us, and you'll take from Barric's fields, but you must stay away from him."

She knew what he said was well advised. It made sense. It was safe. But it hurt all the same. There was something about the closed door to Misthold which frightened her.

William frowned as she stared blankly at the door, and his voice gentled. "I don't mean to hurt you, Rena."

"You are looking after your lord," she said. "I understand."

"It's not just him I'm looking out for," William disagreed, sounding slightly defensive. "He could hurt you too if you let him."

Rena slid back a whole step and nodded. "I understand," she said again, but her voice paled and drifted, betraying her. Despite it all, she'd grown used to Lord Barric, fond of the way he sometimes looked at her. Even with his quick temper, even with his stern pride, she knew him to be a decent man.

"Your message," William said, and touched her arm in gentle reminder. "What did you wish for me to tell him?"

Rena felt as if every stone of Misthold had been stacked upon her chest as she turned at last toward home. "Nothing," she said to William. "Tell him nothing."

The rest of winter turned gray and slushy. Snow came intermittently, never heavy enough to cover the gray or chase away the gloom. It was on a particularly soggy morning that Rena at last received word from her parents. She carried the letter down to the creek and perched on a rock, her eyes racing over her father's thin, elegant script. She did not have to read for long.

They loved her, the letter said. They missed her. They were glad she was safe, tended to, and cared for by her new family. She hated those words—*new family*—but still accepted them as the truth and read on.

"You have made your choices," the letter said. *"And though we will remember you in our prayers, we must live in the separate worlds we have each created. Farewell, Daughter."*

Rena flipped the letter over, knowing she had come to its end but praying other words had been tucked away, perhaps waiting for her on the paper's other side. She felt her own emptiness mirrored in the letter's large white margins, in the empty space that stretched down after her father's stately signature. Though she knew her father could write with vibrancy, letters rich in detail and affection, he had written her only two short paragraphs. The letter had been kind but bland. He had included no news of India, of her family, or how they fared. There were no questions about Nell or Rena's place in England, no show of concern for her day-to-day struggles. He had written with an even hand, focused and controlled.

Rena's fingers pinched the corners of the page. When she'd first come to England, she had felt a hundred doors slam shut on her desperate pleas for food, for work. Staring at her father's letter now was like staring at the slammed-shut door to his study. He had forgiven her for marrying Edric, offered to bring her back home and find her another husband with time, but she had left, and however hard she struggled now she could not wrench open his door. He said they loved her, but he also cast her off.

She was to live her life. They were to live theirs. There was no room to intersect.

As snow began to fall, to nibble at the letter's edge, Rena returned home, the letter still clenched in her fist. She entered the cottage, surprised to find Nell sitting at the table with a middle-aged man who wore a slightly faded frock coat and wide necktie.

"Ah!" remarked the stranger with a pleasant nod. "Here she is."

Rena hovered in the doorway, confused by his presence, until Nell stood and beckoned her closer. "We've been waiting for you," she said, pulling out the empty chair beside her own. "This is Mr. Finley. He is a solicitor. He's come a rather long way to see us."

As Rena took her seat at the table, she realized she still held fast to her father's letter. She smoothed its paper between her hands under the table as she waited for either Nell or Mr. Finley to speak.

Mr. Finley slid on a pair of thin-wired spectacles. "Now that you are both here, I may begin." He rifled through a few layers of paperwork as he spoke. "It seems there has been some confusion about your husband's will, Lady Hawley."

He passed Nell a piece of paper. "This is the will that was found when he died."

Nell's mouth tightened into a frown as she gazed down at her dead husband's handwriting. She placed two fingers, softly, to the paper's edge. "Yes," she said wearily, pushing it slightly away from herself. "I have read it. Everything passes to Sir Alistair's cousin."

"Yes," the man agreed. "According to this will, that would be the case."

Nell's eyes shot up from the paper, narrowing on Mr. Finley. "*This* will?"

He slipped another sheet of paper from his folder and placed it gently in front of her. "This was found after you and your daughter-in-law left India. It has taken some time for us to authenticate it."

Nell stared vacantly at the paper, her eyes straining as she again traced the dips and swells of her husband's handwriting. Her eyes moved frantically from the will to Mr. Finley and back again. "Is it. . .real?"

The man nodded. "Quite real. We tracked down the witness, and it seems to have been written in the same hand as the one previously drafted."

Nell sat back in her chair, her cheeks suddenly flushed, and settled a hand against her temple as if warding off a headache. Stricken by Nell's sudden anguish, Rena grasped the woman's shoulder. "Are you all right?" she whispered. "Do you need him to leave?"

"What does it say?" Nell asked the solicitor in a hoarse voice. "Tell me."

"Your husband's second will is rather. . .unorthodox," he explained slowly. "It seems he and your son joined together to break the previous entailment to the Hawley cousin. The second part was written, rather hastily, after your son had died. It seems the fortune *can* pass to you, Lady Hawley—but only in the event that your daughter-in-law remarries."

Rena felt the blood drain from her face. "Excuse me?"

"There's more." Mr. Finley swallowed deeply. "Mrs. Hawley, you must marry one of Sir Alistair's relatives—one who is, specifically, in the Fairfax line."

It was Rena's turn to feel ill. "I don't understand," she stammered, shaking her head.

The solicitor placed his finger on a line of text and read, "*That my mother's family might finally be reconciled.*" He cleared his throat uncomfortably. "As soon as your marriage license is received," he went on, speaking directly to Rena, "your mother-in-law will inherit all of Sir Alistair's money. And your new husband will inherit Hawthorn Glen."

This time Nell grabbed Rena's hand and squeezed, and Rena was stunned to remember her father's letter was still crumpled within her fisted palm, now beneath Nell's touch. Not even an hour had passed since she'd rushed to the creek, joyous to have found his letter. Now she felt oddly small—just a quick little proviso dropped in the middle of a dead man's will.

She had to marry a Fairfax.

Unthinkable.

She heard Nell saying her name, but all she could think of was the moment she'd told Lord Barric she would never marry again. She had meant those words. They had not been spoken cheaply. But now? If she remarried, Nell would have a comfortable living. Food forever. And if Rena refused? There was a good chance destitution would follow like a clawlike creature wherever they went.

The solicitor fanned out a few more documents in front of Nell. "These are for you to review." He pointed. "This is my address in London should you need to contact me for further details."

His job now finished, the solicitor removed his spectacles and glanced uneasily between the two widows. "Is there. . .anything else I can do for you?"

"No," Nell answered for both of them as she once again pressed Rena's fingers. "Thank you for coming all this way to see us. We just need some. . .some time."

"Of course," said Mr. Finley with a slight, awkward bow. Rena hardly heard him leave, but his words spiraled through her mind until Nell came and knelt beside her chair, angling Rena's chin so she could see her eyes.

"Which relative am I to marry?"

"Rena."

"Charlie, perhaps? He is a Fairfax. So is Thomas."

Yes, her heart whispered. *So is Lord Barric. . .*

She stomped down the thought, remembering how William had barred her entry to Misthold. "You must be joyous," she went on instead. "You stand to inherit a fortune. Your husband has remembered you."

"Don't talk like this," Nell pleaded, dropping her hand from Rena's face. "Tell me your thoughts."

Rena stood in a rush. She couldn't speak. There were too many thoughts, all of them beating like wings inside her mind. "So, this is how it's to be?" Her voice was uncommonly vacant. "From the grave, he sells me off to the highest bidder."

Nell's eyes went wide as she clambered to her feet. "No. It wouldn't have been like that. Alistair loved his family. He loved you."

Rena hated that she was already beginning to doubt that. "Who would marry me except to get the property?" she challenged with a derisive laugh. "Do you think he would be a good man, who would ignore my position to inherit a fortune?"

"And do you think Alistair would have married you off to a bad man?" Nell touched her cheek, a careful gesture. "Do you think I would?"

"I do not wish to be married off at all!" Rena had never yelled at Nell, but her voice bounced off the walls. Hearing the sound of her own ire, Rena broke her eyes from Nell's and shrunk away, feeling smaller by the moment.

When Nell spoke again, she somehow managed to speak reasonably. "Has it not occurred to you that he wanted to make sure you were provided for? Edric was already dead. Alistair knew if you followed me to England, as you said you might, there would be nothing for you here. He wanted to make sure we were both taken care of. He made that possible as best he could."

"Did you miss the fine print?" Rena challenged. "A Fairfax."

"Alistair was very close to his mother." Nell's voice was turning more defensive. "It never set well with him that her family had written her off. He is trying to make that right."

"So you want me to remarry." Though Rena's words were quieter, she still spoke through clenched teeth. "Like the will says. Don't you?"

Nell shook her head. "I don't want you to remember Alistair like this."

Nell hadn't answered Rena's question. Still, Rena considered the few memories she had of her father-in-law. He'd cut in once while Edric was trying to teach her a particular dance, after teasing his son for fumbling feet and an awkward rhythm, although Edric certainly had neither. He had taught her chess and bought her books so she might feel more at home.

He had always called her *daughter*.

But he was also a politician, a man with enough reach and influence to secure a comfortable position in India. He had collected Indian artifacts, positioned them throughout his home as if tangling his world with the broader strokes of another. He was a self-proclaimed nationalist who perked up in his chair whenever he saw his son's imperial red coat. He had always been kind to Rena, true, but he also spoke of the "savages" behind the mutiny. Rena had thought he despised the men for killing women and children, as anyone might, but what if he meant *savages* because of their skin?

"He loved you," Nell said again, more gently, and Rena wanted to believe her. But what if it wasn't love? What if Rena had been nothing more than a curious artifact scooped out of the sand by his son?

"He loved chess," Rena remembered out loud. "And he was always better at it than most. Am I to be his final chess piece?"

"Rena, please. Slow down for a minute. Let's think."

Rena closed her eyes and remembered standing on her father's terrace, watching the red-clad soldiers pass through town. They'd had their orders, always taking, taking, taking.

Her people's land. Their art. Their customs.

Soldiers had already reordered her family's life, pressed her people beneath the imperial thumb, and now she was to be bartered off in exchange for a British fortune. Edric would have shouted at his father before allowing him to pen such a will. Edric had always been different, though. He had married Rena for love, but she realized it was not to be so again.

She shook her head, bitterness forcing its way up her throat like bile. "There is nothing to think about," she answered tautly, then nearly laughed with the wildness of despair. "The sun never sets on the British Empire."

CHAPTER 14

Rena wasn't sure where she was going as she left the cottage, but she moved quickly, passing through town without once meeting anyone's eyes. Twice that day she'd been swept aside by men who called her *daughter*, but she still couldn't decide which strike hurt the most. Past town, she followed the main road, which curved northward, toward the shoals, pressing onward for nearly thirty minutes.

As soon as she had arrived in England, Rena vowed to take care of Nell, and she'd meant those words. She had not so soon forgotten what it was like to watch Nell starve in the back closet of the Gilded Crown, sleeping amid the mold and rotting produce. The woman's hands had turned knobby and somehow older during those weeks, and Rena promised she would never watch the woman starve again.

Still, she imagined Thomas finding out about the estate, how it would be for her if such a man brought her into his house, into his bed, just to get his hands on Alistair's estate, and her stomach turned.

She quickened her steps, breathing heavily through the threat of tears. What wouldn't she give, she wondered, if only to enter her father's house again, to walk over the smooth tiled floor, to see her airy chamber as it had been when she was still a simpler version of herself? Everything felt simpler in India. But then her thoughts turned again toward Nell and nearly gentled—there was an extraordinary dress, she remembered, still folded in a box beneath their bed, purchased with Nell's wedding ring. It was a piece of Rena's home, her life in India, bought at a startling cost. What would Rena give to do the same for Nell, if not more?

Part of Rena already knew the answer.

"Careful!" Stunned by the harsh command, Rena came to a jarring stop and gaped up at Lord Barric, who sat astride his horse, hands tight on the reins as he halted the beast two short paces before her. Slushy gravel ground beneath Samson's thumping hooves, spattering her skirts with dappled flecks like paint. Still, Rena could not bring herself to move aside or feel the least bit afraid of being trampled.

As soon as Barric looked at her, he sensed something wrong in her eyes and dismounted. "Mrs. Hawley?"

She wanted to tell him everything. She wanted to bury her face in his coat, to be held. She wanted someone to know her father had cast her off, just so she wouldn't have to sit in this emptiness alone. Barric placed a hand on her arm as if he could sense she needed steadying.

"What is it? What's wrong?"

She almost told him there was an entire fortune bearing down on her shoulders, and if someone stole her away, they could have it or else she would surely drown beneath its weight. The words were there, on her tongue. But then their last conversation whispered in the back of her mind, and she could not hear her own thoughts above it:

"She's nothing," his uncle had said.

"Beneath me," Barric had agreed, *"a wretched beggar."*

Finally, she looked at him. "I need you to take me somewhere."

He shuffled back as if surprised by her sudden request. "Of course. Where is it you are needing to go?"

"Hawthorn Glen," she told him, and was impressed when Lord Barric didn't so much as flinch at the demand. She wasn't exactly sure what she was doing, what she hoped to accomplish by this. Her wish to see the estate was probably unsurprising, in its own way, perhaps inevitable. If she was to be married off as a transaction—if she really was nothing more than a chess piece—then she might as well see the estate at least once while she was still a free woman.

But she was confused as to why she had asked Lord Barric to take her there. It hadn't escaped her mind, of course, that he was a Fairfax, and perhaps the only one she could trust not to use her if he found out about the will. She was either punishing him, she realized, for what happened at the party, or else she was torturing herself. He was likely the one man in Abbotsville who would never lose his senses enough to do the honorable thing by marrying her; he was also the only one she might consider if she didn't already know it was impossible.

Stay away, William had told her. It was a simple warning, and fair, so why couldn't she listen?

Dropping her gaze, Rena waited for Lord Barric to refuse her request, for surely he would. To carry her off, alone, to an abandoned estate was at the height of impropriety.

But he didn't refuse.

He swept forward, grabbed her about the waist, and hoisted her at once into the saddle. Rena gasped as Samson whinnied and stomped beneath her foreign weight, but then Barric vaulted up behind her and muttered at Samson to hush.

Rena took a moment to straighten the folds of her cloak, covering her legs as best she could to brace herself against the wind. Without warning, one of Barric's arms circled her waist, holding her tightly against him as his other hand took hold of the reins. "You'll want to hold on," he murmured against her hair. "Wouldn't want you unsaddled again, now would we?"

Curling forward, she closed her eyes and clenched the saddle just as Samson took off at a sprint.

Though vacant, Hawthorn Glen was somehow less gloomy than Misthold Manor, with wide blue shutters spanning the length of the building and a swooping balcony up top. Along the edge of the building was an overgrown garden, filled with briars. Someday spring would breathe the brush ablaze with color in a way only Edric, Alistair, and Nell had seen.

Barric pulled back hard on the reins, bringing Samson to a clattering stop along the gravel drive. For a moment, neither of them moved. Barric's hands were still on the reins, unnervingly close to her stomach. Rena angled her head back to read his expression, but he withdrew his arms from her at once, slid down from Samson, and reached up to help her dismount.

Rena felt slightly dizzy even after she gained her footing, as if she was still racing across the heath on Samson's back. Not yet ready to meet Lord Barric's gaze, she turned from him and stepped beyond the reach of his hands.

She studied every detail that made up Hawthorn Glen. There were massive stone steps and imposing statues, mazelike hedgerows, and a sprawling terrace ornamented with a fountain that had been several years dry. Rena craned her neck as she studied each stone, shuttered window, and overgrown vine.

Would someone really take her, she wondered, if it meant inheriting such a property?

Barric cleared his throat behind her. She turned, strangely startled by the sight of him standing in Edric's gravel drive. He still loosely held Samson's reins in his hand as he looked over her shoulder, silently assessing the building. Was he impressed?

"Thank you for bringing me here." She knew she ought to ask him to leave. She'd been unfair to them both by bringing him here. But might he be willing to marry her if it meant securing another estate? She didn't want to know the answer. She didn't want to see the derision in his eyes when she told him of Alistair's will, or, worse, repulsion.

And what if he *did* accept? Could she ever know for sure that he didn't despise her, that he hadn't married a pauper just to secure a prize like the Hawthorn Glen estate?

Barric misread her anxiety and stepped closer. "Do you wish for me to come with you?"

"No," she said and dropped her eyes in shame. She could not tell him about the will, could not guarantee he would not use it against her. "I would rather go on alone from here."

He nodded but didn't move. Then he winced and met her eyes. "I don't want to leave you here on your own."

She was oddly touched by the concern in his voice, the uncharacteristic loss as he shifted Samson's reins from one hand into the other. "Will you wait for me, then?" She attempted a reassuring smile. "I won't be long."

His expression eased at the question, and he bowed slightly to signify he would wait.

Leaving Lord Barric behind her, Rena wandered around the front of the building, her eyes flitting from window to window, attempting to see the halls inside and guess which window might have led to Edric's room.

As she turned a corner, circling toward the back of the building, she found it. Or at least she thought she did. A wide oak tree had grown alongside the stone wall, its jutting boughs nearly reaching a second-story window. In India, Edric coaxed Rena from her own window, and she followed him, her pulse high in her throat. Now she could so clearly picture her mischievous husband, a younger Edric, lifting that windowpane with practiced care. She could imagine him crawling out onto a tree limb and lowering himself, effortlessly, to the ground. It made sense to her. It fit.

She wandered the property, inspecting each detail, trying to puzzle out who Edric had been here. She flexed her fingers as if willing them to be something that could cling.

"Blessed are the poor in spirit: for theirs is the kingdom of heaven." From the warm stone chapel, the parson's words drifted back to her,

carried on the steady wind of many mornings ago.

Rena swayed, lowering herself to a bench. She did not want to remember. She did not want to care. *"Blessed are they that mourn,"* the parson had said, *"for they shall be comforted."* Comforted. Rena bent at the waist and pressed her hands tightly against her eyes. She wanted to shrink from the memory, but the words blew over her like dust. *"Blessed are they which do hunger and thirst after righteousness: for they shall be filled. . . . Blessed are the pure in heart: for they shall see God."*

She dropped her hands and stared at them as she thought through everything, piecing together all the words and prayers she'd heard despite herself. *"And we have known and believed the love that God hath to us. God is love; and he that dwelleth in love dwelleth in God, and God in him."* The parson had spoken those words just that Sunday. For Rena, the reading had been an eerie echo of Edric's missionary friend, who had risked a great deal to marry them in secret—their hands, their very lives, were joined together by the same heavy words spoken from the same thick black book.

But those words meant something, didn't they? They'd followed her all this time, returned to her, unbidden, in moments of distress. They mattered.

God dwelled within her. Could that really be true? How could she ever know for certain that such a God loved her?

Rena stood from the bench and circled back to the front of the house, realizing the air had turned colder in the few hours since she'd left the cottage. Barric must have seen her coming from a ways off, for he was already sitting astride Samson, ambling up the drive to meet her halfway. When at last she came near enough, his eyes searched hers.

"Are you all right?" he asked, and lowered a gloved hand to help her up.

She nodded and placed her hand in his. His grip was tight as he hoisted her up in front of him. He must have felt her trembling, for he banded both arms around her from behind, pulling her back snugly against the warmth of his chest.

"Shall I take you home?" The words rumbled against her from behind.

"No," she said, still staring down at her hands. "Please, take me to the church."

He was silent a moment, and his arms settled more loosely against her. "Did you find what you were looking for?"

"I don't know what I was looking for." But she was suddenly afraid this wasn't true. Maybe she only feared finding what she couldn't bear to seek. The warmth of Barric's arms around her was beginning to feel too familiar.

Barric clicked his teeth to cue Samson, then rode at a rapid pace the whole way back. Rena closed her eyes as they passed the bit of road where his horse had nearly trampled her just a few hours before. Had something changed since then? She knew something had, but she feared it was only within herself.

He steered Samson around the edge of his property, then cut up along the back of town. He was not yet to the main road when Rena set her fingers on his arm. He slowed the beast, leaning his head down closer to accommodate her question over the rhythmic thump of Samson's hooves. "Perhaps I ought to walk from here?" she suggested, craning her neck so her voice would reach his ear. "In case people see."

Though usually he claimed not to care what people did or did not see, he nodded and pulled Samson to a halt. She waited until she was safely on her feet to thank him. "I'm grateful to you, Lord Barric." Grateful, especially, that he hadn't asked her more questions. Perhaps he already knew the answers.

He nodded and gripped the reins more tightly, as though preparing to ride off, but then he met her eyes instead.

"There are at least a hundred things you aren't saying to me, Mrs. Hawley."

His voice wasn't hard, exactly, not accusatory. Curious, perhaps. Commanding.

"There are at least a hundred things you aren't ready to hear, Lord Barric."

A smile neared his lips, followed by a challenging nod. "Perhaps," he agreed, swinging his gaze back to the road. "For now."

Then he galloped off, leaving Rena to walk the rest of the way to the church alone. People in the streets watched her approach, but she didn't mark any of them as she pushed through the wide oaken door and stepped up into the cool stone sanctuary.

"Hello?" Her voice echoed off the buttressed ceiling as if she'd merely answered herself.

She waited, walked the length of several pews, then called again. "Parson Richardson?"

Seconds later the parson emerged through the sacristy door with a book in hand. He approached her with footsteps that thudded loftily.

Later Rena realized the parson did not seem at all surprised to find her there, nor did he ask her if something was the matter. He merely nodded, as if he already knew exactly what she would ask of him, and calmly invited her to be seated.

When Rena returned home, it was dark, and Nell was sitting at the table with a cup of untouched tea, its steam already dwindling from neglect. Chin propped on her hand, the woman stared vacantly at her husband's will. Her eyes were flat and distant, as if she had already committed the words to memory and was now floundering beneath their import.

As soon as Nell spotted Rena by the door, she startled up from her chair, nearly spilling her tea. "I was so worried," she half cried, crossing the room to take Rena's hands in hers. "I am so sorry, Rena. What you must be feeling, it's unimaginable. I know you are angry with Alistair, maybe even with me, but his will—"

"I was baptized today."

At Rena's quiet interruption, Nell's expression opened, slowly, into a look of confusion, then of delight, as if each emotion was unfolding into the other. Rena knew she ought to explain, for there were still a million unspoken words hovering in the space between them, but she could barely manage more than a trembling sigh.

As if sensing Rena's struggle, Nell lurched forward, taking Rena's face between her hands. "My child," she murmured, "this is glorious news. I pray God will strengthen you always, and keep you steadfast in His church."

If she was honest with herself, Rena still wasn't sure what had led her to the church in the first place, or why she asked such an unexpected favor of the parson. Hours before, she'd wished to cleave her grief into smaller parts, into dust, just so it might at last fit in her hands. But then the parson's words came back to her, and snatches of prayers, and the remembrance of a crucifix she'd tried so hard not to see. . .

Rena still worried she'd made a mistake in going to the parson, but she also knew doing so had changed something within her, like diving into a deep pool with no way out. For hours the parson listened as she spoke to him of Edric's death, of Sir Alistair's will, of the letter she finally received from her father. She told him she feared the feelings she harbored for Lord Barric, and feared his feelings even more. And in return he told her stories of prodigal children, of loss and of great sacrifice, of joy that comes with the morning. And he had finally given Rena the answer to her most gnawing question.

"*Their eyes will not be forever closed,*" he promised, and he meant it. "*Jesus lives,*" the parson said. "*And all who are baptized into Jesus—their eyes are opened with His."*

And though Rena still had more questions than answers, though she was still uncertain of what she had done, or why, she believed him.

When Rena finally spoke again, her voice was hushed. "I would marry again." She took Nell's hand. "For you. I would marry long before I would ever again watch you starve. I promise."

Nell sighed. "Rena." She rubbed at her eyes. "We should not make any decisions today. Let us rest for now and face these questions later." She folded the will gingerly, then placed it in the cabinet behind her. "For now, we should both sleep."

Rena did not feel like she could sleep. She felt like her bones were stretching, wider, taller, reaching to get out of her skin. She thought again of her father's letter and wondered what he would say if she wrote to tell him she'd been baptized. Would his remnant kindness fade entirely? Would her family cease their prayers?

She watched Nell begin the usual nightly bustle. Clearing her teacup from the table, then dressing for bed, then looping her silver hair into a long, thick braid. As the older woman sat at the table and prayed, Rena had the oddest feeling she ought to sit and pray as well, but she didn't. Even after everything that had happened, she still couldn't. Everything Rena had ever counted as certain in her life had crumbled, and she could not bear for it to be the same with her prayers.

Barric's uncle sent two more bottles of wine, each vintage worth a small fortune. Barric had already drunk both bottles to the bottom and found he rather liked the taste of his uncle's penance. Still, he couldn't banish the niggling concern that the bottles were more than just an apology.

Standing on his outer terrace, Barric stared pensively at the most recent empty bottle, his fingers curled around the weathered seal on the bottle's shoulder. He'd not heard anything else about the Hawley estate, but he worried his uncle knew more about the matter than he had revealed. He had spent many hours recalling his uncle's story, how he and his father traveled the road to the glen and admired the property even in their youth.

His uncle was not usually a sentimental man. He was a drinker, a man fluent in cursing.

And yet much of his drinking and cursing had come about after Barric's father died. Barric set the bottle down on the rail. He worried the wine was extra incentive to help Uncle George get his hands on Hawthorn Glen. Beneath the tug of family allegiance, Barric almost wanted to help him, but he knew, somehow, it would destroy him if he tried.

When Charlie came to stand beside him on the terrace, Barric took one look at the cigars in his brother's hand and shook his head. "I'm in no mood," he warned him.

Charlie held a cigar out to Barric, dangling it beneath his nose despite the dismissal. "Come," he said grimly. "Someone ought to help me celebrate the birth of my son."

Reflexively, Barric's hand came up and closed around the end of the cigar.

"Celeste has had the child, then."

In answer, Charlie struck a match on the terrace rail. As the tobacco kindled, Barric detected a rich tangle of walnuts and burning moss, as if the trees themselves had been lit on fire. Barric waited for Charlie to puff a few times at his cigar before he spoke again. "When did you find out?"

"Today." Charlie shrugged, but the gesture was sharp, not at all as careless as he wanted it to appear. "Apparently, he was born several months ago. She thought I ought to know."

When Charlie lit the second match, Barric held his own cigar at an angle, watching as the tobacco began to curl beneath the flame. "A boy," he remarked, bringing the cigar at last to his lips. "And so, the world ushers in the next generation of Fairfax."

"Half Fairfax," Charlie corrected, staring up at the sky as he blew a thin line of smoke from his mouth. "If Celeste ever deigns to tell him my name."

"What else did she say in her letter?"

"She thanked me for the money," Charlie narrated, his words clipped. "She said as long as I choose to send it, she will use it, but I am under no obligation. She said I'm free of her and the child."

Charlie's profile was illuminated faintly by the light of his own cigar, his lips pressed tight as he stared out at the trees. "I wonder," Barric mused, trying to lighten Charlie's anguish, "if he'll grow up to be anything like his father."

Charlie stabbed his cigar toward Barric as if the same thought had crossed his mind. "He'd better not."

Sighing, Barric scuffed his shoe along the terrace tile. "Well, what has she named the little scamp?"

"Philippe."

It was strange to hear the baby's name spoken in his brother's familiar voice. Charlie seemed to be living two lives simultaneously—one spent on Barric's terrace, cigar in hand, the other galloping away from him in Paris, always out of reach.

"It's a good name," he admitted.

"Yes, almost as good a name as *Uncle Jack*."

"Ah, I hadn't thought of that." Barric slid a look at his brother as he considered. "Do you think I would be as imposing to him as Uncle George was to us?"

"*Twice* as imposing," Charlie corrected with a half grin. He glanced down at the cigar in his hand, tilted it as he knocked a few ashes to the ground. "Remember when we stole cigars from Uncle's office?"

Barric fell just short of a smile himself. "Of course. You, I believe, were sick for two days."

"He never did tell Father about it."

"Father knew enough."

Charlie slipped into silence, briefly considering his cigar. "Do you ever wish he was here to tell us what's to be done?"

"I make a point to always know what's to be done." Barric's tone was made of iron, carefully constructed, but his eyes traveled down to the valley despite himself, where a thin curl of smoke rose from the cottage behind William's house, where lights glowed like specks in every narrow window.

Charlie followed his gaze. "Have you heard anything else about the will?"

"Nothing," Barric answered. He did not mention he had ridden with Rena out to Hawthorn Glen. That particular encounter felt strangely private. Though Rena had shared very little with him on their ride to the Glen, he could not shake the feeling that she had crossed some inward line, perhaps placed herself more within his reach.

"Are you going to help him get the estate?"

"I haven't decided."

A quick puff of smoke. "And what if Uncle gets the property and then gives it to Thomas? You know how Thomas would lord it over her."

Barric's eyes narrowed. "Everyone is lording something over her," he said, his voice like gravel in his throat.

"Including you?" When Barric didn't respond, Charlie tried a different track. "Do you think she knows there's something amiss with the will?"

Barric gripped the railing as he remembered the way she'd drifted like a wraith around Hawthorn Glen, her eyes that gloomy shade of sorrow. She claimed she didn't know what she'd been looking for, but something had compelled her there. "As if she'd tell me," he muttered.

Charlie's expression sharpened. "You're *angry* with her."

More than anything, Barric wanted to be angry with her. It would have made matters much simpler. But he had held her in his arms as he'd ridden her up to the Glen, and he couldn't lie to himself. They were already rumored lovers, even more so after his Christmas party. It was the one rumor Barric sometimes wished were true, though part of him knew he wanted more of her than that.

Charlie was still watching him, his faint smirk the only reminder that Barric had not answered his brother's question. "What would I have to be angry about?"

"There are many kinds of anger," Charlie replied but didn't press further. "What did Uncle George have to say about her?"

Barric let out a tight breath. "I don't wish to talk about Uncle George."

Charlie tipped his head toward the empty bottle balanced on the rail. Barric had nearly forgotten it was there. "You wish only to drink his wine?"

"I told you I'd stay away from her, and that's the end of it." It was a promise that rang hollower with each passing day.

Charlie puffed at his cigar and shook his head. "With women," he remarked, "there's never an end."

CHAPTER 15

Barric rode through town on his way to his uncle's house to bring him the news of Charlie's unfortunate heir. Charlie said he had no wish to confide any of his affairs to Uncle George, but Barric couldn't hide this from him. Though Uncle George was a scoundrel, he still deserved to know his own brother would have been a grandfather, had he lived to see the day.

"Good morning, Lord Barric." Barric glanced down and found Parson Richardson crossing the road in front of him, a parcel of books tucked beneath his arm.

"Morning," Barric replied, and was about to press onward but found himself pulling on the reins instead. He remembered Rena asking him to take her to the church and suddenly wondered what she had spoken about with the parson.

Of course, it could have been something worshipful, something pious. Over the past few months, Barric had glimpsed Rena's prayerful eyes in church, but he'd only very recently seen her join her mother-in-law at the communion rail. Still, he wondered. Had she spoken to the parson of Edric that day? Had she spoken about the will? Had she spoken of *him*?

As Barric dismounted, the parson turned, faintly surprised to find Barric leading his horse toward him.

"I haven't spoken with you since Christmas," the parson remarked. "I trust you have been well."

"Business fares well," Barric answered distractedly.

The parson angled his head, his eyes keen as he prodded. "Have you stopped to speak with me about business, then, Lord Barric?"

Barric sighed and leveled him with a critical stare. "No doubt you have heard the rumors."

"I have heard many rumors," the parson agreed, motioning for them to walk down the road so as not to draw attention to their conversation. "I put good trust in you that none are true."

Not yet, Barric thought grimly. But if Rena ever confessed to returning his feelings, could he still trust himself to remain an honorable man? He strode beside the parson silently. "What should I do to put an end to all of this?" he asked at last.

"There are only so many options," the parson mused, then eyed Barric sideways. "You are a sharp man. Surely you have considered them all."

"My brother tells me to stay away from her," Barric admitted. "My steward feels the same."

"I see. And now you are hoping I will give you similar counsel."

Barric did not mention what his uncle suggested: that he take her on as a mistress, as many men in his station might have done when enthralled with a woman beneath his class. That Barric had even considered this in moments of weakness disturbed him. "I wish to honor my father," Barric confessed. "His memory, his estate, his title—all are forfeit if I cannot dispel the rumors."

"And what do you think your father would have had you do?"

Barric considered. Perhaps he would have told him not to have gotten into this mess in the first place. Yes, if Barric could wind back time to their first night on the road, might he not have given her money, instead, and sent her well on her way?

"We cannot take suggestions from the dead," Barric said, shaking his head at the parson. "What would *you* have me do?"

"Nothing I think you are ready to consider."

"Tell me."

The parson met his eyes. "Everyone in your world will tell you to be done with Mrs. Hawley. Send her away or stay away or use her as you'd like. But your title means nothing, your money and your influence are *already* forfeit, if you don't do everything in your power to take care of her."

"I gave her food," Barric said defensively. "I gave her shelter."

"Yes, and everyone believes she has already been to your bed."

Barric faltered, shocked to hear the parson speak so plainly about such a delicate subject.

"What will happen to her if you marry someone else?" the parson pressed before Barric could offer a rebuttal. "Things could not continue as they are. But she is a ruined woman, Barric, and will live the rest of her life as your rumored mistress."

"What, would you have me marry the girl?" Barric nearly laughed outright, though the suggestion made him unaccountably defensive, nearly angry. The rumors irritated him now, unfounded though they were. If he ever lost his mind long enough to speak vows to her, his entire reputation would be a pile of ash.

"You cannot support her as you do forever," the parson insisted. "As you well know, something must change."

"So, I am to be shackled in marriage because I once helped an unfortunate widow?" Barric dipped an eyebrow at the parson. "I will not make the same mistake again, I assure you."

"You may find, when things become clearer, that sarcasm will not serve you quite so well as it does now."

"I am grateful for your counsel," Barric said, tipping his head dismissively. "I will ponder what you have said."

The truth, however, was that Barric had no interest whatsoever in the parson's counsel. Had he but told him to send her away or keep his distance, he might have walked away less cynical. But to marry her would be to cast off society, like his great-aunt had done when she'd rushed off with Maxwell Hawley. To do the same, so willingly, would bring mockery down upon his father's legacy.

Still, he couldn't help thinking of Rena's half-joking suspicion, all those months ago, that perhaps there was a Hawley curse which brought about imprudent marriages. Such was not the case for Lord Barric, for he had sworn long ago never to marry half as foolishly as his great-aunt had. But this did not mean he couldn't cast off prayers for guidance and pull her into his arms anyway. Yes, perhaps he'd curse *himself*, he mused—wincing in shame even as the thought came to him—if it meant slanting his lips over hers, just once.

Rena stepped down from the chapel steps amid the usual chatter of morning parishioners. As a rule, she and Nell rarely lingered long after services. Rena was too reserved, and Nell too proud, for either of them to long endure the probing glances of those who mingled in the yard.

They bid their usual good mornings to the parson as they stepped onto the sunlit path that skirted the cemetery. Though the sun was a welcome change, there was still a bite in the air. Winter was hanging to them all by its claws.

As they walked, Rena spent their silence as she had, regrettably, spent much of the service—toiling over Sir Alistair's will. Nell had not mentioned the will or its terms since the night they had fought, but neither woman had forgotten its implications. Like the winter air, it hovered. It followed. It whispered.

On a whim of utmost fatigue, Rena had considered confiding all in Lord Barric. She no longer had Alice as a confidant, and she had kept her distance even from William after their last exchange. Still, she could not bear to tell Barric of the will. She knew—or at least thought—she could trust him, but she also could not erase the image of him standing with Samson beneath Hawthorn Glen's front gate, as if he were already master of its halls.

No, she could not tell him. She was too afraid of what he might say. Or of what he might not say.

Nell hummed a reprisal of one of the morning hymns, oblivious to Rena's toiling, or perhaps trying to soothe it. Over this soft din, Rena heard the sound of shuffling footsteps close behind them. Her fingers tightening on Nell's arm, Rena turned at the hip to see who was following.

Alice froze midstep. Lowering her eyes, she fiddled briefly with the front of her blue pelisse, as if trying to smooth out a crease Rena could not see.

Rena was not sure what to expect from this encounter, and so she deferred, a bit defensively, back to a standard greeting. "Good morning, Miss Wilmot."

"Mrs. Hawley," Alice murmured. Her gaze flicked from Rena to Nell and back again. "I wonder if I might walk with you."

Rena looked uneasily at Nell, but the older woman had already disentangled her arm from Rena's and stepped back. "You two go on without me. I just remembered I need to ask the parson about donations for the spring festival."

Rena highly doubted Nell had any such questions about any such festival, but she allowed the woman her kindly bluff. With a farewell smile, Nell lifted her skirt off her shoes and swept away, leaving Rena and Alice to avoid each other's eyes and reimagine past conversations. When Alice did not speak at once, Rena gestured to the road. "You said you wished to walk?" she asked, trying to help them along.

"Oh yes," Alice breathed, and fell in step beside her. It did not take long for Alice to find her voice. "I was a wretch to you on Christmas," she blurted almost at once. "I wonder that you do not hate me."

"You spoke truly enough," Rena said. "I should have expected no less than what I encountered at Lord Barric's party."

"No." Alice shook her head. "What I said to you was unforgivable.

I have hated myself a thousand times for every word I spoke to you in anger. Lord Barric *cares* for you. Everyone can see it. He looks at you in a way I have always hoped he might look at me, but it isn't to be so."

Rena knew those words were not as unfounded as she once might have thought. She remembered the feel of Barric's fingers as they'd wrapped around her ribs to hoist her up in Samson's saddle, the warmth of his breath against her hair as he rode her all the way to Hawthorn just because she had needed him to. She remembered the way he had looked at her, so concerned as she'd drifted about the property. Perhaps it was foolish to deny his regard. Or perhaps more foolish to hope on it. "I am sorry for causing you pain," Rena said in a smaller voice than before. "I promise there is nothing between Lord Barric and myself."

Alice winced. "But should there ever be. . ."

Rena tried to interject that such would never be the case, but Alice grabbed ahold of her hand and gave it a silencing squeeze. "No, listen. Please. I will marry someone someday. It won't be Lord Barric or any other earl. But someday there will be a kindly and handsome man who thinks I am kind as well, who thinks I am pretty and looks at me the way Barric looks at you. And I will make our home, and we will have a family, and by then Lord Barric will have faded." She paused, bit her lip. "But, listen to me, Rena. If Lord Barric makes you an offer, you must accept it."

Rena closed her eyes and fought off a grimace. "Alice," she said in gentle reprimand.

Alice smiled sheepishly at Rena's slip, evidently delighted to be called again by her Christian name. "Promise me you will consider it," she implored. "That you will consider him, if it comes to that. For what will happen to you five years from now? Or ten?"

"I do not wish to entangle myself with an earl just because of what will happen five years from now."

They came to a bend in the road, and Alice slowed as the road steepened slightly. "You have nothing," she said softly. "Is it so wrong to wish for something? To wish for everything?"

Alice knew more than most about the cost of wishing for everything.

"Your brother gave me contrary advice," Rena noted dryly.

Alice pulled a face. "That's because my brother *is* contrary. Told you to stay away from him for your own good, did he? Yes, well, I've tried that for years, and it's never done me any good."

Rena fought the urge to bury her face in her hands. Sir Alistair's will had once filled her with horror. She had been reminded, unpleasantly, of the girls who worked at the Gilded Crown, how desperation whispered at them to reach into rich men's pockets.

Yet again, Sir Alistair's intentions had been well-meaning. He had sought to fix an age-old rift between two families, to ensure his mother's good name, once tarnished, was joined at long last with those of her own relations. He wanted Nell and Rena to be welcomed back into his family and had made it possible for them both to be taken care of. But if she married under the terms of the will, could she ever know for sure her husband loved her, or cared for her as a person? Could she ever know she wasn't merely money in his pocket, or he in hers? When Lord Barric had stood in front of Hawthorn Glen, she hadn't missed the way his eyes had shrewdly surveyed the estate as any titled man might, silently assessing its worth and merit with a calculating expression. She could not bear for him to look at *her* like that, could not stand for him to weigh her against such a property, and what if she was shown to be lacking?

Alice touched her arm. Rena startled, realizing her thoughts had again turned to Lord Barric. As Alice searched her eyes, Rena considered divulging the entire business of the will, but she drew up short within herself. There was no need to worry Alice needlessly over a legal proviso which might never come into effect.

"I am afraid my husband is fading," she confided instead, a startlingly honest admission. "I used to think of him at every moment, and then every few hours. Now I reach for him sometimes in the night, inwardly, but I cannot find him."

Alice's eyes widened. "But that is because he is not here."

He is with God, Rena finished silently, and while it made her feel better, it also made her feel worse. Rena no longer knew how to grieve. It had been several months since Prince Albert had died, and Queen Victoria had removed herself entirely from society, mourning in a way some feared was madness. Too grieved to attend the funeral, she was now rumored to keep the prince consort's room entirely unchanged, ordering servants to bring fresh water, daily, to her husband's chamber, as if he had never died and still needed to shave each morning.

Rena had felt like that once, grieving beyond her own reason. She had fasted and bowed low on her bedroom floor in her parents' home, begging for release from her own pain. She had crawled through icy rain and mud to find Edric's lost ring, risking death of the cold and striking at Lord Barric when he'd pulled her from her task. Was it disloyal to Edric's memory for her not to grieve so deeply now? Was he fading or was she healing? Would Edric hate her, she wondered, if he knew she had found comfort in the warmth of another man's arms?

Rena ran a hand over her face. "I wish I could know what he would have me do."

She knew, of course, Edric would have bellowed at his father had he known what he intended with the new will. But what of sleeping in alleys? What of Rena's nightmares? What of being a beggar to an earl instead of a wife to a husband? Edric would have bellowed over those things too; nor would he have wanted her to carry on her days in the wildness of uncontrollable grief.

Alice spoke carefully. "I did not know your husband, but I think I know what he'd want. He'd want you to live, Rena."

Rena swallowed the truth of that statement as they came at last to the final stretch of road that led to the Wilmots' cottage. As Rena fiddled with the gate, she paused with her hand on the latch. "The book you gave me for Christmas," she said in a tucked-away voice, "I never did thank you for it."

Alice studied her hands again, twisted her knuckles lightly around each other. "I have hoped it might be enough for you to forgive me."

At the questioning lilt in her dear friend's voice, Rena swept forward and kissed her lightly on the cheek.

Rena was awakened by a swarm of disconnected voices passing by her window. She lay there for a moment, eyes open, holding her breath until the voices were met by others in the distance, then echoed by loud shouts and urgent hollers. Careful not to disturb Nell, Rena slid out of bed, catching up her shawl and slinging it about her shoulders as she jerked open the door.

Three men were tearing past the fence as she stepped outside, their torches lit and held high above them.

"What is it?" Rena cried out, running along the fence so they wouldn't have to slow their steps to answer. "What's happened?"

"Fire!" one of the men shouted, stumbling to a halt long enough to heave out the words. "One of the houses on the other side of Barric's property. If we don't stop it, it could burn the house beside."

The men didn't dare dally a moment longer but went pelting off into the darkness. Rena squinted her eyes toward the horizon, where an orange, writhing glow cast an eerie halo over the farthest tree line. Sleep was no longer an option, nor was waiting for further news.

Rushing back into the house, Rena shook Nell awake. "There's a fire," she explained, pulling on her shoes as Nell rubbed at her bleary eyes. "You stay here. I'm going to see if I might be able to help."

The church bells began tolling in the distance, summoning villagers to rise and assist. Nell sat up straight in bed and grabbed for Rena's hand. "Oh, but you must stay here," she protested. "Stay here where it is safe."

"No." Rena kissed Nell quickly on the forehead. "I must go where I am needed."

And so, clad in nothing but her nightdress, shoes, and shawl, Rena raced out into the midnight chill, her breath catching in her chest as it tasted the sharp air. She followed the voices and torches across the barren fields, toward the trees. Barric's manor still perched like a watchful beast above her, its dreary spires and slanted roof cast almost entirely in shadow.

She allowed the sounds of urgency to direct her steps through the woods until the faint glow was replaced with actual flames and the inferno became visible. Its heavy heat forced its way down her throat as a scattering of workers raced to battle the flames ahead of her, many of them hauling buckets from the creek that stretched behind the property. A little ways off, in a clearing, stood a young woman not much older than Rena, with two small children burrowed against her skirt. The woman's tears fell silently as she watched the walls of her home char and crumble.

Rena knew how it felt to watch her own world burn, to stare in horror, able to do nothing but stand. The flames still licked at Rena's skin sometimes if she let them. The memory of her husband as his emaciated form was lowered beneath a stone of gray, or the feeling of her father's hand as he begged her not to board the ship to England—she observed a similar helplessness in the way this woman ran her hand through her daughter's curls to soothe her. Even though the mother's eyes were flames themselves, she endured.

The people had now formed two lines, from the creek to the fire, passing buckets back and forth.

Rena sprang into action, racing toward the nearest line. "Let me help!" she pleaded. Several men were already in the water up to their thighs, filling buckets and tossing them to the line of workers. A bearded man whom she had seen many times in Barric's field nodded and made room, heaving a bucket into her arms.

The pail was frigid, with water tipping over the rusty rim and soaking her all the way down her belly, but she passed it to the lady beside her and turned for the next. Another pail was hurled at her, accompanied by a barely audible order to hurry. The air crackled around them, thick with heat, clouding Rena's head. Still, she obeyed, twisting back on her ankle as she took the next bucket and the next and the next. All the workers had melded, somehow, as part of the same apparatus. Rena did not mark any of the silhouetted workers at her side, not until a hand clamped tightly around her arm and pulled her out of the line.

"Mrs. Hawley," Lord Barric said. "You shouldn't be here."

Rena pulled back from his touch and accidentally sloshed water down her front. Like the other workers, Lord Barric had clearly sprung from bed to battle the flames. His jacket was gone, his waistcoat disheveled, only halfway buttoned. She stared for a moment at his shirtsleeves, the first reminder that she herself was still dressed for bed.

"But I wish to help," she argued, and handed her bucket, now half-empty, back into the line of workers beside her.

Sweat ran hard lines down the edge of Barric's face. "It's freezing out here. We have no need of you."

The dismissal stung, but only briefly. Though stiff with cold and trembling, she forced herself to speak rationally. "If everyone *else* is risking their death in the cold, my lord, why shouldn't I?"

"If you really wish to help," he urged in a lower voice, drawing slightly nearer. "Go home and pray for rain."

The line of workers continued its relentless course beside them. Shouts were hurtled from person to person as they sought to salvage the ruin, but Rena felt useless, stagnant. She needed to help. She needed to move back in line.

That was when she heard it. An older woman in the other line hissed, rather indiscreetly, "Barric's too busy talking to his whore. . ."

Rena prayed that in the chaos Lord Barric hadn't heard, but then he closed his eyes and stepped back from her. *"Damn,"* he said, then turned and stalked away. At a greater distance, Rena heard him bark a string of angry orders at the men in the creek.

Forcing herself to forget the taste of that familiar, nasty word—*whore*—Rena pushed her way back in line, taking the first bucket passed to her from her left and handing it off to the outstretched hands already waiting to her right.

The rest of the night was a grueling race, and despite their best efforts, they faced the slow agony of a losing battle. Rena's limbs ached from the cold and exertion, her ears hollow drums in the wake of constant, pounding shouting. Still, the blaze leaped out of reach, arching back like a tempest of flame, now twisting dangerously close to the house beside.

The lines began to falter, to disperse. The pail dropped from Rena's exhausted hand and struck the ground with a clatter. She struggled to catch her breath, but her throat felt frozen shut, and the tears in her eyes fell tight on her skin. This time the hand that touched her was tentative, calming. When she looked up, William looked down at her.

"We did our best," he said, his pulse leaping wildly against his throat.

Fresh shouts signaled a jump in danger. Turning, Rena saw Lord Barric, his waistcoat now strewn aside as he clambered up a ladder—up, up toward the roof of the other house.

William let loose a ragged breath, shaking his head. "Ruddy fool's lost his mind."

With hardly a moment's pause, Barric leaped onto the sloped

roof, finding his footing quickly as he reached back down toward the ladder. Seeing what Barric intended, William swore, sprinting toward the ladder to help support it. Sparks rained down onto Barric from the blaze next door, and he angled his arm over his head as if to ward them off. Then, suddenly, someone from the top of the ladder handed him a bucket.

Not just someone—Charlie—who hollered at his brother as if they were invading hell itself. Flinching against the sparks as they hit his skin, Barric emptied the bucket his brother had tossed him, splashing a line of water halfway across the roof. Another bucket was handed to him, and another, all while the sparks fell like fiery starlight onto his skin.

Rena no longer knew what to do, how to help. Some of the other women were clustered tightly around her, their hands dug into the fronts of their gowns as they watched Barric rush to soak the roof. At moments, the sparks that landed seemed like they would surely catch, but he raced to drown them before they could jump to life. She heard a whole host of oaths from the ground, where men and women still scrambled to help in any way, however small.

At last William jumped up onto the roof beside Barric, then Charlie, the three of them lit by otherworldly red as they dashed about to prevent the worst from happening.

Rena's stomach lurched as the other house's roof finally caved, hurling a wall of flames closer to Barric's roof. Before Rena could hear another scream, she covered her eyes with her hands and prayed to God for mercy.

Over time the fire danced lower in the sky, then lower, bowing an arrogant farewell as Barric scrambled like a peasant to subdue it. With William and Charlie's help, he managed to save the roof of the second house, but the first one burned until all that was left was a mountain of smoking rubble.

With a somber expression, he made his way to his now homeless tenants. There was a weeping woman with two young children, an older daughter with dirty blond hair, and a father with a jaw clamped tight like stone. The family gaped at him, the children the barest bit afraid, no doubt awed by the thick sludge of sweat and ash on Barric's brow, or perhaps the blackened blisters that already pulled tightly at his skin.

He assured them that all would be well, that he would find them another place until they could rebuild, that they ought not to lose hope. He gave them the name of a smaller family who might take them in until they found something more permanent. They thanked him desperately and clutched his hand in gratitude, but his mind was too busy to mark their words, too distracted, his thoughts leaping faster and harder than the flames he had already battled.

The workers had already begun to scatter, returning home with downcast eyes and shoulders sunk low in defeat, and for all of Barric's reckless confidence, even he ached in ways his body wouldn't fully realize until morning. He left Charlie waiting by the ruins long enough to sink to the river's bank and drag a palm full of frigid water over his face, then his hair. He welcomed the cold sting of the water as he washed the ash from his skin and watched it swirl away into the creek.

Water still trailing down his shirt collar, Barric walked with Charlie back toward Misthold, their steps wearily slow but straight on course. But then, just ahead, Barric saw a slender shape moving in the distance, shadowed against a gnarl of trees, heading straight in the direction of William's house. Alone.

Charlie saw her at the same moment and shook his head. "Don't, Jack," he said in a weary voice. "Let her be."

But it didn't matter how many times Barric promised to let her be, to stay away from her, because she would always be standing there with those soulful eyes. It was time something was done about it.

Ignoring Charlie's warning, Barric strode to catch up with her. Several other people were milling ahead of her as they journeyed home, their voices bouncing through the trees, unrestrained. Not that it mattered. No one in all of Abbotsville was sleeping now.

Not wanting to be seen by passersby, Barric caught Rena's hand from behind, and she gasped as he pulled her behind a tree.

"Lord Barric!" She seemed unable to form another word, but was breathtaking even in her confusion. Strands of hair had escaped her long braid, and her shawl hung loose over one shoulder, revealing the nightgown beneath. Maybe it was the frenzy of the fire, the utter chaos of the night, the unreasonably late hour, but anything seemed possible. Barric might do anything, say anything he wanted, and it would all seem a dream to them, just like the fire and his foolhardy stunt on the roof.

His first instinct was to order her to leave his property, as he had hoped the parson might suggest when he'd spoken with him. He wanted to tell her to find help elsewhere, to rely on someone else's charity for a change. "*Go.*" He'd said the word once; he could say it again. But what kind of man would he be if he did? His eyes traced her face, and she shifted uncomfortably but didn't pull her arm from his grip.

"You said once that I could cast you off," he finally managed, watching the fear take hold of her eyes. "Ban you from my fields. Certainly it would make things easier if I did."

"Yes," she agreed brokenly. "I'm sure it would."

He considered his hand still curved around her wrist, reminded of how skeletal she'd been when he'd first met her, when dark hollows had greeted him from beneath a hungry set of mournful eyes. One word from him, and she'd flee. She had far too much pride to plead.

But then, again, he remembered the parson's warning. "*She is a ruined woman, Barric, and will live the rest of her life as your rumored mistress."*

Rena spoke when he would not. "You're casting me off, then?"

The despair in her voice crumbled his resolve. He lowered his head, his lips coming within an inch from hers. Breathing in her fear, he told himself to kiss her, quickly, before he could convince himself otherwise. But there were unshed tears in her eyes which made him hesitate. Was she thinking of Edric? he wondered.

His fingers tightened on her arm as he waited for one of those tears to fall, but still she did not break her eyes from his. The opportunity was too perfect, he told himself. No one could see them. No one would know.

If he were any other man, his lips would have already been on her. His uncle's words encouraged him on. *"Such dalliances are to be expected of a young man, especially one of your temper."*

Swearing at the press of his uncle's voice against his wavering conscience, Barric dropped his hands. Ash and soot still clung to his skin, and the raised welts pulled tight as he moved. Ashamed of his own selfishness, he stared briefly at a blister on his hand so he wouldn't have to meet her eyes.

"My lord?" Rena's voice was a mere half breath, laced with confusion. Barric glanced up in time to watch a tear finally slip its place and trace a silent path down her cheek.

"Forgive me," he said quietly, hating that he had hurt her again. "Go home. Sleep."

She seemed uncertain, her eyes darting toward the trees. There were hours of night left, and the darkness seemed poised to swallow them up. "Nell and I could pack our things," she finally offered. "And be gone in an instant."

Barric hesitated long enough to imagine what it would be like if she did as she said. William would come find Barric in his library.

She's gone, he would say, and Barric would follow him to the cottage, set a hand on the doorframe, and glance around the room. All would be bare, bed made, floors swept, nothing left of the women who had once lived there. And Barric knew exactly what he would do. He would swear under his breath and demand of William where they had gone. And when William told him he didn't know, that no one knew, Barric would rein his temper, saddle his horse, and go at once to find them.

Rena still awaited his reply, her face upturned, no trace left of the tear which had slipped her guard and sailed down her cheek. Barric knew there was a good chance she might run, and it had little to do with making things easier, nothing at all to do with the gossips or his uncle or her tattered reputation. No, if she ran, it would be to get away from *him*, from this teetering, almost-moment that seemed to follow them wherever they went.

A *poor, miserable bastard*, Charlie had called him, and he was usually right about such things. "Run if you wish," he said, but the words tasted like ash on his tongue.

Nell was perched by the window, half-asleep in her chair, when Rena returned to the cottage. Pausing in the door, Rena examined Nell's shuttered eyes and the book balanced between the lady's fingers, frowning as she realized Nell had been waiting up for her.

Though Rena closed the door as softly as she could, Nell shot up from the chair, startled from her reverie, and demanded, "The house?"

"Burned to rubble." Rena shuddered despite herself as she slung her shawl upon its usual peg.

Nell nodded as if she expected as much. "You must be exhausted."

"I don't think I could sleep for a hundred years," Rena admitted. She wanted to say more, but the rush of icy adrenaline still raced through her veins, a silent undercurrent tugging her off course. Her nightdress was wet, stiff with cold as she removed it, but her cheeks were hot.

Nell was extra quiet as she sank back into her chair, her hair falling over the chair back like a silver curtain. "Was Lord Barric there tonight?"

Rena pulled into a clean nightdress, which brushed welcome warmth against her skin. "Yes. He stopped the flames from spreading any further."

"Did he speak to you?"

Nell's question was like a net cast over Rena, trapping her in place. She half wondered if Nell could see the places on her skin where Barric had touched her, if all the words he'd breathed had gathered to her and followed her home. Disarmed by Nell's cautious tone, Rena shrugged dismissively. "He said very little."

Nell did not push against the lie, but Rena knew that if she did, her words would shatter like tested glass. Instead, Nell rubbed wearily at her eyes. "Have you told him about the will?"

"Lord Barric?" Rena feigned ignorance. "Why should I tell him anything about it?"

Nell's hand dropped flat on the table, and her voice turned suddenly hard. "If something were to happen to me, what is there to stop you from starving? From being cast out? From having absolutely nothing? What, except for that man's thin charity, keeps us from starving now?"

Rena shook her head, stalling. "I would do as I've always done. Whatever is necessary."

"Yes," Nell agreed. "Has it not occurred to you that this man might have it within his power to save us? If something happened to me, like Alistair, you would have no one."

"But Lord Barric already provides for us."

When Nell spoke, she sounded exasperated. "The will, Rena. I'm talking about the will. Lord Barric is a Fairfax. You know he is."

Rena had known this conversation was coming, perhaps longer than she had admitted to herself. "You mean for me to marry Lord Barric?" She shook her head, her voice strangled in her throat. "What would ever cloud that man's senses enough to enter into such a ridiculous marriage?"

"I would never have suggested it if I didn't already suspect his attachment to you."

Rena could not fake enough naïveté to disagree with what Nell had said. The way Lord Barric had held her that evening delivered a clear enough message, but she sometimes suspected she might as easily be ruined as saved at his hand.

Again, Rena looked to Nell. The woman had survived their last stint of starvation, even gained back some of her weight, but she was still frailer for it. New shadows hung beneath Nell's eyes, pulling at her aristocratic features and making them tired. Though Rena had promised to do anything for Nell, the vow had been made hastily, without having ever been tested in a life of sacrifice. But Rena was no longer a stranger to sacrifice. She knew exactly the cost, the weight, how heavy it felt against her chest. It was all she could do to draw breath beneath its weight, even now.

"You know I would do anything for you," Rena finally admitted, instantly frightened by her own willingness. "Are you ready to command me into an uncertain marriage, knowing I would obey, for you?"

"I would never ask it of you if I thought either of you were indifferent to the other." Nell paused meaningfully. "What really happened tonight. . .after the fire?"

Lord Barric had stood so close to Rena in the woods. She suspected he was vexed by his own regard for her—wanting what he couldn't have—and Rena was not young enough to deny the way he had made her feel in turn, like her heart was clawing up her throat, desperate to get out. Ashamed, she spun away from Nell. "I love your son," she insisted, voice firm.

"We both love Edric. I do not doubt that in the least."

"But you think he is so easily replaced?"

"There are many forms of love. The love you feel for Edric will always be sacred. Tell me you don't care for Lord Barric, and I will never bring him up again. But might he care enough for you to save us both?"

Rena could no longer shoulder the weight of Sir Alistair's will. If she did nothing, Nell might very well die a penniless widow. But could Rena resolve herself to marry a man whose only inducement to accept her came in the form of a handsome estate? Barric wanted her, she knew, but it was despite himself that he did.

Rena sighed as she faced her mother-in-law. She felt as small, tired, and heartsick as all those months ago when she had gathered her things from the train.

"Tell me what to do."

CHAPTER 16

With painstaking slowness, Rena crushed the leaves with a stone. She added tea to the bowl, then dipped a twig into the thickening paste. It had been many years since she had observed the *mehndi* rituals, but she remembered their basic rhythm.

She worked quickly and silently, painting clustered dots and lines on the palms of both hands, then her wrists, then her arms, all the way up to the edge of the choli's short sleeves. The designs were not nearly as intricate as those in the wedding ceremonies she'd attended, nor as dark, but they were traditional enough to bring her some sense of comfort. She hardly knew why she had kept the henna leaves in the first place. She had brought them all the way from India, pressed safely between the pages of one of her father's books.

She balanced her feet on the table, back curved over her bent limbs as she worked. Beneath her steady fingers, sunbursts comprised of tiny dots appeared on the tops of her feet, the tips of her fingers, the prod of each collarbone. She blew on her hands until each symbol was dry, then stood.

Nell sat silently at the table and waited, rising only to help Rena change into the traditional Indian gown which had been bought at such a remarkably high cost. Rena slid into the indigo ghagra then pulled the sari into a loose loop along her waist and shoulder. The blouse beneath was tight, cropped above her stomach to reveal a long line of skin beneath the sari. After years spent donning English fashion, she felt dreadfully exposed, shivering in the moonlight.

Turning from Nell, Rena unwound the cord from around her neck.

Edric's ring, her Indian sands—she could not bring them with her. Not to his room. Not like this. She cupped her palm around both trinkets before placing them reverently in the trunk at the foot of her bed.

"Let him speak first," Nell advised quietly. Her eyes were deeper, more anxious than before. "So that you will know what kind of man he is."

"I thought you already knew what kind of man he is." Rena spoke blandly, shocked by her own appearance when she finally pulled herself in front of the mirror. She looked every bit the world she had left behind—citrus colors and foreign symbols and rich bolts of fabric speckled with gold. Her skin and hair were dark as shadows as she swept the veil down to obscure her own uncertain expression.

Nell settled a thick, gray shawl over Rena's shoulders, her fingers tightening over the rough fabric. "Trust him," Nell said bracingly. "He will not fail you."

The window casements were shadowed all around them, the night beyond still a gaping, black yawn. Rena was becoming more and more uncertain of their plan. To go to a man in the dead of night, dressed in such a way. "What if I am seen? What if I am ruined?"

Nell shook her head. "Lord Barric feels for you, Rena. I can see he does. But he is also afraid, much like you are afraid, and takes far too many risks with your reputation. You must force him to confront himself. To be honest with himself about his feelings."

Rena glanced out the window and sighed. "But what if we are wrong about him?"

"I will pray we are not."

Rena slid her fingers around Nell's. "Then I will join my prayers with yours," she vowed, and slipped out the door before she could convince herself otherwise.

∞

Rena walked at a plodding pace, but she felt like she was racing ten steps ahead of herself. Even when she'd slowed her steps, barely moving, Misthold Manor loomed before her, closer and closer, as if the walls were pushing forward to meet her halfway.

At first she feared she stood little chance of finding Lord Barric's chamber. The entire manor was encased in shadow, each of its endless windows utterly black. But then, as she turned a corner along the eastern wall, she caught sight of one window which was lit with the unsteady glow of a flickering lamp—on the third floor, four windows in from the left, a casement which overlooked the wheat fields.

"It must be," she whispered to herself. "It must, it must."

But she was still doubtful, fearful she would wander the halls like a thief in the night until someone found her roaming. To be thus discovered would be more than ruinous. She would be tossed out into lifelong shame and obscurity far deeper and more humiliating than that which she already inhabited. But she had to try. More piercing than the fear of failure was the ache of desperation, the knowledge that *something* had to change between herself and Lord Barric, and perhaps she had the power to accomplish it.

After a brief search of the grounds, she found the back door Barric had used the night he'd brought her to his study. It opened with barely a creak, ushering her once more into the echoing halls. The manor was still asleep from the lowest hall to the highest, its shadowy corners cradling her as she explored. At last the front hall materialized out of the darkness of a doorframe, even more formidable than it had seemed the evening of the Christmas party.

Saying another prayer that she would not be found—that the room with the flickering lamp was indeed Lord Barric's—she followed the spiraling stairs up, all the while thinking she would surely happen upon a servant or Charlie before she found the room she was looking for.

When she reached the third floor without being seen, she breathed a bit easier. Twice she became turned around and walked herself into a dead end, where none of the doorway cracks were lit from within by the ghostly glow of a lantern wick.

Then she saw it.

Four doors down from the end of a hall, a flicker of yellowish light breathed dim beneath a doorframe.

Drawing near, Rena eased open the door—raw terror spiking within her even as she did—and found a man slumbering on a canopied bed, his evening lamp still lit on the table beside. Terror gave way to amazement, to the nearly incredulous relief of a prayer apparently answered.

She lingered briefly in the doorway, studying the way Lord Barric's chest rose beneath each phantom breath. He had fallen asleep in a state of half undress, his shirt untucked from his trousers and open down the length of his stomach. She could easily picture him falling into bed after battling the flames, too exhausted even to put out the lamp or pull the blanket free beneath him.

Entering, Rena glanced through the casement, studying the abandoned fields below. There she had once stolen grain. There she had been spotted by Lord Barric. There she had worked beneath his unamused gaze.

And now?

She glanced back to where Barric slept and lowered her shawl onto a nearby chair. She began to wonder if Nell's plan to catch him off his guard would truly work or if she was about to destroy herself out of desperation. Her legs shook, but she commanded them to move. She crossed to the bed without allowing herself even a moment to draw breath, and wishing to conceal herself as much as possible, she put out the lamp's already guttering wick, settling the room into a rivaling tangle of shadows and moonlight.

As she lowered herself to the mattress, her fingers fiddled anxiously with the edge of her sari. The last time she had been in bed with a man, it had been her husband's head which rested upon the pillow, his arm the one cast out at that sprawled and slumbering angle. Rena banished the thought as her eyes adjusted to the darkness and traced Lord Barric's unguarded features. His red hair was bright upon the pillow, his jaw a patchy scruff, unshaven since morning. Three hours had passed since the fire, since he had lowered his face toward hers. How certain she had been he would kiss her, but he had drawn away instead. Rena had understood. She knew how it felt to want and not to want with the same breath.

Nell had noticed.

Had he?

Before Rena could stop herself, she reached out and smoothed her fingers down the side of his face. She had vowed never to love another man as she had loved Edric, and so far as she could tell she'd kept that promise—for she did not love Lord Barric *exactly* as she had loved Edric. But did that mean she could not love him? Did it mean she did not love him, perhaps in another way?

Before she could consider the answer to that question, a firm hand clamped hard around her fingers. Rena drew a sharp breath as Barric's eyes shot open, a flash of green in the otherwise dim room. He seemed at once awake and not awake, his hazy eyes startled as they flashed over her veiled face, then lowered to consider the strange, foreign dress she wore.

Nell had told Rena to let him speak first so they might know what kind of man he truly was. Rena waited as she'd been told, mortified to have come to him in such a way. She was frightened he would accept her terms, even more frightened he might send her away in shame.

But Lord Barric was not speaking.

She waited for him to bark at her to get out, as she'd already imagined he might do. Eyes not leaving her, he eased himself up. Weight resting on one elbow, he moved aside the veil from her eyes, then pulled it free from her hair and let it drop to the floor. Rena wasn't sure what kind of expression she wore as he exposed her face to the moonlight. Her breath seemed suspended high above her, her lungs refusing to siphon an ounce of air from the suddenly drafty room.

Barric did not seem to notice. Instead, his eyes dipped to trace the henna patterns on her collarbones, then lower to the ones on her arms.

Then he looked into her eyes.

Without a word, he grabbed her by both arms and tipped her over onto the bed beside him. She scrambled to remember what Nell had told her, to keep to the plan they had set, but Lord Barric's hands sunk into the mattress as he leaned over her, his lips suddenly at her ear. "I always hoped you'd come to me."

Rena opened her mouth to respond, but Barric tipped her face up toward him and pressed his lips against hers. All protests were instantly knocked beyond her reach like they'd been physical things wrenched from her hands. Barric's lips were warm, eager. His skin still smelled like smoke, like the house that had burned to rubble that night, and there was still nothing either of them could do to stop it. This time there were no tears in Rena's eyes as Barric touched her, only a dizzied half awareness as he pressed her down against the bed and threaded his fingers through her hair.

"You are so beautiful," she heard him murmur. "I have always thought you were beautiful."

Rena floundered even more. She knew how it felt to be loved by a man, to be wanted, and she also knew Barric could easily make her forget her own emptiness if she let him. Her heart softening within her, she shifted closer, touching her fingers to the scruff of Barric's jaw as she suddenly returned his kiss.

He released a sharp breath of surprise, his fingers curling around her waist where her skin had been left bare beneath the sari. The warmth of his hand hit Rena like a jolt, but she did not pull back, even as his lips roamed across her cheek, then dipped to press against one of the inky figures on her collarbone.

Yes, Rena thought. This felt right. Much the same as Nell's plan, though her heart knew it wasn't the same at all. What was the name they called her in town? *Edric's Indian whore.* The words twisted the feeling of eagerness within her until it stung and made her gasp. Immediately she stiffened beneath Barric, her throat barely fighting off a sob of shame.

As if sensing her uncertainty, Barric pushed himself slightly up, his body inches from hers as he studied her face. Fingers trembling, she clutched at Barric's shirtsleeves, her eyes pleading with his beneath the arch of moonlight. She tried again to form the words she'd come to say.

"You're. . ." He faltered as if unsure of his own word. "You're *afraid.*"

Rena realized she'd been holding her breath for rather a long time. *Afraid* was far too simple. She was like those fields beyond his bedroom window—razed and barren, remnants of a full harvest brushed by a gust of wind, and there was nowhere she could go to defend herself against it.

As if awakening from a dream, Barric glanced around them, stiffening as he seemed to come to his senses. "Rena," he said urgently, "what are you doing in here?"

"Lord Barric." Her voice was tight but measured. "I've come with a proposition for you."

He gave her an uncertain look, and Rena lowered her eyes, mortification mounting. She knew what he must think of her. It was, after all, not an unusual trick. She'd heard stories of women who had climbed into bed to strong-arm rich men like him into an otherwise impossible marriage. Why should he expect anything different from her? "I've come to offer you Hawthorn Glen," she announced, refusing to sound tremulous beneath his gaze. "Might I be permitted to sit up as we discuss the will?"

As her question registered, his expression darkened. "The. . .will?" Still balanced above her, he paused, eyes drifting down again to her mouth. "You mean to tell me you've come here, like this, to talk to me about money?"

"Will you let me sit up?"

He studied her face, his eyes hard and extracting, until Rena's fear returned. One quick swoop was all it would take for him to dash away her terms, just a touch of the lips. And if she refused him, they both knew he could spread this story to every eager ear in town. The gossips would descend on her like vultures, and all that would remain of her reputation would be a rotting carcass. She was entirely at his mercy.

Shoving himself up by his arms, Barric clambered from the bed, straightening his shirt as he stood. "Hawthorn Glen," he repeated coldly. "What makes you think you have the power to give it to me?"

Relieved by his sudden distance, though not by his darkening mood, Rena pulled herself into a sitting position, taking a similar moment to straighten her hair and tuck her feet beneath her skirt.

"Because I *can* give it to you."

He leveled her with a sardonic look. "Because of the new will, you mean."

"Who told you about the new will?"

"My uncle."

She blinked with some confusion. "What does he know about it?"

"Only that it exists. If you want an even conversation, you'll have to educate me on the particulars."

This was the moment Rena had been dreading. Lord Barric might have been altogether willing and eager to take her to bed as his mistress, but Nell's suggestion of marriage could hardly be seen as a deal in the man's favor. Pressing her hands against the fabric of her skirt, Rena willed herself to speak the words. "I need you. . .to marry me."

To his credit, Barric didn't stagger when she said it, but his eyes narrowed slightly. "What, a proposal you mean? Aren't you supposed to take a knee or something?"

She ignored the barb and explained. "My father-in-law's will is rather shocking. I have to marry back into the Fairfax side of his family for any of it to take effect. Lord Barric, please. We are desperate. If you will only marry me, Nell will receive his fortune. She'll never have to worry again. Never starve. And you can have Edric's family estate."

"Yes," he agreed sharply. "And his wife." Rena dropped her eyes at his curt response, but he went on, pacing nearer to his desk as if he needed more room to think. "So this was the plan, was it? Seduce me into saying yes?"

Rena climbed to her feet, her face heating. "That was *not* the plan," she insisted, though she knew he'd likely suspect as much. "I came to talk about the will."

He froze as if something new had crossed his mind, and his gaze swung back over to her. "Is *that* why you dragged me out to Hawthorn Glen?" He grabbed her by the hand when she swayed back, his fingers tightening as he waited for her answer. "Dangling the prize in front of me, were you?"

"Of course not." Heat pounded into her face. "No!"

"I'm afraid you've overlooked the fact that I have *Misthold*, Mrs. Hawley, which is ten times the estate of Hawthorn. In order for me to even consider biting at your offer, I'd have to want far more than his paltry estate. I'd have to want *you*."

Her voice barely trembled as she challenged, "Don't you?"

When she looked up at him, Barric swore and released her, all semblance of conversation lost in angry accusation. "You know I do. And if I were a dishonorable man, or even a weaker one, I'd take you to bed without a second thought. I'd bed you, then laugh at your terms and tell you to keep quiet about what had happened. And then what would you do?"

She felt her resolve begin to crumble. "You are not a weaker man." His eyebrow dipped in challenge of her trust. "No," she said. "You would not hurt me like that."

Her words did nothing to alleviate his anger. "Does it not bother you?" he growled. "Selling yourself to me like this, to a man who doesn't love you, just so the old lady can have some gold in her pocket?"

Selling herself. A disquieting choice of words, almost as miserable in her ears as hearing him say, so bluntly, that he didn't love her. Her fingers curled into fists as she swallowed both insults. "I suppose it all depends on how much I sell for," she replied, needling him. "Perhaps you think I ought to have taken up work at the Gilded Crown after all."

Her words made him flinch. He pressed forward a step, opened his mouth like he was about to shout something back at her, but then his eyes fell to her trembling hands, and he turned away. "If it's all business," he said, forcing himself to speak more evenly, "why come to me when you might have gone to anyone with a blood claim? Charlie is, after all, a Fairfax too."

"Because"—she fought to keep the grief from her voice—"I trusted you."

Barric fell silent, his eyes ponderous for a moment, and then his expression muted even more as he turned to face her. "Well, if it's all one to you, I will make *you* an offer, Mrs. Hawley. My uncle wants Hawthorn Glen more than anything. He's been scavenging for it for years. And, as a first cousin to Sir Alistair, he has a closer claim than I. Since you've set your terms so prettily, I'll extend them to *him*. It wouldn't be right not to give him a chance, after all. I'll tell him of your offer. If he refuses to marry you, then I will."

New terms now set, Lord Barric crossed his arms across his chest and awaited her reply.

"Your uncle?" she echoed faintly. Her voice sounded as pale as she suddenly felt. She had come to Lord Barric for Nell because she loved her and wanted to see her taken care of. But she'd also come because she cared for him. Because she knew, in some way, he cared for her.

But could she marry his uncle? Did she love Nell that much?

"Family is family, isn't it?" Barric shrugged, his tone devastatingly casual. "It shouldn't matter who you marry, so long as it gets done."

In the wake of the new will, Rena had accused her father-in-law of using her as one of his favored chess pieces; now she felt like she was being shoved violently across the game board. *For Nell*, she reminded herself. *Anything for Nell.* "Yes," she agreed, her voice trailing with loss. She lowered her eyes to the floor. "I am grateful to you for your assistance."

Barric stood silent. She wanted him to say he had regretted his offer, that he would never toss her off to his uncle, that he didn't think so little of her. What would it be like, she wondered, to be married to Barric's uncle, a man twice her age, whom she barely knew? Barric's uncle was also Thomas's father, she realized belatedly. The idea of marrying him made her suddenly sick.

"Then I will speak with him tomorrow," Barric answered coolly. She sensed in his words a clear dismissal, for which she was grateful, if only to escape his cutting eyes. With hardly a nod goodbye, Rena turned and clutched the doorknob.

"Wait."

She paused with the door half-open, one foot already in the hall. As she turned, Barric approached. "By tomorrow you might very well be betrothed to my uncle." He ran his fingers over her hair, softly, as if he couldn't bear not to touch her. "Is there nothing you would want to say to me while you are still a free woman?"

Rena was stricken, suddenly, by how much she wished she might stay there, with him, and not just for the night. What would it be like to hear him call her "wife" each morning? What would it be like to have a husband such as him? It did not matter. It wasn't to be. She had been a fool to imagine Lord Barric cared for her in such a way.

She would not lift her eyes to him, nor could she keep the bitterness from her voice. "I am bound by our contract, Lord Barric." Her voice stiffened with disappointment. "As such, I am not a free woman."

Grimacing at her reply, Barric released her. "Then leave," he said, and turned away.

CHAPTER 17

The sun had not yet risen when Barric saddled Samson and tore out of the stable, straight on course for his uncle's house. His hands were knuckled hard over the reins in a painful grip. He was still furious. Rena had tested him within an inch of his self-control, then had the nerve to say she trusted him. At first he'd been delighted to find her in his bed. If she hadn't gone as rigid as stone beneath him, if he hadn't paused in that moment to look into her eyes, he feared he wouldn't have stopped until he'd had her out of that dress. At first his own weakness had sickened him, shamed him, but now there was nothing left but roiling anger. He thought she had come for him. Instead, she had come in the interest of money.

And then there was the fact she had accepted his horrible terms, that she would marry his uncle because Barric had said it was to be so. As if Barric himself was replaceable, just a pawn in a race for the family inheritance. She didn't trust him—she *needed* him—and Barric was not so swept away that he couldn't see the difference. He knew she was desperate, and he hated that she would willingly toss herself away to his uncle to feel a fraction of control.

"If you will only marry me, Nell will receive his fortune. She'll never have to worry again. Never starve." Barric winced as he remembered her words. That was her motive, the real reason she'd come to him, and in a way he almost understood. He couldn't imagine what it must have been like for them when they'd lived in that brothel, or the terror Rena had felt watching her mother-in-law famish away into nothing. Nell was the only family Rena had left, and both now lived on Barric's charity. And what had he done? Earlier that night, he'd hinted at sending her away,

as if his kindness to her was a whim, a thin line she was obliged to walk every day, and if he was unsettled enough, she'd tumble.

He slowed Samson to a softer pace, his temper relenting. If anything happened to either woman, there was no telling what might befall the other. He remembered the trapped expression in Rena's eyes the first night she'd met him, the useless efforts she employed to sustain herself.

Alistair Hawley's will had thrown the women a rope, and now they struggled to tie it around each other, to bind them both together beyond the reach of destitution.

Of course, Barric had never intended to hand the property, or Rena, over to his uncle. At first he had been testing her, to determine what her real motive was, though he hadn't allowed himself to believe she'd accept such dismal terms. Her instant acceptance angered him despite her stricken expression, and he prodded at her on purpose, insulted her, threatened her, all to get her to stumble and say something that sounded truer to him than the flat words already spoken.

Barric still wasn't sure if she'd come to him because she actually cared for him. Then again, he *was* the only one in the Fairfax family with the title of earl. His jaw tightened at the thought. He didn't know if the plan had been hers or Nell's, or if she would have been relieved had he accepted her terms as she had set them. He knew she felt for him, had recognized it as soon as his lips were on hers—but he also suspected she struggled with her own wantings, that her heart was still cloaked in a widow's shroud.

Yes, there were many things Barric didn't know for certain as he rode across the heath, but there was one thing he did know for certain: there was no way in hell he would ever allow his uncle to marry her.

When Barric finally arrived, he had to wait in the sitting room while the servant rushed to rouse his uncle. Barric paced the length of the room, from window to fireplace, replaying his encounters with Rena over and over in his mind until he felt he'd run mad. The night had been a steady march of endurance. From putting out the inferno, to pursuing Rena in the trees, to finding her in his bed—he felt like he hadn't slept in a century, and daylight had not yet broken.

At last Uncle George descended the stairs wearing his dressing gown and a look of concern.

"Barric," he said, half-breathless as he stopped in the doorway. "What is it? My servant said it was a matter of some urgency. Is it Charlie?"

Barric held up a hand to signal all was well. "I understand the circumstances are. . .strange. But so is my news."

His uncle entered the room, eyes narrowing, then froze with realization. "You've learned about the Hawley will."

Both men stood extremely still. Then Barric nodded.

His uncle drew out a chair and gestured Barric toward the divan nearest the fire. "Sit! Sit!" His eyes were already alight. "What have you learned? Tell me."

Barric eased himself down onto the couch, smoothing his hand over his face as he begrudgingly conceded. "You were right. The property no longer passes to their cousin."

"How grim you look about it," his uncle chided with a broad smile. "That's wonderful news! Whatever could be the matter with you?"

"There is. . .a way," Barric admitted slowly. "A way for Hawthorn Glen to pass to you."

Barric had decided on his way over that there could be no harm in his offering the estate, as he had told Rena he would. Barric would play the dutiful nephew, offering the prized piece of land, and all would be well when his uncle refused.

But what if Uncle George didn't refuse?

Running his hand over his mustache, his uncle perched on the edge of the chair, utterly still as he waited for his nephew to continue. Barric felt the words tangle inside of him, sharp beneath his ribs. If Barric knew his uncle, then Uncle George would never dream of marrying a girl who had come out of obscurity, never ally his title with needless scandal whatever the cost. And why would he? Barric himself had all but laughed in the parson's face at the very suggestion that he marry Rena. And now?

Barric studied his uncle and grimly imagined him waltzing through town with Rena on his arm. How would it feel for Barric to watch him kiss her, to know she went to his uncle's bed as she had so recently come to his? How would it be to know she would never need him again, that she would pass the rest of her days with a man who once played with her out of curiosity?

"I've never been a fan of suspense," his uncle prodded, his voice stern. "Tell me."

Somehow, Barric bit out the words. "You have to marry her."

Uncle George drew back in his chair, his lips pursing with confusion. They were probably the strangest terms he'd heard in all his years. "What on earth are you talking about?"

"If you want the estate," Barric repeated slowly, "then you have to marry her."

"What, the Indian girl?"

Barric gritted his teeth. "Rena," he corrected. "Yes."

Barric waited an eternity for his uncle to shake his head in response. "If I marry her?" the old man repeated, and chuckled awkwardly. "She is a rather pretty thing, to be sure. But to *marry* her? I'd look as great a fool as Edric Hawley." Barric must have made a face, because his uncle held up an obliging hand before he continued. "Oh, I know how fond you are of her, Barric. I don't mean to be insulting. But those are truly the terms?"

"Yes."

"Well, what a bit of silliness. Could you imagine a man of my standing, my age, marrying a young, castaway widow? Of course I feel sorry for her. All alone. With next to nothing."

Barric wanted to choke on his uncle's sympathy. "Do you accept the terms?"

Barric's question awakened his uncle from a passing stupor. The man frowned more distinctly. "Such an unusual offer," he said, shaking his head. "Are you sure there isn't another way?"

"I doubt it."

"Oh, but could you imagine taking a knee for her?"

Nerves frayed with waiting, Barric tried again to corral his uncle into a decision. "So, you refuse?"

His uncle blinked. "Well, but she's Indian."

"So, you refuse."

His uncle seemed disappointed as he realized his own decision, easing back into his chair and tapping the armrest. "Yes," he sighed. "I'm afraid I must."

Barric stood so quickly the divan skidded back a notch. He ought to be frantic, for he had promised Rena he would marry her in his uncle's stead, if it came to that. His uncle had all but scribbled Barric's name on the blasted marriage license, but all he could feel was piercing relief.

But did Rena really wish to marry him, or was he just another in a long line of sacrifices she had made to secure Nell's safekeeping?

His uncle had been speaking, but Barric only snapped from his thoughts in time to hear the end. "Could you imagine the rare looks I would get in town, with an Indian bride?" Uncle George chuckled at the image he'd conjured, and smiled wistfully, until Barric cut toward the door with a sudden burst of momentum.

His uncle rose as Barric reached the door, his expression crumpled with confusion.

"I say, Barric, where do you think you're going? Barric?"

Barric could manage no other reply than to slam the door behind him.

Rena sat on a large branch on the edge of Lord Barric's property, bundled within her heavy shawl, even more distressed than she had been the evening she had gone to his bedchamber.

She had not seen him since that night. No one had, for Lord Barric had entirely disappeared from Abbotsville. His ten-day absence was causing quite the stir, both for locals and for Rena, who was not sure if he had indeed spoken with his uncle, or if he still planned to. William said even Charlie didn't know where he'd gone.

Rena glanced up at the sky. Morning had broken a few hours before, the sky brightening out of its early amber glow. Snow drifted like ash as she stared out at the brittle stubs of dead harvest, thinking of how their world changed color so much faster than her own. Her heart had turned as quickly, she thought—withering from bright Indian summers into gray—but she had only just begun to hope that it might not always be so.

She and Nell both agonized over Barric's disappearance, wondering if this was his way of dismissing her, perhaps because his uncle had accepted her terms and was making preparations for an offer. If such was the case, then Rena would marry a man she barely knew. A man in equal age to her father. What would her life look like if she was forced to move into her dead husband's home with a man who was still a stranger to her?

And if Uncle George refused?

Her thoughts shifted to Lord Barric. He was a man who turned with the harvest: stern as winter, his hair as rusty red as the autumn leaves. But then in other moments his eyes softened into a subtler look which many likely missed if they hadn't held his gaze as often as Rena had.

In the distance, horse hooves pounded a wild, relentless pattern against the frozen ground. The thud rose to a raucous beat, a wall of sound traveling through the branch beneath her and up her stiffened spine. Somehow she knew it was him as soon as the horse pulled up beside her and ground to a halt.

Though she was surprised by his sudden reappearance, she could not bring herself to look at him. Ten days had passed since she had left his bedchamber. Ten days without word, without any indication that he cared for her whatsoever or had kept his word to her. She stared miserably at her hands as she waited for him to speak.

"I've come to congratulate you," he announced without dismounting. "You are to be married."

His dreadful words, spoken without so much as a *hello*, brought her eyes despairingly up to his. Her voice emerged in a rasp of broken sound. "You've spoken to your uncle?"

Barric met her eyes. He seemed disheveled from his ride, with hair windblown and coat spattered with melted snow. Even his cravat was unusually loose. He glanced away as if something in the distance held his attention more than their conversation, but still he answered.

"I have."

Barric's uncle had accepted the terms of the will. The realization struck her like a fist. Rena stood to thank him but staggered sideways on her feet. This was the despair of sacrifice, she realized, the moment when her own life became somewhat less in order to sustain another.

"I am obliged to you," she finally managed, brokenly. "Thank you for speaking my case so eloquently to your uncle."

Barric's eyes snapped back to her, his mouth twisting into a forbidding line. "And you will marry him?" he asked, his voice so low she could barely make out the words. "A man of whose character you know nearly nothing?"

"I know he is your relation."

Barric dismounted at that. "Yes," he agreed coolly. "So is Charlie. So is *Thomas*. Yet you didn't climb into bed with any of them, did you?"

Heat poured into Rena's face, a hot mix of anger and shame. "No," she accepted through her teeth. "I certainly did not."

He tied off Samson to a tree, then approached her. "I want you to answer my question, and this time I want you to tell the truth. Why did you come to me that night?"

Humiliated in every extreme, Rena fell back on a lie. "I would have gone to any man who could have assured me that Nell would be provided for."

He shook his head. "You would throw yourself away to a man who might spend his days despising you? You would share his bed, and let him touch you? Is Nell's well-being really worth so much more than your own?"

"Don't you dare despise me for it!" Her furious words struck as quick as a match, and Barric's eyes widened. "For months I watched Nell grieve and starve, hardly knowing which might kill her first. We slept in *gutters*, Lord Barric. We slept in *alleys*." She broke off, trying to draw breath, but tears welled up within her, and she had to swallow twice as hard to hold them back. "So, you'll forgive me if I am willing to throw myself away for her. There is very little else I have to give. I assure you, the price is not too dear if I never again have to watch her scrub floors in a hall filled with prostitutes."

Barric didn't answer that. With a sharp breath of his own, he dropped his gaze, scuffing his boot heel on the ground. Rena turned to leave but only made it three paces before his hand curled around her wrist and he tugged her back.

"You must be so relieved," she blurted, fighting a wild urge to laugh at herself, at her own foolishness.

"Relieved," he repeated, shaking his head.

"I ruined him, you know. He had been so admired. Respected. You should have seen how people looked at him after he married me. The whispers, I can still hear them, all the horrible things they said about him. About us. He would have risen in the ranks, except his superiors questioned his judgment. Doors which had been opened to him, opportunities he had once lived to explore—all gone. I've done the same to Nell. I've ruined her too."

Barric listened in silence, but she could see his eyes were that softer green she had just been thinking of.

"You think Edric regretted marrying you?"

"It doesn't matter anymore if he did or if he didn't. He's gone." She pulled her arm out of his hand and shook her head as if trying to clear it. "I ought to go," she said distractedly. "I must tell Nell the news."

"If you must go," he said to her back as she passed him, "then I might as well tell you that my uncle respectfully declined your offer."

Rena stiffened and her breath hung shakily between her lips. She turned quickly to face him as if startled from a daze. "He. . .didn't want me?"

"No."

Which meant—

Lord Barric.

Rena hadn't fully realized just how much she wished to marry him—how much she *loved* him—until she fell to her knees with a sob of resounding relief. At first he let her consume the news in silence, standing near her without uttering a word. Then he moved closer, his feet crunching the frozen grass as he drew near. He knelt at her side, pulled her trembling hands from her face, and frowned as he at last uncovered her eyes.

"You're crying," he said and sounded unsure.

She didn't feel the tears or mark them. They fell apart from her, as if they might have been the tears of another person entirely and she was merely their surrogate. They were her father's tears, perhaps, when she told him she must go, when she had broken his heart by leaving. Or Nell's tears, so full of loss, so stoic. Or even Edric's when he had realized he was sick enough to die and leave her with nothing.

"Where did you go?" she finally demanded through her tears. "Why did you leave?"

Wincing apologetically, Barric reached into his pocket and removed a piece of folded paper. "I needed a private audience with the nearest bishop," he admitted. "For this."

He handed her the marriage license—there was his name and hers and the name of their parish. Realization dawned as Rena lowered the document into her lap.

"Forgive me," Barric said before she had time to collect her thoughts, "but I needed to wait the seven days before returning so I wouldn't have the chance to damage your reputation any more than I already have."

Seven days—the required waiting period for marriages by license, a much quicker process than the three weeks needed for the calling of the banns. Which meant Lord Barric had no intention of waiting a moment longer. Rena's heart began beating uncommonly fast.

"And now I have a question for you." He spoke very softly, reaching to clasp her fingers in his. "Why do you think I am going to marry you?"

She dared not hope for more than what she had already suspected. "Because you promised me you would."

"I've broken promises before." His eyes intently awaited another answer from her.

"Because you feel sorry for us?"

He shook his head, his expression turning wry. "I'm not all that altruistic."

Her tone bittered. "Because you want the estate, then."

"*Rena.*"

She choked on the sound of her name, and it was then she noticed how his eyes had softened on her face, how he followed each shift of her expression with unnerving attention.

Drawing back, she challenged, "What, because you think I'm pretty?"

There was a laugh waiting behind his lips.

"You're getting closer," he admitted, right before he tipped her chin, pulled her to him, and kissed her.

CHAPTER 18

Barric rolled onto his side and admired the slope of Rena's back. Her bare skin was only half draped beneath his heavy blanket, and she slumbered deeply, dreaming beside him as if she hadn't slept in weeks. Barric kept time by following the soft lift of her shoulder as it moved beneath each tug of silent breath.

Parson Richardson had not seemed at all surprised to find them waiting for him in the chapel that morning with license in hand. With a shake of his head, the parson glanced over the necessary signature, remarked it was "*about time*," and then summoned a witness with a good deal of haste.

Barric had thought he'd feel uncertain about marrying Rena so quickly, under such conditions. He was surprised at the altar, however, to find the parson could not speak fast enough for his liking. He'd wanted it done. He'd wanted *her*. Rena had been far more measured, he thought. She had lingered at the altar long after Barric had finished his own silent petitions, with her eyes fixed on the cross.

He'd waited for her in the shadowy nave, watching restlessly as she'd at last risen from her knees and come to stand at his side. He had once accused Rena of dangling Sir Alistair's property in front of him, of using him for his money—but as soon as her lips found his in the back of the chapel, Barric had known their marriage was not about Alistair's will or even his own bargain with her. Though he still wasn't sure if she loved him, exactly, he was confident there was far more than money between them.

Barric's fingers moved with the memory, tracing a path from

Rena's bare shoulder down her arm to her elbow. At his touch, she shifted beneath the blanket, her face turning up toward his as if drawn to him even in sleep. Word would have spread by now, he realized as he studied her face. Though he knew the rumors would be brutal, he was glad to know the gossip would never reach her here, in his room.

Their room. It was hard to think in such terms so quickly, but that was the short of it.

People had stared openly as he'd brought her from the chapel back to Misthold—she walking in her quiet way, dignity intact, and Barric following a half step behind, hardly able to take his eyes off her. She had worn the same exotic dress to their wedding which she'd worn ten nights ago, in his chamber, and she wore it like royalty, her back poised to take the whispers.

They'd barely made it through the front door when he'd pulled her into a corner and sought her lips, no thought whatsoever for the servants who might happen upon them. She had been flushed and eager and, he thought, still slightly afraid of him. He hadn't realized how deeply he wanted her until he had her in his arms and there were several dozen stairs left to climb to his room.

He shifted closer to her in the bed, splaying his fingers against the skin at the base of her neck. Earlier, he had wondered if touching her would still make her think of Edric, but *Barric* had been the only name to cross her lips that morning, and he had kissed her until even that word was held far beyond her reach.

Now he traced a hand over his wife's frame, slowly, as if trying to memorize her: the way her hair was scattered down over the blanket, the way her features softened as they pressed against the pillow, the way her hand reached for him, her fingers brushing his chest. . .

He captured that hand, brought it to his lips, and slowly kissed each fingertip. "Don't you think it's time you ought to awaken?"

Far too quick to have been asleep, her expression curved at the jaw, tracing a slight smile. The little pretender. Without opening her eyes, she remarked, "You've been thinking so loudly I could hear you even in my sleep."

"Really?" He leaned closer. "And what was I thinking about?"

She cracked one eye to peer over at him, and whatever she caught in his expression made her lips curl upward. She had an intelligent smile, he thought, with depth behind her eyes. Noticing this made him realize how unfamiliar he was with his wife's shifting expressions, particularly the happy ones. "Do you regret marrying me?" he asked, unsure if he could trust her smiles after everything he'd once counted uncertain between them.

"Oh yes, Lord Barric," she replied, stretching slightly. "That is exactly what I was thinking."

Her idle tone set him more at ease. "*Lord Barric?*" he challenged. "I don't think it's entirely right for you to call me that when I have you in my bed."

She crooked an eyebrow at him. "Just Barric, then?"

He leaned down once more, much closer than before. "Jack," he murmured, pressing the name tightly against her lips. "Just Jack."

In agreement, her fingers touched his face, and he was sinking again, as he had done time and again when he felt her near. He hooked a hand around her back, hauled her to his side of the bed, then heard a door somewhere in the manor clap shut rather loudly. Rena stiffened against him, a hand coming up and bracing against his chest as they both listened. A catapult of shouts echoed through the lower chambers, three voices at least.

Rena sat up abruptly, clutching the sheet against her chest, her eyes wide and suddenly frightened. "Who do you think it is?"

Barric strained to make out words, certain now he heard Charlie's voice. And another voice, far less welcome.

With a groan of annoyance, Barric leapt from the bed, grabbing his scattering of clothes from the chair and pulling into them. "Just. . .wait here," he muttered, fumbling to tuck in his shirttails. "I'm sure it's nothing."

As if to disagree, the door clapped back on its hinge, banging against the farthest wall as Charlie swept into the room. His eyes went wide upon finding Rena in his brother's bed. Stunned into momentary silence, he turned abruptly to face Barric instead. "Er. . .m–morning." He offered a half-repentant smirk as Barric shrugged into his jacket and glared at him.

"So. . .," Charlie hedged when his brother did not speak. He was trying to sound casual, but Rena saw his eyes pinch tellingly at the corners. "I suppose it's safe to say the rumors are true?" Irritation crept further into his voice as he added, "You might have mentioned as much to your only brother."

Barric ignored the accusation, reaching for his boots. "What are you doing here?" he demanded.

"Our uncle has arrived to. . .congratulate you? On your marriage."

Barric shook his head. "Tell him to wait."

"He's on his way up right now," Charlie said, gesturing innocently toward the door. "So, unless you'd like to have this conversation with him in here. . ." He trailed off, tipping his head meaningfully toward Rena.

"You should go," Rena agreed, carefully avoiding Charlie's eyes.

Barric stopped at the bed long enough to brush his lips against hers. "I'll be back *very* soon," he promised.

Charlie held the door for Barric, glancing over with a sly grin as he slipped it back shut behind them. "Honeymoon's over, eh, Jack?"

Giving his brother a slight shove, Barric bounded down the steps as quickly as he could, hoping to intercept his uncle before he got too close to his chamber. Barric muttered an oath as he turned a corner and Uncle George came jogging up to meet them.

"Tell me it isn't true," his uncle commanded, pausing several steps down and gripping the banister at his side. His voice was sterner than Barric had ever heard.

"You'll have to excuse me," Barric replied, refusing to feel sheepish in his presence. "My wife is waiting. Say what you must, but be quick about it."

His uncle paled at his words, falling back another step. "You married her," he said, shaking his head. "You actually married her? No. I can't believe it. You're lying."

"You may ask the parson if you wish," Barric responded blandly. "I'm sure he will give you a full account."

"Have you lost your mind?" His uncle's voice carried through the hall on a bouncing echo, and Barric glanced over his shoulder, up toward the chamber he'd just left. He was certain Rena had heard his words. With a glowering look, he pushed past his uncle, descending the rest of the stairs at a rapid pace. Silenced by his own fury, his uncle followed, with Charlie trailing not far behind.

Barric's mood certainly didn't improve when he rounded the last corner and found Thomas waiting at the bottom of the stairs.

"What is he doing here?" Barric demanded of his uncle.

When his uncle didn't answer, Thomas spoke on his own behalf. "I'm here to see the show," he explained, his expression turning dark. "So, tell me, did you finally give her *exactly* what she wanted?"

"Shut up," Barric ordered, then ushered them all into his study. As they crossed the front hall, a small exodus of servants scattered from odd corners, trying to appear busy.

As soon as Barric had closed the door, his uncle advanced. "I thought I told you to carry on with her privately," he hissed.

Charlie made a sound of annoyance. "Yes," he agreed sarcastically. "Because that's never caused a scandal either."

Barric ignored both remarks. "If you've all come to see if the gossip is true, then my answer is yes. All of it is true."

His uncle leaned forward. "Have you already taken her to bed?" he asked urgently.

Charlie coughed uncomfortably as Barric gave his uncle a flat look, more than answer enough.

"No more clandestine dallying behind the trees," Thomas remarked with a clap of his hands. "At least now you can be civilized about it."

Barric felt his muscles tighten. "You will have a care," he warned slowly, "with how you talk about my wife."

"Perhaps it can be undone," his uncle suggested abruptly. "Annulled."

"I don't wish it undone," Barric argued. "I wish for you to leave."

Thomas's smile grew fiendish. "She's waiting for you up there, isn't she? Haven't quite had your fill of her yet?"

Barric didn't dignify that with a response.

"I think it's best if everyone leaves," Charlie suggested, clapping Barric on the back. "After all, the man has had a busy day."

"And will doubtless have a busy night," Thomas suggested under his breath.

Barric's jaw ached as he ground it tight.

"Did you do it for the estate?" His uncle frowned as he feebly tried to understand. "Did you do it to get Hawthorn Glen?"

"Why should it matter? You said you didn't want the estate."

"Dammit!" His uncle struck again, quick like a viper. "I was not implying you ought to swoop in and inherit an impossible scandal! You've stripped yourself of your own good name, Barric. Why, you've given your father's name to a nobody—you've made her a countess!"

"Why do you think she even married you, Barric?" Thomas attempted a look of mild sympathy. "She's slithered her way into your coffers, Cousin, and now there will be no end of it."

"She did not marry me for my *money*." Barric pounded the words out, though of course he had suspected as much of her the evening before. But Rena's eyes in the chapel that morning had been bright beneath the stained glass, hopeful, holding a silent promise that was sacred, nothing earthly about it. No, money did not paint eyes in such a light.

Thomas's lip curled mockingly. "Yes, I'm sure Edric told himself the same thing right before he took the harlot to bed."

That insult Barric *did* dignify with a response.

He moved before he could stop himself, his fist an unchecked line of motion, striking hard until he felt the cut of Thomas's teeth against his knuckles. It was a satisfying sting.

Thomas drew back with a curse, spitting a spot of blood on Barric's plush carpet. "You think you're so much better than everyone else," he growled from behind his now broken lip. "But look at you. Married to tawdry trash whose only interest is in that property."

If Charlie hadn't grabbed ahold of Barric's arm, if Uncle George hadn't stepped in with a shout and shoved Thomas out of the way, Barric was certain he would have struck again.

"Jack."

All the men turned at once to find Rena poised in the doorway, just as she had been the night of Barric's Christmas party. Only this time she did not seem hurt or torn or at all compelled to run from what she had overheard.

Frowning, she balanced her hand on the doorframe, no veil there to obscure her look of weary disdain. Cut of oriental indigo, her gown was a stark contrast to the wide British paintings mounted on either wall beside her. The curious tangle of symbols still lined her hands and arms, a resilient ink. Lowering his eyes, Barric briefly recalled pressing his lips to each and every symbol not even two hours before.

Charlie was the first to approach her. "Sister," he called her, and took up her hand with that idle grin and gently kissed her knuckles.

She returned Charlie's smile, eyes still half-tired. Then she turned and examined his uncle, who had colored from the neck to the face as soon as he'd seen her enter.

"You want Hawthorn Glen, do you?" Her voice was stone. When he did not reply, she went on. "Take it if it means so much to you that you would allow your son to call me trash. If you would have him call me a harlot because you want it."

Uncle George said nothing. Barric could not recall a time the man had not flung words back in the face of a challenge, but the old man held his tongue as tightly as he held Rena's gaze. In a calm voice, she challenged, "Won't you call me a harlot, Uncle? Like your son has called me a harlot?"

Still, he did not speak. And so Rena crossed the room and extended a steady hand toward him. "Shall we shake on it, then?" she suggested. "And then the property will be quite yours. I'll not break my word."

Barric's uncle considered her outstretched hand. A swirling glyph had been painted in the center of her palm in a dark reddish hue, with dotted tendrils curling around the outer edge of her hand. Uncle George stared at her palm, then braved her eyes with a faltering smile. "The only offering I will accept from this hand," he said at length, taking her fingers in his, "is your forgiveness, *Lady* Barric."

His voice deepened on the title. Thomas was the first to regain his voice, taking a lumbering step forward. "But, Father, you can't just—"

Uncle George held up a silencing hand. "That lip of yours is less than you deserve. Less than I deserve. We've taken more than enough of your cousin's time. It's high time we left him to his new wife." As they all moved to leave, Uncle George caught Barric by the shoulder, fingers pressing tightly as he spoke low in his ear. "By all the saints, Barric, I hope you know what you're doing."

By all the saints, Barric hoped so too.

CHAPTER 19

Barric leaned against the doorframe, watching as Rena danced with Uncle George. It had been six weeks since the wedding, and if he was honest with himself, he still wasn't sure exactly what he thought of his new wife. She was quiet but attentive. She prayed often. And though her eyes had calmed in recent days, less hungry and fearful, he could not fully banish the worry that she might not love him, that perhaps her heart was still tethered to Edric in ways he could not see.

With the beginning of spring, his uncle had insisted on hosting a lavish ball in honor of his nephew and his new bride. It was a bold statement, made in the interest of *letting bygones be bygones*, as his uncle had put it. Half of the guests now danced while the other half whispered distractedly among themselves about the newlyweds.

Some said Rena trapped Barric into marriage, entirely against his will.

Others said he hadn't been able to help himself, that he'd taken her to bed and therefore had little choice in the matter.

Others speculated she married him for her dead husband's estate, or she seduced him to get Edric's money, or they had been too carried away with lust to live apart.

Very few suspected love.

Barric didn't drop his eyes or alter his stare as William came to stand beside him.

A thin veil of silence hovered above them as Barric watched his uncle spin Rena about until she seemed half-breathless and actually laughed. He could tell William wanted to speak, could feel the stillness which descends when one is very deep in thought. He heard a soft exhale of air as William nearly spoke, but then he didn't.

Barric's eyes were still fixed on Rena. "Say your piece and have done with it, man."

William was silent a moment longer before hesitantly asking, "Why on earth did you marry her, Barric?"

Across the room, Charlie stepped forward to claim Rena for the next dance, and Uncle George bowed his tired acceptance. Barric studied his wife as she crossed the dance floor and curtsied to Charlie from across the narrow aisle.

Barric had married her for many reasons.

Because she was stronger than she appeared, and strength always spoke to him.

Because he knew she'd slept in gutters, that she'd sacrificed everything for Nell, and he would never allow it to be so again.

Because he'd found her in his bed that night and was surprised to realize he wanted her there, always.

"Because," he admitted at last, recalling his foolish denial the day he had spoken with the parson, "it felt wrong not to."

"And? Does it still feel right? What I mean to say is, you do have feelings for her?"

Barric shot him a dry look. "I have feelings."

William glanced across the hall at Rena. "Do you believe she returns them?"

Barric frowned at that question. He knew Rena had married him partially out of fear. Fear of destitution. Fear of leaving Nell unprotected. Fear of the kind of life which had already dealt her blow after wretched blow. He also knew she was drawn to him, that her eyes held a certain depth when he looked at her, and that when he kissed her she felt warm and willing beneath his touch. But love was something else entirely, and their bargain still stretched beneath them, a shaky foundation for any marriage.

Could he be certain she returned his feelings? No. But he was about to find out.

Without answering William's question, Barric crossed the floor and intercepted Rena's hand, tugging her away from Charlie in the very middle of the dance. "You won't mind if I cut in," he said softly to Charlie, then pulled his wife decidedly into his arms.

She drew a sharp breath but did not stiffen or draw back from him. She was so beautiful, Barric thought, her shades-of-midnight hair shimmering under the lights. He remembered the times he'd watched her dance with other men—William, Thomas, Charlie. Even his uncle had asked her to dance that night, well before Barric had been able to offer his own hand. Far too often Barric had watched from the perimeter and ached to hold her.

Well, enough was enough.

He smirked down at Rena's startled expression, glad to have caught her off guard. His hands curved around her waist, fingers pressed against her ribs. "There's no escaping me this time, Rena. You're going to dance with me."

The music tugged them together and pulled them apart, a dizzying set of steps, but Rena kept her eyes on her husband. As he met her again at the center of the aisle, he pulled her in, nearly against him but not quite. He held on to her a moment longer than was necessary, until whispers began to drift throughout the crowd.

"People are talking," Rena commented, her voice barely heard over the thrash of the piano.

His fingers slid from her waist, and they were separated, briefly, down the line. She waited the few beats it took to return to him, and as he drew her against him, he paid no heed to the other dancers or those watching.

"Do the whispers bother you so much?"

She closed her eyes and imagined what the guests suspected of her, what they whispered to each other behind their cupped hands. She only loved him for his money, they said. She trapped him into marriage, or else he'd taken her to bed as any man might when overcome by a set of beguiling eyes. Indian witch. . .

"They are like shadows, I suppose," Rena decided, resetting her gaze on her husband. "Nothing of substance."

"Good," he agreed, then leaned down to whisper intimately in her ear. "Let them talk."

His fingers pressed against her waist, and she was struck, not for the first time, by how deep his gaze was. There wasn't a woman from there to Liverpool who hadn't set her cap at him, and yet Rena's expression was the one he studied with such curious attention. Despite everything, she and Barric seemed suited to each other rather well, with their solemn expressions and watchful eyes.

"I want Nell to move into Hawthorn Glen." Those unexpected words jarred her, so she missed a whole step, but Barric's hand tightened as he helped her recover her footing.

"But. . .Hawthorn Glen is *yours*," she answered with some confusion, shaking her head. "It is your reward. For marrying me."

"I don't want it."

"Why?" She frowned as she foresaw his answer. "Because it was Edric's?"

He hesitated at that. "There is something else—someone else— Edric left behind," he admitted, his eyes falling heavy on hers, "which I am much more inclined toward."

She lowered her gaze, knowing well enough that he was speaking of her. "But you already have her, my lord."

"Do I?"

The music ended there, and Barric was obliged to release her, to bow. But she still hadn't answered his question, neither was he satisfied with her silence. Capturing her hand, Barric led her through a side door to an abandoned outer terrace. After so much time spent in the cramped hall, the open air made Rena's breath feel strangely shallow. The trees were beginning to bud above them, smelling of honeysuckle and evening rain. When Barric did not speak right away, she glanced up at the watchful moon, so full it seemed ready to fall from the sky and shatter like a saucer.

"I didn't marry you for the Hawley estate," Barric said at length, his voice tight but controlled. "I didn't marry you because of some daft bargain I made when I was angry. I married you because I wanted you. We could be married for a hundred years, and I'll still not have what I want. Not unless you can say the same."

Rena stood painfully still. She had been so afraid of Sir Alistair's will, angry because it had slated her to marry a man who might never love her. And here was as dependable a man as ever she'd met, and he was looking at her now as if Sir Alistair's will was nothing but a scrap of useless paper he'd sooner throw into the fireplace.

When she couldn't find the words to speak, Barric pulled her once more against him, his hands anchored against her back. "You still love Edric," he guessed in a soft voice.

Yes, she thought, and surely she always would. Not very long ago, her heart had gaped like a chasm, and she'd felt precariously perched within herself, always ready to fall. But her heart had also changed these many months, had grown in ways she was still learning to understand. Now, even amid the sorrow which might always remain, she experienced moments of fullness. Of hope. Yes, even love.

Love for a man whose red hair reminded her of the harvest. A man who was stern and proud but impossibly kind. A man who always seemed to make her lose her footing.

Maybe Edric had been the laughing sort of husband who had once softened her heart.

And maybe Barric was the steadfast sort of husband who could finally put her back together.

When she said none of this out loud, Barric released her. "You told me once you don't belong here. I can understand that. But don't you think that someday you might?"

"I belong with you," she answered at last, as if all of this should have been rather obvious.

This time Barric was the one who remained silent, though his eyes softened at her answer. Drawing closer, he settled his hands onto her shoulders, tracing his thumb against the gentle hollow of her throat until she felt she may never be able to speak again.

She took up one of his hands and pressed a kiss against his knuckles. "Where you are," she vowed, "there it is that I am, my love—and there I will always be."

ACKNOWLEDGMENTS

So many people voiced support and excitement as I wrote my way—sometimes feebly—to this moment. While I am indebted to all mentors, friends, and family members who have cheered me on in various ways (seriously, thank you!), I wish to thank a few people more directly for the production of this book:

Adria Goetz—you told me I was allowed to use all the exclamation points I wanted when I received my offer from Barbour. There will never be enough exclamation points to express how thankful I am for that first phone call when we joined forces, or for all your tireless work since then—you are a remarkable agent!

Annie Tipton—you believed in my book enough to offer it a home on bookshelves, and I am so grateful. Thank you for welcoming me into the Barbour family and for all the publishing gymnastics it took to make my childhood dream of authorship an unthinkable reality.

JoAnne Simmons—infinite thanks for ensuring each word and punctuation mark carried the proper weight. My book is so much stronger because of your vigilant eyes.

Kirk DouPonce—thank you for creating a cover that is both vibrant and slightly melancholy. You brought a small sliver of Abbotsville to life, and it looks exactly as I always imagined.

Elizabeth Davis—someday we'll finally meet in person, and I'll have a big hug waiting for you when we do. Thank you for reading that earliest draft and challenging me to find a softer side of Barric.

Ruth Boeder—for suggesting documentaries about bread making, for educating me on some basics of farming, and for debating, via midnight text messages, the placement of a single comma in my author bio—thank you!

Jenny Maske—my BBC soul sister. My dearest friend. Thank you for being one of my book's earliest readers and for freaking out in perfectly appropriate ways when I realized I was actually facing publication.

Christina MacKenzie—oh Ena. You've read and critiqued more drafts of this book than I can count. Thank you for always, *always* being my first reader, and for slogging through and helping me revise all the wretched manuscripts that finally led to this one—yes, even the ones with vampires.

Mom and Dad—all those Scholastic book orders have finally paid off! Thank you for giving me a childhood in which my shelves were always stocked with books, and for being so excited about my own book that you told people about it before you were *technically* supposed to. I love you both.

Curtis—I hardly know how to say how thankful I am for your unending support and input, and for all the Starbucks runs, and for encouraging me whenever I doubted my writing. I love you so much. (Also, I'm sorry I had to give the parson a name, but thank you for coming up with a plausible, non-sketchy reason for his presence in the brothel.)

Lastly, Jonah and Isobel—my little ones. Someday you might find this book in your hands, and, if so, all I want you to know is this: I love you more than all the books in the world. I love you more than writing. You are my grandest adventure.

ABOUT THE AUTHOR

Naomi Stephens (née Fenker) is a bookworm turned teacher turned writer. She received an MA in English from Indiana University–Purdue University Fort Wayne and now lives in Ohio with her husband, her two children, and a rascal of a dog named Sherlock.

Check Out More Historical Fiction from Barbour!

The Mayflower Bride
by Kimberley Woodhouse

Join the adventure through history, romance, and family legacy as the **Daughters of the Mayflower** series begins with *The Mayflower Bride* by Kimberley Woodhouse. Mary Elizabeth Chapman and William Lytton embark for the far shores of America on what seems to be a voyage doomed from the start. Can a religious separatist and an opportunistic spy make it in the New World?

Paperback / 978-1-68322-419-8 / $12.99

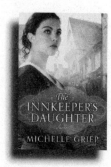

The Innkeeper's Daughter
by Michelle Griep

Officer Alexander Moore goes undercover as a gambling gentleman to expose a plot against the King—and he's a master of disguise, for Johanna Langley believes him to be quite the rogue. . .until she can no longer fight against his unrelenting charm.

Paperback / 978-1-68322-435-8 / $14.99